MALCOLM MACPHAIL'S GREAT WAR

ISBN 978-94-92843-01-2 (Trade Paperback edition)
ISBN 978-94-92843-00-5 (e-book edition)

First published in the Netherlands in 2017 by Esdorn Editions

Copy-editing by John Hudspith
Cover design by JD Smith Design
Interior design and typesetting by JD Smith Design

Cover photographs acknowledgement: Library and Archives Canada/
Ministry of the Overseas Military Forces of Canada fonds: *Smashing
barbed wire with trench mortars. May, 1917* (a001381), *Canadian armoured
cars going into action at the Battle of Amiens* (a003016)

www.darrellduthie.com

MALCOLM MACPHAIL'S GREAT WAR

DARRELL DUTHIE

Esdorn
Editions

PART ONE

CHAPTER 1

3rd of September, 1917
Hill 70, Lens, France

'Boche, sir!'

Private Stringer was pointing. He and Munns were hunched behind their Lewis gun looking downhill, their flushed young faces grim and serious. I followed their lead and I spotted them, a clutch of field-grey figures 300 yards away in the gloom. They appeared to be forming up.

'I can't see a damned thing from this angle,' muttered Captain Ferguson, which was pretty much exactly what I'd warned him of when he insisted we set up here. He stood with his elbows buried in the dirt at the top of the trench, brass-rimmed field glasses clamped to his eyes. 'GHQ says the 1st Guards Reserve are moving into our sector. The general is anxious for some confirmation. I don't need to tell you, Malcolm, that's one of their elite units.'

'So, you reckon the Germans are moving in fresh troops for another counter-attack?' I said. 'It's unbelievable. We took the hill two weeks ago and they're still at it.'

He lowered his glasses. 'Yeah, that's a strong possibility.'

'Well, Ferguson, unconfirmed, albeit far-fetched rumours have it that you're in intelligence. What now?'

Ferguson rolled his eyes. Then he stared at me. I stared back at him. It ended in stalemate. It was eerily similar to how the war had progressed these past few years. 'Alright. I'll go,' I said, finally, with a weary sigh. I tucked my field glasses under my tunic and yanked at the leather strap of my helmet, not that a well-fastened helmet ever helped.

Ferguson clapped me on the back. 'I owe you one, MacPhail.'

'Stringer. Munns,' I said, grabbing my rifle. 'I need to take a closer look. Keep your eyes open.'

'Sir!' They grasped the rims of their tin helmets in a good-natured salute. Munns had his lucky charm, a dog-eared rabbit's foot clenched in his hand.

Cautiously, I crawled out of the trench. An uneasy quiet had descended on Hill 70, but there was always the threat of a sniper lurking unseen, somewhere out there in the wasteland. With that thought in mind, it didn't take me long to work my way around the wired fenceposts and the small rise in the ground that were obstructing our view. I rolled into a vacant shell-hole not thirty feet ahead of Ferguson and the two privates.

Down the slight slope in the direction of Lens' ruined, red-brick northern suburbs, and a huge black pyramid of coal-mine tailings off in the distance, I saw the squad of soldiers assembling. There were more than I expected, maybe fifty of them. I couldn't tell for certain at this distance. The light was poor as the watery sun prepared to set and thick dark clouds were sweeping across. It would rain again soon.

This group was preparing to move. Was it another counter-attack?

A red Very flare shot up into the sullen sky. Someone else had spotted them, too. A minute later a shell whistled overhead, closely followed by others and a succession of explosions detonated in the German lines.

Almost immediately a double green flare soared upwards out of the chaos and began its lazy descent. The Germans were calling for their own artillery to retaliate.

As I stared, there was a massive boom, followed by darkness. Giant shovelfuls of earth were dumped upon me. Then silence, black and absolute, like death.

After a bit I heard voices and felt an arm tugging frantically at mine. I coughed and wheezed as they pulled me free. The damp smoky air smelled fresh and I inhaled deep lungfuls of it. Shakily I rose to my feet, brushing at my tunic. My rescuers shook their heads in astonishment. 'Are you sure you're alright, fellow?'

I pushed them away and in a fog, I stumbled back to where Ferguson, Stringer and Munns were sheltering. One wall of the trench had collapsed. A solitary torn helmet and a blood-streaked timber protruded from the earth. The shell had hit the trench almost dead on. At the sight I closed my eyes.

3rd of October, 1917
3 miles east of Hersin-Coupigny (near Lens), France

The crater-sized pothole appeared out of nowhere. I wrenched the steering wheel to the right, the front wheels shot off the road, and the car slammed to an abrupt stop.

I was on my way from Corps Headquarters to another reconnaissance in the front line, this time as the division's newest intelligence officer, but now my car from the divisional pool was half in the ditch, with a worrisome plume of steam emanating from the hood. My forehead was tender, my ego bruised and, worst of all, I had no idea how I was going to get to the reconnaissance. The general was not going to be amused. I might not make it to a month in my new position. I walked around to take a look at the damage.

Cars! I could see them tearing down the road towards me in convoy, coming from ahead. They were travelling fast.

As they approached they slowed; there were three of them, all gleaming unnaturally, in particular the large staff car in the middle. I say unnaturally because nothing ever gleamed near the front, so it was a dead giveaway some braided cap was on the move.

The cars breezed past, leaving me enveloped in a fine cloud of yellow dust and a growing sense of helplessness. As the large, boxy Vauxhall staff car swept by, I caught a glimpse of a mottled grey and white moustache seated in the back, and I saluted smartly. Some important general out reviewing the troops, I presumed. Then to my relief the motorcade came to a halt. The doors of the first and the third cars opened, discharging a collection of sharply-dressed officers. A private, one of the drivers, hastened towards me.

'Captain,' he said, 'do you require some assistance, sir?'

'Do I ever,' I responded. 'There's no way I can get this contraption back on the road, myself. I'm glad you stopped.'

He nodded, and after conferring briefly with the other drivers, set to work. I climbed into the ditch to help – it wasn't deep – and I put my hands on the hood where the right wheel had plowed into the loose earth. A group of five or six red-tabbed staff officers congregated on the road behind us in a semi-circle, leaning on their canes, and with amused looks on their faces, but seemingly disinclined to join in. No need to muddy *their* boots. They'd probably taken one look at mine and decided to leave me to it.

'Thanks,' I said to the private beside me, who was readying himself to push. 'I hope it still works. Before you arrived, it looked like Vesuvius erupting.'

'Oh, I wouldn't worry about that, sir. Duncan's a genius with motorcars,' he said with a flick of his head in the direction of the driver who first spoke to me. Duncan was now readying himself at the steering wheel.

'Where are you fellows coming from?'

'Cassel up by the Belgian border, sir. We were visiting the field-marshal's residence.' That got me thinking. Their passenger must indeed be an important figure if he was dropping in on the field-marshal.

Perplexed, I asked, 'I understood the field-marshal resides in a château near Montreuil, not Cassel?'

'He does, sir. That's at General Headquarters. The Château de Beaurepaire it's called. The one in Cassel's only his second residence.'

'His second residence! Boy, I wouldn't mind seeing what a *second* residence looks like.'

The private laughed. 'It's nice, sir.'

Private Duncan shouted, 'On three, lads,' and even before I had my back into it, my car's four wheels were resting again on the narrow road. The privates were a handy bunch. Duncan was already peering at the engine; he had a VIP waiting impatiently, so naturally he was pressed for time.

'It's fortunate we happened along when we did,' I heard a kindly voice say. I turned and you could have heard the clunk of my jaw as it dropped open. Field-Marshal Sir Douglas Haig was standing in front of me. The commander-in-chief of the British Expeditionary Force (BEF) was gazing at me with interest.

He stood with both hands deep in his coat pockets, collar upturned, and the wisp of a smile on his face. His blue eyes had a friendly sparkle to them. The field-marshal had that easy grace of a man who knew his rung in life, and knew that others knew it too; commanding an army of one and a half million men can have that effect. I felt about as relaxed as an ant with the shadow of a heel looming over me.

'Sir. Yes, sir. It's very fortunate,' I said, trying to juggle the surprisingly difficult act of talking and coming to attention at the same time. I towered over him, but felt strangely cowed.

'And with whom do I have the pleasure of speaking, Captain?'

'MacPhail, sir, Malcolm MacPhail. I'm with the 3rd Canadian Division.'

'Ah, Louis Lipsett's division. Pleased to meet you, Captain. As it happens I'm on my way to see your Corps Commander, General Currie, about the offensive.'

'The Ypres offensive, sir?'

'Yes, of course, the Ypres offensive. Which one did you suppose?' As there was only one offensive at the moment, and that was the field-marshal's break-for-the-coast push near Ypres, his puzzlement wasn't entirely surprising.

'Seeing as how we're in the line forty miles from Ypres, I just assumed it must be something else, sir,' I stuttered, my knees going weak. Ypres was my cruel introduction to this war. I arrived near that charming Belgian city in April 1915 feeling as exuberantly over-confident as any new private can, and raring to go, ready to save the Empire. Before long I was clinging to life by a string – or in my case a urine-soaked handkerchief clamped to my face – as dense green clouds of gas billowed terrifyingly over us. Even the Germans were awed by their new weapon of horror. And the fighting was still raging. Thanks to Haig's offensive we were into our third major battle there in as many years.

The field-marshal took one of his hands out of his pocket, and straightened what looked to me like a textbook example of a straight cap. 'Right you are, Captain, you're not there at present, but the war moves quickly,' he said with a wink. 'You'll be pleased to hear we took Polygon Wood, though.'

'So, it's going well, then, sir? The offensive?'

'Yes, it is. Quite well indeed. The heavy rain in August was a setback, naturally. However, the intelligence staff inform me enemy casualties are close to a hundred thousand and German morale has never been lower.'

I caught myself frowning. Our own casualties were reportedly a hundred thousand. It was a bloodbath, a slaughterhouse. But then I remembered Haig's intelligence chief. He had a reputation as the eternal optimist; he certainly wasn't the sort to let reality intrude on a good plan. Not that anybody at GHQ could be accused of much experience with reality. Which, when I thought about it, was a major part of the problem. 'That's excellent news, sir,' I said, 'but I understood our own casualties are also quite heavy?'

Haig looked me in the eye. 'What you must understand, Captain, is that in every stage of this wearing-out struggle, losses will necessarily be heavy. But we must persevere.'

'Of course, sir. Might I enquire if that's where we come in?'

At that moment I saw the colonel lurking behind him, ramrod straight with a pencil thin figure. I would have recognized him anywhere; I never forget a weasel face, particularly one cloaked in red tabs and with gold scrambled eggs on his cap. He was the very colonel I'd had an altercation with last week.

There was a shout of triumph from Private Duncan. My motorcar was putting happily away. The field-marshal greeted the news with visible enthusiasm, likely because it afforded him a polite escape from this obstreperous captain from the colonies and his impertinent questions.

'Best of luck, Captain. I'll mention your name to General Lipsett when I see him.'

'Yes, sir. Thank you very much for the assistance, sir,' I said, as Haig turned and left, the colonel and a sea of minor uniforms scrambling in his wake.

'The captain's a big man. Lipsett has got himself a crew of proper lumberjacks,' I heard Haig remark to the colonel, as he strode back to his car. The colonel said something in response that I couldn't make out.

I looked over at my own car. Whatever magic Private Duncan had conjured up had done the trick. Incredibly, it appeared no more battered than before, and it was running. The reconnaissance was on. And that was a relief. Were it not that the field-marshal appeared to be toying with a new plan for us, I might have been happier. Since arriving on the continent, *my* plan most days revolved around staying alive and hoping the war would end, neither of which seemed more likely with each new plan dreamt up at GHQ. The very mention of Ypres had set off the bludgeons in my stomach.

At the front line the weather was unsettled and the wind had blown in another shower. I stood in Totnes trench, to the south of Lens in the Méricourt sector, and only a few miles from where I'd almost been buried alive. Today the German 5.9s were shelling the rear, Quebec trench, and our support lines. Every so often, a stray shell landed perilously nearby with a sudden boom and a geyser of dirt. One very much like the last had killed Ferguson and the two privates. Lipsett had appointed me as poor Ferguson's replacement the very next day.

'Sir, that's the dug-out. There, straight ahead,' instructed the corporal, as he helped me adjust the field glasses. There was a narrow gap between the two rough timbers that ran along the top of the trench and when I held the glasses up close to it, I could make out the protruding mound in the earth 500 yards away, on the enemy's side of No-Man's-Land.

'And that's where all their officers were spotted?' I said. 'Doesn't look terribly special.' It had a decent amount of wire strung around, but that wasn't unusual. In fact, it could have passed for every other dug-out in this section of the line. Apparently, appearances were deceiving. One thing both the corporal and I knew was that German officers stayed well away from the trenches unless duty absolutely required it, so it was more than your average dug-out – but what? Were they planning an attack?

'I know it doesn't look like much, sir. But that's where we're seeing them... every day the past week, at least one, and usually several more.'

'Have they been carrying maps? Do they appear to be studying our line?'

'It's hard to tell, sir. Usually we see them enter and leave, but it's difficult to make out what they're up to once they're in the bunker. In another hour or so, you can see for yourself. For some reason they tend to arrive in the evening.'

'Fine,' I replied, and took another look. I had plenty of time. I was planning to stay with the battalion overnight.

One of the planks in front of me shuddered violently, as if someone had taken a hammer to it, and there was a brief crunching noise. I knew exactly what it was; it was the sound of metal shredding wood. The plank was thick, and the distance long, but the bullet hadn't missed the gap by more than a foot. I didn't stick around to look any closer. Hand on my helmet I sank down below the lip of the trench and the corporal did the same.

'That was close,' I said. 'That Fritz is a scarily decent shot.' I'd barely noticed the sudden crack off in the distance. Rifle shots were as commonplace as air in the front lines, perhaps even more so, what with all the gas and high explosives that were displacing it these days.

The corporal had an explanation. 'A sniper spotted you, sir. He must have seen a flash from the field glasses.'

'Yes, probably,' I agreed. 'Let's come back in an hour as you suggested. It'll be dusk by then.'

Which we did. And it was. A light rain had begun and there were gusts of wind.

Peering off across No-Man's-Land I felt like I was staring into a well, straining to see the bottom. 'How can you tell if it's an officer in this light, Corporal? How can you see anything, for that matter?'

'Your eyes will adjust, sir. Watch for the helmets of the others. They always straighten up momentarily if an officer passes.' The corporal may have been barely twenty, but he'd learned a few things along the way. 'And if you look through the wire, there – a hair to the right of the entrance – they're silhouetted for a second as they duck to enter the dug-out.'

Within half an hour I had a chance to test his story. I saw four or five helmets bob up, one after the other, along the length of the trench. The soldiers opposite us were a disciplined lot: Prussians, of course. And then for a brief moment I saw a figure stooping, and illuminated as promised by the light from the dug-out. He was slipping his helmet under his arm and he looked like he was carrying a case. It was his rigid bearing that gave him away. He was an officer all right.

We staked out the dug-out for another three miserable hours, but saw nothing else. By the end, I was wet and cold, and I couldn't care less whether the entire German General Staff turned up out of the blue. The reconnaissance was inconclusive. Something was going on over there in that dug-out, but what? I was going to need a new strategy. The thought led me back to my conversation with the field-marshal. He'd said very little, but enough to know there was a good chance we were heading for an even bigger mess.

CHAPTER 2

6th of October, 1917
Château Villers-Châtel, Villers-Châtel, France

'Why the frown, sir?' My assistant was asking.

'Thinking, that's all, Sergeant.'

'About the offensive at Ypres? The attack on the 4th at Broodseinde went well, sir. The German losses were reported as very heavy.' I didn't contradict him.

The Aussies, together with the New Zealanders and the Brits, had surpassed themselves. They'd grabbed another chunk of the crucial ridge line surrounding Ypres.

'The casualty count might have been in our favour, Smith, but we lost heavily as well. And you realize Passchendaele and its ridge are still to come. Apparently, it's been pouring non-stop ever since the attack at Broodseinde. The whole area's barely at sea level to begin with, and seeing as how all the bombardments have destroyed the irrigation channels, it must be one big, muddy cesspool by now.'

'Perhaps the field-marshal will call off the offensive? Due to the weather.'

'Perhaps,' I said, without much conviction.

Once, life at Château Villers-Châtel had been very pleasant, I thought, as I gazed at the crowded confines of the small, elegant room I shared with Smith and two other officers. We arrived only yesterday at our new divisional headquarters, and already I had visions of sitting out the war here. The realist in me knew better. As Smith correctly deduced, my surprise encounter with the field-marshal was still fresh in my mind.

My office was on the first floor, not far from the grand wooden staircase leading downstairs into the main hall. Our room was painted a delicate robin-egg blue and with its fancily-adorned ceilings, and graceful French doors leading to a balcony, was absurdly dainty compared to the four oafs who presently occupied it. Cramped into this space were four matching army desks and chairs, and half a dozen filing cabinets. The chipped walls were plastered with the maps and paperwork so vital to running a modern war, none of which added to the charm.

A captain entered the room, sat down, and threw me a surly look.

'Afternoon, Tibbett. Shouldn't you be out counting guns while Fritz is eating?' I asked. I knew how much he disliked the casual informality that pervaded the Corps. In the absence of any real entertainment, bugging Tibbett was one of my few diversions. When we first met, his disapproval of me, written so obviously on his face, had only led me to redouble my light-hearted efforts to rile him.

Paul Tibbett was English, not that I held *that* against him. It was his air of condescension that I really hated, as if I were a lucky sod just to be breathing the same air. No doubt it stemmed from some insecurity; the result of a flawed childhood, or other such drama. Frankly, I didn't care. His spectacle-endowed clerk's face was soft, round and meek, much like his voice – unless he had something important to say. And then every sentence concluded by pitching irritatingly higher, as if to underscore his undeniable superiority. To top it off, he was a teetotaler, and that was never a positive sign in my book. He did have one redeeming quality; he was a competent enough divisional Counter-Battery Staff Officer. Not that I ever gave him the satisfaction of admitting it. Secretly, I entertained myself by dreaming he was a German spy, infiltrated into our ranks with the sole purpose of ruining our good spirits. That was patent nonsense, of course; no German I'd ever met possessed so little humour.

To his right sat his colleague, Lieutenant Benoît DuBois, whose brow now furrowed in apparent deep concentration. I could see from the strains on his mouth, he was holding back a laugh.

13

Benoît was a French-Canadian from Trois-Rivières. I'd shared more bottles with him than I cared to remember. He was a bear of a man and, if anything, that tired cliché did him an injustice. I'd known plenty of bears who would have thought twice before taking on DuBois.

He had curly brown hair, a trifle long by army standards, and a rough, friendly face set on oxen-like shoulders. His arms hung like lamb joints from each side of a well-toned chest and well-fed belly. All this was anchored on wide hips, and two lithe, powerful legs. If anyone was a lumberjack it would have been DuBois. Why he was a counter-battery officer, and not out with the infantry, was a great mystery. I asked in a round-about way, on several occasions, and got no more than shrugs and jokes in return. If I was in some elite front-line German regiment, I would have cut tail and fled at the mere sight of Benoît barreling down upon me.

Benoît's years in the army had done little to lessen the expressive, almost nasal, Québécois accent that seasoned both his English and his French. I found it utterly charming, although it didn't always make him easy to understand. British officers hearing him speak for the first time regularly did a double-take, glancing at his uniform again, just to see if they'd made a mistake. On the other hand, I'd seen French officers do much the same. I considered him a good friend.

By the time Benoît got around to suggesting lunch I was famished. I was slightly self-conscious my reputation in certain circles as the glutton of the division wouldn't be done much good if I led the charge. So, I sat and ignored the gurgling coming from my abdomen. Tibbett looked up after one particularly egregious rumble, but didn't dare say anything.

As we rose to leave, I said, 'Keep at it, Sergeant,' to Smith, who was putting the finishing touches on the day's intelligence summary. 'I'll be back forthwith,' I lied. I had absolutely no intention of rushing the highlight of my day.

As we approached the officer's mess I knew we were in luck. My nose seldom led me astray and it told me that Madame Jeanne was running the ovens this afternoon. She was an elderly French lady who, once or twice a day, came to the château to cook. I never found out the genius responsible, otherwise I would have put him up for a medal.

I was on my very best behaviour with Madame Jeanne. For her part she seemed genuinely pleased I was so enthusiastic about her cooking. As it was, army food had improved a great deal since Verdun and the Somme. Perhaps the generals were taking to heart the truthful old saying that an army fights on its stomach. More likely it was simply a case of fewer mouths to feed.

'*Messieurs, avez-vous envie de manger? Un peu de nourriture?*' she questioned as she approached. Were we interested in a little food? It was one of those rare times my high school French rose brilliantly to the occasion. Madame Jeanne wielded a huge ladle and was pushing a trolley atop of which rested a monstrous, black, cast-iron casserole.

'*Oui, un peu plus* (yes, a little more),' I responded, smiling at my own pathetic joke.

Benoît rattled off several sentences, of which I think I understood three words. I glanced over at Mme. Jeanne. She looked equally puzzled, but in a mist of steam, she began ladling out a thick brown sauce chock full of what looked like mushrooms and carrots, with a meaty chicken thigh on top.

'*Le coq au vin,*' she said, by way of explanation. Chicken with wine didn't begin to describe the rich aromas that were wafting up from my bowl. With the huge chunk of crusty white bread and large tumbler of red country wine that followed, for a long moment I was intensely happy to be in France. I relished these moments. They were few and far between.

DuBois sniffed at the wine skeptically and took a mouthful. '*Pas mal, pas mal,*' he said, after swirling it noisily around in his mouth.

'Of course it's not bad,' I said. 'You'd drink anything, anyhow,' I told him with a twinge of guilt. I knew I was referring more to myself than to him.

He ignored me. 'What I don't understand, Mac, is why you're so worried. The offensive is going well,' he said, returning to our discussion of the morning. 'I remember how we tunnelled under that ridge near Ypres…'

'Messines Ridge.'

'Right. And put nineteen mines under the Boche trenches. It blew them to smithereens. There were almost 10,000 killed. They could hear the explosions in London.'

I shrugged. 'Sure, but that was in June. Now it's October, it's become one huge painful slog in the mud and Haig is searching for reinforcements. Surely you recall Ypres, Benoît? Do *you* want to return? That's why I'm worried.' After the elation about Messines it had been all downhill. The war cabinet debated. The army's preparations moved at the pace of maple syrup in January. And the German Fourth Army – forewarned – littered the countryside with hundreds of impregnable concrete pill-boxes. The offensive didn't even resume until the last day of July. Then, the August rains began: the heaviest in years.

He lifted his head to stare across the table at me. Sensibly, he then returned to his food. 'This is the food I keep telling you about, Mac,' he managed to spit out, with a full mouth, slurring his th's like they were d's, and food sounding like foot. '*La cuisine de ma grand-mère,*' he exclaimed with delight. A thick trickle of sauce ran down into his beard. Her cuisine or not, his manners would have appalled his grandmother.

With a napkin I brushed at my own clean-shaven face to give him the hint. Facial hair, especially moustaches, were *de rigeur* in the BEF. Almost every officer, senior or otherwise, had one. Beards were less common. DuBois, living life to the fullest, had both. General Currie, like me, was moustache-less. He probably didn't have a clue what *was* or *wasn't* "de rigeur". As for me, I couldn't care less about army etiquette, I wasn't senior anyhow, and I certainly wasn't going to make myself a bigger target for a German sniper by growing an irritating lap of hair on my lip. Naturally, in the dry, warm comforts of an HQ there was no risk from snipers; a fact that was not lost on most senior officers.

'You should have seen them, Benoît,' I was saying, 'they stood there in their gold braids and red caps, with their proper names and polished manners, doing absolutely nothing to help. Most of them couldn't fight their way out of a paper bag. And Field-Marshal Haig...'

'Ah hum,' said a voice I recognized. 'I thought I might find you here.'

General Lipsett had come from the rear. I was caught with my proverbial pants down, or more accurately, with a mouth full of semi-mutinous talk and a half-eaten chicken bone.

'Sir,' I managed to choke out.

'We're going ahead tonight,' said Lipsett.

'Yes, sir, most definitely. I'm heading down there after dusk,' I replied.

'Good. You've got me intrigued whether the Germans are up to something near this dug-out of yours.'

'I hope I'll have an answer for you, General, after tonight.'

'Well, I'll hear tomorrow, either way. Good luck. In the meantime, enjoy your chicken, gentlemen. And MacPhail...' I looked up at him. 'You might do well to remember our earlier discussion.' Then he disappeared as rapidly as he came.

I exhaled, a deep, long, frustrated sigh.

Benoît stared at me inquiringly.

'You remember I told you about my candour with that dim-wit of a colonel from GHQ last week?'

'Wixley-Wexley?'

'Almost. Whatley-Wigham. Anyhow, afterwards the general reminded me that a certain decorum and discipline was expected of officers – particularly those who wished to remain on his staff.' Benoît shook his head understandingly.

The aerial photographs at Corps HQ hadn't revealed much more than my reconnaissance; the enemy was adding to his artillery. And there'd been a few heavy bombardments recently. It wasn't much to go on, but if an attack was coming, I wanted to sound the warning well in advance. So, I took my suspicions and paper-thin evidence to the major and argued we should send a raiding party in the hope of capturing some prisoners, and maybe some documents. He took it to the colonel and soon the whole question was in General Lipsett's hands. To my surprise, Lipsett quickly agreed; he didn't want to get caught off guard any more than I did. It was commonly thought the Germans would hit back hard after their whipping at Hill 70.

Smith and I were going to the line tonight. If the raid went well, we'd return with some useful intelligence early tomorrow morning.

'Well, Benoît,' I said, as we drained the last drops of our wine. 'Unfortunately, I see no alternative but to return to our fight against the Hun, and in your case, Tibbett. When you're starving in some stink-hole in Ypres, you'll remember this meal.'

He grinned. 'You worry too much, Mac. I'm sure it won't come to that,' he said. He rose and I followed.

I wasn't going to ruin his mood, so I said nothing. Benoît wouldn't have seen danger standing on the edge of a cliff. But after what I heard from the field-marshal, I sure did.

As we passed through the doorway into the main hall, I turned on a whim and returned back through it. 'Hang on a minute,' I called out over my shoulder.

A minute or two later, I re-emerged, to be greeted by a hoot of laughter from DuBois when he saw the plate heaped with food I was carrying.

'So, you couldn't resist,' he said. 'You're thin now, but you'll be bigger than me if you keep eating like this.' At 200 pounds and six foot two, I'm not exactly a lightweight, even if DuBois thought otherwise.

'No, no, it's not for me,' I replied.

We climbed the stairs and entered our office. Smith looked up as I walked to his desk, and I placed the dish in front of his nose without a word. From the astonished look he gave me, I knew his gratitude would go far. That was just as well, seeing as how he wouldn't be sleeping much in the next day or two.

'You're welcome,' I said, 'Eat up. There's work to be done.'

I sat down, and began to review the latest reports from the line, scrutinizing the aerial photos with particular care. 'Sir,' interrupted Smith, 'you ought to see this... the day's intelligence summary from 2nd Division.'

I read it quickly. Almost at the bottom, I spotted it: TRAIN MOVEMENT WAS ABOVE NORMAL YESTERDAY AFTERNOON... UNUSUAL TRAIN MOVEMENT WAS ALSO NOTICED ALL DAY – TRAINS GOING IN BOTH DIRECTIONS.

'Additional train movements, eh? Yes, the Germans could be moving in reinforcements,' I said.

'Our raid tonight is looking increasingly important, sir.'

'Yes, yes it is.'

It was pointless to dwell on that now. Yawning dramatically for Tibbett's sake, I stood up, and announced I was going to take a nap. 'Finish that off, Smith, then I suggest you do the same. You'll need your wits tonight. Come to think of it, Tibbett, perhaps you should rest also.' With his weary groan in my ears, I beat a hasty withdrawal.

I bunked in the château's round tower, one of two that flanked the central hall of the L-shaped grey stone house. Since moving in, I'd had almost no time to admire my quarters. There wasn't much to admire: two metal-framed beds filled most of the room, and a wooden trunk, containing the bulk of my earthly belongings, was pushed underneath one of them. The room itself was a peculiar pie-slice shape, with the end bitten off due to the staircase running up the middle. A quaint rectangular window at shoulder level offered a nice view of the trees to the back and some welcome light. As I crawled into bed, the thought came to me that I hadn't even seen my bunk-mate. With the hours I was keeping I might never.

Dinner was a more subdued affair than lunch – Mme. Jeanne wasn't there, she must have been at home cooking for her grandchildren – and I only picked at my food. Even DuBois noticed.

'Are you feeling alright, Mac?' he asked.

'Sure, Benoît, full from lunch, that's all,' I said. I smiled at him uneasily.

Deep down, I was apprehensive. I wouldn't be going out with the raiding party, but in the front-line trenches anything can happen. I knew that all too well. And I was very conscious that due to my zealousness – there was no other way to describe it – some of the men crawling out through the wire tonight might not return. It was a solemn thought, and it didn't do much to awaken a healthy hunger.

With dinner behind us, I said good-bye to DuBois, and headed out the main door where Sergeant Smith was waiting. A stately driveway looped into a large cul-de-sac before the main entrance. As always, there were several vehicles parked outside, not always neatly, and there was a tent from the days of a field ambulance company, pitched incongruously off the right wing. Rain, little care, and the feet of a legion oblivious to the charms of a château had left the grounds noticeably down-at-heel. A car with driver stood idling at the bottom of the stairs. We quickly descended and got in. The driver asked: 'Are we ready, sir?' and I replied: 'We are.' With that, and in a spiral of smoke, we set off.

'You okay, Smith?' I asked, after we'd driven for a couple of minutes, surprised my chattily-predisposed assistant hadn't said a word.

Smith was along to translate. He spoke very good German having learned it from his parents, the Schmidts, who long ago had immigrated to Canada. German speakers were few and far between – at least on our side of the line.

'Fine, sir,' he curtly replied. He was in no mood for a chat: nerves maybe. Neither was I. Our trip to the line would take no more than an hour and I had a lot to mull over.

After my encounter with Haig I'd done a lot of thinking, and I can't say I liked my conclusions. Officers are a tight-lipped bunch by nature, and anyone at a headquarters – in other words, those most likely to know anything worth knowing – were the least likely to tell. Still, you didn't have to be a genius, or even an intelligence officer, to see the overall direction.

The Ypres Salient was a meat grinder and Haig's latest offensive was chewing up men like I'd once seen a bear devour a hare. The field-marshal had sixty odd divisions at his disposal, and the bulk of them were already active in the Salient, or had been. If he needed fresh troops there were only so many places to look. In six months, the Corps had taken two of the toughest positions on the Western Front, and my guess was the generals weren't going to let us rest on our laurels. Haig had virtually said as much. His visit with Currie was no coincidence. *It couldn't be, could it?* I'd have to pray the job in the Salient got done before we were needed. I was not looking forward to revisiting "Wipers".

As a young fresh-eyed lieutenant, I'd once plucked up my courage enough to chance the ridicule and ask a sergeant – a grizzled, stocky man by the name of Higgins – why they all called it Wipers. Like any smart-ass lawyer, I probably thought I already knew the answer. For the typical Anglo, Ypres doesn't exactly roll effortlessly off the tongue. But the sergeant paused for a long while – so long I thought he was going to ignore me, drew on his cigarette, and then finally raised his weary blood-streaked eyes to mine. 'Well, sir, that's because it's where we all get wiped out.' I was convinced he'd hit the nail on the head.

Morosely, I turned my head and gazed out the window at the dark countryside, catching fleeting monochrome images as the car jolted its way along the small country roads.

CHAPTER 3

7th of October, 1917
Méricourt sector, Lens, France

It was very dark. By the reckoning of my battered but trustworthy Borgel wristwatch, it was a few minutes past twelve o'clock. The raiding party was preparing to leave.

There was an officer, two non-commissioned officers (NCOs) and ten men – thirteen souls. I'm not superstitious, but I was glad for the weather. The night was ideal for a foray into enemy lines; the wind was picking up, and it was drizzling and overcast. There was no danger that a shard of moonlight would spill off a rifle barrel or bayonet.

The weather was one of the reasons why we were pressing ahead. Only days earlier, 2nd Division had replaced us in the line and that should have made it their raid, but General Lipsett said that was far too risky. We had a detailed plan, and we were ready, while they weren't. It was a principled stand and I admired him for it.

'So, you're Andrews?' I said to the lieutenant.

'Yes, sir. I'm leading the patrol tonight.'

I'd heard good things about him. He was from the scouts and surprisingly young, younger than most of the wiry types who were standing around waiting for him. They were all scouts and the elite *fleur-de-lys* scout patches were readily visible on their sleeves. They were loaded down under what seemed like a dizzying assortment of weaponry.

21

'Are you sure you need so many weapons, Lieutenant? It's only a reconnaissance. What are you carrying, exactly?'

'It's best to be prepared, sir,' he replied. 'Oh, we have rifles – naturally – also pistols, bombs, knives, cudgels, and probably a half-dozen other things tucked away, even I don't know about. And these.' He held up the palms of both hands, fingers extended, in front of my face. In his eyes I saw a cold seriousness.

It took a special breed of soldier to be a successful scout. It was one thing to master the skills. It was quite another to launch oneself over the parapet into No-Man's-Land in the dark of night, on a patrol that would land you deep in the enemy trenches.

'Look, you know the bunker from studying the maps and the photos. We need to gather information and hopefully a prisoner or two, preferably officers. If it turns out to be better defended than you expect, forget about it. The last thing I want is to lose half of you in a skirmish, and for nothing. Remember, it's a red Very flare if you need the artillery.'

He nodded. 'Yes, sir, I think we should be able to manage that. Give us an hour or two. I'm not sure how long it'll take to get through all the wire, but usually it's a quiet stretch, this.'

I felt like an over-protective mother, admonishing her children to be careful before they went out for a night on the town. Only these men might not be coming home at all. A patrol into the enemy line was about as dangerous as it comes.

Usually, we let off an artillery barrage when a raid went out, just to keep Fritz's head down. But so as not to frighten away anyone of importance, we dispensed with it tonight. The weather was with us.

'Good luck, Andrews,' I said, and I gave each man a nod, and a fleeting pat on the shoulder, as they filed by.

Smith and I followed the party out of the bunker and down the trench 30 yards. We turned right into a communication trench, a sap, linking the front and second-line trenches, and emerged a minute later in Totnes trench. It was wet going. There were trench mats, a rough flooring of sorts that look a lot like wide-planked ladders lain end-to-end. However, this makeshift floor was shin-deep in water, and mud was oozing up through the parts that weren't.

We walked past a bulky sentry who stood forlornly under a small overhang. He was peering sideways out into the darkness, his greatcoat stained black from the rain and his collar upturned to catch the worst of the wind. His helmet was tilted rakishly forward with the brim low over the eyes, a look that had become a virtual trademark in the Corps in the last six months. It lent a visible toughness to his appearance that surely would have enticed some of the girls back home. More practically, it allowed the water to pour off somewhere other than down the back of his neck. Soldiers were nothing if not practical.

I saw the blue rectangular patch of the 2nd Division on his arm. When he turned briefly to glance at us, as we trundled by, the insignia of the 24th Battalion was visible. They were the Victoria Rifles from Montreal.

The drizzle was turning into a downpour and the wind was blowing hard. While I felt for the lads' discomfort this was very welcome. The German sentries would find the weather equally foul.

The first of the scouts scampered up the trench wall and slid over, a dark shadow that disappeared from sight almost immediately. He was promptly followed by the next. Lieutenant Andrews raised an arm to bid us farewell, glanced briefly at me, and then disappeared after the others into the sheets of rain that were now pelting No-Man's-Land.

I climbed up a step or two and peered cautiously over the parapet – more than one soldier, in a moment of carelessness, had lost his life to a sniper this way – but seeing nothing but darkness, we quickly retreated to the warmth of the dug-out.

As dug-outs go it wasn't bad. It was almost entirely underground. Despite that, I had to bow my head only slightly to pass under the heavy wooden beams that reinforced the ceiling. It was unmistakeably not a French design. Above ground, sandbags were piled high to protect against the artillery, although they wouldn't have held a direct hit from a 5.9 howitzer or, even worse, one of the heavy trench mortars. Short of that, it was the safest place in the line.

Coming in from the cold and the rain, I immediately felt the warm air from the coal stove that was burning in the centre of the room. A stove-pipe led up, and to the rear, where the smoke was funnelled away so as not to reveal the dug-out's location. There was nothing the Germans relished more than shelling anything that might be a headquarters.

Despite the warmth, the air was heavy: a mixture of damp earth, smoke, food and the smells of men who'd gone unwashed for far longer than those at home would consider civilized. With the departure of the raiding party, the main chamber was empty, save for the duty lieutenant and two privates, one of whom was talking on the field telephone. Away from the entrance and the main chamber, four small rooms – cubicles really – had been built with rough wooden planking separating them from each other. There were two on each side with a corridor down the middle. Two were filled with bunks and another with a table, some cabinets, and a few chairs. The last was a small medical post. It had a couple of beds and was manned by two orderlies. I popped my head through the doorway and greeted them with a quick wave.

I returned to the main room and plonked myself down at a table in the corner. Smith was engaged in conversation with the lieutenant; something to do with artillery codes. Sergeant Adam Smith. I couldn't help but laugh – what parent would name their child after an economist, famous or not? They must have had some inkling of his character, for watching him now, he was obviously buoyed by this dull material. Then, the reddish-brown earthenware bottle occupying a prominent place on the table caught my attention.

It was *jenever*, or what the English referred to as Dutch gin. It wasn't bad stuff and a nip of it might do me a world of good. I was nervous. I picked it up, and it seemed full. That was a stroke of luck: *Bols*, it read. That was the real stuff from neutral Holland. How it got here was beyond me; liberated from the Germans probably, who themselves had pinched it somewhere in Belgium – their gentlemanly behaviour early in the war had deteriorated. If truth be told, so had mine.

After more than two and a half years on the continent, I was well acquainted with the local tipples, and a little *Bols* would have hit the spot quite nicely. Reluctantly, I set it aside and went over to one of the privates to rustle up a cup of tea. If things went well with Andrews and his patrol, I might need that bottle before the night was out – and a lot more than I needed it now.

I yawned. My short nap earlier this afternoon was wearing off. I sipped at the strong dark tea and glanced over at Smith. He had rejoined me; proving you can discuss artillery codes for only so long. A year ago, I wouldn't have even known what they were. It was a sign of the times, the army was changing.

It was a fine thing, too. While no one ever accused us of lacking in spirit, the short-comings of an over-reliance on bravery in trench warfare became woefully apparent not long after arriving in Belgium. I'd seen the sorry results. Fortunately, we had a few good leaders and an eager, almost boyish, willingness to learn. Naturally, change came easier when you weren't tied down by centuries of tradition. Not everyone in the Imperial army saw that as an advantage.

I still recall a starch-encrusted officer sniffily describe us as, "that shabby lot", and I couldn't blame him. We'd come a long way from the early years, though, even if the average Canadian soldier's deference to authority, or lack thereof, remained a festering sore for some in the army hierarchy. That was why it was so nice to have the Australians around, they made us shine. Lightning, I was taught, tends to strike the most exposed object and, as lightning rods, our raucous Aussie friends performed their role brilliantly. It was a shame Colonel Whatley-Wigham couldn't find some Aussie to harass.

'It's a strange job, ours,' I said to Smith, making a stab at conversation. 'We struggle to bring some order to all the information flooding in, yet we're running around like idiots trying to garner even more.'

Smith bobbed his head as if my ramblings were perfectly understandable. 'It's a real juggling act, sir.'

'What do you think of this work, Smith? In intelligence, I mean?'

He considered the question. 'I like it. The army is much more professional these days. There's so much detailed planning and it all relies on intelligence. I feel like I'm in the centre of the war, sir; that what I'm doing makes a difference. More than if I was simply holding a rifle in a trench, at any rate.'

It was true. The bumbling amateurism of a year or two ago was disappearing and intelligence had become critical to the entire war effort.

Smith continued. 'Surely, you must feel the same, sir? After all, when you were in operations it was mainly about logistics. And now you're in a position to make a real difference. There are not many captains that can say that.'

Thoughtfully, I rubbed my chin. 'You know I hadn't thought about it like that, Smith, but you have a point. I was simply going to say I was surprised by all the paperwork.'

'You were a lawyer, sir. I wouldn't expect you to be afraid of a little paper?' It was an amusing and perilously saucy rejoinder from Sergeant Smith. A month with me and he was already sarcastic.

I let it pass and I sighed. 'No. It's not the paper I'm afraid of, Smith. What terrifies me is what's *on* that paper. That, and the fuming generals; not to mention the bullets, bayonets and shells I still have to contend with. And to think, in civilian life, I considered a day in court to be a perilous undertaking. What a difference a war makes.'

Smith smiled.

KABOOM. The shell went off with a deafening crash outside the dug-out wall beside me.

I was propelled head-first into one of the rough wall timbers that supported the whole structure. Thinking back on it later, I felt the shock waves before the sound even registered. I was a little tense, I guess.

Stunned, I lay crippled on the moist dirt floor for a long moment. Then I realized where I was and what had happened. My forehead was wet. I raised my hand, and turned it reflexively to my backhand, as if to wipe the sweat from my brow. When I glanced down, I was shocked to see it smeared in blood.

'Sir!' cried one of the medical orderlies I'd seen earlier. He'd materialised seemingly out of nowhere. 'You're wounded.' Smith stood, with a concerned expression, looking down at me.

'And here I thought, sitting in a dug-out, I might return without a scratch,' I replied. My heart was racing. I felt a mite queasy at the sight of so much blood – my blood.

'Don't you worry about that, sir, we'll have you fixed up in no time,' the orderly said, helping me into a chair. 'Every so often Fritz lobs one over to see if we're awake.'

'Thanks,' I mumbled. 'Good of him to think of us so. I hope we can return the bloody favour.'

As the orderly cleaned and bandaged my left temple, I thought back to my last real wound, a souvenir from the Somme. That one eventually got me out of the trenches and into the château, and it was tempting to think what my latest scratch might lead to. No, no matter the twist I put on it, the context of this particular mishap wouldn't do anything for my reputation. Ridicule was most likely. I put my head back, and my feet out, and tried to relax.

It was 1.27 a.m. I'd just glanced at my watch again. With a start I heard a machine gun start up. I was more than a little jumpy. TUF-TUF-TUF rang out. It sounded like a German standard issue MG08. A Maxim. I prayed it didn't mean bad news.

I rushed out of the dug-out, through the communication sap and down Totnes trench heading towards the lookout post. A flare shot up in the distance. It began its relentless, slow descent to earth, wobbling uncertainly, much as my boyhood spinning top did on a table when it ran out of energy. The flare's white light was pure, and yet harsh at the same time; not unlike how a snow bank, covered the night before in a fresh blanket of bluish white snow, could gleam so very brightly in the midday sun that you had to avert your eyes. As the flare wobbled to and fro on its descent, its glare mercilessly lit up No-Man's-Land in front of me.

In my haste, I nearly toppled a soldier as I ran up the few steps into the lookout post. I thrust my face up to the sheet iron plate fastened at the top. In it a long slit gave an excellent view of the terrain in front of us. 'Smith!' I bellowed.

'Sir?' came the baffled response from behind me. He'd been quicker than I expected. With irritation I noted his voice was calm and steady and, most infuriatingly of all, not out of breath.

'Ah, good, you're awake,' I bluffed. 'Get the artillery to let off a few salvoes. And hurry!'

As I peered through the slit, I could make out very little despite the illumination from the flare. In the distance, a line of wire was visible; it was ours. There seemed to be nothing moving. The rain was driving down with such force that the ground was a dancing tapestry of splashes, as if the water-soaked earth was literally spitting out the deluge that was coming down upon it.

Our artillery started up. I felt the concussion of the shells being fired and saw the bright flashes almost immediately as they dropped in and around the German trenches, not more than 500 yards away.

The rain dimmed the effect from where I stood. That was misleading I knew, the effect on anybody caught unawares in that trench would be devastating.

'They're here, Captain,' said Sergeant Smith. Smith had returned, but amidst the din of the weather and the field guns I'd heard nothing.

Emerging from the look-out post, I spotted Andrews and his party trudging through the trench. A couple of sorry-looking Germans were drooping along in front. They must have entered the trench further along. I followed them to the dug-out where I made my way to a drenched but grinning lieutenant. 'Well sir, it went like clockwork. I think they were all trying to keep their heads dry,' he said. 'We didn't have any problems until the bunker; a young lieutenant there was a bit over-zealous… it's funny how the young ones are always the most unpredictable,' said our twenty-two-year-old firebrand.

I didn't bother to ask what happened to the German lieutenant – I had a sneaking suspicion I already knew. I couldn't blame them.

'I have no casualties to report and we have three prisoners. One is a captain. He appears to speak decent English. I also have this,' he said. With the adrenaline dissipating, his tone became noticeably more formal, as he remembered he was in the army. He handed over a black leather map case and I opened it immediately. There was a thick sheaf of papers in the middle pocket. I quickly rifled through them.

There were three detailed maps and I took a look at one. On it were drawn various artillery emplacements, both ours and theirs. Ours I knew. Tibbett and DuBois would be thrilled, however, to see what the Germans had and where. And the artillery lads were always keen to know what the enemy knew about their own positions; no one liked having a bulls-eye painted on their head.

I whistled. 'Andrews, you and the scouts have outdone yourselves tonight. This looks like great material. I'd like you to pass on all the details of your raid to Sergeant Smith, once you get back to battalion headquarters. And then make sure you get a good night's sleep. You deserve it. You all do,' I said loudly, turning to face the others. 'I'll be sure to tell the general what you've accomplished tonight.'

Suddenly, Andrews noticed my bandages. He must have seen them when I turned. 'You're wounded,' he cried.

'Just a scratch, Lieutenant, just a scratch,' I said, acutely aware I was the only one wounded despite having remained in the dug-out all night.

'Sergeant Smith, would you accompany Lieutenant Andrews and these two over to battalion HQ?' I asked, gesturing at the two German privates. 'See what you can get out of them. I'm going to take a crack at the captain right away. Andrews tells me he speaks English so you'd best concentrate on them. And keep a very close eye on this,' I said as I handed him the case. 'This might get Tibbett into quite a lather.' Smith looked intrigued. 'Not that that would require much,' I mumbled under my breath.

I turned my attention to the captain. He sat despondently at the corner table where I'd motioned to Andrews to leave him. He had fair hair, a thin waxed moustache and a face I could best describe as gaunt. His features were perfectly symmetrical. He had a solid dependable air about him that women undoubtedly found handsome. The moustache looked absolutely absurd – though who was I to criticize Prussian facial hair fashions?

And he was obviously Prussian. Not only did his tunic display the insignia of the 1st Guards Reserve Division, an elite formation from Prussia, he looked as only a Prussian can – not dissimilar from the majestic bald eagle sitting high in a tree and arrogantly surveying his domain. The captain's normal proud bearing was frayed a touch. His ignominious capture, and being prodded at bayonet-length through the rain and mud by a private who probably just as easily would have shot him, could have had something to do with that. Still, he had a dignity about him in the circumstances I couldn't help but admire.

'Hauptman,' I said, addressing him by his German title as I approached. Before he could respond, I grabbed the jenever bottle and poured out two full glasses. I pushed one towards him. Then I pulled up a chair, sat down, and offered him a cigarette. He grabbed it with a mix of enthusiasm and desperation. I lit it for him. He inhaled greedily – after the night he'd been through I could certainly relate.

'Don't look so glum,' I said. 'You're one of the lucky ones, you've made it out of this war and with your skin intact. Cheers.'

I raised my glass to him, and he responded with a formal nod of

29

his head, and raised his glass as well. I drained the glass and looked expectantly over at him. He hesitated, and eventually did the same, whereupon I refilled both glasses.

'You're obviously not from around here,' I said. 'Where are you from?'

He brightened. That was good. He understood English well enough and he didn't seem inclined to play the sullen prisoner.

'Danzig,' he replied, which sounded awfully truthful to me. The interrogation was off to an excellent start.

'You know, I've never had the pleasure. Perhaps after the war you can take me around. I'd take you around the dug-out, but there's not much to see.'

'You're Canadians?' he enquired.

'We are indeed. You can probably tell from our rugged good looks,' I clowned, trying to ingratiate myself.

Cautiously he smiled. 'You're all so big.'

He was right, we were. We were a good head taller than almost all the Germans I'd encountered, and the English and French were no different. Field-Marshal Haig could be forgiven for wishing he had a few more lumberjacks in his merry band.

'It's all because of our healthy air, I expect. Until we arrived at Ypres, that is,' I said, unsure whether he'd pick up on my oblique reference to the German gassing we'd suffered in 1915 – it had been just our luck to be at the receiving end of the first-ever gas attack.

'Yes, I know,' he said seriously. 'This war leads to the worst in man.' He spoke English well – for a Prussian – and his heavy German accent was more amusing than distracting. In happier times it would have been reason enough for a little good-natured teasing. I didn't disagree with what he said, though.

'You must miss your family?'

'Yes, I do. Very much.'

'Show me them.'

He took out his billfold and from it, a picture folded in quarters. With great care, he methodically unfolded it, and placed it on the worn table in front of me. 'My wife Else, and my two little daughters, Ensel and Katryne. They are in front of our home.'

'They're absolutely beautiful.'

'Do you also have a wife and children?' he asked.

I hesitated. This wasn't a topic I'm normally keen to discuss. In some perverse way it seemed alright to talk to him about it, a total stranger and an enemy to boot. 'I did,' I said, 'a wife, that is. But we never had kids. She died more than three years ago, in the summer of 1914. Her name was Kathryn. Almost the same as your daughter.'

He pursed his lips sympathetically and raised his glass. I did the same.

The bottle was three-quarters empty and it was approaching 3.30 a.m. when I decided to get down to brass tacks.

'Horst, you know I was puzzled why so many officers visit this bunker where young Andrews found you. Sure, you have a nice view of our trench-line, but it's not without its dangers?' I said. That's the beauty of a bottle of jenever; you find yourself on a first name basis long before you might otherwise.

'Ah,' he said. 'It really is very simple, Malcolm. We are being replaced next week, and our young lieutenant just received a whole case of pear schnapps. Imagine that, a whole case. He has,' he began to say, and then corrected himself, 'He *had* important relations in the *Kriegsrohstoffabteilung*.' I knew a little German, but I must have looked puzzled. 'You know, the raw materials department. Our lieutenant friend was not a very pleasant man, but his pear schnapps... well...' He left the thought hanging.

By the time we finished the bottle, we were each feeling worse for wear; and I was definitely feeling the dumber of us both. All the heightened activity had boiled down to a standard trench rotation, much as we'd done last week, and a case of pear schnapps. My report was going to require some serious creative embellishment.

Luckily for me, artillery Hauptman Horst Gruendemann was thoughtful enough to bring his attaché case with documents and maps to what was officially an observation of our lines, and unofficially a schnapps tasting. I should have felt relieved there was to be no attack, only a darker cloud was circling: Haig's plans for us in the Salient.

CHAPTER 4

9th of October, 1917
Château Villers-Châtel, Villers-Châtel, France

'Bloody hell!' I muttered to myself, after glancing fleetingly at my watch. It was 10.05 a.m. and the staff meeting had already begun. It wasn't the first time I was late to a meeting, and I hoped this time my recent nocturnal duties might grant me a reprieve. We might even hear some good news from Ypres: such as the objectives were taken, or Haig had called off the offensive. I was clutching at straws, I admit.

'Ah, the walking wounded have decided to join us,' exclaimed General Lipsett on seeing me ease through the door, sinking any hopes I had of silent anonymity. There were snickers of laughter; petty retribution for past jokes of mine. The general watched as I slunk across the room and eased into a chair at the far end of the table.

General Lipsett had a good sense of humour, which I appreciated; except when I was the butt of it. At the moment, it was his temper I feared most. He prized punctuality. And results.

'Sorry, sir,' I stuttered, breathing hard from the run downstairs.

'We really ought to get you into physical training, MacPhail. You sound like you're seventy.' The snickers grew louder. Some of those present were enjoying my discomfort a tad too much, I thought.

To my relief, our senior staff officer, Lieutenant-Colonel Hore-Ruthven, called the meeting to order. I'd missed next to nothing, but in typical army fashion, enough to get lambasted for it anyhow. Then the colonel asked Tibbett to speak. Apparently, this was not going to be my morning.

'Thank you, sir,' said Tibbett. 'Thanks to Captain MacPhail, we have determined precise firing locations for most, if not all the German batteries in the Méricourt sector.'

I sat bolt upright in my chair. I wasn't sure I'd heard correctly. The entire room was staring at me – again – this time without the smirking grins.

Lipsett seemed to wink in my direction. Then he rubbed an eye with a finger leaving me in doubt. I was still a little light-headed after my exertions of two nights earlier.

Tibbett continued: '2nd Division has already undertaken several counter-battery shoots…'

I let his words buzz on like a bee gorging itself on apple blossoms. It surprised me; Tibbett was not one to share credit, not if he could take it himself. Maybe he was resigned to sharing his oxygen supply, after all.

I've always found staff conferences to be a necessary evil, but that didn't mean I had to like them. Typically, each officer gave a succinct summary of recent developments in his department, and came away with an extensive wish-list of new tasks. Operating on the theory that the less said, the less likely additional work would be thrown in my lap, I kept my contribution to a minimum. Tibbett had covered my back admirably.

I did mention the upcoming German troop rotation. Also, I reported what the prisoners from the 1st Guards Reserve told us: they believed they were going to Flanders. No one said a word.

I repeated it, changing the wording so nobody would misunderstand. 'Due to the heavy casualties from our Ypres offensive, the Guards anticipate being called north as reinforcements.' Nothing. Lipsett and Hore-Ruthven were as mute as the rest of them. It made no sense at all. Was I the only one fearful we were to be reunited with the 1st Guards across the wire? Or worse, going up against them in an attack?

Mercifully, Hore-Ruthven tolerated few deviations, and developments were largely routine, so the meeting wound up well before 11 a.m. DuBois grabbed my arm as I went to leave.

'Lipsett was very pleased, Mac,' said Benoît.

I shrugged. 'I hope so.'

'I was thinking about this whole Ypres offensive,' he said, slowly. Someone *had* heard my guarded warnings. 'Perhaps the French will come and help?'

'Oh no, I don't think so. The rumours have it the whole damned thing began when General Pétain begged Haig to attack. You remember General Nivelle's offensive in April and May?'

'At the Chemin des Dames, in the Champagne? Of course.'

'And you remember what happened.'

'A big disaster. The French soldiers, the *Poilus*, were baa-ing like sheep as they left their trenches.'

'Right. And there were 190,000 dead and wounded, and afterwards whole units mutinied. An entire division even deserted.'

'Nivelle got sacked.'

'True, but the damage was done. The French Army was a mess. And everyone feared the Germans would catch on. It came as godsend when Haig launched the offensive in June.'

'And that's why he launched the offensive?'

'That's what I think. That and the Admiralty were lobbying hard to retake the ports at Oostende and Zeebrugge, to relieve the U-boat menace.'

'So, no French reinforcements?'

I shook my head.

'Captain MacPhail!'

It was General Lipsett. He and the colonel had concluded their brief post-meeting conversation.

'Wait a minute, Captain, I'd like a few moments of your time.'

'Certainly, sir,' I answered, not sure whether to be pleased or concerned.

While his accent sounded upper-class English, Lipsett had been born Irish, and I had no reason to doubt it, having been at the muzzle-end of his fierce temper more than once recently. He had a low tolerance for fools. It was something he'd evidently decided to overlook in my case, temporarily, at least. He'd made it abundantly clear that my accession to the intelligence section was on a "trial" basis, even if he worded more tactfully.

'Does it still hurt?' he asked. He gestured towards my bandaged forehead as we strolled down the corridor to his office.

'No, it was more the shock than anything, sir,' I replied, lightly touching my temple. As a matter of fact, it hurt like hell, but I wasn't about to admit that to anybody, especially not the general.

'There are a few things I'd like to tell you,' he said, immediately after we settled into our chairs in his spartan office. Sadly, he seemed intent on skipping vital refreshments like tea, or even a biscuit from the tin box in the middle of his desk that I knew was home to assorted delights. He and I plainly differed on what constituted necessity, so long after breakfast, and so far before lunch. I kept my mouth shut.

It certainly wasn't an office anyone would have thought belonged to a major-general. When I was in the trenches, I always equated a general's domain with pure luxury. This was far from that. The ornate furniture belonging in an elegant room like this was nowhere to be seen; the general's desk and armchair looked like stock army fixtures – of the nicer variety, not like those I was using. There was a painting of rolling hills and quaint woodland prominently displayed off to my left – presumably so both the general and his visitor might appreciate it. I guessed it was some place in Ireland. Otherwise, there was a regimental standard I didn't recognize, and several photos of the general posing with other officers. One, judging by the helmets they were wearing, was taken in Africa during the Boer War. Another had Lipsett standing erect beside the Prince of Wales.

'First of all, I had the occasion, yesterday, to speak briefly with Colonel Whatley-Wigham,' he said, without as much as a word of introduction. He hadn't invited me to critique his interior decorating. 'The colonel told me the field-marshal was able to assist you with some car troubles a while back. He also insinuated he overheard you taking an insubordinate tone.'

I began to sputter. Lipsett lifted a hand to silence me. 'I trust that's an exaggeration on the good colonel's part, but I hope I don't have to remind you again of the importance of showing appropriate deference to your superior officers.'

'No, sir,' I mumbled.

After a long pause, he came to the real topic. 'As of this morning, we've been reassigned from the First Army to the Second,' he announced. I didn't say anything. 'Are you alright, Captain? You look ashen.'

I nodded. So it *was* to be Ypres. 'Yes, sir,' I murmured. There was nothing to be done.

'You're certain?'

My chin went up and down. And my stomach followed. We were being thrown into the quagmire.

Until now we'd served under General Horne's First Army in the Lens-Arras sector, the site of our big battles at Vimy Ridge and Hill 70. The Second Army, commanded by General Sir Herbert Plumer, was well into its fourth month of the offensive in the Ypres Salient. There was one small salvation.

'We're off to Ypres, but we're not joining General Gough's Fifth Army, then?' I asked.

The Fifth Army was active on the left flank of the Ypres offensive. Many in the know thought that if we were going anywhere, it would be there. I had no desire to repeat the experience of the Somme, the last time we'd fallen under Gough's command, or to come anywhere near his bullying chief of staff Major-General Malcolm. Malcolm was widely despised in the BEF, and it was a sentiment I shared – despite the name.

He sighed. 'You're nobody's fool, MacPhail. That was a considerable risk, in my opinion,' he said, and paused abruptly. Pensively, he looked off through the windows to the trees outside now being showered with rain. After a moment, he came to a decision.

'Now, and this is *not* for general consumption, Captain,' he continued, 'but I have it on excellent authority that General Currie told General Horne in no uncertain terms that he and the Corps were not enthusiastic about serving under General Gough. I'm told General Horne relayed that to the chief of staff, and he informed Field-Marshal Haig. Upon reflection, the field-marshal has decided we will join the Second Army rather than the Fifth. I think you'll agree that's rather fortunate.'

'Wow,' I managed to utter. This was potent stuff. No officer took refusing to serve under another's command lightly. In its harshest light it could be seen as mutiny or, at the very least, insubordination on a scale far worse than I'd been accused of. General Currie must indeed be in Haig's good books.

The attack on Hill 70 was Currie's baptism by fire as Corps commander. We took the objectives and German casualties were three times our own. Crucially, Haig's plan to divert enemy resources from Ypres was masterfully accomplished, no doubt explaining his forbearance with our new commander.

'Wow, indeed. I trust I won't be hearing idle chit-chat about this in future, Captain,' he said, with a glare that penetrated right through me. 'Secondly, now that I've satisfied your curiosity, I'd like you to...'

'...get my ass up to Ypres,' I said, finishing his sentence.

He smiled thinly – a good thing for me, not every general would have taken my upstart interruption so magnanimously.

'And?' he asked. There was a long moment of silence. In an uncharacteristic loss for words, I pondered what he could be driving at. With his elbows on his desk, and hands clasped together under his chin, he gazed fixatedly at me. I started to feel claustrophobic.

'You know, I didn't put you on the intelligence staff for your pretty face alone,' he said, finally. 'Let me show you something. In strict confidence.' After rummaging in his drawer he passed over a single sheet of paper.

It was marked PERSONAL & SECRET, and dated today. It was from Corps HQ addressed to General Lipsett personally, "*in accordance with instructions received from the Corps Commander*". Personal and secret, that was unusual.

At the top of the page was a short excerpt from an order entitled: SECOND ARMY O.A.D. 654. My eyes raced down the page... "The Canadian Corps will be utilized for one of the following purposes:"... here it came...

The first option was to support Gough's Fifth Army. *That couldn't be it, not given what Lipsett just told me.*

Then I saw option B: "To secure the Right Flank of the Second Army by the capture of the ZANDEWOORDE-GHEULUVELT and BECELAERE Spurs." That made more sense. Yet I was puzzled.

The critical ridgeline that was the initial objective of the offensive began near Messines to the south of Ypres. It then curved to the right and upwards like a reverse "C" – to the north – in a rough 120 degree arc. The arc ended near the village of Passchendaele. However, four months into the offensive, and after numerous major battles,

Passchendaele and the remaining ridgeline still weren't taken. Securing a ridge currently in German hands seemed a bit premature.

'Sir, either there's something I'm missing, or this makes about as much sense as making reservations where we should dine once we get to Berlin,' I said.

'Be that as it may, Captain, that's what I have to go on,' he replied. 'So, my question stands. Once you get your *ass* up to Ypres, what exactly do you propose to do? Particularly now that any semblance of fine dining in the area is a thing of the past,' he added, with a wry grin. Just like the general to knock me down a peg or two.

'Well, sir,' I began, 'I suspect you'll want to know where we're apt to end up, what we'll be tasked with doing, and as much information about that task as possible in order to begin preparations. And should I happen upon it, you'd love to receive the entire German order of battle with their exact current locations.'

'Finally, a good idea.' He paused for a moment, during which time he gave me a bemused look, and then added, 'And based on your *vast experience* of these matters, Captain, what is your assessment of where we'll end up?'

I ignored his subtle gibe. He asked my opinion, so now I planned to give it to him. He might not be too pleased at my conclusions.

'Forgive me for saying so, General, but it's starting to look frightfully obvious. For four months, the brunt of the attack has been against the Messines-Passchendaele ridge. Right now, the two ANZAC Corps are spearheading the advance. Either, they succeed in the very near future, or they'll be replaced by fresh divisions. Frankly, I'm afraid we're Haig's first choice as replacements – sorry, I meant to say Field-Marshal Haig's first choice. I think our orders will soon involve a major attack. And if I read the map correctly, there's only one place that can be, and it begins with a P.'

He sat, digesting my comments. 'You're probably not aware of this, but today at dawn a fresh attack was launched. We'll know by the evening how it turned out.'

'We can only hope for the best, sir. We may not be needed. However, you asked what I should do in Ypres. Well, I think liaising with the Australians, and getting as much information on their sector as possible, would be a good start.'

38

'And presumably you have an idea where you'd like to begin?' Lipsett asked.

I couldn't put my finger on it, but I had a sneaking suspicion I'd just been led by the nose to a conclusion, and course of action, General Lipsett had long since determined.

'Coincidently, sir, I met someone from II ANZAC Corps, actually, it was the 3rd Australian Division, at a conference a few weeks ago. I should be able to arrange a billet with them, I reckon.'

'The way you phrase it, MacPhail, makes it sound like a jaunt to a house of ill repute. It's fortunate I needn't worry about that, given the absence of any women with our Australian friends.'

'If you knew Aussie women, sir, you wouldn't worry in the least.'

The outlines of a smile appeared, and he lifted the lid on his tin box. Turning it, he pushed it slowly towards me. Greedily, I reached out, but then hesitated. An image of my curly-eared black Labrador came to mind, straining eagerly for a biscuit I was holding up as a reward. I didn't hesitate long; General Lipsett's treats were always very tasty, I was starving and, besides, my black Lab never turned down a treat I offered. In war-time, self-respect was an over-rated attribute. Not like self-preservation. If I valued that, this was the moment to put my tail between my legs and run.

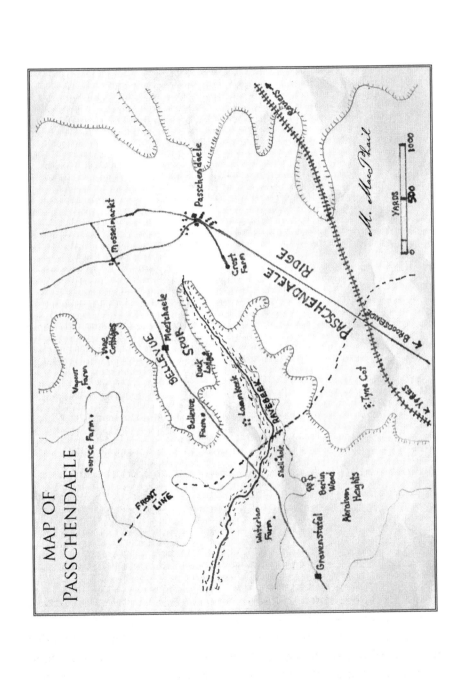

MAP OF
PASSCHENDAELE

Soure Farm

Vapor Farm

Vine Cottages

Source Farm

Mosselmarkt

Passchendaele

BELLEVUE SPUR

Meetcheele

Crest Farm

Bellevue Farm

Dock Lodge

Laamkeek

RAVEBEEK

Snail Hole

Waterloo Farm

Berlin Wood

Gravenstafel

Abraham Heights

Tyne Cot

PASSCHENDAELE RIDGE

← BROODSEINDE

← YPRES

FRONT LINE

YARDS

0   500   1000

M. MacPhail

CHAPTER 5

11th of October, 1917
Train station, Arras, France

The whistle blew shrilly and the train began to inch forwards. It laboured furiously to pull itself into motion, as if at every turn of a wheel it might not make it to the next, rather a lot like I'd felt this morning getting out of bed.

Seated across from me in animated discussion, even at this hour when talking was absolutely the last thing I wanted to do, were two officers from the division. By army standards it wasn't particularly early, but I'd never been one for army standards, and especially not after a send-off from DuBois and a couple of others that had lasted well into the night. It didn't help that I was heading to Ypres and action. And the officers opposite me seemed determined to not let me forget why that was.

'The Australians got clobbered again on the ninth, eh?' said an earnest looking lieutenant from the artillery. I figured he was on his way to make preparations for their imminent move.

'Oh?' said the other, also an artillery lieutenant. 'It was a debacle I gathered, but I didn't hear the details. What happened then?'

'The captain told me there were almost 7,000 casualties. Imagine that, 7,000 in a single day. And they ended up no further than their starting lines,' said the first. 'The barrage was a bleeding disaster. I guess the weather hampered putting enough guns in position. And what they did shoot was wildly inaccurate.'

'It's nice to know what we're getting ourselves into,' said the other, smiling bravely.

The bulk of the casualties were British – from the 43rd and 66th Divisions – but other than that, the lieutenant's brief account was sadly accurate. The Ypres offensive was bogged down.

At the Corps conference yesterday afternoon, General Currie formally relayed the news we were being ordered to Ypres. DuBois said the response was distinctly underwhelming; not that anybody, least of all Currie, would be surprised by that.

As the train moved northwards towards Belgium, the terrain levelled off and the small hills and ridges that enlivened the countryside around Arras gave way to a stark flatness. The trees, now predominantly brown and yellow in their autumn colours, thinned out and I began to see a monotonous succession of blackish brown fields, punctuated by the odd farmhouse or a lone tree. There were mainly sugar beets and potatoes grown here, I was told. The war hadn't come to this corner of Northern France, but staring out the window, it took little fantasy to picture these desolate sodden fields as a muddy shell-torn battlefield.

We were approaching Hazebrouck, the last major town before Belgium, and the skies outside assumed a uniform greyness. The wind was blowing and a light drizzle streaked the carriage window. The sun that I glimpsed as we departed this morning had long since retreated. All in all, it was a thoroughly depressing sight. Even the weather was warning me off. The good news was that the thumping in my head was almost gone, and I was starting to feel hungry.

The train largely emptied at Hazebrouck, including the two young lieutenants, who departed in a rush of friendly good-byes. 'Best of luck, gentlemen,' I said, hoping I didn't sound too grumpy – I hadn't exactly been a model of affability during our journey.

As the whistle blew and we started out on the last leg to Ypres, I began to consider what lay ahead, now that my brain was shaking off its rum-induced state of cataleptic stupor.

I knew what General Lipsett wanted – anything and everything to make it easier to hit the ground running, once our commanders gave the orders we both knew were coming. There were really only two possibilities: either we were to shore up the line, or we were going on the attack. But, what had Haig said? *"I'm visiting General Currie to discuss the offensive"*. So, that really left *one* possibility. We were going to have to slog our way through the ridgeline that was stymying everybody else, and Lipsett would want to hear from me how best to do it. Given that no one had yet figured it out, I was going to be busy. The general wasn't one for excuses, regardless how well-intentioned the efforts.

Haig's grand Ypres offensive was designed to force the decisive breakthrough. Not for him the "bite and hold" operations like the victories at Vimy Ridge, Hill 70 and Messines. The field-marshal was dead-set on something far more ambitious. His plan was to cut through the semi-circle formed by the German Fourth Army who, entrenched on the high ground of the ridge, were punishing Ypres with their heavy guns. Once through them, there would be a push for the coast. This would isolate the German forces caught between Ypres and the Channel coast to the left, and gravely threaten their position to the right.

On paper the offensive didn't seem outlandish. Back in June I don't think it was. On the ground, in mid-October, things looked a lot different, especially as the ground had turned to mud. After a half dozen major battles, and months of fighting, it didn't take a great strategist to conclude that the element of surprise was long gone. Casualties were piling up fast, and the plan needed an urgent overhaul. Any possibility of still breaking for the coast was pure fantasy. But then we were dealing with GHQ. And I didn't see the likes of General Charteris, Haig's intelligence chief, or Sir Launcelot Kiggell, his chief of staff, mustering up the courage to inform the field-marshal even if his pants were on fire. It was infuriating. No, it reminded me of two bulls going at it until one, or both, succumbed; with the only difference being one bull was up to his waist in mud. And soon, I feared, that bull would be us.

'I wasn't sure you'd make it,' I cried out upon detraining at Ypres station, where Captain Dan Banting of the 3rd Australian Division, stood waiting for me. He was leaning against a black Ford so covered in mud that determining its colour was more a matter of judgement than eyesight.

'Bloody near didn't,' he replied, and waved me over to the car. 'Get in, we'll talk on the way.' I threw my helmet and my small canvas duffel bag with socks, some underwear, a shirt and a few toiletries into the back and got in. My trunk remained behind in France, but the corporal responsible had solemnly assured me that it would be sent along later, together with the divisional luggage. It was an assurance I might have been more concerned about had the contents of my trunk warranted it.

'I'm impressed,' I said. 'I didn't realize the car had finally made its entry Down Under. Of course, you needn't have gone to so much trouble washing it all up for me.'

Banting snorted and stomped on the gas pedal. I hoped I hadn't irritated him too much. He was an affable looking man – much like his personality – with a broad mouth, wide friendly eyes and rugged features, all capped by a set of fiercely wild eyebrows that somehow didn't look out of place and accentuated his natural expressiveness. I glanced over at him. He looked haggard, scruffier than when I saw him last, and obviously frazzled – exactly what a few weeks in Wipers will do to you.

'What ran into you?' he asked, with a toss of his head in my general direction.

My bandage was gone but an ugly looking bruise remained. With my cap removed it was all too visible.

'A bulwark,' I replied.

'Looks painful,' he said. 'How's the bulwark faring?'

I grunted. Banting was concentrating on avoiding a column of soldiers.

'So, tell me... you're on the verge of a major breakthrough?' I said, more out of hope than good sense.

'Ask me after tomorrow. We're attacking again. That's why I'm a little rushed.'

'I hadn't noticed,' I said. I had, of course, but I didn't think rubbing it in would help.

'One thing's for sure. It's all too haphazard for my liking. Haig is breathing down our necks to take Passchendaele and he's not taking no for an answer. The Brits got nowhere on the ninth. Well, you'll see for yourself, shortly.'

'So there's no hope the whole thing will be called off?' I asked.

'Called off,' he exclaimed. 'No, I don't think that's going to happen. I overheard Monash talking, and apparently Plumer and Gough argued to close the campaign several days ago. Haig would have none of it. No, we're to take Passchendaele, come hell or high water.'

'From what I hear, it sounds as if both are applicable.'

We roared down the Rue de Lille and bumped across the cobblestone causeway at high speed, barely avoiding another column of soldiers marching into the city, not to mention a couple of massive potholes, or German shell-holes; it was hard to know for certain. Either way, running into one of them would have ended our little ride very abruptly. I was thankful I hadn't taken the lieutenants up on their early morning offer of bread and sausage.

We passed through Ypres' medieval southern gate into the city proper, and then made such a sharp right, I had visions of entering the city in an overturned car, my face plastered to the passenger-side window, as we slid across the road. Fortunately, Banting tooted loudly before turning; a group of soldiers in file was hugging the ramparts. I caught a fleeting glimpse of one as we thundered past; he appeared strangely unruffled. That revealed either a great deal about Australian bravery or, more likely, he was simply accustomed to Australian driving.

In a screech of brakes, Banting announced, 'We're here.' It was none too soon.

A dilapidated two-story grey brick building was built into the ancient ramparts that encircled most of the city. Almost all the windows were missing and even the doorways stood open. What had once been the garden, between the wall adjoining the street and the building itself, was now roofed over with a makeshift assortment of wooden planks and tarpaulin, from which numerous stove pipes of varying lengths and sizes protruded. At the front, running along the top of the old garden wall, was a jumble of telephone cables. Outside, on the muddy dirt road, a gaggle of uniforms stood slouched, smoking and drinking, and watching us with undisguised curiosity.

'It's quite the château you have here,' I said, thinking forlornly of Château Villers-Châtel and Madame Jeanne. I heard Banting sigh, in an exasperated sort of way.

It was only a short ride. There'd been no need to make a race of it, I thought grumpily. Now, as the adrenaline subsided and I started to think of food, my stomach began doing cartwheels. I pointed to the field ambulance parked outside. 'Is that for me?' I asked, as I shakily dragged myself from the car.

'You're looking a trifle pale, Malcolm. Come in. I'll introduce you and show you your lodgings.'

Inside, the divisional HQ was no more hospitable than its outer shell – *squalid* came to mind. We walked along a cold dark corridor on the main floor, before descending a few steps. From the maps on the wall, and the activity within, it appeared to be an operations room.

Banting cleared his throat, in precisely the sort of way you do to get someone's attention, and announced: 'Gentlemen, let me present Captain Malcolm MacPhail. You'll be interested to know he hails from the King's coldest colony. And more recently from Arras.'

'Welcome, mate!' I heard shouted a few times, accompanied by animated waves. The Aussies weren't the sort to get caught up on decorum, which suited me just fine. And they were friendly. I smiled back.

'That's Lieutenant-Colonel Jackson over there,' Banting said. He pointed to a corner table where a lanky, younger looking man with an impressively bushy beard sat. 'He's our GSO1.'

The GSO1 was the senior staff officer just as Hore-Ruthven was ours, and like him, Jackson was also English – due to their experience most senior staff officers in the Dominion forces were. That wasn't always unequivocally welcomed, especially not by the independent-ly-minded Aussies.

'Come on. I'll introduce you.'

As we approached, Jackson turned, and after the niceties were completed, said: 'So, I expect you're here to see what you're getting yourselves into, Captain?'

'Well, we were rather hoping that you'd capture Passchendaele before that became necessary, sir,' I replied.

'Yes, I can imagine,' he said. 'We'll do our best, won't we, Banting? A pleasure to meet you, Captain. But if you'll excuse me, I have a great many things waiting.' And with that he went back to more urgent matters.

'I'd have thought both he and the General would be up at the front, reconnoitering?' I said with a frown, after we stepped away.

Banting grimaced. 'You might think that. Neither of them have actually been to the front, as it happens.'

'Really?' I said.

He shrugged. 'Come on, let's get your things away. You'll have plenty of time for more introductions later.'

I followed him up the steps and down a corridor, where we soon descended a deeper flight of stairs into what felt, and smelled, like a cellar. It was damp, dark, and musty, and smelled an awful lot like my grandparents' cellar, where as a kid I always liked to poke around. Of course, the advantage of my grandparents' cellar was that I didn't have to spend the night. Nor did they keep several large unwashed Australian louts and countless rats in it. It was something I hadn't adequately appreciated at the time.

'Your quarters are right over there, in the corner, Malcolm,' Banting said. He waved to a dark recess in the room where I could make out the bare outlines of a wood-framed bed. It might have been the light, but I could have sworn it was crooked. Sourly, I considered whether it would hold me.

'You shouldn't have gone to so much trouble, on my account,' I grumbled.

'Oh, it's nothing,' Banting replied. 'Knowing you Canucks feel most comfortable in the great outdoors, I first asked about a shell-hole. Unfortunately, they all appear to be taken at the moment.' I saw Banting was wrestling to maintain the guileless look he'd assumed.

'I think you'd better call me Mac,' I said. 'Only my friends treat me this well.'

'Alright, Mac. Before you get too comfortable though…'

'Oh, I don't think I'd worry too much about that. I hope I can return the favour sometime.'

'Well, that's something to look forward then,' said Banting. 'In the meantime, we're taking a patrol up near the front lines. Do you want to come?'

'I wouldn't miss it for the world.'

We passed through the Menin Gate. It was the sole exit from the north of the city, a fact the Germans were well acquainted with. Consequently, that made it one of their favoured targets. Haste might have been warranted, but the going was slow as the road was heavily congested with marching soldiers and an endless procession of pack animals, carts, and vehicles. I'd offered to drive. Banting had turned me down – something about not knowing the way. Danger aside, my stomach was happy his pedal foot was temporarily tamed. And it gave me a chance to look around, although I was shocked by what I saw. The city I remembered, the attractive, prosperous looking one of early 1915, and later the shell-torn version of the spring and summer of 1916, was now completely obliterated. Of the great Cloth Hall and the Cathedral, only eerie skeletons of stone remained, jutting out as lonesome reminders of what had been. Even the ruins were ruined. Ypres had been razed to the ground and piles of grey stone, and the odd timber, were all that testified that this once, incredibly, had been a vibrant city.

As we exited the Vauban ramparts I looked by chance to my side.

'It's still there,' I exclaimed. 'Who'd have guessed?'

'What's still where?'

'The straw in the lions' mouths, or hadn't you noticed?'

'Oh, you mean that tale about the Germans not returning until the lions ate the straw?' said Banting. The Germans briefly occupied the city in 1915. When they left, the townsfolk had put straw in the mouths of the two lions that sat astride this gap in the ramparts. The superstition was that the Germans wouldn't return, until the lions had eaten the straw.

'Yeah, exactly. Seems to have worked so far,' I said.

'And here I thought *we* were the ones keeping the Germans out. Now it turns out to be the lions…'

Compared to my trip from the station it took an eternity to make the 2 ½ mile journey to the village of Zonnebeke. It was a blessing in disguise as it gave my innards a much-needed respite. The narrow dirt road was not only clogged with troops, animals and other vehicles, but pockmarked with shell-craters that the engineers were labouring furiously to repair; almost as furiously as the Germans were endeavouring to create new ones. I was fortunate Fritz took a well-deserved rest of his own during our journey. It left me with little to do but look out the window, not that there was much to see.

Once out of Ypres and its carpet of stone, the landscape became a veritable wasteland, a dark tribute to the war-making skills of man and the cruelties of nature. Of the little copses of trees, the farmhouses, the hamlets and whole villages I recalled, nothing remained. At most, a disfigured tree stump, or a fencepost now and again, to provide a reference on the endless horizon and every so often, the remains of a tank or a truck or, once, the unmistakable corpse of a horse sunk awkwardly into the muck. The grey sky hung like a blanket low over the battlefield. From the ground wisps of black and white smoke curled upwards as the occasional shell landed. As far as the eye could see the ground was mottled with craters. Even from the road I could make out the water that filled them. I couldn't imagine there was another place on earth to rival this in its misery.

We arrived just outside the village, or the little that remained of it, unspeaking, still slightly awed by what we'd seen. I opened the car door, pleased to get out. As I inhaled my first breath of open air in the Salient I gasped in disgust, quite loudly I think, for Banting quickly asked, 'Are you okay?'

It hadn't smelled particularly fresh in the car, but I'd written it down to my Aussie friends and a tough few weeks. However, an awful stench now overwhelmed me and I put my hands on my knees and my head down deep, and I felt like I was going to retch. Thankfully the feeling passed. But the smell remained; a nauseating mixture of earthy tones from the dampness and the mud blended with the acrid sweetness of cordite from the guns, the oniony stench from the traces of mustard gas still lingering in shell-holes, and the putrid odour of decaying bodies, excrement and God knows what else. It was the smell of hell itself.

To keep my mind off the smell I turned to Banting. 'Those guns there,' I asked. 'Are they to be used tomorrow?'

'As far as I know, why?'

I pointed to the small stack of shells lying on the ground beside each of the three 18-pound field guns that were lined up not far from each other. 'They won't be shooting long with that miserly pile,' I said.

He shrugged. 'I know, but we haven't had much time. And, as you might have noticed, it's like pissing in the wind to get a shell up here.'

I was going to point out that the single timbers on which the guns were mounted wouldn't hold them for long. Not when they began firing. And particularly not in this mire. But in a flash of tact I didn't think I had, I bit my tongue. It was probably all they could lay their hands on, I thought solemnly.

In a group of perhaps a dozen we headed off along the single wooden duckboard, westwards, in the direction of Tyne Cottage, only a speck on the map. Banting had told me their 9th Brigade would attack from there, tomorrow at dawn. I was thankful to be walking on solid ground. How the best part of a three-thousand-man brigade would make it along this narrow wooden pathway, in short order, in the early hours of the morning prior to the attack, was another matter.

After we walked in single file, in silence, for almost twenty minutes, a large group of soldiers came walking towards us. Seeing as how they were carrying stretchers, I stepped off the duckboard with one foot to allow them easier passage. I regretted it instantly. My foot sank away into the mud up to my knee. Somehow, I didn't lose my balance, but my boot and leg were sucked into the glutinous earth and were not leaving of their own accord.

'She'll be right, sir, just give me your arm.'

An Australian private had come to my rescue. After a lot of exertion on his part, and grunting on mine, my leg – boot and all – came free with one great *ploop*.

'Thanks,' I said, as I pulled myself together. 'This isn't any old ordinary mud you have here.'

'No, that it isn't, that's for sure,' he replied. 'I've seen men sink right away in it and that's no joke. I'd keep to the duckboards if I was you, Captain.'

I thanked him again, also for his advice, and we moved on. I could see it was a considerable relief to the platoon sergeant. He was undoubtedly counting the seconds we stood immobile out in this ocean of sludge. Not that the chances of surviving a shell were any greater when moving than not, at least I never thought so. It may have felt differently to him.

From a distance I heard a mournful braying. As we approached I saw the poor beast. Its legs were swallowed by the mire all the way up to its belly and it was straining terribly to pull itself from the quicksand. The mule had strayed inadvertently from the planks of the timber road that crossed our little path, perhaps from the shock of a shell exploding nearby. Weighted down by the shells on her back, she had sunk quickly into the soft viscous mud bath that Flanders fields had become.

As we neared, I saw the driver pulling frantically at the reins of the animal, as distraught as the beast itself. We passed and I saw he was English; I couldn't make out his unit. He was crying, tears pouring unashamedly down his face. The mule was fixated on him, her big eyes bulging in terror and he spoke softly trying to reassure her – or was it himself. I wanted to stop. Instinctively, I knew the futility of doing so. Our troop marched remorselessly on and so did I. In despair and embarrassment, I turned my head away. I could feel my eyes welling. My legs marched, with a mind of their own, mechanically onwards.

We arrived, not long after, at what I took to be Tyne Cottage. It proved to be nothing more than a ramshackle barn that was somehow, miraculously, half intact. Scattered around it were a collection of five or six concrete pill-boxes, all heavily pitted by artillery and small arms fire. I could see the Aussies were using the largest one as a dressing station. Astonishingly, the rain had ceased, and there was a row of men on stretchers neatly lined up beside each other on the ground outside, waiting to be attended. Banting's division took the position only last week. The fight had been a fierce one.

I looked around to see where Banting was, and I spotted him conferring with a couple of officers. They were all bent over a table and looked to be studying a map. Occasionally, one would straighten his back and gesture forwards with his hand, while talking animatedly, as if describing a feature of the torn landscape in the direction of Passchendaele. As I watched, the gesticulating became more and more frenzied. I walked over, curious as to what they were discussing.

'Fuck me dead! The bloody Poms were supposed to be further. How could they not know where they were? Are they blind? Damnit! What a complete cock-up!'

I was surprised to hear Banting doing the cursing. Until now I'd never seen him in anything other than upbeat good spirits.

51

MALCOLM MACPHAIL'S GREAT WAR

Tentatively, I called out: 'Hey, Dan!' As I drew nearer, I said, 'I don't suppose you'd mind translating that last thunderstorm?'

He waved me over and stabbed his finger at the map. 'The 66th Division were supposed to be here, after that mess of an attack two days ago. Instead,' he moved his finger down the map to illustrate, stabbing another point repeatedly with his finger with such ferocity I could hear it, '...they're here... 200 fucking yards further back. And to top it off, they hadn't even figured it out after two bloody days! Imbeciles. Our patrols only discovered where they *really were* this morning.'

'And?' I asked cautiously, not completely grasping why 200 yards was bothering him so.

'AND,' he said. He was in quite a lather. 'That means the artillery are going to have to adjust their barrage in the first crucial minutes. Instead of moving their sights 100 yards ahead, every eight minutes, now they're going to have to do it in four. Otherwise, the 9th Brigade's attack in this stretch will fall behind the rest. That leaves the infantry with precisely half the time to cover the same distance, but in this same stinking mud. If they hope to keep pace behind the barrage, that is. You know as well as I do, if they don't keep pace, they'll get blown to bits when the Jerries run back to their guns. What a monumental cock-up!'

CHAPTER 6

12th of October, 1917
The Ramparts, Ypres, Belgium

Everyone at the Aussie headquarters in the Ypres ramparts was on edge. The initial reports from the battle were coming in. At first, an excited optimism permeated the air as ground was steadily won. We knew that the cost would be terrible. But as the afternoon wore on the pace slowed. Then came the shocking news that the 9th Brigade, and soon others, were retreating.

Aside from cursing, and my ears were ringing from the expletives, there was nothing to be done. I saw it first in their downcast eyes as the news dribbled in. By nightfall, drenched in water and mud, exhausted and dazed by their ordeal, the first survivors arrived at headquarters. The battle was lost and with it my last dash of hope. Courage had taken them far, but the Australians were a spent force.

The next afternoon, when I cautiously inquired, Banting told me they had less than 4,500 men in fighting form – barely six battalions out of a force of twelve. Of the New Zealanders I heard only a little. It was more than enough to know they were equally battered. Later, one of the Australians, in a whispered aside, confided that the Kiwis had suffered their worst loss of the war – by far. I figured I knew all too well how they felt.

By day's end the final terrifying casualty toll from the attack on the

53

twelfth was tallied. It was another slaughter. Between the Kiwis and the 3rd Australians some 6,000 men were lost, and there were surely thousands more killed and wounded on each side of the seven-mile wide advance. To make matters infinitely worse, Passchendaele and its ridge were still firmly in the hands of the German Fourth Army's *Gruppe Ypern*. Unless Haig reconsidered, the inevitable loomed.

14th of October, 1917
Hazebrouck, France

When the shouting started, I glanced surreptitiously around the room. It was a select gathering. There was Major-General Watson, the commander of the 4th Division, accompanied by a lieutenant-colonel I didn't know; Currie's chief of staff Brigadier-General Radcliffe together with a stiff-looking major and, of course, Lieutenant-Colonel Hore-Ruthven. And then there was me, outranked as usual and, once again, out-dressed.

Despite the best efforts of an enthusiastic, pimply-faced private deep in the catacombs of the Australians' HQ, getting the mud, and especially the stink, out of my uniform hadn't been an unmitigated success. I figured my best strategy was to stay out of the way. If you're looking to avoid stray shrapnel, it's always prudent to keep your head well down. I wasn't formally invited to the conference – and gate-crashing this kind of event wasn't done – but Lipsett had asked me to attend yesterday when he called. 'Come and give me a report. I won't be far from Ypres, and you might as well sit in on the conference while you're there,' he told me. So here I was, in Hazebrouck, where the 4th Canadian Division had its newly installed headquarters.

Normally, this was a pretty self-assured bunch. Now they were all sitting stiffly erect in their chairs like junior cadets, unspeaking. Their eyes, and mine, were fixated on the plain white wooden door at the end of the room. Behind it, a volcano had erupted.

General Currie was raging. 'PASSCHENDAELE,' he roared. 'What's the good of it? Let the Germans have it, keep it, rot in it! Rot in the mud!'

My heart sank. This didn't sound good. The others looked grim.

Naturally, Currie had been out to see for himself. That was the problem with making the effort to reconnoitre, most times you didn't like what you saw. Come to think of it, that was perhaps why General Monash and his colonel hadn't bothered. I most definitely didn't like what I saw. If only Field-Marshal Haig had taken the time; it might have saved us all a lot of trouble.

Currie continued, 'There is a mistake somewhere. It must be a mistake! It isn't worth a drop of blood!'

I could only imagine how Lipsett was coping; he'd been singled out for this private chat. For that, most in the room were rather grateful, regardless what their jealous looks said five minutes earlier. Whatever Lipsett was saying seemed to be working, as we didn't hear "old Guts n' Gaiters" erupt again.

The men had given him the nickname. At first, I thought it was a wink and a nod to the old expression of "guts for garters", so I asked a veteran sergeant. He explained, in more detail than I cared to hear, how 19th century serial killers in London used their victims' guts to make garters, before eventually letting drop that the nickname referred to the general's pear-shaped figure and straight-laced discipline. I was relieved when he finished.

I arrived a little before eight-thirty, shaken by the drive and the emotions of the past couple of days. Early this morning I said my farewells to Dan and my new Australian friends, and wished them well. Under the circumstances there was little else I could say.

The Australians had kindly lent me a car and driver. I could have sworn it was the same mud-splattered Ford I sat in earlier; certainly, the hand imprint in the passenger side door looked vaguely familiar. As to the driver, I'd gone out of my way to assure Banting that he was *far* too busy to even contemplate driving me to Hazebrouck. Having neatly side-stepped that hazard, I was feeling rather pleased at how diplomatically I handled it. That was not long before I realized that I'd actually thrown myself in front of a bus – in the form of a fast-talking private from Perth who, making precious few concessions to his pale and silent co-pilot, endeavoured to set a new land speed record in the Ypres-to-Hazebrouck run. I'd barely staggered into the headquarters building, after a rushed 'see-ya, mate' followed by a spray of gravel, when General Lipsett saw me and waved. He immediately ushered me into a small room along with Lieutenant-Colonel Hore-Ruthven.

Once seated, Lipsett stared at me. Then slowly and without making any attempt to conceal it, he inspected me from top to bottom. 'Well, MacPhail, at least you won't have to worry about messing up your uniform,' he said cryptically. Hore-Ruthven was crinkling his nose, but didn't say anything. Then Lipsett got down to business. He wanted to know everything. This wasn't a moment for diplomacy and, in all honesty, I'd had my fill of diplomacy for the morning. So, I told him.

I told him about the rushed preparations, the lack of shells and guns, the poor communication and inadequate logistics. I told him of guns sinking helplessly into the sludge because there weren't enough timbers to make a stable firing platform, of shells disappearing without exploding because the fuses weren't designed for the blubber, and of the bravery of men going into battle, exhausted before they even got to their starting lines. I even told him about commanders conducting a battle on a field they'd never seen, relying, almost as if it were by osmosis, on a single strand of telephone cable. I didn't leave much out. Hopefully I hadn't overdone it.

When I was finished, the general furrowed his brow, looked thoughtful, and then asked but a single question: 'The battlefield, the mud – is it really as bad as you say?'

I simply nodded.

By the time the conference officially began, at ten-thirty sharp, we all had a good idea what would follow. Fortunately, Currie had blown off some steam. Anybody that hadn't heard him minutes earlier would have dismissed out of hand any talk of a foul temper, although his introduction surprised me.

He began very evenly, noting that the recent march discipline was lax. 'Columns should not halt in towns,' he said, with a stern look. He immediately followed this up by remarking, 'mounted men should dismount when halted.' I waited… listening for the punchline that must surely be coming. But it didn't arrive.

Currie was always a stickler for discipline. That was one of the reasons why the senior British commanders had gradually warmed to us after our high-spirited entry into the BEF; the other was we won battles. The discipline didn't make him especially well-loved amongst the men, although Currie was far too shy, aloof, and ungainly to be a soldier's soldier: not like our previous commander, the dashing General Byng. Byng overcame his noble English roots and won the troops over with a cheerful informality. Currie was a fine general, but I sure hoped he'd drop this nit-picking when the Corps got to Ypres, or the mud would truly be flying.

Quickly, he shifted gear to the topic everybody was waiting for – perhaps it was his way of breaking the ice. 'Gentlemen, we are to take Passchendaele. So that is exactly what we are going to do.'

My stomach hung there in mid-air. *Passchendaele.* So that was that. *Alea iacta est.* The die is cast. There was to be no miraculous reprieve, or last-minute change of plan. For him, and for us, there was nothing to be done. Get on with it. Like we always did.

The general's tone was matter-of-fact, but underneath it you knew there was a backbone of steel. He may not have liked the orders, but he was going to clear the ridge of the Germans and what they, or anybody else thought, had absolutely nothing to do with it. If Crown Prince Rupprecht had been listening, I'm sure it would have sent shivers down his spine; it certainly did mine, although for altogether different reasons.

I looked up at the cracked plaster ceiling. At the time it seemed like some kind of lousy metaphor for what was unravelling in the Salient. Banting was right. Haig was hell-bent on taking Passchendaele. The grand strategic plan of breaking through to the coast was long since in shatters. Even his chief of staff Sir Launcelot, who'd never seen a battlefield in his life, aside from the well-manicured rugby pitch at Sandhurst, must see that – although, on second thought, he struck me more as a croquet man.

Rising to the occasion, some obsequious soul at GHQ came up with a stirring new rationale for capturing the ridge – it was essential to gain higher positions in advance of winter. Which was preposterous. The transparent stupidity of it was almost laughable, but then I thought of the Aussies. No, it was simply Haig being bull-headed. He'd stubbornly continued the offensive at the Somme against better judgement, and it sure looked like he was doing the same thing again. So much for learning from your mistakes.

Ironically, the field-marshal had made changes for the better in this war, but throw a bit of red in his eyes and he wasn't a jot different than your average Spanish bull in a ring. Curiously, I'd been accused of a little obstinacy myself. Just last week some red-tabbed army bureaucrat had called me a pig-headed sod, but then I wasn't a field-marshal. Besides, I'd been right. I sure hoped Haig was.

Something in Currie's tone jolted me back to the present. It might only have been the sudden realization that what he was saying was shortly going to be of vital concern.

'I would like General Lipsett and General Watson to consider a plan of attack as soon as possible,' he said. 'In all probability the attack will be carried out in three phases. The first two phases will be carried out by the 3rd and 4th Divisions, and the last, namely the actual assault on Passchendaele, will be the responsibility of the 1st and 2nd Divisions.'

Lipsett and Watson looked on impassively, not altogether dissimilar to DuBois after he'd consumed his second bottle of the evening. Benoît, it must be said, usually seemed more at peace with himself than they did now – being half comatose can have that effect. Gamely, I attempted to follow their example, even though I was already strategically planted in an inconspicuous corner, and my Ypres bouquet along with me.

Then I heard Currie explain that we were to take the left of the II ANZAC positions. The 4th Division was to be on the right.

I perked up. So, we were to relieve the New Zealanders. I'd never met many Kiwis, but I reckoned they couldn't be half bad if they managed to co-exist in the same neighbourhood as their rowdy antipodean cousins to the south. Right when I was on the cusp of recalling the capital of New Zealand – I felt it bouncing around on the tip of my tongue – I heard my name.

'Captain MacPhail returned this morning from the 3rd Australian Division, where he bivouacked for several days. He had an opportunity to see the Australian positions, and their preparations, as well as to follow the battle at General Monash's headquarters. Before the conference, he mentioned a number of interesting things. I think they might be worthwhile hearing, especially with regards to the last item.' Lipsett glanced inquiringly over at Currie and Watson, who both nodded their assent, and then turned his eyes to me: 'Captain?'

Stuck somewhere between Wellington, Christchurch, and Auckland, I'd been a couple of continents away from hearing the last item. I inhaled deeply, and assumed a look of profound concentration. That should buy me some time, I hoped, and lend some weight to my forced spontaneity. Now, if only I could determine what the hell the subject was. I was right back in 12th grade science class again.

Luckily, in the depths of my reverie, I'd caught something about how critical it was that ammunition be delivered to the guns. I decided to wing it from there. 'Thank you, sir,' I said, more-or-less in the direction of General Lipsett, as I stood to address them. 'I think that was an excellent point.' No harm in going with the flow, I figured. A compliment sometimes went a long way in making friends.

'From what I observed with the Australians, there were not only too few guns, but they had very little ammunition prior to the barrage. Clearly there was insufficient time to prepare. The roads and tracks were woefully inadequate to transport the guns and the sheer volume of ammunition and material required. The ground is very, very poor. It's really impossible to describe without actually seeing it. My uniform may give you some indication.' There was some rustling around the table. 'Partly as a result of the ground, and the rushed preparations, many gun positions were only makeshift constructions. Most of the guns half-submerged themselves in the mud after repeated firing. Following the attack, a number of Australians complained they hardly noticed the barrage.'

'Captain MacPhail…' It was General Currie. 'It was lieutenant, I believe, when I spoke with you last?' God, the man had the memory of an elephant. Of course I remembered him. It was almost a year ago, sometime in the winter of 1916, if I recalled correctly. How could I ever forget?

'Yes, sir, I'm surprised you remember,' I replied.

'You're not easy to forget, MacPhail,' he said, and then to Lipsett, 'You've got yourself a good man there.'

Lipsett smiled politely. He had a look that said he was holding something back. A little voice whispered in my ear that it would be better if it remained that way. Unfortunately, it was in my ear and not in the general's.

'Stubbornly impertinent at times, sir, but not unamusing, no, I

59

wouldn't say that,' I heard him remark. There were muted chuckles from the others.

Before I had time to contemplate exactly what that was supposed to mean, Currie continued, 'That sounds vaguely familiar. Getting back to the question of the guns, however, Captain. Do you have any observations about the pace of the barrage?'

'Well, the artillery was on an eight-minute per hundred-yard pace as you know, sir, with a 100 yard lift,' I said, lapsing effortlessly into army jargon. 'But the infantry had a great deal of trouble keeping up. The conditions are truly atrocious. Keeping that in mind, I think it would be more effective to use a fifty-yard lift.'

That was one of the invaluable things I'd picked up being a lawyer, how to make saying very little sound like a lot. In plain English what I said was fairly simple: the guns would normally begin firing at a point not far from the taped starting positions where the attack would begin. Then, every eight minutes, they would lift their fire to a new line 100 yards further than the last. The creeping barrage was a technique we'd used to great effect at Vimy Ridge and elsewhere. I'd simply proposed that they halve the distance. At least then our infantry, struggling through the mud, wouldn't be miles away from the falling shells. With any luck, that would prevent the enemy from being cocked, and ready, and machine-gunning them as they approached.

'That's very helpful, Captain, thank-you for your contribution,' said Currie.

After my surprise performance the meeting passed remarkably quickly. I think I'd resigned myself to the inevitable. In the army it was better just to get on with it, not that there were many other options. At least we wouldn't be making the same errors twice… not if Currie had anything to say about it. And for the first time in three days my stomach was settled, the air was fresh, and lunch was imminent.

'Why don't you stay here tonight?' said Lipsett, as he prepared to leave. 'Take a bath, and you can travel on the bus tomorrow morning with the other officers from the division up to II Anzac HQ, to view their model of the front. I hear it's quite impressive.' My smell must have been a few shades worse than I feared if a bath was the first thing that sprang to his mind. Not that I minded. I would have killed for a hot bath. There was even the prospect of a warm meal, and if Lady

Luck was really in my corner, a bottle of rye or one of those decent French reds.

'Thank you, sir,' I replied, hoping not to sound too pleased. I was grateful all the same. 'And I expect I should then carry on to the Kiwis?'

'Full marks, Captain. I'll have Major McAvity arrange something for you with their headquarters staff. Assuming you're not in with some Kiwi, already?' he said, his voice full of innuendo. I shook my head. 'Fine. You know the task, so get on with it. And do try to think about your personal hygiene, MacPhail.'

On an afterthought he turned to me again, and looked me in the eye. 'None of us wanted this, Captain. But we will get it done. I'm depending on you.'

'Yes, sir. And we will get it done, sir,' I replied. I knew, from Currie on down, we would do what we had to do. And the first thing I had to do, was figure out how to storm a muddy rise saturated with barbed wire and machine-gun blockhouses.

CHAPTER 7

17th of October, 1917
Shell-hole, approximately 300 yards northeast of Berlin Wood, Belgium

I peered out of my hole ever so cautiously. I kept my head well down, my chin resting in the soft clay. Even at this range a sniper had been known to put a bullet through a man's head. I looked across the flat and torn landscape and saw perched, like an ominous but very thin grey cloud lying low, almost north-to-south across the horizon, the infamous Passchendaele Ridge.

Somewhere in the middle of this vista, must have lain the name-sake village I'd seen marked so prominently on my map, a mere mile and a half away. Of it there was nothing to observe, not even with the powerful Lemaire field glasses I had the good sense to borrow when I was in Hazebrouck. Flowing down from Passchendaele in my direction was a once insignificant stream, the Ravebeek. It was flanked on either side by spurs of the now infamous ridge jutting out like malignant tumours towards us, as if nature itself was lending the enemy its own potent defences.

Rising, five hundred yards ahead and off to my left, was one such outgrowth of the main ridge. It was the Bellevue Spur. Atop it lay the forest of wire and the chessboard of concrete pill-boxes that had shattered the New Zealanders. To my right was the backbone of the main ridge bulging outwards in my direction. There the 3rd Australians had shared a similar fate to the New Zealanders. It too was cleverly peppered with concrete blockhouses, machine-gun nests and barbed wire. And not far away, directly in front of me, ran the Ravebeek. Swollen by the rains and mutilated by the incessant shelling, it had flooded its banks and a 600-yard swath of land smack in the middle of our advance had become a watery swamp, an impassable morass even by the undeniably brutal standards of the Salient.

This presented at least two main difficulties that I could see. First, it meant that our attack on Passchendaele would need to be broken into two forks, one on either side of the Ravebeek. Not only would that dilute their combined hitting power, it would put each arm well within the range and sight of machine guns on the opposite ridge. Secondly, the Germans knew this. They would concentrate all their formidable firepower on the two approaches to the left and the right of this once-innocuous little creek.

To make matters worse, beyond the ridge line and further into German-occupied Belgium, well sheltered from my sight but whose deadly presence was never far from mind, were the formidable Boche batteries of field guns, howitzers, and mortars. As if attuned to my thoughts, I heard a Jack Johnson from a 5.9 inch howitzer roar over-head. I saw it detonate in the distance in a huge greasy plume of black smoke. That was part of the problem; as things stood now, the Boche could see us and our artillery a lot easier than we could see them. Of course, it didn't help if you bunched all your guns together like the Aussies had; that was asking for trouble.

I turned to the Kiwi lieutenant, from the Otago regiment, whom a helpful Major Wilson at the New Zealand HQ had insisted accompany me on my daily visits to their lines. "Lines" was a fanciful word for the front-line in the Salient, I'd discovered. It wasn't so much a line, as a series of roughly adjacent, and very water-logged shell-holes, manned by grim-looking types who in civilian life you'd have given a wide berth. It was enough to make me miss the trenches. There were a lot of things missing in this putrid mire, but shell-holes certainly weren't one of them.

The lieutenant's name was Stewart. He seemed like a decent enough fellow although he kept to himself. I liked that. He was touchingly apologetic after he learned who I was, and what I was doing here, when I landed without warning two days ago on his doorstep. 'We feel terrible about it, sir,' he said. 'We've never lost a major battle until now, you know… We did our best, but it rained like the dickens and the barrage was...'

'…as helpful as an umbrella in a hurricane. Yes, I heard,' I said, quietly finishing his sentence.

He shook his head. 'Actually, it was worse than that. After the artillery shelled our own assembly area, it seemed like they ran out of shells… at least we didn't notice them much anymore. The lads joked that the only time they were on form was when they were shelling us.' He was right, it was a whole lot worse. I sighed sympathetically.

Fielding only a single division, the Kiwis had sensibly omitted any numbers from their nomenclature. The 1st New Zealand division was therefore simply *the* New Zealand Division. It had a certain ring to it, I thought. There was no danger confusing them with anybody else. Not like us, with a three in front of our name. Before you knew it, you were having to explain: 'No, very sorry, we don't have a clue where South Lancashire is,' or even worse; that it was *really, truly* our good pals, the 3rd *Australians,* who ransacked the bar.

But now I wanted to know something. 'That sergeant who mapped out the wire right before the attack. Travis, I believe his name was, that's him behind us, or not?' I asked Stewart, and pointed at the little group of soldiers who were accompanying us. 'Can I talk to him?'

Stewart waved at him and Travis climbed quickly out of his hole. With his back bent well forward and rifle in hand, he slogged his way over through the mud, before jumping in with an audible sigh of relief.

In another life, I could have pictured Sergeant Travis as an earnest shopkeeper, wearing a white apron and greeting his customers by name, with a smile and a twinkle in his eye. He wasn't much more than twenty-four, twenty-five, but his wide forehead and receding hair made him appear older. Either this war marked the end for you, or it was a jump-start into old age.

After a few introductory words from Stewart, I took over. 'Sergeant, I understand you led a patrol out onto the Bellevue Spur a night or two before your attack. If I heard correctly, you warned that the wire was a lot worse than any of you were expecting.' He nodded resolutely, so I kept going. 'I'd be very interested if you could tell me about that, and perhaps show me as well?'

'Well, sir, it was exactly as you say. After the patrol I reported back that the wire, especially around the pill-boxes and strong points, had been reinforced a great deal. There must have been a good ten to twenty feet of wire entanglements in front of all the bunkers on the Spur. And it was all new. The artillery bombardments hadn't touched it. At the time everybody seemed interested to hear, but at the end of the day, nothing much came of it. I can tell you, sir, getting through twenty feet of wire with a machine gun or two spraying at you is simply mad.' Then he paused. 'If I may?' he enquired politely, pointing at my field glasses. I offered them and he quickly trained them on a spot ahead and slightly off to our left. 'Here, have a look, sir, those pill-boxes, there. You can see for yourself.'

Sure enough, just barely visible in front of a cluster of four or five concrete bunkers 500 or 600 yards out, marked Laamkeek on the map, were two rows of fence posts and great sugar spins of wire. If the other pill-boxes looked anything like these, I knew they were going to present one huge headache when it was our turn to tackle the Bellevue. From the lack of lead around our ears, it appeared that the unit manning this particular strong-point didn't have a sniper active. Otherwise, I might have been less worried about the future, and more about the present.

'And what did you do about it, during the attack, I mean?' I asked. At that moment Fritz lobbed off another Jack Johnson. This time it screamed very low over our position and exploded only a couple of hundred yards to the rear, forcing me to repeat the question.

Travis exhaled loudly. 'There wasn't a lot we *could* do, mostly they mowed us down. We took a few pill-boxes, but the wire won most of the time.' Evidently, the preferred BEF tactic of sending in waves of soldiers was not likely to be an overwhelming success in such conditions; at least if you defined success as having anybody left at the end of the day. Not that I was extremely confident such a banal detail was even a consideration to all in the upper echelons.

Slowly, but surely, I was getting a feel for the ground. The whole exercise was definitely not making me any more confident. I had a few obstacles to add to the maps, and the impressive 1:400 scale *maquette*

65

of the terrain displayed at Corps headquarters, and a lot to think about. Like what to tell Lipsett. It was time to head back.

We began the slow and arduous journey to the rear lines. The Kiwis had only got as far as constructing a duckboard track to Abraham Heights, a mind-numbing 900 yards behind us; so that consigned us to an exhausting trek through the sludge.

My boots reached almost to my knees. That was small comfort, as it seemed as though at every third step I ended up to my thighs in the goo, requiring a vigorous struggle to free myself. After ten paces I had the balance of a one-year-old and I was panting like a stallion in heat. At least one thing was going our way, our Jack Johnson postman appeared to be enjoying a break. It came as quite a relief when I finally put a foot on solid ground. The relief quickly evaporated when the unmistakable gut-wrenching stench of the decomposing body I'd stepped on enveloped us. Ypres was no place for the weak of stomach; weak of mind, perhaps, but not weak of stomach.

After my first nauseating re-acquaintance with the Salient I'd been determined to be better prepared. So now I smothered my mouth and my nose with a handkerchief. Inexplicably – it couldn't have been foresight – I'd thrown it into my duffel bag in Villers-Châtel when I was packing, and had stuffed it in my coat pocket when I arrived at the Kiwis. I stepped off again into Lake Ypres.

I was rather chuffed I'd finally found an appropriate use for the four white linen handkerchiefs my parents had sent me months earlier. They were from the Hudson's Bay department store. You had only to look at them to know they were good quality. A lot better than I would have bought, but I can't imagine having bought them at all. I pictured my father and mother standing in the fancy new sandstone store on 7th Avenue discussing the matter at length; she was pointing out how frightfully dirty it was "over there" – it was a good thing she didn't know the half of it – and he was repeating the sermon I'd heard so often on the advantages of buying a quality product. At any other time, a conversation like that would have driven me stark-raving mad. But wading through this foul quicksand, just the recollection of them gave me a warm glow. I felt a touch guilty that I'd been so exasperated when I first opened the package. 'What the hell I am supposed to do with these? Polish my rifle?' I'd shouted at DuBois, as he and a few others looked on in amused curiosity at the contents of my parcel. *I must write soon.* It had been ages since the last time, and if the post ever caught up with me, I probably had a stack of letters as thick as my fist by now.

It was about this time, right as we were passing Berlin Wood that the heavens released their load. But then it was always raining in Ypres.

Normally my Aquascutum trench coat was as impervious to rain as I was to forsaking a drink. But now the water was pouring off my helmet like it was Niagara Falls and my coat's well-padded shoulders were showing signs of saturation. I'd shelled out an exorbitant £3 12s for it at a little shop on Jermyn Street on my last leave in London. Even though that was the better part of a week's wages, it was possibly the best purchase I'd ever made. Which made me think, perhaps my father's little sermon hadn't entirely gone in one ear, and out the other.

All told, it took us not far off two hours of plodding exertion to make it to the first improvised infantry track. By that time, I was ready for the slag heap. I could only imagine how they must have felt going the other way, with only the prospect of a lead-filled attack ahead.

Once on the firm planks of a duckboard, I found I could devote my attention to something other than not simply keeling over. I was astonished to see a torrent of activity all around. It helped that the rain had slowed to an even drizzle. I was even more astonished when a group of pioneers from my own division barrelled past, timbers in hand. It was hard to believe, it had only been three days since I heard old Guts n' Gaiters give his preliminary orders and the area was already swarming with Canadians. Normally I'm not one to liken my countrymen to insects, but what I saw would have put any self-respecting anthill to shame.

It seemed that everywhere I looked there were soldiers on the move: building track for the light railways, so indispensable in replenishing the guns; laying new bath-mat tracks for the infantry and plank roads for the many pack animals and carts. Soon the guns would follow. Later, DuBois told me that General Currie had gone so far as to commandeer a saw mill and a forest, (in France, I was guessing, the Belgian forests having less wood in them than my family's Christmas tree), to provide the necessary timber. We shuffled along, taking it all in, unspeaking… each of us lost in our private thoughts. The coffee must have been gone, for Fritz was behind the breech of his guns once more, doggedly determined to make up for lost time as the shells began exploding again with tiresome regularity. None of us paid overly much attention.

I'm not entirely sure why I reacted the way I did. Flanders fields were a constant cacophony of noise. If it wasn't the rain, it was the artillery or the machine guns or the snipers, and mixed in with it all were the sounds of men and animals – too often these were the moans and shrieks from those who were wounded and who lay unattended, somewhere out there, alone, in the desolation. Perhaps it was the plaintiveness of his call that jolted me out my stupor, the sheer desperation of it that led me to look closer. Whatever it was, I motioned for Travis and Stewart to halt. Ignoring their obvious puzzlement, I stepped off the bathmat track and began wading purposefully in the direction of the cries, towards something that bore an unmistakable likeness to the corpse of a horse and an overturned wagon off to our left.

From this lower vantage point I could vaguely make out a man, and he was still alive. He was shouting hoarsely, his arms flailing wildly above him, excited as he too had seen me. The mud had swallowed him to his midriff. As I approached I waved and looked closer. I squinted when he finally came into full view, and my brain whirred insanely, to process what my eyes were seeing. I could make out his elegant spectacles – I'd shamelessly teased him about them – flung off in his panic. They were hanging helplessly from one ear. It was Tibbett. I hated to admit it, but I was very glad to see him.

I roared to the Kiwis to come help, and they did, with an alacrity that astonished me. We set to work freeing him from the morass in which he was slowly, but inexorably, sinking. It took the five of us, several planks from the cart, and more toil than my pay grade usually demanded, before we finally tugged his feet from the quicksand.

'Tibbett,' I exclaimed, when it was done. 'Whatever are you doing here?' Looking at him sandwiched between two of the New Zealanders, with an arm around each of their shoulders, and they around his waist, I felt oddly protective of him. Shorn of his haughty airs he had the look of a small bird who'd fallen abruptly out of its nest.

'It was a shell,' he said. 'We didn't hear it coming.' It was a story I'd heard before, from everybody I'd ever met with the same experience and who had lived to tell about it. Not that there were more than a couple; the odds were decidedly not with you. 'One minute we were here with the three of us setting up a microphone. I went back to the cart to get the wire, and next thing I knew, I woke up ten feet away with my legs almost completely submerged. It was rather fortunate I went in that way and not the other,' he said. I bit my tongue.

He rattled on. I'd never heard him talk so fast. 'No matter what I did, however I moved, I kept sinking further away. In another hour or two, I'm certain I would have been completely under. Thank goodness you came when you did.' As the adrenaline began to subside, he asked, 'I presume the other two are gone? I couldn't see them. I shouted until my lungs ached.'

I glanced around. Other than the horse and the remains of the cart, I could see absolutely nothing of the two soldiers he was with. There was only a large shell hole. The detonation had erased any visible evidence I could see from up here. I had no inclination of climbing in to investigate further. I shook my head.

Once back on the duckboards I asked him the question that had first sprung to mind – his previous answer only increasing my curiosity. 'I'm still puzzled why on earth you're here? Microphones, you said?'

'Oh yes, Colonel McNaughton is very taken with these new sound-ranging techniques. We're becoming rather proficient in pinpointing the location of the enemy batteries. Really, it's quite brilliant. Simply measure the sound of their guns firing at several different locations and then, based on a precise measurement of those locations and the time it takes each instrument to register the same sound, triangulate where the sound is originating from. With a few microphones and an oscillograph, we...'

'An oscillo... what?' I asked, interrupting him mid-stream before I got hopelessly out of my depth. I knew of Lieutenant-Colonel McNaughton. He was Tibbett's boss at Corps headquarters. He was gaining a real name for himself for the counter-battery work they were doing, seeking out and destroying the enemy's artillery. Naively, I always assumed that observation, aerial photographs and documents like those we captured at Méricourt were responsible. Science class, for the second time this week, was catching up with me.

He smiled. 'An oscillograph,' he said, coming back to life. 'Oh, in its most rudimentary form it's nothing more than a device that can measure and record – interestingly enough using film in our case – the sound waves made by a shell being fired.'

'Simple, keep it simple, Tibbett,' I said. 'Remember, I've been breathing this air for a week now.'

He laughed. 'Well, how's this, then? We listen for a gun to fire with our microphones and then record exactly when each microphone heard the exact same shot. Take the coordinates of the microphones, mix it with a little math and *voilà*, within five minutes we can inform the artillery lads where they should be firing to destroy that gun.'

It was my turn to laugh. 'Thanks Tibbett, it takes a smart man to distill things into a format even I understand.' Halfway out of my mouth I was suddenly aware I'd let down my guard with him, as I'd never done before. It felt like walking half-naked into the Grace Presbyterian Church on 15th Avenue. Quickly I kept talking. 'So, you were here placing one of these microphones according to some plan the colonel drew up?'

'Yes, exactly.'

We talked some more and then walked beside each other for a long time in silence.

After a while, he turned towards me. 'My father will kill me if he hears of this,' he said quietly. 'You don't know what he's like, he pulled a considerable number of strings to get me my commission, what with my physics study at London University and my spectacles. My brother, he's the athlete. Tennis, cricket, rowing, there's little he doesn't do well. Naturally he studied at Cambridge. Classics. Worst of all, he's already a major.' He paused and I thought he'd finished. Apparently, it was just to breathe. He began with renewed passion. 'Other than recalling Tom's exploits, I don't hear much else when I'm home on leave. My father's always preaching on about how wonderful he is. He simply couldn't let it go when he heard that I'd been assigned to a Dominion division. Sorry, that wasn't terribly tactful of me.'

'Listen Paul,' I began. I don't think I'd ever called him by his first name before, but I'd never wrestled him out of the mud before, either. 'In case you hadn't noticed, there are a lot of people here who would like nothing better than to kill you,' I said, waving an arm in the general direction of the German lines. 'Somehow I think they're of more immediate concern than your father!'

70

He smiled. 'That's what I like about you, Malcolm, always that quick humour.'

I was momentarily stunned. I'd always thought he detested me, and my jokes even more.

'Apparently, you haven't done much to enlighten your father. You might point out sometime that we colonials keep getting stuck with the biggest messes to clean up. To which you might add, the reason being is that we actually get the job done,' I said. 'Unlike certain other divisions, including those your father seems to hold in higher regard,' I muttered as an afterthought. 'He should be very proud of your work.' Uneasily, I smiled. I realized I'd been doing some preaching of my own. Tibbett nodded thoughtfully.

'And where would we be without you, Paul? After all, most of us from the Dominions can't even pronounce oscillograph, let alone spell it!' He smiled a watery smile. My compliments had made him uneasy.

'I wish I knew how I could repay you, Malcolm,' he said effusively. I don't know what it is about narrowly escaping death, but it was doing Tibbett a world of good.

'Mac, call me Mac, Paul. That would a good start,' I said. 'We can discuss payment another time,' I teased.

It was dark by the time we arrived at the moss-covered concrete bunker at Canal Bank – the days were getting shorter. Canal Bank, so-named for its proximity to the Yser Canal was roughly a half-mile north of Ypres. For some curious reason, I couldn't begin to fathom, it was where the Kiwis had planted their divisional headquarters. Thinking back on it, it made the Australians' dungeon vaguely resemble Buckingham Palace, although I was far too tired to devote much energy to the comparison. I inhaled some rations when I had the chance, although I hardly bothered to taste them. That was always a wise policy with rations anyway. I was ready to call it a day.

We arrived cold, exhausted, drenched to the core and filthy in a way I didn't think possible after so much rain. Strangely, though, I felt good. Tibbett was sleeping in a temporary cot beside me, shocked, but otherwise unharmed from the day's experiences. Sergeant Smith would arrive tomorrow. I was looking forward to that. He and I, and an unnamed officer from the Corps, were to open an intelligence headquarters here in the Kiwis' cozy bunker. I hoped he would bring my trunk, I thought dreamily, as my eyes fluttered in out of consciousness – I could sure use some dry socks.

CHAPTER 8

23rd of October, 1917
Ten Elms camp, Poperinghe, Belgium

Ten Elms camp was not terribly impressive, a motley assortment of drab-coloured canvas tents fiercely regimented into a precise grid-work of long rows and columns, such that only an army could be responsible. In the centre of this tent metropolis were a handful of hastily constructed wooden structures. A couple of them were quite large, although I wouldn't go so far as to call them proper buildings. A far corner of the camp was dedicated to the massive and astonishingly detailed outdoor model of Passchendaele Ridge. Even at this hour, a little before nine in the morning, it was already being studied by various officers and NCOs brought here to do just that. Apparently, his Royal Highness the Duke of Connaught, the former Governor-General, had dropped by only yesterday to have a gander himself; it was the kind of thing that appealed to men brought up on model train sets.

The camp was located on the northwest outskirts of the little town of Poperinghe, or "Pops" as most called it, itself tucked away five miles behind Ypres. Poperinghe had been spared the worst of the shelling, and with the capture of Messines Ridge it was mercifully out of sight, if not out of range, of the heaviest German guns. With the departure of the 2nd ANZAC Corps HQ, it was here that the Canadian Corps had established its headquarters. I'd heard talk that Pops possessed a comfortable all-ranks club in the main square where, word was, you could enjoy a hot cup of tea. It all sounded terribly racy. Myself, I was of the opinion that the Salient required considerably stiffer refreshment than tea.

Close to the camp entrance, I was surprised to see two Lewis guns mounted on poles and surrounded by an obviously makeshift log barricade. There was a group of four soldiers loitering around it with a relaxed casualness so I strolled over to them. They'd naturally seen me long before I saw them, but pretended they hadn't. As the realization sank in that an encounter with an officer was inevitable, they turned and gave me four of the sloppiest salutes I'd had in a long while. I slopped back. That was easy enough to do, saluting had never been my strong suit.

'You lads are going to have to work on those salutes. I know a general or two who might take it quite personally if he'd seen that pathetic display.'

'Sir,' they said, straightening up and beginning to look nervous.

Pointing at the machine guns I said, 'You realize, it's been a bad duck season this year?'

They stared at me as if I was wearing a *Pickelhaube* and doing a tap dance. Finally, the shoe dropped and one, a corporal, began to smile: they were obviously from the city. 'That's alright, sir! We're after bigger game. Gothas mainly.'

'Gothas! I didn't know they ventured out here? Bagged any yet?'

They'd all noticeably brightened since their initial tense moments, recognising, I guess, that I wasn't intent on imposing any cruel new misery upon them.

'No, sir, not yet,' said one of the others. 'We've seen a few in the distance and they dropped some pineapples on Vlamertinghe, just down the road from here, two days ago.'

'The weather helps,' said another, gesturing to the dreary overcast skies that were intermittently spitting rain.

The private was right, the overcast skies made it tough for the aeroplanes. Still, I had seen them off in the distance. On top of which, the intelligence summaries from the Australians regularly reported that low-flying planes were machine-gunning their troops, sometimes in groups of as many as fifteen. That was the problem with low hanging clouds; the pilots had nothing to do up above, and strafing enemy troops was a worthy alternate pastime.

The massive, ungainly, twin-engine Gothas were an altogether different story from the other aeroplanes. They were slow and their sheer size made them a target even these lads ought to be able to hit. Which is why they typically attacked at night. Of course, if you missed, or your pea-shooter failed to bring it down, you had a considerable problem. A single Gotha carried fourteen 60-pound pineapples. That was enough to level the privates' little barricade several times over and most of the camp with it.

Without any bombing machines to fend off, the privates and the corporal were primarily concerned with monitoring the approach road to camp. I noticed from their faces they had spotted something. Shortly thereafter, I heard it as well. It was a large staff car approaching at speed, a Vauxhall D-type and it positively glinted. That could mean only one thing.

'Speak of the devil,' I said, straightening to attention. 'Well, lads! Here's your chance to show your spit and polish.' We all saluted, suitably smartly, as the car crunched past on the gravel track heading towards the centre of the camp. I could see clearly through the back windows and I blinked when I glimpsed the by now all too familiar, mottled grey-white moustache; it was Field-Marshal Haig. What's he doing here? I wondered. This was supposed to be a conference of the Corps commanders; nobody had said anything about Haig attending. Thankfully he appeared to have left his stiff-necked colonel at home.

'I'll leave you to your Gothas, then. Good luck, but hopefully you won't be needing it,' I said to the Lewis gun squad. I prepared to hasten over to the largest of the wooden barracks, where the action was palpably heating up. This time they saluted crisply. In good spirits they called out, 'Good-bye, then, sir.'

As I approached the barracks, I saw a familiar face from the division and I called out to him. He pivoted, hesitating as he made out my face, and then waved exuberantly. His name was McAvity. For a long while I'd mischievously spread the word, to great hilarity, that he was a dentist fleeing a malpractice suit. Finally, in a burst of exasperation, involving *my* teeth and the threat of *his* fist, he convinced me that wasn't the case. Of course, he being a major, I would have immediately taken his word for it, anyhow. Since then we'd become quite friendly. That was just as well. He was not only my superior officer, we worked together far too often to be at loggerheads.

'Malcolm,' he said. 'What are *you* doing here?'

'As it happens, Sir Malcolm,' I replied, with a salute, 'I too have been invited – sort of. As usual, I'm not entirely sure why. I briefed Lipsett yesterday.'

Malcolm was a name that had some pedigree in our division. It began with our old commanding officer, Major-General Malcolm Mercer. He'd been killed at Mount Sorrel. Major Malcolm McAvity was the second, and I was the third. I just had to make it to major to give it the ring it deserved. My elaborate report, notwithstanding, I don't think I'd scored many points with the general last night. An attack was simply going to require meticulous preparation and stolid perseverance. I think Lipsett had hoped for more from me.

'I presume the whole thing is still on?' I asked cautiously, knowing the answer even before the words passed my lips.

'I'm afraid so,' said McAvity.

'Do you know who I just saw arriving?' I asked. Without awaiting a reply, I added, 'Haig. That's right, Sir Douglas himself.'

'That pretty much seals it, I'd think. I don't think the field-marshal would make the effort to come up here, merely to say "Sorry chaps, thanks for the splendid efforts, but I'm calling it off".'

'Hmm,' I replied. I'd concluded the exact same thing ten minutes ago when I saw his Vauxhall glide by. Hope was a funny thing, though. You clung to it even when there was none.

'One thing you might not know about, MacPhail, are the conferences on the 16th,' he said provocatively. Who knew what and when, had become a bit of a game for us – we'd been away from the front lines for far too long.

'Oh, you mean a week ago, at Corps HQ and Anzac HQ, when General Plumer came to visit?'

'Right. But do you know what he and Currie discussed?'

'No, not offhand,' I said, unhappy to be in the dark and curious as to what he would say.

'As it happens, I was at Corps HQ at the time. I also happened to speak with a lieutenant-colonel who heard it all.'

'Well, spit it out man,' I said. 'I've got a war to fight!'

'Alright. Apparently, Currie pleaded with Plumer to convince Haig to call it off. He warned him that there'd be 16,000 casualties. Can you imagine? 16,000! That's twice the size of Fredericton.' McAvity was from New Brunswick. He was right, it was a stunning number.

'And then?' I asked.

'Plumer was quite sympathetic. He really seems to be a decent general. But the orders were plain, according to Plumer,' he said resignedly. And then with real feeling, 'God-damn Haig!'

I pursed my lips and slowly exhaled. I didn't know how old Guts 'n Gaiters came up with 16,000 casualties, but it was a depressing number.

We chatted a while longer and then decided to move inside before the conference began. It wouldn't have been particularly auspicious if the field-marshal and half-a-dozen generals were promptly on time, while the captain and the major were too preoccupied with each other to be punctual.

General Lipsett spotted us immediately. He summoned us over with a flick of his head. He was talking to Batty Mac, the commander of the 1st Division, General Macdonell.

After excusing himself, he said, 'I was curious when you two might deign to present yourselves.' As always with the general, it was never entirely clear whether it was a question or a statement. Likely both, knowing him.

'We were discussing the field-marshal's sudden arrival, sir,' I said. Convincing Lipsett was not unlike breaching the German lines, in both cases it didn't do to vacillate.

'The field-marshal? You mean Field-Marshal Haig?' he asked, in a puzzled tone.

'Yes, exactly, sir. He arrived forty minutes ago,' I said, suddenly full of bravado.

'Ah-ha,' he said slowly, and then paused, thinking about the implications of what I'd said. 'It's a good thing the two of you are purportedly in intelligence. Otherwise, I might be tempted to assume this was a clever feint to cover for the fact you've been gossiping like old women, and forgot the time.'

There was no pulling the wool over Lipsett's eyes.

10 a.m. came and went with no visible sign of the Corps Commander or his mysterious guest. I could feel the raised eyebrows – this was more than a little unorthodox, particularly with a stickler like Currie. Minutes later, the eyebrows went through the ceiling as the field-marshal, cane in hand, marched into sight, with Currie following on his heels.

Their faces spoke volumes. That was an over-worn expression, at least to my ears, and beloved of my mother. I can't say I'd ever encountered a clearer example than with these two. The field-marshal looked as resolute and aloofly unperturbed as ever, while Currie had the tense features, narrow eyes and pursed mouth of a man who'd chomped on an under-ripe lemon, or more precisely, I guessed, a mud-locked Flemish village.

After the briefest of introductions from Currie, Haig began to speak. 'Gentlemen, circumstances have arisen that render it imperative that Passchendaele Ridge must be taken at all costs. I know the Canadian Corps can take it, and my mission here is to ask the Corps Commander to do so. I feel I should tell you he was opposed to doing so.' Castle Mountain (aka General Currie) standing beside him didn't bat an eyelash. 'I have been able to meet his objections and to agree to what he considers necessary. I may say he has demanded an unprecedented amount of artillery to cover your advance; and this I have promised. I would like to explain why this attack must be made and perhaps someday in the future I may be able to do so. At present, I simply ask you to take my word for it. The necessity is imperative.'

I still had my qualms, but it was a classy gesture. The commander-in-chief was as close to God on Earth as most of us would ever know, yet he'd come here in person to *ask* the Corps to take Passchendaele. He obviously knew a thing or two about motivating men, if not strategy, I thought sourly.

Haig remained the entire conference, a polite observer to the detailed, but remarkably abbreviated briefing and discussion led by Currie with uncharacteristic verve. Then he departed, with the customary fanfare, to inspect our immensely popular battleground model.

When I was ten there was nothing I loved to do more than play with my set of intricately-detailed lead soldiers, made by W. Britain, out in the garden behind our house. I would have died for a sandbox like this one – so I could understand the inherent attraction.

I waited around with McAvity outside as the generals and staff officers climbed into their respective staff cars and raced off. General Lipsett had offered me a drive back to Canal Bank. I was more than happy to accept, though I quickly realized that in the pecking order of Lipsett, Hore-Ruthven, and McAvity, MacPhail was destined to join the chauffeur in the front seat.

The shortage of intact real estate being as it was in the Ypres area, the division had moved into the Kiwis' old digs yesterday, mildew and all. As a seasoned inhabitant of the bunker, I'd astutely taken advantage of the confusion as one HQ moved out, and another in, to lay claim to one of the better rooms to bunk in. It was a classic fog of war manoeuvre, as I explained later to Sergeant Smith, though his eyes fogged over when I mentioned von Clausewitz.

'So, that's that,' I said to McAvity, before we left.

'It would look that way,' he replied.

'Shame, though, that Currie didn't demand an unprecedented amount of booze to accompany that artillery,' I said. 'Or perhaps that's to be our reward?'

CHAPTER 9

26th of October, 1917
Assembly area 1,000 yards northeast of Gravenstafel, Belgium

Cold was a state of mind, I kept telling myself, but my homespun logic was having precious little impact; being half-asleep wasn't helping matters. Stamping my feet, and rubbing my arms to get the circulation going, I felt like an eighty-five-year-old in a blizzard. It was the sort of coldness that only high humidity can cause. The kind that doesn't hit you like a brick wall, but works by stealth, seeping unfelt through your clothing until, finally, when they're saturated, it reaches your bones – and then doesn't leave. While it wasn't truly raining I could have swum laps in the mist. They say Eskimos have more than twenty different words for snow and I imagine the Belgian vocabulary must be equally rich when it comes to rain.

It was pitch dark and the luminous dial on my Borgel indicated that it was approaching 4.05 a.m. – I'd meticulously synchronised my watch as instructed – and the last soldiers were being lined up in the assembly areas to have their gear checked and the plans explained one final time. NCOs were circulating through the ranks. Through lack of sleep or shaky nerves, some had forgotten to attach their muzzle protectors, or weren't standing where they should be. They were being reminded about it in no uncertain terms, with whispered shouts unleashed only inches from their faces. The battle I'd been dreading was about to begin.

Then it began to rain. As usual, rain was a description that didn't cover it by half. The barrage of water that was coming down made our own feeble attempts at barrages seem just that. 'Well, boys, welcome to Wipers,' I heard a corporal grumble to his platoon. A few, the veterans who'd made it through Vimy Ridge and the Somme, grunted indifferently. The others looked on, apprehensively, in silence. They had heard the stories ever since the rumour got out we might be heading here and knew that the rain was only the beginning.

Cleverly, somebody had decided to fix ZERO hour at a less predictable time than at dawn a few minutes after the hour or the half-hour. That constituted the standard attack drill. The Germans, not being entirely dim-witted, had long since picked up on this quaint practice and, as the sun prepared to rise, would regularly shell the front on the hour and the half hour hoping to catch-out a force mustering to attack. It was a tactic that had worked more than once. Absurdly, it had taken our side an indecently long time to figure out that their side had our side completely figured out. To me it seemed pretty simple, but the gears of the BEF ground slowly.

Our guns went off together, timed perfectly to the minute, if not the very second, in a great deafening crescendo of noise; the ground positively rumbled under our feet. There were an impressive 235 of them, of all calibres, dedicated to the division's front alone. Behind us the flashes they created illuminated the skies as if dawn were breaking, colouring the low hanging clouds in a sinister, moving potpourri of yellows, oranges, and reds. In the light of the explosions, and through the streaming rain, I could make out criss-crossed streams of bullets from the heavy Vickers belt-fed machine guns – each pumping out 500 rounds a minute into targets far out in front. It was 5.40 a.m. on October 26th, 1917. The attack had begun.

The officers and NCOs were shouting now, marshalling their troops, even as they began moving forward, anxious to keep to their timetables and under the curtain of iron falling 150 yards ahead. It would move in precisely eight minutes, leapfrogging 50 yards ahead and, after four minutes do it again until the objective was taken, or they had run out of shells. Naturally, I knew there were many others responsible, yet I felt strangely content my advice to Currie had been noted.

I imagined a similar scene must be playing out along the entire front. To the left of the Corps, the British 63rd Royal Navy Division was to advance simultaneously, to protect our flank from counter-attacks and the dreaded enfilade fire: machines guns raking our troops from the side. To our right, the 1st Anzac Corps would do the same.

The British Army must be a lot more pressed than was generally known if they were drafting in the Navy to do their dirty work. Understandably, some army-types might call it pure genius.

The thrust of the Corps was a broad swath on both sides of the Ravebeek – in the shape of a V – heading directly to Passchendaele. As Currie had succinctly described, almost two weeks earlier in Hazebrouck, we were the prong to the left of the Ravebeek. Our attack would run up the crest and along both slopes of the pill-box infested Bellevue Spur. This would be the widest part of the advance, requiring two of our three brigades to attack along a long 1000-yard front. It was ground I knew all too well after days spent reconnoitering it; I swore I knew every miserable yard. To our right, and on the other side of that bloated creek, the 10th Brigade from the 4th Division would fight its way to the ridge top and then along the main ridge towards the village.

Despite the conditions, the first minutes of the advance were progressing well. There were few signs of a German response. They certainly couldn't have been sleeping with the racket the artillery boys were making. I turned and began my journey back to the Capitol.

Those farcically named ruins in the mud, a mile or so from Gravenstafel, lent a semblance of shelter and, more critically, well-connected telephone wires to the 9th Brigade. The brigade had its headquarters there.

Thanks to the well-prepared infantry track, it was only a short walk back to Gravenstafel. There, a car stood waiting to take me and a couple of other drenched souls to headquarters.

When we arrived, there were half a dozen officers and other ranks in the main bunker. The voices were calm. Somehow, that made me only more aware of the sense of excitement, the same nervous tension I'd felt with the Australians as their attack began to unfold. The Brigade commander, Brigadier-General Hill, was energetically explaining something to a major from one of his battalions. I slipped over to listen. He was bent over the table, which occupied a good portion of the available space, and was pointing at the map that occupied most of it.

'Our observation post confirmed the report from the artillery observers. Our troops are entering them,' he was saying. I looked closer and could see his finger rested on the pill-box concentration just below the crest of the ridge closest to us. That was very good news; it was only 6.30 a.m. Fifty minutes in and we were well on our way to the red line denoting the first phase objective.

In the hour that followed, the first reports from the field trickled in. I began to see cautious smiles replacing the anxious looks from earlier. In desperation the Germans were shelling their old positions on the Spur, but large groups of prisoners were arriving. The frowns returned momentarily as a wounded officer was brought in. He reported stiff resistance on the Spur's right slope. Heavy machine-gun fire from the fortified Crest Farm machine-gun nests on the main ridge were holding them up. Crest Farm was on the far right side of the Ravebeek, close to Passchendaele. But then came the welcome signal: the 4th Division had taken all their objectives. They were pushing patrols out to Crest Farm.

Around eight o'clock, a young signals private barged noisily into the room and we all looked up. From the sight of him I knew his tidings were not what any of us wanted to hear. 'Sir,' he said, addressing the general and drinking in huge gulps of air, 'The 58th and most of the 43rd are back at their jumping-off lines!' The Boche artillery and machine-gun fire were driving them back.

'Damn and double damn,' shouted the Brigadier. As curses go I've heard worse, but I understood Hill's anxiety all too well. His two battalions formed the centre of the attack. Without them the advances of the 8th Brigade on the left and the 10th on the far right, would be at grave risk. The entire attack was in the balance. If matters didn't improve, and quickly, not just Lipsett, but Currie himself would be having his guts for garters.

The General looked around the room like a caged animal until his eyes alit on me. 'You, Captain,' he called, impatiently waving me over.

'MacPhail, sir,' I replied. In fact, I'd already introduced myself to him earlier this morning as I had to all the others.

'Right,' he mumbled. I could as easily have said, *Kaiser Wilhelm, sir,* and he wouldn't have noticed.

'You don't appear to be doing much.'

I was preparing to quibble, but the look he threw me was convincing enough to suggest silence was preferable.

'You know the terrain,' he said. I did. I wasn't entirely sure how *he* knew that. Without as much as a confirming nod from me, he blazed on, 'I need you to get up there as fast as possible. Survey the exact situation and get back to me like the dickens. Clear?'

Anything other than a yes wasn't in his play book, but I'm not the sort to always play by the rules. 'And reinforcements, sir?' I ventured bravely, thinking the obvious.

'Yes, the 52nd is reinforcing, a fresh advance has been ordered.' The 52nd was the battalion held in support for situations such as this. 'But I need to know exactly what's going on up there. Report to the Camerons' HQ at Waterloo Farm when you're finished; they have a telephone there. Now get going.' Snatching a rifle, a satchel with ammunition and my helmet, I hastened to the door.

All told, it took me the best part of an hour to reach the tip of the Spur. It was still raining – tamely compared to its earlier ferocity, but the going was tough. The slippery gummy slime, and occasional shreds of wire, pulled tirelessly at my boots. I fell twice. The Boche continued to lay down a barrage on the central approaches to the Spur, so I veered to the left, avoiding the worst of it. Now I was coming up on the crest. I made sure to steer well away from Bellevue Farm, or where I figured it must be. My mental map I was so confident about was fogging over.

The Farm's formidable concentration of pill-boxes was, untaken as far as I knew, and I had no desire to tackle it on my own. If ever I'd entertained any notions that an appointment as divisional intelligence officer meant a cozy sinecure full of warm beds, baths and food, they were being severely disabused.

A shell came whistling over in my direction, so low it almost seemed to graze the ground. Soldiers' superstition said that you never heard the one that got you, but that was an easy thing to say when there was no one around to contradict it. I certainly wasn't about to take any chances. I sprang into the crater ahead of me – to my surprise it was occupied.

A young soldier sat hunched over, directly opposite, staring with the most innocent big brown eyes, as if I'd landed from the moon. In some ways I had, coming from brigade headquarters. He wouldn't have looked out of place in a schoolyard. However, he sure did here. He couldn't have been more than 18 and I was convinced he was a lot younger – though if he lied when he joined up, he wasn't likely to confess that to an aging captain who, at 28, must have seemed positively ancient to him.

He was in the 43rd Battalion, the Cameron Highlanders. The connection wasn't difficult to make after my eye fell on the kilt he was wearing. That was hard to miss even at my age. Of all the impractical absurdities I've ever seen, wearing a kilt in the pouring rain, in this soupy bog, topped them all.

I nodded to him. He perfunctorily returned my glance before nervously looking away. I saw he was trembling and it wasn't from the cold. His arms were shaking, wrapped tightly in an embrace of the Lee-Enfield he clutched to his chest. He was holding it so fiercely I feared he might set it off, perhaps even in my direction. Ignoring the danger, I moved closer.

'It's not a bad hole you have here, Private,' I said. And it was true, it wasn't. It was deep, the earth was firm as far as shell-holes go, and there was only a smallish puddle of water at the bottom.

'Yes, sir,' he replied.

'What's your name?' I asked.

'Philips, sir.'

'And where are you from, Philips?'

'Digby, sir. Digby, Nova Scotia.'

'Now, that's a place I've never been. What's it like? I imagine you're out on clam-bakes whenever you can,' I said. 'Well, at least you're not far from the water here in Ypres,' I went on, hoping for a laugh or even the glimmer of a smile.

'Yes, sir,' he said, deadly serious.

'How does a lad from the Maritimes end up in a unit from Winnipeg?'

'Mother, sir.'

This was going nowhere. 'Mind if I move over there beside you?' I asked. Not awaiting an answer, I crawled over next to him and lay on my side. 'Least now I can look out in the right direction,' I fibbed.

At that moment a shell exploded. It was near enough that we were both doused in a shower of wet mud which rained down on our helmets and soaked our coats, and something harder. It bounced off my shoulder and lay grotesquely next to my boot. When I took a second glance I was pretty certain what it was: part of an arm. I looked Philips in the eye, trying to engage him before he noticed, and kicked desperately with my foot to push it off into the water.

He didn't see it. But he was shaking so badly by this time I almost thought he was having a seizure. I put an arm around him and firmly squeezed his shoulder. 'You know, when I first arrived, I was scared too. I still am,' I said. 'There's no shame in that. Being scared keeps you sharp. But look, you've had all sorts of training and I can see you're a fine soldier. I bet you can handle that rifle better than I can.'

He looked doubtful.

'You miss home?'

He nodded.

'The sooner we dispatch with this bunch, the sooner we'll be there,' I said smiling. 'Who else is here?'

'A bunch of us Camerons, sir,' he replied. A complete sentence – that was encouraging – as was the news. We still had a foothold in the centre of the ridge. The battle wasn't lost yet.

'I really need to find your commanding officer,' I said, 'Do you know where I can find him?'

'That'd be Lieutenant Shankland, sir, the captain's gone missing. I expect he's somewhere over there,' he said, motioning off to our left and ahead. 'They're about 40 yards in front of two pill-boxes.' I guessed the concrete bunkers he was referring to were stormed in the first hour or two, when things looked a lot brighter than they did now.

I was about to respond when, out of the corner of my eye, I saw movement. I turned, ever so slowly, to lie flat on my stomach, and peered gingerly over the brim. Sure enough, clearly visible despite the rain and the smoke, were ten shadowy figures in grey, perhaps more. Inexorably they moved towards us. They were crouched low with rifles in hand and walking abreast of each other. I could see their *Stahlhelms*. They weren't more than 100 yards away.

DARRELL DUTHIE

I slid down the mud wall to the bottom of the crater, breathing hard. My helmet was now well under the lip of the shell-hole and I grabbed my Lee-Enfield with both hands. 'Boche!' I whispered fiercely to Philips. 'When I start firing, you shoot like you've never shot before,' I commanded. I looked him directly in the eye. 'Are you ready?' His chin bobbed affirmatively.

We wormed our way upwards on our bellies using our elbows and legs, the wooden stocks of our rifles clasped with two hands in front. Reaching the top, my eyes just cleared the rim and we assumed firing positions. I planted my feet in the earth for more grip and glanced over at Philips. He looked across anxiously, awaiting a sign from me.

Grasping the butt tight against my shoulder, I closed my left eye and squinted down the barrel at the nearest of them, close to the middle of the group. With the bead on him I adjusted my aim, sliding the small dot carefully into the centre of the little 'u' of the rifle sights. I paused, held my breath ever so slightly, and then squeezed the trigger. The figure crumpled to the ground. Almost immediately there was the retort of a shot beside me. I saw another grey shape collapse. A trained rifleman, it was said, could shoot 30 aimed rounds a minute from a Lee-Enfield. I didn't come anywhere close to that, but I was working the bolt with a desperation and an oiled ease I've seldom known. Within a minute it was over. My heart was pounding like a jackhammer. Empty brass cartridges lay scattered around.

The Germans were gone. We hit a few before they turned tail and fled and that was a decisive victory in my books. It had been a long time since I'd fired a shot in anger. I was pleased I hadn't deported myself like a total baboon.

I looked over at Philips and gave him a huge smile. I was more than a little relieved at the way things worked out. 'Well, done, Private Philips. I knew you were a natural with a rifle; you could teach me a thing or two.'

He was grinning from ear to ear. 'Thank you, sir.'

'I'm pleased that I can report back to the general that this part of the part of the front is in good hands,' I said, only half jesting. 'I do have to find your Lieutenant Shankland, however.'

'Yes, sir, I know. Thank you,' he said, still grinning. It was an astonishing transformation.

87

'Good luck! And good-bye, Philips.'

'Good-bye, sir,' he called cheerfully.

I crawled from the hole, hesitated briefly as I turned to give him a final wave, and set off in the direction of the two pill-boxes he'd indicated.

THUMP.

The shell fell only scant yards behind me. Instinctively, I dived forward, into the crater that lay before me. I landed head-first, my helmet falling to one side and my face coming to rest at the bottom of the hole in a cesspool of mud and water. I waited there for the explosion which, amazingly, didn't come. The shell was a dud. *Luck was a mighty fine thing to have.*

Pulling myself from the blubber I looked back expectantly, waiting to see Philips waving, with an exuberant grin on his face. But I saw nothing. I clambered out of the hole to get a better look. Still there was nothing, absolutely nothing in this empty pockmarked wasteland. 'Philips!' I called and then again. No answer came. The only sounds to be heard were those of the shells whistling overhead and the explosions a little further on. And then the realization hit. In my heart I knew what had happened; the shell had hit him mid-ships. Dud or not, it had ripped his fledgling body asunder and buried it deep in the muddy depths of Flanders, miserable yards from where I now stood shaking like a leaf.

I felt empty. My head, my limbs, my entire being, were buried under a great numbness. I don't think I've ever felt so drained in all my life.

'You okay there?' It was a soldier calling. He shouted again. He'd seen my dive and the shell landing. He was hollering from a few holes away.

I woke sufficiently from my shock to curtly wave. I stumbled towards him. I was lucky he'd called; as it was I was a sitting duck for any German grandmother with a rifle.

'Sorry, sir,' he said, as I reached him. 'I didn't realize you were here, Captain. I thought maybe you were Philips or one of the others.'

'Philips is dead… a shell,' I mumbled.

The soldier shook his head with evident sorrow. 'That poor kid, best shot in the unit. I saw you and him take down that patrol.' He sighed. 'I don't know why his parents ever let him sign up.' It was a damned good question.

I grimaced. 'No, neither do I. They won't be seeing him ever again, I'm afraid.' I paused to shake my head, as if that would clear the whole miserable scene from my mind. 'I'm trying to find your commander, Lieutenant Shankland,' I murmured.

'We're dug-in in front of two bunkers further up, he'll be there. Keep your head down, sir, there are some nasty machine-guns not far ahead.'

I thanked him and headed out, anxious to make time, and glad for anything at all to keep my mind off young Philips from Digby.

Before long I reached the captured bunkers, forewarned by a mine-field of corpses in olive green and kilts. As I covered the last few feet they made way for field grey. Not far in front of the pill-boxes, two Lewis-guns were positioned and a fair-sized group of soldiers. They were deeply entrenched with a good view down the Spur in the di-rection of the Germans. Incredibly, I'd missed Lieutenant Shankland. The first two Camerons I encountered told me he'd left only minutes earlier. He'd gone back to battalion HQ to get reinforcements.

'Damn,' was all I managed to say, albeit with real feeling. The sol-diers looked as if I'd tossed a grenade into their hole instead of a curse. I'd risked life and limb to get here, across this macabre morass, and it appeared to be for nought. I wiped the face of my wristwatch clean on my sleeve as best I could – 9.37 a.m.

'Sorry, sir,' they replied, obviously bewildered; first by the sudden appearance of this mud-drenched captain whom they didn't know, and then by my foul temper on learning that Shankland had departed.

'No, that's alright,' I said a little gruffly, 'I was hoping to see him, that's all. Who's in command then?'

'Lieutenant Ellis, he's over by that Lewis gun. Keep your head down, sir, there's Germans in the trench ahead.'

Following their advice, I ran low and fast across to the machine gun. 'Lieutenant Ellis, I presume,' I said, sliding in beside him without warning. 'I'm MacPhail. General Hill sent me.'

He looked as surprised to see me as the two privates had, but recovered well. I could see he was wounded.

'Welcome, Captain,' he said. 'I would have been even happier to see you with 50 men at your back.'

'I bet. That's the reason for my visit. No one actually knows you're here. But thank God you are. I hear Lieutenant Shankland went back to HQ for reinforcements. Tell me about your situation.'

'Well, it's not too bad,' he began. This was one unflappable fellow: wounded, under sporadic shell-fire, outnumbered by twenty to one, with a gaping hole between his position and other units on both his left *and* his right, and *not too bad* is how he summarizes it. 'We dispersed a big counter-attack not long ago. They were forming up ahead, over there,' he said, and pointed to a lower lying area 500 yards forward. 'We hit them hard and they didn't make it far.'

'You've got good defensible positions here. What about the Farm?'

'The company commander, Captain Galt, took a few men to capture it, but we've heard nothing for hours.'

'So, it's likely in German hands. And you've got a troublesome trench in front?' I asked.

He nodded, 'That's right, but with a few more men and machine guns I'm sure we could break through. The Germans are shelling the hell out of the Spur, even with their own men all over it. But that whole stretch, there,' he said, motioning with his hand, 'it's a dead spot, it's shell-free. Send a couple of companies through and we'd be on our way.' I looked closer; it was the lower left slope of the ridge and impossible to observe from where the Germans were.

Presumably, that was what Shankland would relay when he got to HQ, assuming he made it. If he didn't, that made it all the more crucial I get back myself. I had a few things to tell General Hill, not wishing he endanger his guts, unnecessarily. One thing was as clear as a sunny day in the Rockies: if we didn't regain the initiative soon, this attack was going to be an unmitigated disaster. Then, a lot more than just the General's guts would be in danger.

I grilled Ellis for another couple of minutes, told him what a great job they were doing in the most inspirational tones I could summon, and bade him an abbreviated farewell. I hoped it would be a quick run back to battalion HQ at Waterloo Farm. It was.

The lieutenant's route was as good as promised. Barely half an hour passed before I stumbled into Waterloo Farm and my second former German bunker of the morning. It had been reincarnated as a headquarters. You had to give the Boche credit, they made some seriously robust bunkers.

Shankland had made it back too and, predictably, his appearance was like a bolt of electricity in a pond of sleeping frogs. When I arrived, the air was still buzzing. Hope had returned.

A large group of men, rallied from those who'd fallen back to HQ, was making ready to leave, as was the dauntless lieutenant himself, to return to his embattled company. Lieutenant-Colonel Foster of the 52nd was there. He was in furrowed discussion with another colonel whom I took to be the Camerons' CO. It was a maelstrom of activity.

'Get me a line to Brigade headquarters. I need to speak with General Hill,' I commanded the private manning the telephone.

'Sir, the line is reserved for urgent matters only, for use by the battalion commander.'

Only after the promise of a bottle, and an improvised but serious threat involving my bayonet, did he relent and put my call through.

'General Hill?' I began awkwardly. 'Yes, hello, sir. It's Captain MacPhail,' I stuttered, conscious of the static and the crackle on the line. It felt as if I was using a bullhorn to bridge the distance back to the Capitol. 'You've heard we still have a position on the Spur. Yes, indeed, sir, it's wonderful news. I've just returned from Lieutenant Shankland's company... yes... yes... I completely concur with the lieutenant's assessment,' I said. Hill had asked whether sending reinforcements up the left slope was advisable. I barely had my two bits in before the general spoke again.

'If I might add one thing,' I interrupted, doggedly persevering in the face of the general's proclivity to rattle on. 'I spoke at length with Lieutenant Ellis, who was left in command, and I surveyed the situation myself. They are held down by fire from a trench dead ahead of them. Ellis is convinced, and I agree, that with additional men they could overwhelm that position. In fact, if we reinforce up the left slope as Lieutenant Shankland suggests and take that trench, it would allow the Camerons to sweep to the right and back, to help the 58th... yes... very true, sir... we could then attack the remaining strongpoints at Bellevue Farm and Laamkeek, from behind.'

General Hill had instantly grasped what I told him. I glanced at my wrist: ten minutes to eleven.

CHAPTER 10

30th of October, 1917
Duck Lodge, Bellevue Spur, Belgium

I slept poorly: recurring visions of Private Philips, grinning idiotically and jauntily waving farewell like the schoolboy he was, haunted my thoughts as they had the last four nights. I tossed and turned in my bunk, dropping in and out of consciousness in the last precious few hours I had to rest. Yesterday's orders that I was to remain with the front line battalions to "reconnoitre, advise and assist as required", hadn't added to my inner peace.

Smith and the others were enjoying the comforts of the Canal Bank bunker – thinking about it, I'd been unjustly harsh with my hasty dismissal of the accommodations. But that was prior to my stay at the Grime Inn, otherwise known as Waterloo Farm, where a dry bed – even for officers – was a luxury. Meanwhile, I was more nervous than I cared to acknowledge. The second phase of the attack would begin today.

Miraculously, it wasn't raining. There was what is euphemistically called a stiff wind. To anybody other than an Eskimo, it was bloody freezing.

The attack four days ago, on the 26th, had been touch and go. At 11.30 that morning orders went out to Lieutenant-Colonel Foster of the 52nd to send a company to relieve Shankland, Ellis and the forty-odd men with them on the Spur. Just after one o'clock, the whole battalion was thrown in. The waiting was agonizing.

Finally, word came; the German defences on the right slope were beaten into submission. They'd been caught from in front and behind. It was exactly as General Hill and I had discussed. Not taking it lying down, the Boche counter-attacked later that afternoon, and into the night. Unprepared for the sheer stubbornness they encountered, they dribbled off each time. The key centre of the attack was secured.

On the far-right, the 4th Division and the 1st Australians had both been ordered to take Decline Copse astride the Ridge, and the main rail line running north from Ypres to Roulers, which they did. But then, in the sort of comedy pantomime you saw in the movies, with one character saying, 'Oh, I thought you had it,' and the other, to laughter, 'No, I thought you did,' the Germans, as was their wont, sneaked back in; and that was decidedly *not* a laughing matter. The 44th Battalion was obliged to do an encore the next night. This time they stayed firmly put. It was the sort of botch-up Banting and I would have resolved in a flash.

After a day and a half, the casualty list was a lengthy one. The Camerons alone reported more than 300 killed, wounded and missing, roughly half their initial strength. For the 600-odd yards they'd advanced, it was a heavy toll. There weren't any reliable figures for the German casualties, but I reckoned they weren't a quarter of ours. Admittedly, we'd taken hundreds of prisoners, but they were alive and largely unharmed. In the mixed-up arithmetic of this war, that probably counted as a draw, so to GHQ it was a victory. I had a tough time seeing it that way.

My feelings aside, we had graduated from the red line to the blue, our next objective on the deceptively short, but brutally hazardous path to Passchendaele. It reminded me all too much of swimming lessons, and the time I ran home bursting with pride that I was no longer a Tadpole, but a Minnow – not realizing until later that a minnow was rather small as fish go, and getting to a level commensurate with my parents' ambitions was going to be a tough and lengthy affair.

Up early this morning, if not by choice then by circumstance, I saw the troops assemble, the barrage thunder, and the attack commence – this time from the shell-marked confines of Bellevue Farm. The 9th

Brigade had fitted out one of the German bunkers as a report centre. Other than the names of the fresh units that came in relief, the plan was little altered from four days earlier. You could have criticized that as lacking imagination, were it not for the fact there was no other way to go to get to Passchendaele, a salient detail not lost on our foe.

On the low marshy land to the left of the Spur, a battalion of the 8th Brigade was to advance through the charmingly, but wildly inappropriately named Woodland Plantation, subdue the strong-points at Furst, Vapour and Source Farms, and push on until they reached another outgrowth of the ridge called the Goudberg Spur. Across the Ravebeek on the right, the terrain widened, and three battalions of the 12th Brigade were to wrestle further along the Ridge, almost to within spitting-distance of Passchendaele itself.

Once again, I was up to my calves in the muck, in the centre of the advance, straight up the Bellevue Spur. The 49th Battalion from Edmonton was to take the left side of the Spur, and the Princess Patricia's Canadian Light Infantry, the right. Kindly, the model train adept's daughter, otherwise known as Princess Patricia of Connaught, had lent the Patricias her name. It was rather a shame the Duke wasn't here in person to see them in action, I thought.

It was a little before 7.15 a.m., and together with a signals officer from the Brigade, four runners, and six men carrying a Power Buzzer and accessories, I arrived at Duck Lodge.

Some wit had so named it, there naturally being neither a lodge, nor ducks. There was, however, an ominous-looking pill-box squatted across the land, glowering like some imperious medieval regent sitting on his haunches, and surveying his minions in the swamp below. At roughly waist level, thin dark eyes peered out, commanding the approaches. Its massive walls, buttressed by concrete and steel rods, were as the shell marks made clear, impervious to all but the very largest of our shells. As for ducks, the only ducks around here were either in the belly of some fat Fritz, or had flown the coop three years ago. It suggested an innate intelligence evidently lacking in us two-legged creatures.

To underline my point, a couple of hissing Jennies flew over, doing justice to their name. With their deadly velocity, they had come from the 105mm field guns, and were available in a variety of flavours ranging from high explosive to shrapnel to gas – all much feared by the infantry.

Unfortunately, we were not the only ones up early; the German artillery crews put in long days as well. By my reckoning, it took them exactly 3 minutes to begin shelling this morning, and they were still at it. If they knew the havoc they wrought, I'm afraid it would have encouraged them to even greater lengths, Germans being as they are.

Well prepared for the battle, I was packing my own heavy artillery, my .45 calibre Webley revolver. It had the stopping power of a mid-sized freight train; the only drawback being that if you missed the first time, there was a good chance you were already on your behind, so powerful was the kick. Alternatively, you could avoid the whole recoil problem and simply bludgeon somebody. It was a multi-faceted weapon.

I took it and weighed it thoughtfully in my hand, reassured by its heavy solidness. The company of mopping-up soldiers was still warily circling the bunker. Jaundiced, perhaps, by two and a half years of war, they seemed to me over-cautious. The Patricias had taken Duck Lodge twenty minutes earlier – I'd seen most of that fierce fight, with my own eyes, from Bellevue Farm.

Inching along, ascending the light incline of the Spur's right slope, they endured a hail of lead of epic proportions. It was too much for many. From afar, the Patricias advanced as specks, even at the maximum magnification of the Lemaire field glasses I still carried. Pillars of earth from the exploding shells enveloped them. Regularly, a couple of specks remained behind, motionless. As they approached, and I could make out the figures more clearly, their ranks were shattered by a spray of gunfire from the Lodge, the crest of the Spur, and Graf House 500 yards further along – as well as from across the valley.

I watched the survivors, shooting as they went, throw Mills bomb after Mills bomb. The machine-gun nests encircling the bunker fell one-by-one. Thankfully, the artillery had done its work, and the wire was cut. Finally, as if they'd done it a thousand times before, although it was likely nearer the first, they laid down a fierce fusillade of rifle and Lewis gun fire against the pill-box. With the defenders dazzled by the fireworks, a couple of soldiers slipped unseen up to the grey monstrosity, and pitched grenades through the bunker's gun slits. Hands held high, a handful of shaken-looking prisoners emerged.

After that, mopping-up seemed a useless pastime. But there were strict orders. It wouldn't have been the first time that a strongpoint was taken, and the shock troops moved on, only to discover survivors re-emerging with new fire in their bellies and bullets in their chambers.

CRACK. The bullet hit me in the side.

I hadn't paid much attention when I first saw them, thinking they were corpses. But one of the grey-clad bodies, in a shell hole not 50 yards away, had lifted himself to his elbows. He was glaring down the length of a rifle at me.

Raising my arm with a jolt I fired quickly, oblivious to the recoil, or even where the round went. Screaming, I broke into a mad sprint towards him, my revolver arm extended. My finger pulled at the trigger as fast as the heavy pull would allow. I could see him plainly now, moustache and all. He was fumbling frantically with the bolt of his rifle, cowering at this mad bison tearing down upon him.

I was almost on him. His bolt was closed again, and he'd regained the composure to aim. The dark round point of his barrel was fixated on my chest.

A shot rang out. But my momentum kept me going.

I saw the jagged, finger-sized hole appear in the middle of his helmet. His head sagged, followed by the rest of him. The shot had been mine.

I slowed to a stop, hands on my knees, panting like I'd run the 100-yard sprint.

I raised my head and stared at him. He lay inert, in that horrible, awkward posture that is natural only to those who have died a violent death.

Only then did I think to look to my own wound. I felt it on my right, and I looked down expecting to see a large, dark, expanding blot staining my trench-coat. But I didn't. Dropping the Webley, I ripped open my coat, and rashly clutched at my side, desperate to find where I was hit.

My hand came away with my respirator, pierced through the goggle and the cloth at the back, by a bullet. I began to laugh.

'Sir, are you alright?' It was a soldier from the Patricias who stood beside me.

I looked at him, my face glowing warmly from the run, and the adrenaline, and I smiled, stupidly. 'Yes, I'm fine. Just glad to be here,' I said.

'That was very brave, sir.' He looked at me with an expression of undisguised awe on his face.

I smiled again, 'Thanks,' I said, unable, or perhaps unwilling, to dispel his admiration as the unvarnished truth surely would have. 'Help me turn him over, would you?'

Dispassionately, we went through the pockets of the man who single-handedly almost ended my campaign, and my life. He was a sergeant, from the 465th Regiment.

He was not what you'd call a crack shot, by any stretch. The 465th were one of the three regiments of the 238th Division, equivalent to one of our brigades. I knew full well the 238th Division had replaced the battered 11th Bavarians not long before. His papers revealed nothing of interest. So, we left him, one body amongst far too many, and not one I'd be mourning.

I scooped up my Webley, and opened the 6-round cylinder, more out of morbid curiosity than any well-ingrained soldierly instinct. It was empty. I whistled softly and then walked over to the pill-box.

The pill-box was a place of horror. As I entered the outer chamber I was met with a scene so shocking that, in the time it took my eyes to adjust to the darkness, it shattered the detachment that comes from being surrounded by death in a place like this. Tens of bodies and their parts were strewn about. A large pool of blood, not yet dry, lay in the middle. Every surface of the room seemed to exhibit traces of the bloodbath. Suddenly, I saw a body move, and I shuddered. Inexplicably, I was moved more by a sign of life, than by its absence.

Before I could say a word, two privates picked the soldier up, and began gingerly moving him outside to be treated. I turned to escape to the open, if not the fresh air of the Ypres Salient.

As the last of the bodies was removed, a private of the Patricias, who was standing around outside, began talking in a loud voice, to no one in particular, 'And to think, I could have been at the Lekkerboterbeek, by now,' he said. The Lekkerboterbeek was an objective of the 5th Canadian Mounted Rifles on our far left – he must have seen it on a map. I hoped there was a punchline coming. Quizzically, I looked at him.

'Roughly translated, that's the Yummy Butter Creek,' he explained, sensing correctly that none of his audience had a clue what he was rambling on about. 'My parents were Dutch,' he added. It was a biographical detail that he shared widely, I presumed, lest someone think he was German.

I smiled wanly, and there were a few tepid laughs.

There was nothing here remotely resembling butter. I couldn't imagine it was any different a thousand yards to the northwest at the Lekkerboterbeek. Unless perhaps it was the mud. That shared an oddly similar consistency to soft butter. If you'd lost both sight and smell, and were therefore blissfully unaware of its vile brown putridness, a weak comparison could be made.

Come to think of it, though, I was largely inured to the stench of the air. Whether my stomach could handle the fresh stuff was another matter. I saw the signals officer and his men working feverishly to set up the Power Buzzer. Curious, I moved over.

Modern war was fast becoming a war of technology. I hoped that at twenty-eight I didn't automatically disqualify for this brave new era; I definitely had some catching up to do, if the last few weeks were any indication.

'Lieutenant, how does that work, exactly – the Power Buzzer?' I asked.

'It's quite a neat gadget, actually,' he replied. 'In the absence of cables, it's obviously impossible to send any wires or telephone traffic. At least not without one of those new-fangled wireless sets they have at Brigade, right?' He glanced briefly over at me, seemingly for confirmation, though it might just have been to see if I was pulling his leg with my query.

I shrugged affirmatively.

'Right,' he said, reassured. 'Well, the Power Buzzer can send a signal for a relatively short distance through the ground, from two metal probes. That's what's underneath those two wires, there,' he said, pointing. 'We'll be transmitting with Morse code to our reporting centre at Bellevue Farm, who will then re-transmit it to Brigade HQ. The only problem is that the Germans can overhear it, if they're close, and if they're listening. So it's best to keep the messages short, or better yet, encrypt them. Until the engineers get a cable up here, and that hopefully won't be long, it's a good temporary measure, and a lot better than the signal lamps or the runners, for sure.'

I shook my head in wonder, but he seemed to suspect I was being critical about the pace of the engineers. 'They do their best, sir. It won't be more than a few hours.'

'No, I agree, they're doing their best. They deserve medals, all of them,' I said. I certainly wouldn't have wanted to follow in their footsteps.

Aside from the obvious sanitary issues, the problem with being at Duck Lodge was that I had the impression I hadn't a clue what was going on, an impression I soon discovered was entirely accurate. That the Patricias were held up by the massive pill-box 500 yards forward, smack in the middle of the critical high ground near the hamlet at Meetcheele was obvious, but little else. The rest of the offensive could have been playing out in Namibia for all I knew. Every so often a tidbit of news would trickle in. Assessing how the Patricias were doing, let alone the 49th, was agonisingly drawn out. I could almost sympathise with our information-starved commanders.

That left us in the "Advanced Brigade Reporting Centre" broadcasting appeals for stretcher-bearers, something I wouldn't have thought necessary given the Corps Commander's infamous casualty estimate of two weeks earlier.

Finally, at 9.24 a.m. – we noted the time for the log – a runner came in brandishing a message. Seeing me first, and noting my pips, he handed it over without a word. The Patricias had taken the Meetcheele pill-box!

'Send: CREST OF HILL TAKEN. LARGE PILL-BOX SURRENDERED. OUR MACHINE GUNS ESTABLISHED,' I ordered one of the signallers, with excitement in my voice, repeating verbatim the contents of the message. There was no denying it was a crucial breakthrough. That pill-box held up the entire advance on the Bellevue Spur.

A half-hour later, a scout sergeant by the name of Mullin, who I only afterwards learned captured the pill-box single-handedly, passed through with confirmation. He was en route to Waterloo Farm to report the details.

By lunchtime I'd largely regained my hunger, following the morning's suspense, and the initial shock of seeing Duck Lodge. That was a good thing, too, as the Boche had considerably left a well-stocked pantry and plenty of fresh water – the latter, perversely, was a real collector's item in the water-logged Salient. Looking at the bounty of edibles I could only dream what German rations looked like before the blockade.

Not wishing to tempt fate, or my constitution, I took a thick chunk of bread and a good length of sausage, and some water, and went outside to eat. The sausage was of a sort I was unfamiliar with, but it smelled delicious.

It was a decision I promptly reconsidered at the sound of a Hissing Jenny. Say what you might of Duck Lodge, it had the undeniable merit of possessing 5-foot thick walls. In the midst of another bombardment that gave it a certain magnetic attraction to those of us fond of our own skin. Retiring to a rough table in one of the inner rooms, I was savouring a mouthful of the garlicky sausage when my mind – in one of the circuitous deviations it is prone to – wandered to GHQ, and the Château de Beaurepaire. Haig was surely well into the port and cigars at this hour, I thought sourly. I savagely ripped away another mouthful of bread with my teeth.

My reputation to the contrary, I was never particularly happy looking busy when I wasn't, and the feeling of being distinctly under-employed grew by the hour. At last I decided to venture out. I wanted to see what I could make of the 4th Division's progress, opposite us, on the main ridge line. Perhaps I might get a vague impression how the overall attack was faring. Looking through the slits of the bunker was as illuminating as trying to read a book through a keyhole. One thing I did know, a burst of machine-gun fire in my direction from Crest Farm, or thereabouts, would not be a positive sign. Optimist that I am, I kept my head low, and my hopes high.

Steel helmet or not, I was relieved by the absence of lead in the air, and even more by the sight of men moving around, and beyond, that strongpoint guarding the gates to Passchendaele. The initial reports of it falling appeared to be correct. The soldiers I saw had to be ours; there was less chance of Germans running around in the open there, than of the German empire adopting the Union Jack.

Around two it began to pour – again. As it looked presently, or unless the water ran out up above, my swimming lessons of old might soon prove invaluable. That was the thing about the Salient, water was never in any shortage, unless you wanted some to drink.

In the next few hours there was meagre progress. The Patricias and the 49th Battalion soon began to dig in for the inevitable counter-attacks. When the actual order to consolidate came, I knew it was time to leave. The attack had run its course for today.

The light, such as it was, through the mottled sea of dense grey clouds sailing above, was fading fast as I began to pick my way through the shell-holes on the journey back to Waterloo Farm. Already I could hear the cries of the wounded all around.

They moaned softly, in desperate isolation, as a dark curtain fell on the fields. I was cold, on edge, battered by the day's experiences, and the sounds unnerved me. I hated to imagine their despair as the last rays of light dimmed, and any hopes of help faded with them; the prospect of a cold, lonely and horrifying night still ahead. Many would be fighting their final battle, against the mud that sucked them deeper into their holes until, when their last ounce of strength ebbed away, they would slip helplessly into the shallow pool of water at their feet. There the water would fill their lungs until life left them and Flanders became their home forever.

Occasionally a shell would fall with a whistle, followed by a long moment of silence, and then a deep concussion. They seemed to accentuate the eerie silence against which a dark symphony of moans and sobbing played on, pierced at intervals by the shrill notes of a scream, as pain and desperation overcame one of them.

Descending the gentle slope of the Spur, I pulled a respirator over my face. I'd scavenged a replacement before leaving. In the dark and alone, I was afraid I would miss the signs of gas before it was too late, or simply stumble into a hole where it lay swirling at the bottom in deadly wait. The German gunners had pounded this slope all day. They'd largely abstained from using gas on the ridge where their own troops were dug in, but they had no such compassion when it came to our lines. Under the rubber mask my own methodic breathing lent a bizarre ghostliness to the setting, as my eyes darted to and fro beneath the scratched goggles, searching for a bathmat walkway that might hasten my travel.

After an eternity, I arrived at Waterloo Farm more tattered than when I left. Promptly, I joined the others there to carry on the business of war. Doing what had to be done: my duty.

CHAPTER 11

6th of November, 1917
Watou, Belgium

'Aren't you a sight?!' Lieutenant-Colonel Hore-Ruthven cried when he spotted me the next day, on October 31st, as I wearily stumbled into the grounds of the Canal Bank bunker. Soon after, Tibbett also appeared out of nowhere, sporting his very best impersonation of an undertaker. On seeing me he brightened visibly. He was genuinely glad to see me, and vigorously shook my hand for what seemed an unconscionably long time, talking non-stop the entire while. After I wriggled free – my circulation not being what it was two weeks ago – and the pleasantries wound down, I broached the question I was dying to ask.

'So, tell me, how are we doing?'

He glanced at me with a look of puzzlement: 'You were there, weren't you?'

'Yeah, getting shot at, shelled by half the German army, and my life generally made miserable,' I replied. 'That's one of the things about having your head in the mud, you tend to miss the big picture.' Naturally, I picked up a few things at battalion headquarters prior to coming back, but I wasn't about to undermine my dramatic story.

His eyes widened perceptibly when he examined me closer. Presumably, he noticed the prominent hole in the side of my trench coat for the first time. 'You actually *were* shot,' he said in disbelief, as if he couldn't believe I'd been telling the truth. It was either that, or he thought I led a remarkably charmed life.

'Luckily, the Fritz mislaid his eyeglasses, or it might have been my last visit to this charming pile of concrete,' I said. 'It's a shame about the coat, though; it was a perfectly good one, too. Cost me a fortune.'

Still shaking his head, Tibbett began to recount the details of the advance. 'You likely know we made decent progress on Bellevue Spur, although a tad short of the blue line. On the far left, it looked dicey for a while. A group of the Mounted Rifles under a Major Pearkes took Vapour and Source Farms, but they were left hanging for the longest time – essentially isolated, and without reinforcements. Currie ordered them to hold the line. And incredibly they did,' he said, again shaking his head. 'Unfortunately, the Royal Navy and 58th Divisions didn't end up offering them much support.'

'Well, I guess that answers the question why Wellington didn't feel the need to ring up the Navy before Waterloo.'

He laughed. 'Up the ridge to Passchendaele we managed to take all the objectives, including Crest Farm, early in the day. It was a little tense whether you lot were going to come through in the middle, otherwise they might have made it even further.'

'And the positions have held through this morning?' I asked.

'Yes, and now we're only a few hundred yards from Passchendaele.'

That was almost a week ago. In the meantime, we'd consolidated the front, moved headquarters to Watou, the complete 3rd and 4th Divisions were replaced in the line by the 1st and the 2nd, and only now did my feet look like they belonged to a human being.

Sorting out my feet was the most trying experience of the week. I rubbed them regularly with whale oil, and combined with keeping them dry for several consecutive days, it eventually worked wonders. My boots were pretty much a write-off, not that I had replacements at hand.

I was up early this morning. Which is about as much of an under-statement as saying that autumns in Ypres can be moist. Inexplicably, it wasn't raining.

The third phase of the attack was to begin at 6.00 a.m., and yesterday Hore-Ruthven had come to me with an unusual request. A "young" staff officer from the British IX Corps wished to observe the attack. He was scheduled to arrive here at 3.00 a.m. and I was to accompany him. So instead of a decent night's sleep with the not uncomfortable prospect of following the battle from the warm, dry and shell-free divisional HQ, I was to play tour guide in the muck. It was a mystery how this little chore ended up on my doorstep. No doubt my vast experience of the battlefield played a role, I reckoned, in a smug moment. Later, after I reflected on it, I realized one of my superiors simply thought I had nothing better to do.

The *young* staff officer turned out, in fact, to be my age. Looking at him, he might even have been a year or two older. His name was Bernard Montgomery and he was a captain. That was a stroke of luck, as it would spare me the cramped formality accompanying a more senior English staff officer. He looked dashing, an effect greatly accentuated by my own lack of dash.

While my welcoming smile wouldn't exactly melt hearts, it was the best show I could muster at this hour. Promptly I addressed him as 'Bernie', testing the waters. A little premature familiarity was always an excellent litmus test for officers. There were really only two basic types: the first, even if they didn't particularly appreciate being acquainted on a first-name basis, would smile and get on with the business at hand. The second, mortally wounded by some sense of improper etiquette, retreated into a shell and might as well be directing traffic at Hell Fire Corner. From the tenseness in his face muscles I knew I'd made Montgomery uncomfortable, but he responded graciously.

We took a car from Watou, passing through Ypres, and went a mile or two up the road towards Gravenstafel, where we were obliged to dismount, and walk the remaining three miles or so to Boethoek pill-box. It gave us some time to talk.

'...the whole art of war is to gain your objective with as little loss as possible,' Montgomery was saying. I glanced over at him in the midst of his discourse. He had a solid but serious air, and a whopper of a nose that bore an uncanny resemblance to the triangle I'd used in geometry. Clean-shaven, his fierce dark eyebrows furrowed deeply as he made his points. In the course of a three-mile walk they proved to be rather numerous. He was what you might call opinionated. But then again, so was I. It made for an animated conversation.

'That's interesting,' I interjected, as he paused for breath during a particularly long monologue. 'The battalions you'll see today have practiced their attacks several times already on a taped course. Naturally...'

Breath regained, Montgomery nodded energetically, as if agreeing. Or it could have just been impatience. Either way, he waved me quiet in a manner that left few doubts that my two pennies' worth were disturbing his train of thought. Evidently, he had more to say on the subject.

'As chance would have it, I've actually written a manual on this very topic. It's called, "Instructions for the Training of Divisions for Offensive Action",' he explained.

'It's a snappy title,' I blurted out.

He smiled thinly, and I hastened to make amends. 'I'd be interested in reading it, if you wouldn't mind sending me a copy?'

He seemed pleased at that. Thankfully, we arrived not long afterwards at the Boethoek pill-box. Pill-boxes, this autumn, were very much in vogue as a location for a headquarters, and Boethoek was no exception.

The 6th Brigade from the 2nd Canadian Division was preparing for three of its battalions to go into action. There was not a great deal to see and, in the confined space, we were plainly getting in the way. So, I motioned for Montgomery to follow and I led him up to Abraham Heights. From there we had a much better view in the direction of the jumping-off lines. I neglected to mention it was also a lot more hazardous.

A group of soldiers from the 31st Battalion passed by in file. They were from my home province of Alberta. Seeing us, they made an attempt of sorts to salute, which from my angle appeared suspiciously similar to waves.

I turned to observe Montgomery. True to form he was returning the salute with a crispness that was utterly superfluous. I decided not to bother mentioning the shared roots.

'Fancy that, a Tommy staff officer, up here,' we heard one say, after they'd passed. 'Probably looking to see how it's done,' said another, and they all laughed softly.

'Spirited bunch,' said Montgomery.

'Yes, they are,' I said. I couldn't help but adding, 'With good reason, don't you think?'

He stared at me blankly.

'You know, having taken Vimy Ridge and Hill 70 since April…,' I mumbled in explanation. Montgomery looked as befuddled as if I were recounting the exploits of the army of the Duchy of Liechtenstein – which, as far as I knew, didn't even have an army.

It was exactly the sort of rankling obstinacy that tends to really perk me up. 'And now we have the battle for Passchendaele,' I exclaimed with a flourish in the direction of the village. 'The troops may not like it, but they're still proud the Corps gets selected for all the choice assignments no one else in the BEF seems *capable* of doing.' It was a touch undiplomatic, in all honesty. But a light bombardment was wasted on Montgomery. To get through to him required a full-blown von Schlieffen plan. Besides, there was a difference between writing manuals and winning battles.

At 6.00 a.m. under a dark, but astonishingly clear sky, the guns went off with a roar that could have woken the dead. I was anticipating it, but even so the deafening intensity surprised me afresh. Through my field glasses I could see that the troops were already racing forward, virtually sprinting towards the pulverising rain of shells falling only 150 yards in front. They must have had quite a breakfast.

For Montgomery's sake I pointed forward. 'Off to the right that's the main ridgeline. The 28th, 31st and 27th Battalions are to take the village, and advance just beyond it. In the middle, the 1st and 2nd Battalions will take the remaining strong-points along Bellevue Spur, and then advance onto the main ridgeline left of Passchendaele. They've got the longest distance to cover,' I bellowed into Montgomery's ear. 'The Bellevue Spur is that high ground, there,' I added, motioning in the direction of our now infamous spur.

Montgomery nodded, clearly mesmerized by the spectacle that was unfolding.

'On the far left. You can't see it from here. There's a strong-point called Vine Cottages. A company of the 3rd Battalion will attack it.'

106

The words were barely out of my mouth when green flares shot up to our left and our right. They were prearranged SOS signals to the enemy artillery to commence their bombardment. In my experience the Fritz gunners seldom needed much encouragement, and so it was again. In less time than it would take the captain to reiterate the title of his manual, I saw explosions on the Spur. A minute or two later our starting lines on the ridge were also under bombardment. But Fritz was too late I noted, smiling. The waves of attackers were already gone, the first of them even now running up against the shell-torn German front lines.

We watched in fascination as the rows of soldiers disappeared from our sight, obscured in dense swirling wreathes of mist, and the smoke from our artillery, and theirs.

'Shall we get back to the bunker?' I asked Montgomery. 'It won't be long before Fritz begins shelling the approaches and the support areas.'

Well before 8.00 a.m., came the momentous news that the village of Passchendaele was taken.

By 9.00 a.m. all the objectives were secured. 'Congratulations,' said Montgomery, who'd been uncharacteristically silent since we returned. He'd missed nothing as the morning progressed. But his silence might have had something to do with an offhand remark I made. I'd said; 'The problem with theory was that when theory and reality met, in-evitably it was reality that was left standing'. Certainly, from what he described, we'd done everything in his little manual and more, and the casualties were still piling up. The instructions might have been fresh from the presses, but an urgent rewrite seemed unavoidable, although I didn't say that. Montgomery was a decent man, I decided, irksomely self-assured perhaps, but nothing a spell with the Corps wouldn't resolve.

'Thanks,' I replied. 'We're not done yet, I'm afraid, but we're a step closer. Are you sure you wouldn't like to join us at this late hour? Spruce up your life with a little excitement?'

Right when I was thinking nothing could budge the granite impas-siveness of his jaw, he smiled broadly, his first of the morning.

The apprehension on the faces of the brigade general and his staff had softened, and cautious smiles shone through like rays of sun on an overcast day. The all-important objectives were taken. The price would be all too clear tomorrow morning when the casualty lists were complete. Like me, they were acutely aware the next phase – the fourth – wouldn't be long in coming.

That was one of the problems with this whole damn Ypres offensive, it just kept going. And so it seemed with Passchendaele. Once past the red and blue lines, and before today's objective of the green line was even tackled, a stippled green line had emerged on the maps. What would happen if we made some real ground? We'd only advanced a mile and a half, and already they were running out of different-coloured pens.

CHAPTER 12

11th of November, 1917
Crest Farm, Passchendaele, Belgium

There was no reason for me to be here – it was rash, and possibly a bit stupid if I was honest, even if I had assured the colonel otherwise to get his permission. Like bees from a hive that had been violently whacked from its tree, the Germans were in a buzzing frenzy to exact their retribution. Their stings, when they came, were fierce and rang out day and night. Behind the ridge to the north, and beyond the range of our own mud-encased guns, were countless batteries of the deadly 77mm and 105mm field guns. Further back were the heavy howitzers, like the 5.9s and the 203mm cannons, capable of lobbing a high explosive shell almost six miles. However, I felt the need to see this spot with my own eyes. This Flemish village had occupied most of my thoughts, and all of my exertions for a month, and it had demanded far more from others.

The attack on the 10th for the remainder of the high ground north of Passchendaele – the infamous stippled green bulge on the maps – had succeeded, barring the wearily predictable failure of the 1st Imperial Division on our left. With it the last piece of ridge-line facing Ypres that remained in German hands was captured. It fell astonishingly quickly. A rag-bag of disorganized and demoralised German units ceded the ground with surprisingly little resistance and surrendered in their hundreds.

Their generals, ensconced in comfortable quarters to the rear, took it less lightly. It was an unwritten rule of war; the further you were from the front, the more fervent you became. In the streaming rain the muzzles of five entire German corps pulverised the ridge for most of the day. They inflicted heavy casualties. In one of those instances you might be tempted to call poetic justice, but was really just plain sad, they obliterated untold numbers of their own men as they stumbled back to the prisoner cages. Whole wings of enemy aeroplanes swooped low with their machine guns blazing. But their counter-attacks, when they came, failed. The price for this ground was far too high. We were digging in to stay.

DuBois had cheerfully volunteered to accompany me when I told him of my sightseeing plans. I'd been careful not to ask outright, not wanting him to feel obliged to join me, but I'm sure he sensed I wanted the company.

We walked all the way from Ypres. It took us close to four hours. The Londoner who bemoans the congestion of Piccadilly Circus has never experienced the Ypres to Mosselmarkt road. DuBois, judging from his frequent muttered curses, appeared to wish he'd never experienced it either.

It was a fortunate thing the Germans were no longer on the ridge, for the corduroy plank road and the duckboards were packed solid. Soldiers and supplies plodded forward, and stretcher-bearer after stretcher-bearer – often German prisoners conscripted for the task – passed them as they went, bearing their sorry load for the field hospitals in the rear.

Arriving in Passchendaele we headed for the church, and finding none, ended up at a cellar instead. A private from the 20th Battalion ardently insisted this was the church. It was only after DuBois found a cross in the rubble that we believed him.

'It's not much to fight for,' said DuBois.

'No,' I agreed. 'There's not a single solitary building that's left intact. Village sounds more worth fighting for than rubble, I suppose. When the war's over, it'd be a wonderful spot to build a château, though. Look at the view, Benoît.'

At the rear of the church cellar, the hill fell sharply away, giving a wide panorama of occupied Belgium to the north, visible to us for the first time since 1914. Down the steep muddy slope, I could see the shell-holes manned by a soldier or two, their helmets and rifles jutting out from under their groundsheets, their sole bulwark against the worst of the weather, and the preying eyes of the enemy. The groundsheets offered no such protection from the bullets and shells.

From the church, we walked down the hill in the other direction, back towards Ypres. It took us less than five minutes to reach Crest Farm. There, we sat near the remains of one of the dozen or so machine-gun nests, and gazed out across the Salient. The ground was ripped apart and strewn with equipment of all sorts, tangles of wire and bodies – the latter mostly German.

'You see the machine guns, Mac; they're all pointing the wrong way. The Seaforth Highlanders used the Boche's own guns to beat off his counter-attacks,' said DuBois in obvious admiration.

It was hard to believe that five days earlier, in the other direction, what for us had been an easy five-minute stroll, had consumed shells by the tens of thousands. Far worse, it had cost hundreds their lives or their limbs.

'That's Ypres!' said DuBois, surprise lacing his voice. The billowy grey blanket that had been nailed across the horizon since I arrived here nearly a month ago, had lifted its veil ever so slightly. Save for an occasional spot of rain the visibility was shockingly good.

'The cathedral and the Cloth Hall,' I said. 'It's funny, you know. They look much better from here than they do up close. It almost makes you wonder whether the Germans didn't bother to completely raze them, just so they'd have something to aim at.' I sighed. 'Of course, we've been fulfilling that role for the past month.'

Benoît shrugged. 'You don't have to be much of a shot to hit something from here.'

'No, more like shooting a herd of caribou with a Lewis gun, you mean. Of course, that's pretty much what happened.' I shook my head. 'It's amazing, Benoît, how much closer everything is from up here on top of the ridge looking down, than down there looking up, don't you think?'

Across the Ravebeek and its swamp, to our right, the water-glazed, shell-pocked, brown mound of the Bellevue Spur dominated our sight. I shuddered when I glimpsed Duck Lodge virtually opposite us. Even a half-blind Tibbett without his spectacles on could have picked off the figures wandering around. And I suspected he was as handy with a rifle as I was with an accordion.

DuBois borrowed the field glasses, and peered off in the direction of the pill-boxes at Meetcheele. 'It's a miracle we took this you know,' he muttered.

'I'm inclined to agree,' I said. 'I'm not sure we *would* have a couple of years ago.'

DuBois lowered his glasses, and cocked his head.

'Sometimes I marvel at the changes we've undergone, Benoît. Do you remember how it was in the beginning?'

He nodded. 'Yes, wild charges, seat-of-the-pants planning, and rifles that jammed.'

'Right, and it wasn't what you'd call overwhelmingly successful most of the time.'

'No, it wasn't, Mac.'

'But look at us now, we're a well-oiled machine. And all the new tactics and technology. It's enough to make my head spin. I'd never even heard of an oscillograph until two weeks ago. It's been an incredible transformation.'

'All thanks to Byng and Currie, if you ask me,' said Benoît solemnly.

'They sure didn't have much to work with,' I said and we both laughed. We'd been in the first contingents sent overseas.

'I never understood, Mac, why we've changed so much, and the Imperial divisions so little.'

I smiled. 'Well, we had a lot more to improve on, I expect!' Benoît nodded. 'Seriously, though, we were eager to learn. And it helps we're not third-generation dockworkers, or coal-miners since the age of fourteen...'

'...with the son of the Earl of Ketchup as our superior officer...'

'Exactly. And with a red-faced sergeant-major, bellowing in our faces, that we're sorely mistaken if weasels like us think we're going to up-end three-hundred years of regimental tradition,' I added. 'No, we're used to thinking and fending for ourselves.'

'Which is why it took two years for most soldiers to learn a decent salute?'

Benoît was always quick-witted. I liked that. I wouldn't have wanted to face off against him in French.

'You have to admit, Benoît – and don't tell the general I said so – but saluting is not the most productive activity imaginable.'

'The Aussies definitely agree with you there, Mac,' he said. The rambunctious Australians remained a blight in the eyes of the average Imperial officer. In comparison, we were the picture of docile civility.

Benoît picked up the field glasses and went back to studying the Spur. After a length, he murmured softly, 'It's a bloody miracle.'

He couldn't see me, but I frowned. 'There was a good reason why Currie was so generous with his casualty estimates,' I said.

At that, he put down the field-glasses again, and turned to face me. 'Did you hear any news?'

'No. Not yet. They're still compiling the lists.'

'Yesterday, there were more than a thousand, they say.'

'I reckon there must be fourteen or fifteen thousand in total, likely more,' I said grimly. The boyish grin of Private Philips flashed in my mind. Fifteen thousand was so many that it became an abstraction, not like Philips, whose face I would never forget. However much I lamented it, no sane man could bear the burden of fifteen thousand Philipses. If the politicians and generals had, perhaps this blasted war would never have begun.

'But Haig got his victory, eh?' Benoît said, his h's absorbed in the softest of whispers. I smiled to myself. I'd always loved the way he pronounced 'hAig' – almost as if it were a chronic disease.

'Yes, yes he did,' I replied dreamily, my mind elsewhere. Then I turned to him. 'It may be victory, but it sure doesn't feel like one, does it? Do you think this war is ever going to end?'

Benoît said nothing and I looked away.

'Benoît?'

There was a pregnant pause, and the delivery must have seemed like it would never arrive, for finally he asked, 'Yes, Mac?'

'We did everything that was asked of us. But what was asked, was it worthy of everything that we did?'

He nudged my elbow. Without speaking he passed me a flask.

Greedily I swallowed a generous mouthful of a fiery spirit I couldn't place. Benoît was good that way.

PART TWO

CHAPTER 13

15th of December, 1917
London, England

From behind I heard a shrill scream, and I pivoted.

The green lorry was bearing down upon me at high speed, with an urgent TOOT-toot, TOOT-toot, TOOT-toot and a screeching which seemed to go on and on until I felt it in my marrow. Through the windscreen I saw the red-capped driver, his ruddy features twisted in anxious contortions, the milk bottles stacked up behind him in wooden crates rattling wildly against the top of the cab. Ten feet... nine feet... eight...

I swivelled and sprang. Back to the sidewalk, literally two or three feet away, an eternity. I did it with the reflexes born of combat, unthinking.

In a blast of wind, the lorry whooshed by, and I sank to the ground, still embracing the lantern post. A woman knelt beside me. The sharp, sweet scent of roses from her perfume stirred me, and I thanked her.

On my lips I could almost taste the lantern's metallic lead paint. But all was well and I was on leave. I was still feeling a little giddy about it.

I've always found London to be an exciting place; exciting in an exhilarating, uplifting, glad-to-be-alive sort of way, as opposed to the kind that has you pressing your helmet flat on your head and your body even flatter while some Fritz machine-gunner takes it upon himself to put more holes in you than adorn a slice of Swiss cheese. Mind you, until the English get around to driving on the right side of the road, it could be equally hazardous.

I was staying at the Connaught. After an extensive study, I largely picked it on the basis of its all too familiar name, although apparently that was new. In retrospect, I should have spent more time studying the room rates. The hotel itself had been around for years, a hundred and two to be precise, according to a brass plaque mounted behind the white-haired doorman, and some rusty mental arithmetic, including the last three of them at war. The Germanic-sounding Coburg Hotel had met its demise at the altar of 1917 xenophobia. Name changes were all the fashion in certain circles this year, I gathered, including even the Royal ones. On the face of it, the King's case seemed stronger than the Coburg's: there was no arguing that the House of Windsor sounded more sympathetic than that of Saxe-Coburg-Gotha. Besides, the latter might all too easily be confused with the big bi-engine German birds my friends at Ten Elms were hunting, and which this season were periodically dropping their loads over London.

The toll the Connaught was taking on my pocket book was momentarily overshadowed by the almost childish joy I was experiencing residing in it. My sojourn so far was one of the pleasantest I've ever had. Knowing that my two weeks leave would end in a few days, I resolved to not think about the cost, or my guilt, the two being hopelessly intertwined. The thought of my leave coming to an end, however, was a dangerously double-edged sword. So, I tried to blot that out as well, usually at the expense of my pocket book. It left me in contortions of the sort Bobby Leach must have experienced going over Niagara Falls in a barrel.

This morning I enjoyed a full English breakfast. There was something distinctly civilized to be said for starting one's morning with eggs, toast with butter, a "rasher" or four of bacon as the English quaintly insisted on calling it, together with some brown beans in sauce, and half a fried tomato. Civilized, was not a word I would have readily associated with the coarsely textured black mound accompanying it. Black pudding, I was told. Without putting too much of a point on it, black pudding had strong associations with a couple of other things, neither of which were even remotely edible.

After breakfast I strolled down Mount Street. I was deposited several minutes later in the lush green of Hyde Park, although to describe it as such, in mid-December, was a stretch even by my imagination, particularly as there was often a light dusting of snow in the mornings – one of the primary reasons I enjoyed going so much.

At this hour, the park was quiet and I enjoyed sitting on a wooden bench and contemplating life which, at the moment, felt rather good. Thanks to a stunning German victory at a place I never heard of called Caporetto, the Ypres offensive had been unceremoniously terminated and eleven British and French divisions were hustled off to Italy to help. Haig kept his promise to Currie, and soon after our fourth and final attack at Passchendaele, we were making our way back to the area of Lens in France. I wasn't sorry to leave. By the time we departed, General Currie's outlandish casualty estimate had proven horrifyingly accurate. And I'd known more than a few of them. Leave couldn't have come at a better time. I was doing my best to forget it all, only in the quiet moments it came flooding back.

If the grand plan was to wear down the enemy, then presumably a key to the plan was that he be worn down before we were? All I knew was that after Passchendaele I sure felt worn down; the Corps was definitely worn down – hell, the entire BEF was worn down. It was almost too much to hope for, that the Germans felt equally bad.

I pulled the lapels of my trench coat more snugly around my neck and watched my breath fog the clear dawn air. Not long after arriving at Waterloo station from the coast I traded in my old Aquascutum for a new Burberry. It proved even more expensive than its predecessor, despite wasting an entire afternoon shopping around for a better price, the Scottish blood in me getting the upper hand. The Aquascutum had served me well, but regardless of what the cleverly worded advertisements might have you believe, its protective qualities did not extend to bullets, and it was time for a change. I also bought a couple of elegant new uniforms.

That particular investment had everything to do with the bolt from the sky that General Lipsett himself had divulged two weeks earlier: my promotion to major. 'Don't make me regret this. We'll make a soldier of you yet, MacPhail. Remember that with the ladies in London,' were his final words, delivered with another of his cryptic smiles, leaving me to ponder what precisely the one had to do with the other. What I did know was that major meant a crown to replace the pips on each shoulder, as well as an extra dollar a day pay. Even so, at $5 a day, my next leave was unaffordable until somewhere around 1920… unless there was a sudden promotion to field-marshal in the offing I was unaware of.

Never before had I felt so carefree here. After the Salient, the noise and hustle and excitement of this great city held few surprises anymore. I'd seen humanity on the brink, and somehow that made me long for the simple things of life. I wandered aimlessly through the streets, my thoughts gloriously free, pausing when whim would have it to peer into a pretty shop window adorned for Christmas, or to warm my hands around a hot cup of strong black tea. Until a newspaper headline caught my eye.

BOLSHEVIK RUSSIA
SEEKS PEACE WITH
CENTRAL POWERS

'One penny, sir,' said the bright-cheeked lad who was selling them.

I paid up and tucked it under my arm. This was not the kind of news I was hoping for. The Bolshevik revolution, of only last month, gave the Germans a golden opportunity to shift forces from the East to the West. If there was even a sliver of truth to rumours of peace treaties between the two, we'd be up to our necks in fresh Germans in the time it took General Ludendorff to pin on his medals in the morning. The New Year hadn't even begun and already I wasn't looking forward to it.

Newspaper in hand I steered along Sloane Street towards the Grenadier, a little pub I'd discovered in Belgrave Square. I considered their meat pies one of the triumphs of the British Empire. They washed down splendidly with a pint or two of Burton ale. I discarded the newspaper and its litany of problems, half unread, and took a walk over to the National Gallery.

After dark, London streets turned treacherous. Especially for the single, well-dressed officer in uniform. The first couple of times I felt horribly provincial, shyly turning away from the rolling English hillside thrust in my face, greeting the oily grin, and painted suggestive eyes with embarrassed silence.

Now, one such lady ambled towards me; she'd spotted me from afar. Hoarsely, she whispered, 'Those are beautiful brown minces you have, love.' I failed to see how my brown eyes had anything to do with the matter.

'Thanks,' I mumbled, and moved on as quickly as my patina of dignified nonchalance allowed. Strangely, the determination I was an unwashed colonial didn't awaken the usual curiosity as much as add fuel to their ardour. I had a sneaking suspicion a particular sub-set of Londoners knew our generous pay scales better than we did ourselves, and I was beginning to grasp how it was that one man in five had V.D.

Naturally, I'd eyed a few beauties in the street, or standing across the bar, sparkling vivaciously as they conversed with some red-faced, thickset, Greek deity of fifty-five. For some reason, storming a machine-gun nest seemed inherently easier than risking an advance on any of them. Either there'd be a miracle on the Thames in the next three days, or I'd have the long trip back to Lens to fashion a suitably erotic tale of my adventures.

I was tired after a day of fresh air and exercise – it was strange how it was the fresh stuff that always wore you out. So, after a light dinner, I made my way back to the hotel and its delightful bar. Part of its charm was that it was still undiscovered by the Aussies, thereby ensuring it kept its charm. It also meant I needn't worry about being hit on the back of the head with a well-placed chair. For some reason it was heaving at the seams tonight. I soon realized that might have something to do with it being a Saturday night. It was the sort of detail that was as good as irrelevant at the front.

The bartender Ted saw me slip in. Given the throng, that was a sensation in itself. He greeted me with an enthusiastic wave and a, 'Hello there, Major MacPhail,' hollered across the crowded bar so as to escape no one's notice, making me momentarily feel like a minor celebrity.

Vera, one of the servers, took my arm. 'This way, Major, I have a nice table for you over here in the corner.' And in an act vaguely suggestive of something from the Old Testament, the crowds parted and I was ushered to a comfortable corner table for four. Ted and Vera were by a considerable margin the friendliest bar staff in the Western Hemisphere. More likely, I was simply the best customer they'd had since the Tsar and his entourage were last in town.

It was a good table. But sitting by my lonesome when half the room could barely find the space to plant two feet in close proximity to each other, was more uncomfortable than I would have thought. When I noticed the two captains enter, and gaze hopefully in my direction, I beckoned them over and offered a seat.

'Thank you, sir, that's very kind of you, it's packed to the gunnels in here,' said one, a short slender type with glasses, of whom it was hard to believe he'd made it through any form of pre-enlistment medical screening. 'Perhaps we should order?' Short he might be, there was no disparaging his manners.

When I saw the huge tumbler he'd ordered for himself, and nothing for us, I reconsidered. I was even more puzzled when he glanced furtively about. Then he poured a third of his glass into mine, and a third into his companion's.

I stared at him, my own manners momentarily forgotten.

'Dora,' he explained.

'Dora?'

'Mmm. The Defence of the Realm Act.'

'Ah ha,' I said, speaking the words, but understanding nothing.

'Under the provisions of the act it's an offence to treat others to a drink.'

'You must be kidding,' I said. I stared at him afresh. 'It's illegal to buy a guy a drink? In the middle of a war!?'

'Welcome to Lloyd George's England.'

'Well, I'll remember not to treat him should our paths cross, but in the meantime, cheers.'

They were decent fellows. The Scotch whisky they were buying was much better than decent. In fact, I was all but ready with my new "judge a man by his drink" litmus test, when I recalled the swill I'd been known to consume, and summarily shelved the idea.

'Seeing as how you're sitting on my chairs, and I'm drinking your whisky, why don't we dispense with the ranks for the time being? I'm Malcolm MacPhail.'

The short, skinny one, Ewan Turner, was in tanks as it turned out. I should have guessed. It was either that or he cleaned artillery barrels for a living. He was back from the great battle at Cambrai. It began spectacularly ten days after we'd cleared the ridge, and ended in bitter stalemate ten days later.

The other, Niall Richardson, was on the staff of the Fourth Army. With his crisp uniform and red tabs he looked every bit the role. The way he told it, it had become an army in name only. After the Ypres offensive ended most of its units were divvied up amongst those needing reinforcements, like so many spare parts. That got me thinking.

'Tanks, eh?' I said, a touch cynically. 'I've never seen one yet that didn't have a passionate bond with the mud.'

Turner laughed, 'I know. I know. Passchendaele you said, right? That was a mistake even attempting to use tanks there, the terrain was completely unsuitable. You should have seen them at Cambrai where it was drier. Almost four hundred strong, we cut through the German lines like they were putty. We penetrated more than four miles in a single day. You must have heard about it, the church bells were ringing all over England?'

'Oh, and here I was thinking that was to mask the noise of the tanks,' I said.

Richardson chimed in, 'No, no, Malcolm, that couldn't have been the case; by that time they were all broken down.' He was proving himself very adept at hit-and-run barroom banter.

We snickered wickedly, but Turner was refusing to sound the retreat. 'Sure there were a few. But that's to be expected with any new technology. Admittedly, it's a case of one step forward and half a step back sometimes.'

'Or more often, one jolt forward and half a day of repairs in the back,' I added. Out of the corner of my eye I could see Richardson wiping furiously at his nose. His mouthful of Scotch appeared to have taken a wrong turn at my last comment. Turner was looking a trifle frustrated, and not nearly as well lubricated as our nearly empty glasses or his two chirpy drinking companions would have suggested.

'Seriously, Ewan. I don't understand how, after a breakthrough like that, the battle was lost?'

'Oh, the usual. Shoddy preparation and no reserves to exploit the advance, mainly. The Germans skewered us brilliantly when they counter-attacked.'

I smiled and said, 'Another text book case of snatching defeat from the jaws of victory,' and then downed the last of my glass.

'Tell us about you, Malcolm; you don't usually get one of those for sitting at a desk?' Richardson said, pointing at the white-blue-white coloured ribbon sewn on my chest. It was the Military Cross. I'd had it since the battle of Mount Sorrel. An extra water canteen would have been more useful.

'Well that's a long story from a long time ago. It was probably the reason I got my commission, that and the fact most of our officers were killed or wounded. But you'd be astonished, Niall, to hear where my desk has been in the past two months. Suffice it to say I was stuck in the mud almost as often as Ewan's tanks. I can't say I was ever as thirsty as I am now, though.'

They chuckled. Richardson went off to order.

'Well, here's hoping that next year will bring salvation,' toasted Turner, after the glasses were topped up.

'Slim chance of that with the Bolshies up to their mischief,' muttered Richardson.

'That's a worry for later, lads,' I said. 'Drink up!' There was no point in spoiling a nice evening with sombre geo-political predictions. Leave was meant to blot those sorts of things out, along with all the other unpleasant memories and worries. Last night, for the first time since Passchendaele, I hadn't woken with nightmares.

The noise in the bar was getting to that comfortable pitch, slightly shy of rattling the windows, when the brass ship's bell behind the counter put a loud warning shot across our bows and left my eardrums vibrating for minutes afterwards. It was last call – a recurring problem I'd been experiencing here in London.

Only then did I spot the thin dark moustache and beady eyes staring at me from across the room. It was Colonel Whatley-Wigham.

CHAPTER 14

13th of January, 1918
St. Emile sector, Lens, France

The night was cold, crisp, and almost windless; exactly the sort you'd expect in mid-January in Northern France. It was early evening, but already it was very dark. The sun had set an hour ago. The ground was frigid and hard, and we were making good time. We shuffled along in single file, in silence, pausing periodically to listen.

Occasionally, the snow-covered serenity of the scene was shattered by the sharp retort of a sole German gun, not far from us, propelling its deadly parcel of steel and high explosive miles into our rear.

The raid's commander, Lieutenant Jucksch, signalled to move on.

It felt odd being back in the trenches. That is to say, in a proper trench, not the miserable string of watery shell-holes we made do with in the Salient, which offered next to no protection, but enough misery to last a lifetime.

Most people presume the front line is a neat series of trenches, with two long ones running perfectly parallel, separated by a narrow, wire-strewn patch of No-Man's-Land. In the endlessly see-sawing fortunes of war, the reality was always more complicated. Take where I was: Commotion trench.

Commotion trench began well behind our front lines and extended diagonally from left to right, moving north and to the east on my map. After a stretch it intersected with our front-line trench, Nuns Alley – some soldier's humour immortalized on the trench maps – and left our lines into No-Man's-Land. There it was filled in. After several hundred yards the trench resumed, this time on the German side of the wire. It continued on northeastwards, where it soon crossed the Germans' front-line Cinnabar trench, at almost a right angle. Then, ambling on further afield, it headed into their support lines near Cité St. Auguste, a small village northeast of Lens.

The trench was dug as if its designer wished to sketch a parapet of battlements from some great castle deep in the soil. There was a cunning cleverness in the many zig-zagged corners he'd drawn. They would provide cover for the trench defenders, and a broken line of sight for any attacker, should ever it be breached.

Jucksch had chosen carefully. Commotion trench had a tailor-made entrance into the enemy front lines, and he intended to use it. If he had his way, the Germans' troubles tonight were going to be far worse than mere commotion.

I remembered the last raid I was involved in near Méricourt. Coincidently, it was less than a mile away, on the other side of Lens. In three months little had changed in Lens and its surroundings. It was the same bleak, uninviting, war-ravaged industrial landscape I recalled all too well. The snow was a welcome change.

We exited Commotion trench before our wire and slipped through a gap. Ahead was No-Man's-Land. The trench was filled-in delineating, for the moment, the Western Front in this area of France. Now, out in the open, we cautiously picked our way across the shell-pocked landscape until there was a flurry of hand signals. We halted.

The German lines were only yards ahead. There, Commotion trench – Commotion sap, as it was called – resumed. A jumbled forest of barbed wire blocked the entrance to the German side as surely as any brick wall would have done. Two lone sentries were keeping watch, no doubt cursing their luck as their companions further back ate, and slept, in the warmth of a dug-out.

We sank to the frozen ground to wait. Lieutenant Jucksch crawled forward. An unwieldy 10-foot-long tube of ammonal was balanced ever so carefully in his hands. It was the same powerful high explosive the tunnellers had used to blast apart Messines Ridge. We hoped it would demolish the wire that blocked our path.

Jucksch's plan was bold. There were four groups of six, and two officers, all from the 58th Battalion. They were farming lads mainly, from central Ontario. After blasting the wire, three parties would rush forward along Commotion to where it crossed the German Cinnabar trench. Then, they would fan out to block the other three approaches; in front, to the left, and to the right. If reinforcements came, and they would I was solemnly assured, they would come from there. The fourth party, in their wake, was to tackle the large dug-out before the intersection, and the stragglers left behind. With any luck, we'd seize some prisoners and some useful intelligence.

I should have sent Smith, but newly promoted lieutenant or not, he was down with the flu. Largely thanks to my strongly worded representations, the man had just received a coveted commission from the ranks. But almost before he had the pips on his shoulders, he was lying on his back, moaning deliriously. It was either a hell of an act, or he was seriously under the weather.

This gave me a splendid opportunity to dirty my new trench coat, and tempt fate again, I thought grumpily. Hore-Ruthven, not a man to waste words unnecessarily, had nodded in approval when I told him my plans. In a display of social niceties I didn't think he believed in, he went so far as to engage me in a short chat about the sights of London.

On reflection, Hore-Ruthven's approval was probably the reason I was here. Overcome by a sudden light-headed insanity, I volunteered to accompany the raiding party, promising to stay out of the way. Any sane soul would have remained safely behind at battalion HQ. I was beginning to question whether Passchendaele hadn't rattled something seriously loose up above.

We sprawled only yards from the enemy wire, in three rows, on the frozen ground. I barely dared to breathe, let alone move. Speaking, of course, was unthinkable. I heard guttural voices now and then. The sentries. Every so often, the Boche gun would go off, and I jumped involuntarily each time.

Lieutenant Jucksch looked imperturbable, although it probably only looked that way. He was lying on his stomach with an unholy long tube of high explosive precariously outstretched in his arms. If it wasn't placed precisely in the middle of the wire, it wouldn't work. And it was a very tricky business pushing ten feet of metal tubing into a tangle of barbed wire without being heard. Ten yards away there were a couple of Fritzes who would shoot him, and the rest of us, in a flash, if only to relieve the boredom.

My legs were exhibiting the classic first symptoms of hypothermia when Lieutenant Johnson, the second-in-command, nudged me. He pointed a finger towards my wrist, probably not believing what he saw on his own. I turned the watch for his benefit and held it close under his face. The Borgel gave 6.57 p.m. We'd lain here for more than an hour.

On the other side of me was a brawny soldier. He was fidgeting with his bayonet and I looked closer. His hair was closely cropped, thereby emphasizing his massive broad forehead, which had all the subtlety of a fair-sized boulder and looked about as strong. Cauliflower ears, and a stubby crooked nose, jutted out from under his helmet. He had the same fearsome lines as the Mark IV tank, but without the looks, and that made him an exceptionally fine man to keep behind. A couple like him, and the Hindenburg Line might as well be manned by housewives. I certainly couldn't fathom him getting stuck in the mud, thinking suddenly of Turner, and the tanks. He gave me a toothy boxer's grin when he saw me observing him. I nodded in return.

WHOOSH. The detonation was not so much an explosion as a tornado of air. It sucked hard, and then blew out over us with such violence that it took my breath, and damn near my helmet. A second of stilted silence followed. Then, in a cascade of noise and light, four Stokes mortars and a couple of Vickers machine guns blasted into action, and we leapt to our feet.

The Stokes is a light trench mortar, and invaluable to the modern infantry. Manned by only two, they consist of a short metal tube on a tripod and forearm-sized bombs, all items which are easily portable and quick to put into action. A Stokes mortar could put down a shower of bombs, and that was precisely what they were now doing. Flashes were erupting in the German trenches. I could see them to the left, the right, and ahead of the Commotion-Cinnabar junction.

'It's called a box bombardment,' Jucksch explained during the briefing. 'The Germans will be boxed in with fire from all sides. Our first three units will move 50 yards or so down each trench. The Stokes and the machine guns will be firing just beyond their positions. If all goes well, we'll completely seal off the whole junction, and everything in it.' He had a wild grin on his face. Fritz was not going to be pleased.

Ahead I now heard rifle fire and Mills bombs.

We were running up against the first outpost. Lieutenant Johnson was frantically marshalling his squad forward, with me right behind, Webley in hand. 'Watch for the wire, Major,' he warned. I grumbled, thinking he'd confused me with a paraplegic crossing the road. There were a few strands of wire left, but the ammonal had done its work. Once in the trench we came to a half dozen bodies. I stepped over them and pushed on. They were German.

The eager young lieutenants weren't visibly overjoyed with the news I came to reinforce them. They were obviously of two minds as to what kind of support a middle-aged staff officer from division might offer. Evidently deciding very little, they assigned me to the mopping-up party. It was most likely a case of out-of-sight, out-of-mind, and most important of all, out-of-the-way. I couldn't really blame them.

Past the bodies, we arrived at a dug-out built into the trench wall where a soldier on one knee was firing around the corner, and into the dark opening below. Others stood ready with Mills bombs in their hands. One, having taken the pin out, apparently let the safety lever slip accidently. Coolly, he disposed of it off to the side. It exploded with a loud bang on the dug-out roof.

I heard Jucksch shout down, '*Raus! Steigen Sie aus!*' It must have been the right thing to say. Almost immediately, raised hands preceding them, grey steel helmets began emerging.

Unexpectedly, one of them began to run, overcome by a sudden madness. He sprinted towards me, and away from the large group of soldiers clustered around the dug-out. Behind him two of the lads raised their rifles in our direction, but I was dead centre in their field of fire. There was a shout, 'Look out!'

The German had a crazed, desperate look on his face, and he was running straight at me, his last obstacle before freedom. I was bringing up the rear; the lieutenants had entrusted me with that. His right arm was pulling at his side and I knew exactly what for: a bayonet.

At moments like this instinct grabs you. Instinct and training. And in my case, anger. War had instilled a weary fatalism in me, like most everybody who'd spent any time on the front lines. But I'd seen far too many friends killed or wounded, and the fanatic zeal on this soldier's face triggered a roaring rage in me.

I could have shot him, but we needed prisoners, not bodies.

So I lunged forward and thrust myself towards him with an evening's worth of repressed energy, and too many years of painful moments. I got only a couple of steps in, but it was enough for decent momentum and I brought my head down, and braced my right shoulder for contact. We smashed together like two locomotives colliding at speed. Only I was 200 pounds, and angry, and he was maybe 140, and just desperate. He slammed into the trench wall, the force of my momentum and my body squeezing the air out of his chest and the movement from his limbs. My forearm, Webley in hand, come to a sharp rest on his scrawny neck. My eyes dared him to move. With that, he sagged, and became as docile as a lamb. He'd be sore for a while. I holstered my Webley.

'Jesus,' I heard someone say. 'And here I thought all they did at headquarters was shuffle paper.'

Then, ahead and off to our left, there was the sharp crack of rifle shots, and the gentle thump of grenades. The Germans were trying to break through; to come to the aid of their cornered comrades. We didn't have much time.

The last of the Germans climbed from the dug-out. They were herded to one side by the bayonet of the erstwhile boxer. A soldier climbed cautiously down into the enemy post, his bayoneted rifle gingerly leading the way. He re-emerged almost immediately. 'They won't come. There are still six of them bastards there!' he shouted.

Without a word the corporal of the squad stepped forward. As if he were playing softball, he lobbed a grenade through the opening with a smooth underhand. When it went off, two others followed, and then two more. We didn't have time to play hard-to-get, and in case they hadn't noticed, there was a bloody war on.

Jucksch signalled we were to retreat. My unit took up defensive positions along the cold trench walls. Before long the three blocking units, and a cluster of prisoners, filed past in quick-time. We turned and followed.

'Well done, Jucksch,' I said to him, once we were back in our trenches. A newfound silence had settled over the sector, and snow was falling. It was spookily quiet after what had gone before.

'Thank you, sir,' he responded. His keen eyes were gleaming. He was on the short side, but not scrawny. His neatly trimmed dark moustache suited him, despite making him look older, though that might well have been his intention. Only his intense pointed eyebrows, and the bounce in his step, hinted at the pent-up energy within. I didn't need much of a hint; I'd seen him in action.

'Are there any casualties?'

'None, sir.'

'A brilliantly planned raid, Lieutenant, and perfectly executed. Congratulations.' I made no attempt to hide my pleasure. An unexpected bonus was that Jucksch spoke German. That was going to make the interrogations an awful lot easier.

At battalion HQ the mood was one of elation. I felt it too. There were eleven prisoners, at least thirteen enemy dead, and not a scratch on the raiding party. Even the dead-weight from headquarters had emerged unscathed, and with a prisoner of his own. Knowing my comrades-at-arms, that was going to cost a couple loafers at headquarters a dollar or two in lost wagers. And for once, I felt confident the enemy casualty count was a conservative one.

For a so-called pencil pusher, I was spending a God-awful amount of time in the trenches the last few months. But this was worth it. Hopefully the prisoners would have something useful to say.

The next morning when I returned to divisional headquarters I found Smith at his desk again. His sallow cheeks had all the colour of a codfish belly. It wasn't so dissimilar to his normal complexion that I was overly concerned.

'Any news here?' I enquired, after we covered the preliminaries, and I told him about the raid.

He paused briefly. 'Lieutenant DuBois is hung over.'

'News, Smith. I said NEWS!'

'Captain Tibbett is also.'

That *was* news. Tibbett's adventure in the Ypres mud had made a brand new man of him. 'And Fritz?' I asked cynically. 'Or is he hung over as well?'

'No, he's just pissed off, I expect, sir,' he replied, without blinking.

131

I smiled. 'According to the prisoners we captured – they're from the 220th Division – they're here for a rest. That doesn't suggest they're up to much of anything, at least anything General Lipsett need be concerned about.'

'You know, sir, the Germans are calling this area the Ypres sanatorium.'

'Well I can certainly understand wanting to get out of Ypres for a few days,' I said, chuckling to myself. 'After some raids like last night, they may want to reconsider their plans for a spa, though. At least if rest is what they're looking for.'

In reality, I figured Fritz wasn't sleeping well at all. Not knowing if he'd be poked awake with a bayonet, or bombed, shelled, or kidnapped while his eyes were closed had a way of doing that to a man. That was precisely the idea. We were prodding the Germans with a dozen patrols, and a raid or two, every night. General Lipsett was insistent we keep our guard up.

'You know the Germans and the Russians agreed to an armistice? And that a peace treaty is in the works?' I asked Smith.

'Yes, sir, I read about it. And the Boche are now moving their armies to the Western Front.'

Of course he knew. You had to be deaf, dumb and blind – and even then the odds were against you – not to know that it was a question of time before a reinforced Boche army would be knocking at the door. I really hoped it wouldn't be at ours. One problem, among others, was that Fritz seldom knocked; a Flying Pig, Jack Johnson or Hissing Jenny was usually the first you heard of him… if you were lucky.

'Perhaps that group of officers, the ones we spotted studying the maps over near Cité St. Auguste, were only familiarising themselves with the front,' said Smith. From his words I sensed he too was afraid of the coming German offensive.

'Perhaps. But this bunch last night, said the talk was they were to be relieved – by the 1st Guards Reserve, no less. I don't have to tell you what a new division means, that one in particular. Especially when you know how badly the Boche want this ground. I'm afraid the chances of an attack just went up.'

'At least they'll be missing a Hauptman,' said Smith. Flu or not, he didn't forget much – least of all, the fruits of our last foray behind enemy lines, at Méricourt.

'Very true,' I said. 'I expect Hauptman Gruendemann is enjoying the good life at some comfortable POW camp by now. Of course, if all our new recruits are any indication, the Germans have long since replaced him. That bloody division just won't leave us alone. We cleaned their clock in the Hill 70 attack and they keep coming back for more. It boggles the mind.'

'That's because they're all new recruits, sir.'

Which was true. I remembered how desperately eager I was when I first arrived. I also remembered it hadn't lasted long.

'New recruits or not, Smith, they're coming. Sooner, or later, the Boche are coming. And we had better be prepared.'

CHAPTER 15

23rd of February, 1918
Château d'Acq, Villers-au-Bois, France

The morning's intelligence reports from GHQ were unequivocal: new German divisions were reported all along the British front.

'And do you have any indications of an attack being prepared opposite us?'

'No, sir. None.'

'I hope for your sake, you're right, MacPhail.'

General Lipsett stood in front of me, agitatedly smoothing the hair on the back of his head. He was entertaining an important guest this afternoon, so he had multiple worries. Colonel Hore-Ruthven was a couple of steps behind, listening intently to my briefing.

'We have a lot of patrols out, sir. They've noticed nothing out of the ordinary. Nor have we identified any new units. The Boche artillery is more active than usual, though.'

'Might I suggest you look into that, then, Major,' Lipsett said testily.

'Yes, sir. Of course.'

'We wouldn't want to miss anything would we? I'll see you this afternoon.'

'Yes, sir. I'll be there,' I assured him. Not that my saying so made the slightest difference. That wasn't how the army worked. And with the mood the general was in, this was no time to overlook his "invitation".

Afterwards, DuBois took me aside. He'd been watching.

'Don't worry, Mac. He knows it wasn't your fault. Everybody is feeling the pressure, including the general.'

'Thanks, Benoît, but it feels like I'm a footstep away from sentry duty in a trench.'

Château d'Acq wasn't the Connaught by any stretch, but it was hands down the best accommodations we'd had in months. My room faced the garden courtyard and the gate, and while it wasn't terribly large, I had it to myself – an almost unheard-of luxury. The château had a modern feel to it I didn't readily associate with a château, most were old dumps these days. This one was in excellent condition, as if the hardship of the times had somehow passed it by.

As usual, DuBois summed it up in his characteristically restrained, '*Pas mal. Pas mal du tout*,' reserved for anything that met his fancy. 'Whatever happened to French exuberance?' I protested indignantly. 'We Anglos are supposed to be the stuffy ones. What about *Magnifique! Incroyable!* Surely, your vocabulary must extend a little further than, "*pas mal*", Benoît?' We both smiled, pleased this detour in the campaign had brought us here. I planned to enjoy it while it lasted – in this war, anything good never lasted long. Once the Boche got going, just staying alive was going to require all my energies.

The first night in Villers-au-Bois, I sat outside with a small group on the tree-covered hill at the back, passing around a bottle of rum. Sadly, the château's owner had taken an axe to many of the trees, and sold the timber, leaving the wood in a state of mild desolation. The army, no stranger to desolation, had gleefully filled the gaps with those woefully ugly, corrugated steel, half-barrel shaped Nissen huts to house the myriad staff a headquarters brings with it.

The air was chilly – it was late February after all, and I shivered despite my coat and gloves. It only made the sharp rush of warmth from the rum all the more pleasing as it burned its way down my throat. There wasn't much conversation. We merely stared at the clear, star-filled sky and thought our own private thoughts, feeling a strange peace, of sorts. Lens was a paltry six miles to the east. When I thought about it, those six miles encompassed everything that man was capable of: in all of his wisdom and, these days, in all of his folly. It was a sobering thought – even with the rum.

I had no time to dawdle and certainly not to philosophize. As it was I was late. Tibbett would be regretting he'd asked me along to visit his battery.

'You'll find it quite interesting,' he said when he first invited me. 'We're going to a battery of heavies, the 60-pounders. We use them a lot for counter-battery work. You might find it useful, Malcolm.'

I didn't dare inquire, but after the overnight reports on more enemy shelling and Lipsett's thinly-veiled orders, I had to concede he might be right. Also, Tibbett was boyishly keen on showing it off – this was his work. A flippant rejection wouldn't have done our blossoming friendship any good at all, I thought, swallowing uneasily at the description. So here we were.

Tibbett had borrowed a staff car, another Ford, and I let him drive. It gave me some time to reflect. The general was riding me mercilessly. He seemed to hold me personally responsible for every twitch the Germans made. Particularly their surprise raid a couple of days ago. *How the hell was I supposed to know?*

I'd brought a flask of coffee and a *baguette*. Admittedly it was a calculated risk; any Aussie behind the wheel and second-degree burns would have been a given. Thankfully, Tibbett remained true to character and we toddled along like two old women on a Sunday drive, arriving at the battery late, but dry and unharmed.

A simple wooden sign with hand-painted white letters greeted us as we drove into the small wood where the guns were concealed amongst the trees: FRITZ'S EXPRESS SERVICE – SPECIALIZING IN HIGH EXPLOSIVE, SHRAPNEL, & GAS. DELIVERY GUARANTEED. It was the sort of gallows humour you saw a lot around the front.

'So, Paul. What have you got in mind for us?' I asked, as we stepped out of the car.

'I thought we could first look at the guns. Then I need to discuss a shoot. You'll remember those recent aerial photos, the battery of 77mm field guns near the railway embankment? The ones that have been causing so much trouble? Well, I'm hoping to put an end to that,' he said firmly. He had a look I'd never seen before. If I didn't know him better I would have called it fierce.

He went on, 'I spoke with a Lieutenant Parkes on the telephone. Ah, that must be him, there.'

And, indeed, a cheerful looking lieutenant was striding up, grinning broadly and looking for all the world like he was pleased to see us. It was a welcome change. Two staff officers from headquarters more often than not elicited a reaction varying from indifference to disgust, however charming my smile.

'Major. Captain. I'm Lieutenant Parkes. Welcome to the 36th Howitzer Battery.'

We smiled and thanked him.

'Have either of you visited the artillery, recently?' he enquired.

'It's been a while, I'm afraid,' I replied.

'Fine. Then I think it would be best if you listened to the sergeant for a minute, for your own safety. We've had some trouble recently from gas attacks. Do you both have your respirators with you?' We confirmed that we did. Tibbett looked like he had a severe case of indigestion. I understood completely; the *baguette* that had slid in so nicely during the drive was weighing like a soft brick in my gut. God, I hated the gas.

'These attacks, Lieutenant, have they become any more frequent?' I enquired. *It won't be long now before the Germans throw half of Prussia at us,* said the voice in my head.

'No, we've been spared at this location, but several others were hit recently. They're trying to get our range. Naturally, we do our best to reply in kind.' Then he frowned. 'Do you think they're coming, sir?'

I paused, contemplating the question. Finally, I answered. 'Yes, Lieutenant. They're most definitely coming. But don't worry, we'll be ready.' It was my turn to comfort him. 'Fritz will be more than a little nervous about taking us on,' I blustered. From my cool confidence he looked reassured. I was anything but.

The sergeant must have been nearly thirty-five, going on fifty. From the pockmarks and scars on his face, he looked as if he'd fought in every battle since the Boer War. He was plainly in fine form. It wasn't every day he had an opportunity to lecture two officers like they were bug-eyed eighteen-year-olds just off the boat, and he was going to make the most of it.

'I don't care if your eyes are falling out, your goggles are fogged up, or you think it's a false alarm; don't remove the mask until I give the all-clear,' he commanded. 'You may have pips on your shoulders, but the gas is an all-ranks killer.'

'That's a blessing, at least,' I said. 'With the snipers, I always feel like I'm being unfairly singled out.'

'Sorry, sir, I didn't mean anything by it,' he said, even if his expression suggested otherwise.

'Right. Well, continue then. I'm sure my pips will be over it soon.'

'The Boche often use phosgene, and particularly the infantry still get hit by it a lot. It's invisible and smells a bit like old hay, not that you'd want to smell it. An extremely potent killer when inhaled. The masks work fine against phosgene gas, but you need to put them on quickly. Remember, if the alarm sounds, drop everything and get your respirator on.'

'And mustard gas?' I asked, feeling a touch impatient with my assigned role as the clued-out staff officer. 'What about that?'

'Right you are, sir. Since our attack at Ypres last year we're seeing more and more of it. If you have any skin exposed mustard burns like hell, afterwards, not to mention blistering. But I see you're both wearing coats and gloves. Keep everything on and well buttoned. In large concentrations it can soak through clothing and even masks. Don't worry, you need a lot more than a few shells for that to happen.'

'Well, that's a considerable relief, isn't it, Paul?' I said, and looked over at him. Tibbett's good spirits of the morning had discernibly evaporated. From what I saw on his ashen face, relief appeared to be the last thing he was feeling.

'I should add,' said the sergeant, not wasting any time getting on with his lesson, 'mustard is very heavy and usually sinks to the low ground. Up at Passchendaele a lot of the shell holes were filled with it.'

I hardly needed a reminder. It wasn't easy to forget those cesspools of mud and water. Nor the rancid garlic stench coming from gas that was coiled here and there, in deadly wait, at the bottom.

The sergeant continued, 'The Boche call it the yellow cross. That comes from how they mark their shells. They regularly combine mustard gas with an explosive charge in shells so it disperses better, the mustard being so heavy. Mustard gas is a big problem for us because it doesn't dissipate quickly. That's why both sides use it against the artillery. Unless there's a good stiff wind, the stuff settles and then we either have to clean everything, move, or both.'

'And is there anything we should do, if attacked?' I asked.

'Keep your masks on and well fastened. Also your clothes. Avoid any exposed flesh, otherwise it'll burn it. If you feel some, or breathe it in, get your gear on and respirator fastened, although a touch won't kill you. It's best to seek some shelter. But remember, the gas will settle in the low spots. You could do worse than sitting in your car, unless they happen to throw a few high explosive rounds along.'

'Most reassuring, Sergeant. So it's a question of damned if we do, damned if we don't? Always a fine pickle to be in.'

Which, when I thought about it, was precisely the word I'd been searching for to describe the sergeant – the sour personality, at least. The look on his face wasn't dissimilar, either.

The lieutenant walked over to us again. The artillery sergeant, having successfully delivered his monologue of horror, said a few brisk words of farewell and took his leave.

'Uplifting fellow,' I said.

Parkes smiled knowingly. 'He's an experienced man. Good to have around, and the men seem to adore him.'

'Must be his warm nurturing side.'

The howitzers were lined up on the easterly edge of the little grove, each dug into a pit, with camouflage netting draped in the trees above. Any gun not hidden from the prowling eyes of the aircraft was a certain target. Lining both sides of each pit, like sandbags, were walls of large shells stacked five or six high, with more piled neatly behind.

A host of sparrows was frolicking in the tree tops, oblivious to the sergeant's lecture, diving fast towards the foliage – despite the wintery temperatures some remained – and pulling up just as quickly. It looked like a lot of fun. I'm not particularly an outdoorsy type, but it was nice to see some wildlife. The only wildlife I'd seen near Lens was rats and there are only so many rats you can see before you've had your fill.

Tibbett hadn't exaggerated, the 60-pounders were impressive. Their wheels alone reached to an average man's shoulders, and the massive barrels were as long as two men lying end-to-end. According to Lieutenant Parkes, who offered to give me a tour, it took a crew of ten to keep one of them operational, with as many horses required to haul it. I began to see why the sergeant felt picking up and moving was such a chore.

'And how far do they shoot?' I asked.

'Oh, generally six miles or so. Some of the newer shells go as far as seven. And a sixty-pound shell like these, well, they pack quite a punch when they arrive.'

'I bet they do. Hopefully Captain Tibbett will ensure they arrive where they're supposed to.'

At that moment Tibbett came over to join us. He'd gone off to discuss the shoot on the 77mm field guns with the battery commander. He'd asked if I wanted to come, but I declined. 'No, that's fine, Paul. Once you start talking coordinates, trajectories and shell velocities, I'd be lost, anyhow.' For some reason I found a curious pleasure in playing second fiddle to him. The tight protective cocoon he'd once woven for himself was fraying quickly since Passchendaele. But I still had trouble believing he'd emptied a bottle with DuBois.

There was a whistle, and a shell landed 200 yards in front and off to our left, with a loud plop.

A dud. I'd seen enough of those not to flinch a muscle. I turned to resume my conversation with Lieutenant Parkes.

'GAS! GAS! GAS!'

I fumbled at the clasp of my haversack and ripped the respirator out and over my head. My helmet fell to the ground. As I made to pull at the straps I glanced at Tibbett and I saw he'd dropped his helmet and his mask.

Cursing, I leaned over and fished the respirator from the ground.

'Stand still,' I ordered, and I pulled it over his head. Behind the thick rims of the goggles and his spectacles underneath, his eyes flitted nervously back and forth. I pulled the straps to tighten it, only to discover that I pulled too hard – he was flapping his arms – so I loosened them a bit. I stepped back to inspect it. It looked alright.

'Looks fine,' I shouted and gave him a thumbs-up.

It was then I felt the burning in my throat and prickly searing in my eyes. I coughed and blinked hard a couple of times. Oh, damn… *my* straps.

With both hands I pulled frantically at them and the mask tightened against my face. Cautiously I breathed in. I coughed again a little. My eyes were watering but I could still see.

Tibbett quickly looked me over – too quickly – and responded with a weak thumbs-up of his own.

Two more shells went off, again with a loud plop. I could almost see the plumes drifting up from where they'd landed, joining with the others. Mustard gas being close to invisible that was as much a figment of my imagination as thinking the war was over. For some reason, confronted with the invisible wreaths lazily circling in the field, I felt little fear, only a mysterious enthrallment of sorts. There wasn't much of a wind, a gentle whisper every so often, but such as it was, it was blowing from west to east and thus away. Still, as more shells ploughed into the earth a dense cloud would be forming, and as it grew, it crept ominously closer.

Parkes strode over to the gun crew who, not long before, had been in the midst of cleaning the long steel barrel. The other crews, with their masks on, were gathered around their officers. I looked at Tibbett. He looked back.

'Tell them to shoot back,' I said.

'I can't be sure they're from the same 77s,' he responded.

I shouted, 'Maybe not. But it beats doing nothing.'

Tibbett moved over to Parkes and the commander. The commander must have preferred action to inaction too for the discussion was a short one.

One of the masked soldiers began furiously winding at a wheel on the cannon closest to us and its barrel slowly elevated as he did so. Another began manhandling a shell half the size of him over to the breech.

'Shrapnel,' explained Tibbett when he returned. 'To catch the crews in the open. The high explosive will come later. Perhaps even gas.'

'I hope your information is correct.'

'It is,' he responded, with a conviction I found heartening. 'The captain assured me they could hit it.'

'Yeah, not knowing they'd be doing it in a mustard cloud,' I said.

Within minutes the first gun erupted, closely followed by the others, leaving me winded and mildly dazed from the fire and the thunder and the smoke.

The Germans were still shooting short. They knew something was close, but they hadn't got the range yet. There mustn't be any observers, I thought. The sky was free of planes and there wasn't a balloon in sight. Of course, through these accursed goggles it felt like I was viewing the scene from the bottom of a lake. The Germans could have parked a Zeppelin in front of my nose and it's doubtful I would have seen it.

The balloons were hugely annoying. Fritz would tether them somewhere and then stare down uninhibited into our rear lines, seeing everything, and directing his artillery by field telephone. Our machine guns were as good as useless against them – they were too big and too far away – although many tried, more out of frustration than anything. Even the planes had their hands full trying to bring down the big ones. Billy Bishop got the Military Cross for destroying one near Vimy last year.

The enemy gunners were firing blind. I had healthy respect for them; if Fritz had your range, then you needed to be well away, or deep underground. As an artillery man those options weren't on offer, which made it one of the most lethal jobs on the entire front. It was almost enough to make me glad I'd enlisted in the infantry.

'They haven't got our range,' I shouted in Parkes' ear, who by now had met up with us again.

'No. But this is not a good place to be if they shoot any shrapnel or high explosive,' he replied, or as near to it as I could make out in the din from the guns. The 60-pounder in front of us exploded again, jerking backwards while a huge piston recoiled then returned, smoke spiralling from its breech as it was thrown open to be reloaded.

I pictured the mustard cloud starting to roll in, wisps already enveloping a couple of the howitzers. I didn't need much of an imagination, only a good memory – and that I had.

Tibbett motioned to me. 'Malcolm, let's go. We need to move back,' he roared in my ear.

I didn't see the purpose of it – if high explosive began hitting the wood there was no shelter back there that would be worthy of its name – but I followed dutifully, thankful to be a little further away from the gas.

Soon the guns fell silent and Parkes reappeared. I expect he had strict orders to ensure no harm befell the two officers from division.

In the field they sometimes feared headquarters almost as much as the enemy.

'Fritz gave it up five minutes ago,' he informed us. 'We kept at it awhile to finish the job.'

'So they *were* Tibbett's 77s,' I cried out, astonished that for once all the pieces had fallen into place.

He noisily cleared his throat. Mine was feeling dry as well, not to mention sore. 'No. Not necessarily, but's there's a good chance.'

'And when can we take off these blasted masks? I'm going to smell like rubber for a week.'

'We're lucky the wind's picked up, we should escape the worst of the gas. But leave them on for the moment, half the field is still in a cloud.'

By the time the sergeant signalled the all-clear by clanging on an empty shell casing, we were nearly an hour behind schedule. Normally, I wouldn't have given it much thought, but Tibbett and I were required back at headquarters.

We removed our coats, gloves, haversacks and helmets in case they'd been contaminated by the gas, and threw them in the back. My throat still felt raw.

'Damn, of all times to get gassed,' I cursed as we pulled away, after some hurried good-byes. 'Lipsett is going to eat us alive.'

'Do you think so?' said Tibbett, more for politeness' sake than because he really wanted to hear the answer.

'Count on it. When you see who our visitor is you'll understand.'

We couldn't have been more than twenty-five minutes late when we pulled up to the white wrought-iron gate of Château d'Acq. I drove.

However, the courtyard was crowded, and worst of all, our guest of honour was in full view conversing with Lieutenant-Colonel Hore-Ruthven, and a colonel I knew all too well.

'Damn,' I muttered under my breath. 'Follow me, Tibbett.'

We slipped through the gate, and along behind the ten-man quarter guard from the Royal Canadian Regiment – Benoît's unit – who were standing stiffly at attention.

'So nice of you both to show up, MacPhail,' hissed Lipsett, who turned up out of nowhere, his eyes flashing. He'd cut us off as we made for the gap in the group of officers awaiting an audience.

'I'm sorry, sir, we were in an artillery duel, and attacked by gas,' I murmured.

He did a double-take, and glared at me with a look that could have melted the Columbia Icefields, searching for a sign I was jesting. Seeing none the fire in his eyes dimmed.

'You're both alright?' he asked, traces of concern tinging his voice. We both nodded meekly.

'We're fine, sir, thank-you,' I said. I hoped I was. I must have swallowed three or four mouthfuls of mustard.

'I thought you both looked a little green around the gills,' he said, and left to return to our guest.

'That was close,' I whispered.

It didn't take long before he returned, our medal-encrusted visitor with him, and I saluted smartly. The commander-in-chief's bright blue eyes twinkled like those of a kindly uncle.

'Field-Marshal, this is Major MacPhail, my intelligence officer.'

Haig deliberated for a moment, and then I saw his eyes widen. 'Good afternoon, Major. Actually, Louis, I believe Major MacPhail and I have already met. He had motorcar troubles at the time. I see he has the same robust look to him.'

In a devil-made-me-do-it moment, I blurted out, 'I expect it's all the healthy air we've been getting of late, sir.'

A sound you might best liken to an exasperated sigh came from Lipsett. 'The Major had a somewhat trying morning at the front,' Lipsett offered, gently. His eyes, however, locked on me, were blazing. Colonel Whatley-Wigham, leering over the general's shoulder, looked as if I'd belched in the King's face.

The field-marshal nodded politely, and quickly moved on to Tibbett sensing, perhaps, here was a man genetically incapable of anything other than conventionally correct replies.

'Still up to your old tricks, Major?' said the colonel as he returned my salute.

'Sir?'

'I've got my eye on you, just so you know.'

'Yes, sir. I have noticed,' I replied. It may not have been the response he was looking for, for in his eyes I saw a thunderstorm blow in, before he moved on.

Shortly, the circus wound down and Haig and Lipsett disappeared inside for what surely would be a fascinating tête-à-tête. Hore-Ruthven left not long thereafter accompanied by Whatley-Wigham. Sadly, it wasn't in the direction of the front lines.

'Why do you suppose the field-marshal's here?' I asked a captain by the name of Willis, who was standing beside me.

'Beat's me. There's no new offensive planned? Or is there?' I could hear the nervous uncertainty in his voice.

'Not that I know of, but then again, these things have a way of sneaking up on you.' It was also what I worried about: if we weren't getting attacked, then High Command would surely be busy planning an attack of our own. That was how things worked. Neither option was very palatable. 'I suspect Fritz is going to have us in a wringer long before we get around to any new offensive,' I added.

It had been billed as a social call. But since when did the commander-in-chief drop in for tea with a divisional commander? With the Germans poised to go on the attack, you'd have thought Haig had more important things on his mind, however nice tea and biscuits with General Lipsett might be. On the other hand, perhaps not; I presumed the general's tin box of treats would be wide open this afternoon. That would be reason enough for me to take the afternoon off.

DuBois ambled over. 'What happened to you two? Lipsett was steaming.'

'Not much, some casual sightseeing at the artillery. Tibbett would love to tell you about it.' It was pure theatre, of course. I cleared my throat, thinking first of the gas, then of Whatley-Wigham, and finally of Lipsett's eyes boring into me.

'And hAig, what's he doing here?'

'That, my dear Benoît, is the *question du jour*. One thing's for sure, his *wearing down the enemy* strategy is succeeding brilliantly, at least from Hindenburg's perspective.' I let him ponder that for a second. 'Did you realize with their fresh divisions from the East, the Germans will soon outnumber us? Haig must be plotting something; heaven forbid it involves us.'

'And *les Americains*?'

'Sure, every bit helps, but we all know they're not exactly battle-hardened. I can't help thinking how things would stand if the BEF hadn't battered itself to a pulp the past two years.'

'Well, thanks to Currie, at least we're not jumping off the cliff like the rest of the army,' added Willis. Seeing the puzzled looks he went on, 'You know, the latest hare-brained scheme to reduce each division from 12 battalions to 9, and then use the surplus battalions to create new divisions. By a happy coincidence, it requires thirty percent more generals.'

'You may have our commanders' dirty little secret figured out, Willis, but you obviously understand very little about smoke and mirrors,' I said.

'Or elastics,' added Tibbett, the physics graduate. 'You can easily enlarge an elastic by a third or more, all you need to do is stretch. It's the same concept.'

'*Exactement*, it's brilliant,' interjected DuBois. 'You take 60 divisions, cut a little off each, create some new names, and *voilà*, you have 80 divisions. The Germans, now outnumbered, are so fearful they simply run away.'

We all smiled. It was either that or cry.

By late afternoon, the discussion turned to what it turned to most days. When and where would Ludendorff's hammer blow come? The divisional staff were an eclectic bunch, but most had seen action. We all knew the Germans would hit hard. As the intelligence officer everybody looked to me for answers. So, when the château doors suddenly opened, and Haig and Lipsett emerged, I was relieved. Until I remembered the look Lipsett gave me. He'd been livid.

Haig and Lipsett now looked as cheerful as might be expected after a comfortable afternoon at Château d'Acq plying themselves with sweet delicacies. I would have been more reassured had Haig looked worried. There were too many in the BEF who saw the current calm as an opportunity to rest while the storm clouds gathered. Haig should be out cracking the whip. *Lipsett certainly was.*

Lipsett walked the field-marshal to the gate, and I could see the cameraman poised, ready to preserve the moment. I was no closer to figuring out what Haig was doing here – field marshals didn't drop in on a whim – but I had my suspicions. A rare photographer being on hand didn't do much to alleviate them.

CHAPTER 16

15th of March, 1918
Vimy Ridge, France

Benoît was along to translate. As far as I could make out, I was along to translate the translator, which made about as much sense as anything else in this war. However, I'd volunteered. It was a splendid opportunity to escape the sharp tongue of General Lipsett for a day.

The former French Minister of War, Général Auguste Roques, was coming all the way from Paris to Vimy Ridge to inspect the defences. You knew it was important if someone of his stature was going to journey 125 miles from the capital to saunter around in the mud for a couple of hours, knowing full well lunch was apt to be a sober affair, and bully beef and biscuits the main course.

Not that there was anything wrong with the bully beef. I'd acquired a real taste for it. Apparently, the Germans liked it as well, so much so, a few jokers occasionally threw a tin or two of Fray Bentos into their trenches. After recovering from the initial shock, the German sentries and their buddies emerged from their shelters shouting in English, 'More! More!', and were quickly obliged. By the time every Fritz in the trench was standing around clamouring for another shower of bully beef, the Mills bombs followed. It was cruel, granted – but less so than a *flammenwerfer*, I thought.

We set out from Villers-au-Bois at a little past nine o'clock,

147

anticipating that we'd arrive at Vimy Ridge well before ten. Already I felt like I'd put in a full day. At 5.30 this morning two separate raids by the 4th and 5th Mounted Rifles went out. The second one was especially large, almost 200 soldiers and officers were involved. Were it not for Smith going down to observe, I wouldn't have slept a wink. As it was, I was up early to hear the details, and to put together the day's intelligence summary.

The Germans in the line were adopting what General Lipsett was prone to call an aggressive stance. He was fond of that sort of jargon. In plain English, they were raiding a lot, and sending over far too many shells for my liking, or anybody else's, least of all Lipsett's. That usually signified one thing – the Boche were priming for the attack.

In my experience, the Germans are a pretty obdurate bunch, but they pale in comparison to the likes of Currie and Lipsett – it was a lesson this group was going to have to learn the hard way. Sitting back and taking it wasn't exactly our generals' style. They ordered that we hit back hard. After a month of replying with three shells for every one of the Germans', and two raids for every one of theirs, I had the impression the message was sinking in.

We were hardly in the car when Benoît asked me straight-away, 'Hé, Mac, the attack, is it coming soon?'

The question didn't particularly surprise me, more that he was doing the asking. Everybody was feeling tense and even the laid-back giant from Trois-Rivières was seemingly not immune.

'I'll tell you what I told Lipsett, the enemy is prepared for offensive operations.'

'And how do you know this?' he asked.

I was ready to say, *fingerspitzengefühl*, but held back. DuBois was a big fan of intuition; on the other hand, he wasn't such a big fan of anything German. 'There are a lot of signs. They're raiding aggressively, their artillery is a lot more active, and their planes are fiercely protective of their skies. They definitely don't want us to see what they're up to. So, of course, they're up to something.'

He waved a finger in the air as if to demonstrate he wasn't convinced. 'Yes, but that's hardly conclusive.'

'You're right, it's not. However, in the past month or two, they've done almost no work on their own defences. Either they're lazy as hell – and these are Germans we're talking about, Benoît – or they're not planning on being there for long. They've also built a lot of new artillery positions, and plenty of supply and ammunition depots to accompany them.'

'So, you think it will be shortly?'

'Yes.' Then realizing he was awaiting an explanation, I continued, 'For weeks the prisoners have all said they're preparing for an offensive. They're being trained to push deep and to rapidly exploit their successes. Their divisions from the East arrived long ago. Many are at railheads merely waiting to get the signal where to go. Frankly, everything indicates their preparations are complete. And time is decidedly not on their side, not with the Americans coming in large numbers. They know that, and so they have to attack, and soon. And they will.'

'*Fantastique,*' he murmured, making it sound like a curse.

I hesitated, debating whether to mention it. 'You know what concerns me?'

He turned his head, grinning mischievously. 'What we're having for dinner tonight?'

'Right, besides that. What concerns me are these new *stosstruppen* companies. Shock troops.'

'You mean what they call us?'

'No, they call us *sturmtruppen*. Storm troops,' I said slowly, clearly enunciating the German so as to highlight the difference. Where Benoît and German were concerned it was a waste of perfectly good air, but I couldn't be faulted for trying. 'Anyway, the gist is the same. The *point* is, Fritz has decided he wants some shock troops of his own. He's assembled his best men and trained them to aggressively infiltrate the lines. They'll obliterate us with the artillery and the *stosstruppen* will attempt to penetrate deep into our rear, bypassing any strong points.'

'And you believe they might succeed?'

'You remember the Passchendaele Ridge? How we encircled the pill-boxes and let the mopping-up troops deal with the holdouts? It's the same idea, but on a much grander scale. There are some weak divisions in the front. Not everybody has dug themselves in with the same sense of urgency. The boy scouts could have done a better job in many cases. If they hit the weak spots, there's no telling how far they'll get.'

'It's a good thing you don't have kids, Mac, they'd never go to sleep after one of your bed-time stories. And are they going to attack here?'

'That's the big question, Benoît. We know they're coming but no one seems to have figured out where, including me. When this is all over, some heads are going to roll at headquarters, I can tell you. On the other hand, this being the BEF, I guess even that's not certain,' I said caustically. 'If it's any consolation, the prisoners we took this morning knew nothing about an imminent attack. So perhaps we'll be spared for the moment.'

'Try not to get blue in the face, but what if you're wrong?'

I sighed. 'Lipsett is grilling me daily: is the attack coming against us, or not? I told him, "not yet". If I do get it wrong, I'll be the next thing stuffed into one of your 60-pounders.'

Benoît perked up at that. 'You know, I'll do my best to have you shot off somewhere nice,' he said.

I moaned, conscious I sounded like Banting in one of his off moments. 'I'm serious, Benoît. If I make one mistake Lipsett is going to have *my* guts for garters. He was terribly angry about my so-called "insubordinate attitude". After only one little joking remark to the field-marshal! He said I'd been warned. It didn't help that Whatley-Wigham turned up to rub it in.'

Benoît bobbed his head sympathetically. He'd heard it all before – likely far too often. 'Whatever did you say to that colonel to get him so angry at you?'

'Nothing! I merely politely pointed out that based on the intelligence, it was precisely the opposite of what he was saying.'

'Ah. So you made him feel like a complete idiot?'

'Benoît, he *is* a complete idiot.'

Benoît sighed. 'I have no idea how you ever made it to major, Mac.'

Lipsett's wrath, however, was no idle fear. He was breathing down my neck and Currie was surely breathing down his. As a result, I was getting scant hours of sleep. But it wasn't solely because of the general. Everyone was relying on the intelligence section, and every scrap of information had the potential to be significant, so I was working from dawn till dusk, and usually longer.

This morning's raids were a great success. I was heartened to hear there wasn't so much as a hint we were to be on the receiving end of

General Ludendorff's fearsome battering ram. Lipsett even permitted himself a watery smile when I told him.

Vimy Ridge loomed large like a giant black molar stuck in the earth, dominating the countryside for miles. Struck by the scene, my mind inexorably drifted back to last April. It had been a glorious victory, the first since the bloody stalemate of the Somme, virtually a year earlier. The elation was overwhelming and it was easy to forget how heavy the price was. Fighting for the first time together in a major battle, the Corps had done what others couldn't, and dislodged the Germans from this pivotal redoubt. The larger offensive failed, like so many before it, and as the belligerents pummelled away, the victory was losing its significance – except for those of us who were there. Vimy wasn't the strategic triumph that would change the war. Nonetheless, it was the crucial dead-bolt guarding the last remaining coal mines of Northern France still in French hands. General Roques was not leaving Paris simply to get away from the traffic.

We doggedly edged our way up the steep winding road to the summit, the car's engine whining at the exertion, and Benoît softly clucking in encouragement. Already I could see that a lot had changed. New trenches, dug-outs, machine-gun entrenchments and artillery positions cut through the moonscape of shell holes left from the battle. There was nothing growing, save for the thorny thickets of brambleberries and rose bushes encircling each position. Except, the thickets were neither brambleberries nor roses, but barbed wire.

There was no sign of the French yet. I could see a few of our officers, congregated in a waiting pattern, and we set off to join them.

'Who's that?' asked DuBois, as we approached, referring to a thin, energetic-looking man. He was dark-haired, and even with the obligatory moustache, looked young for his rank.

'That's Brigadier-General Radcliffe, Currie's chief of staff, the BG GS,' I replied. 'You know, the last time I saw him was back in October, in Hazebrouck.' Actually, his full name was Percy Pollexfen de Blaquiere Radcliffe. Learning it required as much study as your average Latin verb. God knows how the half-illiterate British army administration coped.

'The BG GS: The Brigadier General, General Staff... I've never seen him before, you know,' he said.

'He's a Brit. He's supposedly very efficient,' I remarked. 'Of course, one look around here and you'd be hard pressed to conclude otherwise.'

I introduced Benoît to the general. We also met the others, including a cheery major from Corps HQ as well as a fearsome looking lieutenant-colonel who commanded the battalion manning the ridge.

'Remember, speak slowly and enunciate clearly,' I counselled DuBois after I motioned him aside.

'*You're* telling *me* how to speak French?'

'No, I'm just trying to avoid any misunderstandings with our allies.'

He exhaled audibly in frustration. It beat a fist to the nose. In the past my remarks were known to elicit that kind of primal reaction, and under the circumstances, it wouldn't have been entirely unwarranted.

By eleven the French arrived, three gleaming staff cars strong.

Général Roques had a head that a statue carver would have wept in joy at, all full of sharp lines and equally sharp corners, ending in a pointed grey goatee. I was introduced as the *chef d'intelligence*. While this was a title considerably more inflated than my modest role, I could see it made an impression on him, for he nodded seriously as he returned my salute, and shook my hand, looking me square in the eye as if I were a man worthy of measurement.

The inspection began on the crest of the ridge and the sweeping vista of the Douai Plain provoked an excited flurry of conversation amongst the French. Even from a distance, the surroundings of Lens were not picturesque – mind you, compared to the Ypres Salient it was a veritable Garden of Eden – with pointed grey mounds of mine tailings and the rickety towers of coal shafts readily visible. The French were talking coal mines and railways. The first, the coalfields, stretched in the form of a thumb laterally across this part of France and Vimy Ridge, and the Lens sector, were the gateway. Losing the collieries would be catastrophic. The second topic concerned the main railway and road from Amiens in the south up to the town of Béthune, a little north of where we stood. Losing them would slice the BEF in two, a calamity perhaps even more disastrous than losing the mines.

Radcliffe was doing his utmost to demonstrate that neither would occur on our watch. He hurried our guests from trench to dug-out to machine-gun post, and then on to the artillery batteries – 72 on the ridge alone, I heard to my surprise. It was a blistering pace and I secretly hoped Radcliffe's confidence wasn't all show.

I'd warned Benoît that he shouldn't belittle this as a leisurely excursion. As I saw him furiously gesticulating with his hands, and his head turning left to right, and back again as he endeavoured to translate some nuance, I knew he'd be cursing that he hadn't listened to me. I was, however, dead wrong about lunch.

The French must have taken the initiative themselves. There was something to be said for a people who were fighting the war of their lives, but for whom lunch was of equal import.

At the *Aubergerie de mon père* I stepped through the crooked wooden frame of a doorway built for gnomes, and had to bow my head so deeply that my chin came to rest on my chest. My pupils strained as they acclimatized to the darkness within.

A beer barrel of a woman in an apron greeted me. Her fat face was glowing crimson from the heat and the excitement, and she shot short bursts of welcome at me in rapid French, and handed me a flute of bubbly champagne. I smiled appreciatively in return. Behind her stood a pretty young girl holding a silver tray with a couple of filled glasses on it, likely her daughter – though, even in the gloom, the resemblance was a weak one, at best. I smiled at her and she shyly averted her eyes.

Inside, the small restaurant was lit by candles. Most of the tables had been pushed to the middle of the room to form a single long rectangular table now resplendent in white linen. An event like this didn't come often and the family looked like it had pulled out all the stops. Three vases of fresh-cut flowers adorned the table; my knowledge of flowers being only slightly less developed than my command of Chinese, I hadn't a clue what variety they were, but they did look pretty. The windows were far too small to let in much light, even on a day significantly less sombre than today, and I couldn't help thinking the collection of antique kitchen utensils, dusty wine bottles and assorted knick-knacks that obscured them didn't help. The decorator had correctly concluded there was nothing to see outside, anyhow. The faded yellow walls, dark wooden beams from another century, and dim lighting, created a warm comforting ambiance. I found it appealing.

There were twelve of us: five Canadians including our adapted Brit, and seven Frenchmen. This being an army occasion a natural hierarchy had developed. The important people including the two generals, their aides, and good old Benoît, sat at the end of the table furthest from the door, and it trickled down from there. I was at the gutter end, so to speak.

A *capitaine* from the French First Army, Aurélien Lafontaine, sat beside me. He was an amiable sort, allowing me to instantly deduce he was not Parisian – that and his peculiar accent. As it turned out, he was from the south, the city of Toulouse. His long-winded intro-duction was delivered in an unforgiving tempo. Only by concentrating intensely did I make out that he had something to do with machine guns, although his cadence was a sure give-away when I thought about it. It didn't take long before he insisted I tell him everything about the guns we were using. He was especially intrigued by our motor-ized machine-gun brigades, as well as Currie's plan to bolster the machine-gun battalions in each division. I can't imagine how he came to hear of it – I didn't know the details myself. Still, I was pleased to oblige, and divulged all that I knew. It made for a short conversation.

Valiantly, I started off in halting French, but quickly discovered my vocabulary of vegetables, household items and farm animals wasn't quite up to the task. If anything, his English was worse. Happily, he understood more than he spoke, and we soon settled into an easy pattern whereby I spoke English, and he responded in French, but not before I insisted he moderate his breakneck pace. After the third glass of champagne we were babbling away like we'd known each other for years.

'What's this?' I asked, as the young girl placed a plate with a pinkish slab sprinkled with a dark jelly and three thin slices of toast in front of me.

'*Foie gras*,' he responded. I could see from his greedy eyes that wait-ing for his general to dig in was going to require the sort of fortitude that had protected Verdun.

I watched discreetly as he very precisely sliced off a bite-sized corner of the slab and smeared it roughly on the toast. He then dabbed a little of the jelly on top with his knife, and took a dainty bite. I followed his example. It was rich and creamy and unctuous, with a gamey flavour I couldn't place. The jelly added a sharp, subtle touch of acidity, and together with the savoury crunch of the toast, this morsel melted in my mouth in perfect harmony.

'Wow!' I exclaimed, my English vocabulary suddenly feeling as inadequate as my French.

'*Oui*,' he responded, smiling. '*Attends*.' His eyes twinkled as he gently pushed a glass of a viscous, deep yellow, tinted wine towards me, and jerked his head upwards in the universal language of *drink up*. I took a sip.

'*Sauternes*,' he explained, and laughed, seeing the awestruck expression on my face.

Sauternes meant little to me, but I'd just discovered my favourite wine in the entire world. It kept its ranking all of twenty minutes, until the next course arrived.

At the time I found it curious, the wooden case that had been unloaded with such gentle care from the trunk of one of the French cars, and brought gingerly inside. Why would the French be carrying a box of grenades – for that's what it looked like – in their cars? And bringing it into a restaurant!?

The answer lay in my glass.

'*Un Château Margaux de la millésime 1900*,' announced Aurélien proudly, when the glasses were filled, and the bottle and decanter placed before us. My first sip lasted so long that he began to look concerned, and he asked, '*Ça va?*'

The corners of my mouth pressed upwards, and I gave him one of those sloppy, bewildered, blissful grins as if it had been my first time which, in a way, was not far from the mark. Sitting across from Général Roques, Benoît appeared to be having the time of his life, and, sipping at his own glass of this heavenly wine, he likely was. It was a long, long way from the trenches.

By the time lunch finished I was ready for bed. Instead we piled into the cars to drive to the front to continue the inspection. It gave me time to admire the French constitution, and bemoan my own.

The afternoon saw us visit a dizzying procession of defensive works, trenches, fortified artillery positions, dug-outs and more. I didn't envy Benoît having to stumble along and feign a semblance of alertness

155

while doing so. Thankfully for him, it transpired that General Radcliffe spoke decent French, therefore his role as translator was hardly crucial. Mine was even less so, and I tagged along as a tourist for the most part, imparting some ream of information every now and again, so as not to leave the impression of being a total vagabond.

Yesterday, in a flash of foresight, I boned up on our defensive works, thinking this was the sort of trivia ideally suited to impressing our French guests – only time would tell whether the real thing would impress Fritz. He was an altogether more exacting customer. The statistics, at any rate, were stunning.

In three months we'd laid enough barbed wire in our sector to stretch from Vimy to London and back again. As to trenches, there were so many, had they been built in a straight line, they would have gone all the way to Amsterdam with sixty miles to spare for any wrong turns along the way. It seemed a lot of effort to keep Fritz at bay.

Général Roques nodded at intervals during the inspection, but his face was otherwise impassive, to the point of being inscrutably so. 'What do you think?' I asked Aurélien. 'Are we passing muster?'

'*Bien sûr*,' he replied, recounting he'd seldom seen the general look so ebullient.

'Now that you mention it, I can see why you'd say that,' I said, thinking perhaps I'd misunderstood. Or, it could simply have been that Général Roques was a Buddhist monk in a prior life, and not given to showing emotions.

Abruptly, at around seven, I felt a nervous excitement among the underlings, and soon an eruption of frenzied salutes and handshakes signalled that the party was taking their leave. The French crowded into their Renaults, and tore away at speed, the oily grumble of motors echoing after them – late dinner plans in Paris, probably.

By the time we were back at Château d'Acq I found even the thought of eating dinner far too onerous, which could have been the afternoon's lunch speaking. More likely, it was the stream of messages from GHQ. They warned that an enemy attack was imminent. I headed off to report to Lipsett.

CHAPTER 17

26th of March, 1918
Château d'Acq, Villers-au-Bois, France

The rumbling roar grew louder. To the south, a fiery red line, low to the horizon, traced its way further south through the darkness until the glow became a pinprick, and my eyes could see it no further. The ground was shaking under our feet. All hell was unleashed.

'Holy Christ,' said someone. His voice was quavering. The distant thunder rolled on like a storm that never ebbed.

I looked over at Tibbett who was standing beside me, a glowing red stripe reflected in the glass of his spectacles. His face was taut and expressionless, drained of emotion.

'It's begun,' he said quietly.

I nodded, but he didn't see me. We stood together in a row, all looking southwards, all mesmerized by the sight. I felt a dull, pulsating pit in my stomach. Others came to join us. It was a quarter to five in the morning.

The second shout roused me when I recognized my name being called. 'Major MacPhail,' somebody was bellowing, off near the court-yard gate. I left at a fast clip.

'It's to the south of Arras. At the Somme,' said Hore-Ruthven as I approached. 'Have we seen any sign of enemy movement in our sector?'

'No, sir. I don't know for sure,' I stammered.

'Then you had better get on with it, MacPhail. Forthright,' he said. Which I did.

The news from our battalions was reassuring: our lines were quiet. Our sister divisions reported the same. And then around one o'clock – finally – news came.

'The infantry attack has begun, sir,' I said, as I rushed into the room, brandishing a signal. 'The Third and Fifth Armies are under attack across their entire front. It's sheer chaos. There are no reports of any activity from our lines, yet.' The general was standing in the dining room. Many of the staff stood in little groups, or were clustered behind the desks that were hastily propped here and there, working.

Lipsett was calm, and he reflected on my words. I stood before him, breathing fast and heavy, my heart thumping. 'Fire the projectors,' he said. 'Inform the other divisions.'

Tibbett and DuBois looked at each other. The signaller left first. They followed immediately afterwards, along with a handful of others.

'That should keep them occupied,' said Lipsett, his eyes blazing defiantly.

'Sir?'

'Gas,' he replied. 'Four thousand drums on our entire front. From Hill 70 to Méricourt, we're going to flood them in it. If they want to attack, let them get through that first.'

'I'd like to launch some raids, as well, sir,' I said. 'To hit them where they're weak, keep them uncertain, and to probe their intentions. Better they worry about us, than the other way around.'

Lipsett stared at me for a moment, thinking. 'Wait until the gas is dispersed, and then do it. But keep me informed.'

I turned away.

'Major?'

'Yes, sir?'

'Good thinking.'

That was five days ago. Five long days of much work and even more worry. The raids went well. But there was no German attack. Not here. Not yet. The clock was still loudly ticking.

Today began well enough, at least in that fleeting moment after declaring victory in my daily struggle to hoist myself out of bed, and right before my brain kicked in to remind me of the mess we were in.

Gough's Fifth Army crumbled, its centre nearly dissolving in a half-panicked retreat on the first two days. German losses were heavy, but within three days they battered a dent thirty miles wide and fifteen miles deep into our lines, and crossed the Somme. By midday yesterday they'd penetrated as far as twenty miles.

'The Fifth Army is folding like a house of cards,' proclaimed Tibbett, as I poked my nose into the small room which served as our office.

'With General Gough in command? Are you surprised?' I asked. I was hoarse. I wished he'd waited until I drank at least a single, extra-strong cup of Blue Ribbon tea before assailing me with the day's crop of innuendo, rumours and occasional fact that passed for news.

'To be honest, it was the weakest part of the whole line,' I said, in a feeble attempt to be fair.

Only fairness had nothing to do with it, I thought. Naturally, our generals had their redeeming qualities. In civilian life they might even have been upstanding citizens. Their grandchildren probably idolized them. The soldier, though, lives in a black and white world. Balanced precariously between life and death there's no room for the meaningless platitudes that pass for civility or politeness back home. As far as I was concerned, either you had what it took, or you didn't. From what I'd seen in the BEF, the latter group was heavily over-represented. And a pleasant manner didn't redeem you by a long stretch.

'He should have been sacked two years ago,' offered DuBois. He was never one to waste an opportunity to share his opinion. I agreed with him.

'Someone likes him well enough they keep finding a new army he can run into the ground,' I said, my morning ill-humour getting the better of me.

'Haig you mean?' suggested Tibbett.

'Well, if it's not Haig then he truly does have friends in high places,' I responded. 'But it's ironic, don't you think?'

'What is?'

'Our commanders. Most of them wouldn't last a week if they were bagging groceries at the Banner Grocery Store, but commanding an army...'

'Why do you suppose everyone wants to be a general? You don't get shot, and you never get fired,' said DuBois. We all nodded knowingly.

Little did we know, a day later, Gough would be relieved of his command. It was another fine example of too little too late, much like the general's planning.

Tibbett shook his head, his face twisted in worry. 'If something's not done and soon, we'll lose both Arras and Amiens. You know what that will mean?'

'We'll be in deep doo-doo,' piped in Mason, a red-headed captain from operations who dropped by to chat.

'If Amiens and Arras fall, we'll be completely cut off from the French. Not to mention losing our supply depots, the train hubs, and the main north-south roads,' added Smith, superfluously. He was right, of course, which was why my first instinct this morning had been to dive under the covers again when it all came flooding back to me.

'Is there any bloody tea around here?' I asked.

'We're going to be in deep *doo-doo* sooner than you think if you lot don't stop sipping tea and gossiping like elderly women, and get to work,' snapped a familiar voice from behind. It was Lieutenant-Colonel Hore-Ruthven. He was standing in the doorway looking none too friendly.

'Sir!' we mumbled, like schoolchildren caught in the act of eating candies in the library.

Hore-Ruthven was never so testy – I guess we were all anxious. How long would it be before the Germans' mailed fist came our way?

I looked around the room after he left, still hoping to spy a full teapot somewhere in the clutter, or better yet, coffee. However elegant the surroundings it never took the army long to turn it into a pigsty, explaining perhaps the preference to put us in a pigsty to begin with. The walls were papered with enough trench maps, barrage maps, intelligence summaries, reports, lists, logs, and orders to create a proper fire trap. Then there were the clapped-out wooden chairs, desks and cabinets that were propped into the room like it was the closing-out sale at Al's discount furniture mart. I'd seen flea markets that looked

160

better. I sniffed the air; and smelled better too. Self-consciously I snuffled at my armpit – it seemed okay.

Small it might be, our room sure beat bivouacking in one of the draughty Nissen huts out behind the château. Usually the smell wasn't any better out there, and pneumonia was an ever-present danger.

Shortly before dinner Smith called out, 'You better look at this, sir.' I could tell from the tone in his voice he thought he was on to something. He was even more of an eager beaver since becoming lieutenant. I had only little old *moi* to blame for it.

I walked across the room – which took all of two seconds – and peered over his shoulder at the report. It was from the 7th Brigade.

'You're right, Smith. We'll put it in the intelligence summary. Better yet, I think it's best if I report this straight away. Where's the other report, the one from earlier?' I enquired, and grabbed impatiently at the sheets he proffered, and made for the door.

As it happened, I ran into Hore-Ruthven only ten feet down the corridor – he'd been loitering all day near our office, so this was not quite the coincidence it seemed. I passed him the first page.

He read it aloud. 2PM – MORE THAN 20 TRAINS ON THE DOUAI-LILLE LINE, NEARLY ALL GOING NORTH.

'And this one as well, sir.'

5.10PM – ABNORMAL TRAIN MOVEMENT NORTHWARDS ON DOUAI-LILLE LINE, AND CONSIDERABLE MOVEMENT IN ENEMY FORWARD AREA ON FRONT OF LEFT BRIGADE, he read. He looked up from the paper, frowned and asked, 'So, what do you think?'

'That many trains. All going north. It pretty much has to be Ypres. Nevertheless, it surprises me. Why would the Germans attack there when they're having so much success on the Somme between Amiens and Arras? I'd have thought they'd continue to pour in troops down south, or even here, near Lens.' For no good reason I can think of, I then put my neck under the guillotine and added, 'As to the movement on our front, I don't believe it's anything worth worrying about, at least for the moment.'

He nodded. 'Hmm. I dare say there's a good chance you're right about Ypres. I'm calling Corps HQ shortly. I'll ask General Radcliffe to inform Major McAvity as well. They may want to send it to GHQ.'

McAvity had flown the coop not long after Passchendaele to become chief intelligence officer for the Corps. Two major Malcom M's in one division was clearly one too many. I was pleased for him and I suspected his promotion to lieutenant-colonel wouldn't be long in coming.

Two clerks came out of an office down the hall and turned in our direction, their loud voices echoing cheerfully until they saw the colonel and me, whereupon silence reigned. The army has an uncanny knack for ruthlessly repressing any form of spontaneous frivolity, though neither of us actually said a word.

Hore-Ruthven pulled me to one side as they passed. 'Is there anything else I should convey to General Lipsett?'

'According to a prisoner from the 23rd Infantry Regiment they have a thousand gas cylinders wired to fire. The battalions in the line would be advised to keep their masks at hand.'

'I'll pass that along,' he said.

'I'll be needing one myself, if my room doesn't freshen up soon.'

He arched an eyebrow. It was a very English way of noting that he was not amused. 'You *could* try opening the window.'

I grimaced, in an embarrassed kind of way. Ever practical, our colonel was.

'One other thing, MacPhail. Don't let the Germans' gains blind you to their losses. The Fifth Army may have lost a lot of ground, but they're making the Boche pay for it in blood. His supply lines will be stretched to the limit. And reinforcements are on the way. It wouldn't surprise me if the Germans wind down their attack near Amiens, and attack elsewhere. That's why Ypres is a good possibility.'

'I didn't think about it that way, sir.'

'I thought not. That's why I'm telling you. You may also not know that General Currie sent the 1st Motor Machine Gun Brigade down to join the Cavalry Brigade in plugging the gaps. It doesn't look much on paper. But twenty armoured cars with two Vickers machine guns apiece, that alone will help.'

'I suppose it will, sir. Not long ago I met a French captain at Vimy who was positively lyrical about the concept. Lots of firepower with great mobility, according to him.'

Actually, Lafontaine had called it the future of warfare. At the time it seemed preposterous. I suspected the wine was going to his head. Perhaps it wasn't as outlandish as I first thought.

'On that subject, sir, do you think we're next? To shore up the line, I mean?' It was the same impossible question that everybody always asked of me.

He inhaled deeply, and I knew I had my answer.

'I don't know for certain. If I had to hazard a guess... yes, the odds say our turn is coming.'

'Great,' I murmured with a distinct lack of enthusiasm. 'Out of the frying pan and into the fire.'

'We're not out of the frying pan yet, MacPhail,' he countered.

With the Germans on the warpath, two divisions in reserve, and the 4th Division and ourselves holding a preposterous ten miles of front; we most definitely weren't.

The night sky was clear but for a few wayward clouds sailing purposefully across the vast midnight-blue canvas stretched above our heads. It had been another long day in a long blur of days and nights since the *Kaiserslacht*, the Kaiser's Battle, ruptured the uneasy stalemate. Smith and I ventured outside to stroll around on the hill behind the château for a spell, to cleanse our minds. I was looking forward to a peaceful half hour before we turned in. Following several warm days, it had cooled noticeably, and this evening it was distinctly crisp, not that I minded. My head was anything but cool.

At first, I paid it little heed. From a distance it was no more noticeable than a swarm of bees on a summer day, buzzing lazily around a garden full of pollen-ripe flowers. Before long the innocuous buzzing grew louder and more insistent, until finally it was supplanted by a harder, harsher, pulsating drone that was unmistakably mechanical. And that could mean only one thing...

The dark shape was passing above us. I could practically hear the pilot cackling. I pictured him thrusting his goggled head out of the plane and glowering down at us. Smith and I stood motionless, captivated by the loud hum and the sight of this ugly giant bat as it floated effortlessly by, captured for a fleeting second against the light of a quarter moon. 'Damn,' I muttered.

'What's it doing here?' whispered Smith. It was a needless precaution, as you couldn't have heard a drill sergeant in the racket it was making.

With a start I heard a loud concussion and saw a sudden bright flash down by the gate. Then another, less than a hundred yards from where we were standing. I staggered as the shock from the blast hit me, momentarily blinded by the flash of light. Confused, I looked around. Smith had been at my side. Now he lay on the ground. The full force of the detonation had caught him.

'Smith!' I shouted. 'Are you alright?'

To my relief he gave me a weak thumbs-up. He said something, but his response was lost in the malevolent buzzing of the plane. Luckily, we weren't 20 yards closer. We were luckier still it was high explosive, not shrapnel.

I ducked, involuntarily, as another blast went off, this time further away.

'You're sure, you're okay?' I inquired as I knelt beside him. He looked dazed. His coat was covered by a shower of dirt and his right cheek was bleeding. It was only a scratch. I brushed at it with my handkerchief before giving it to him.

'Fine. I'm fine. It was so sudden, it just blew me off my feet.'

Another explosion went off, this time in the direction of the town. The plane was dumping its load, seemingly at random, perhaps hoping to hit something of importance as the crew searched for targets, not realizing they'd passed a big one. The bomb that had thrown us about had missed one of the artillery huts by a hair. The windows were gone, half the corrugated steel wall was blown in, but the hut still stood; it reminded me of a tale I was once very fond of involving a wolf and three little pigs. The wolf lost that one too.

General Lipsett, with his tunic off, and hatless, stood in the courtyard of the château where most of the staff were milling around with the hapless disconcerted looks of those roused brusquely from their sleep. He shook his head when he saw us. 'Always in the middle of the action, MacPhail. I might have known.'

'It was a Friedrichshafen, sir,' said Smith. 'A medium bomber.' He looked on the verge of briefing the general on the plane's specifications when, abruptly, he stopped. Maybe he'd heard me groaning. There might be a handful of things the general wanted to do at 11.00 p.m.; I was dead certain hearing the wingspan of a Friedrichshafen medium bomber wasn't one of them.

Lipsett tipped his head to Smith in acknowledgement, sensing I'm sure that the whole experience had left him rattled.

'Well, I'm glad you're both alright. Let's hope he doesn't return. Good night, gentlemen,' he said, and turned on his heel. My guess was that he wasn't off to bed; he was burning the midnight oil as well.

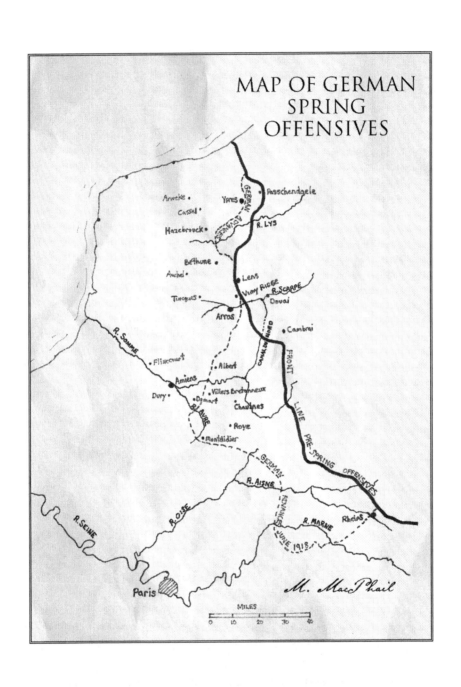

MAP OF GERMAN
SPRING
OFFENSIVES

Passchendaele
Arneke
Ypres
GERMAN
Cassel
R. LYS
Hazebrouck
ADVANCE
Béthune
Auchel
Lens
Vimy RIDGE
R. SCARPE
Tincques
Douai
Arras
CANAL DU NORD
Cambrai
R. SOMME
FRONT
Fliancourt
Albert
Amiens
Villers Bretonneux
LINE
Dury
Démart
Chaulnes
PRE-SPRING
Roye
R. AVRE
Montdidier
OFFENSIVES
GERMAN
R. AISNE
R. OISE
ADVANCE
R. SEINE
R. MARNE
Rheims
JUNE 1918

Paris

M. MacPhail

MILES
0   10   20   30   40

CHAPTER 18

16th of April, 1918
Sains-en-Gohelle, France

The band of little men sawing logs in my throat was hard at work. I felt dreadful.

My bed offered scarce solace for the aches, pains, cough and roaring sore throat I'd had for three days running. The flu was going round. I dressed slowly, methodically straightening my tie in the mirror where a sallow-looking character with huge bags under his eyes stared woefully back at me. After pulling on my second boot I felt winded, and I dropped back prone onto the bed where I was sitting, my head momentarily spinning.

I wasn't feeling any better about the latest news from the front, either. None of us were. Some were downright angry. They had every right to be. Passchendaele had been abandoned.

General Plumer had ordered a withdrawal from Passchendaele and its ridge, the oh-so critical ridge that had cost so very, very much. In a grave tone the field-marshal had implored us that it was "imperative" to capture it. It "must be taken at all costs" he had lectured at Ten Elms.

Six months later, without so much as a shot, Plumer's legions put their tails between their legs and beat a hasty retreat. We left it in their hands and they gave it away. It was infuriating. I tried not to get too worked up about it. I was feeling queasy enough as it was.

We heard the news the day before and talked about little else.

'Listen, I hate to say it,' I said, at a heated moment in the conversation, hoping the contrarian streak in me wasn't going to lead to a bloody nose, 'but abandoning Passchendaele and the ridge was sensible from a military perspective. It's a simple question of geometry. Manning a half circle requires a lot more men than manning its diameter. And lately manpower is a scarce commodity. Plumer really had little choice other than to withdraw.'

'And we all know why manpower is scarce,' growled Lieutenant Hannigan, his face glowing red, 'because of the tens of thousands of men it cost to take the bloody mud-hole in the first place! And to give it up without as much as a whimper!?' Normally Hannigan was a mild-mannered, ideal son-in-law sort that the artillery, for one reason or another, seemed to attract. He lost a lot of men at Passchendaele, and it didn't take a clairvoyant to see it weighed heavily on him. He wrote a great many letters home.

The lawyer in me knew I was on the wrong side of this discussion. Intrepidly, I plugged on. 'You're right. But holding it wasn't the answer. Since the Brits hollowed-out their divisions they're in no state to defend the Salient, *and* to prevent the Boche cutting through to Hazebrouck and the Channel ports... at least not without French reinforcements. And they don't seem to be coming.'

Ludendorff's encore was to strike in the north. With supplies and communications stretched, his *Operation Michael* along the Somme had ground to a halt – for the moment. The British cavalry and the Aussies stoically rebuffed the last attack there, in front of the little town of Villers-Bretonneux, at the gates of Amiens. But then Ludendorff shifted gears. Hoping to cut the Ypres Salient off at its neck, the Germans attacked along the river Lys in a broad swath astride the French-Belgian border, heading to the coast. It was only a week ago. Their progress was distressingly rapid.

'What was the point of taking Passchendaele in the first place, if it's not even worth defending?' asked Tibbett, not usually one to throw pebbles in the stoup. Nor to ask questions, I thought with surprise. He was more accustomed to answering them, even those a would-be questioner hadn't yet asked.

'I completely agree,' I pleaded, 'but look at Gough at the Somme. He had the same calculation to make as Plumer, and chose differently.

It was an outright disaster. Gough held on to indefensible positions when he should have pulled back long before, and fortified behind the Somme. Why didn't he? Well, leaving aside that we're not talking about Napoleon...' I paused briefly to cough, and let the throbbing in my head subside. 'I'm sure popular opinion in England played a considerable role. All those families who lost their sons taking that ground didn't want it given up without a fight. Only that ended up costing more lives.'

'Yeah, and in comparison, Passchendaele was easy come, easy go. Especially with the colonials doing all the work,' sneered Hannigan. He was bitter, and it sounded harsh, but we all understood. I didn't reply.

'I'm no strategist,' DuBois began. Predictably, the very idea of a six-foot-four broad-shouldered General DuBois waving his cane in the air was greeted by raised eyebrows. 'But explain this to me. If we all get killed taking a couple of miles of ground, that leaves too few left to defend it. Therefore, we give it back to the Boche the moment he comes knocking. At the end of the day, we're dead, and the High Command has no more land than they had before. Wouldn't it be a lot easier to line us up in two long rows, and let us shoot each other, until one side remains?'

I shrugged, wearily. DuBois had a talent for plain language, assuming you made it through the language barrier. God, how I wished Field-Marshal Haig could have listened in. I don't imagine they taught anything so sensible in military strategy at Sandhurst. If they had, we wouldn't be where we were.

'By the way, Benoît, what you're suggesting, it's called trench warfare,' I said. 'Only if it's going too slowly, then one side launches an offensive.' None of us were in a good mood.

At the moment, I had fresh worries.

'Major, you're holding the rifle away from you like a spoiled diaper.'

'I'm sorry, sergeant. I was afraid I was going to puke on it.' He looked at me dubiously. With a keen intuition he moved on to softer marks, like Tibbett, whose Lee-Enfield was casually pointed at an angle that could have taken out me and half of General Lipsett's staff at the slip of a finger. I wasn't being flippant with the sergeant; I truly felt miserable. I should have been in bed. But there was no time for that. Everyone with a pulse was needed.

Along with the transport units, and the entire divisional staff, I was enlisted – press-ganged was another word that came to mind – in the "last resort" reserves. If General Currie had realized the dregs he was recruiting with this idea he wouldn't have bothered. Alongside two new brigades formed in the desperation of the moment from the engineers, tunnelling companies, and every other man not already in the line, we made up the line of last defence. In hockey it could be likened to sudden death overtime. In particular, the sudden death part of it bore an uncanny resemblance. Anyway, here we were, the 3rd Division's finest, doing musketry training on a barren and frosty field in the morning mist. It was not going especially well.

'No. No. NO!' shouted the sergeant, frustration getting the better of him. The Lee-Enfield was continuing to get the better of Tibbett. 'Captain, it's elementary physics.'

I perked up at that. I couldn't wait to hear the high-school educated sergeant from Etobicoke lecture our budding Max Planck on the subject – this might be fodder for literally months of entertainment.

'It's Newton's third law. The force of the bullet's momentum requires…'

'…an equal and opposite reaction,' interjected Tibbett. For the first time all morning he looked in his element.

'Very good, Captain. That's the recoil. To offset it we need a counter-recoil. Otherwise the rifle is going into the mud, and without a rifle you'll be at best useless, and at worst, dead. That's where your shoulder comes in. So, you need the butt tucked in nice and tight against it before you even think about squeezing that trigger. Pretend you're cozying up to your girl.' At which point he proceeded to help Tibbett with the mechanics of how that worked.

Who helped out when the actual girl was involved, was a thought-provoking question – best left for another moment. I couldn't ever remember physics being quite so entertaining.

Finally, with the acrobatics of holding a rifle behind us, we got down to some actual shooting practice. We were facing off against a couple of menacing-looking cut-outs 200 yards distant, perched in front of a small dirt incline. Our first wave stepped up to do battle. The sergeant was peering down-range with his field-glasses. From the savage curses it sounded like the Hun was putting up a stiff fight.

It wasn't long before the magazines were empty, and the reinforcements were ushered forward.

The sergeant stood behind me, watching. I took careful bead on the middle German, right in between his exaggerated bushy black moustache and his *Pickelhaube*. And then I sneezed. My shot went whining off into the dull grey sky. I only hoped that some general of ours wasn't underneath. That exact thing had happened to a luckless British Tommy. He'd almost killed his own brigadier, and it wouldn't surprise me if he'd been in the trenches ever since. Not an example I wished to follow. The sergeant groaned loudly.

Determined to redeem myself, I took a deep breath. Mechanically my arm worked the bolt, up-back-forward-down, and I aimed and shot. The last time I'd fired a rifle was with young Philips on the Bellevue Spur. That was an eternity ago. My mind elsewhere, I fired off four more rounds in quick succession.

'Congratulations, sir,' said the sergeant. 'You've got yourself a German.'

'Thanks, Sergeant. I hardly need the rifle, coughing at them would have done the trick.' He smiled the taut, joyless smile drill sergeants are born with and I thanked my stars I was a major.

'I'll remember that when we're up close in bayonet drill, Major,' he said darkly, and smartly marched the two steps over to a couple of the lads from operations. They'd seen some action and it showed. Evidently, I'd joined A Company. If only we managed to avoid any friendly fire from B Company, I figured we'd do okay.

By lunchtime, my shoulder was ablaze, and ached like a tooth had been pulled – however improbable that might sound from a biological perspective. I would have put it down to the rifle's recoil, only it was the wrong shoulder. It was going on two years, and I'd honestly half forgotten about it, until this damned flu. I knew a few old soldiers, nursing old wounds, and reliving their old tales with whomever would listen. I wasn't anxious to surrender my last delusions of youth – and flu or not, there was nothing wrong with my imagination – by slipping into that elderly ward. Lunch, in any event, couldn't have come at a better moment. While I didn't have much of an appetite, the few rays of midday sun seemed to have a medicinal effect.

A group of other ranks from the divisional train had arrived by lorry, and were boisterously enjoying the sun and the peaceful setting, and what must have seemed like an afternoon of leisure. They were oblivious to the sergeant from the 4th Mounted Rifles who, by now, was scrutinizing them with a practised eye. On the heels of the hapless but high-ranking divisional staff, a few naïve privates were surely an appealing prospect to him.

Bored with our own adult discussion I shuffled over in the soldiers' direction. Judging by the cheery voices, morale was not suffering in the slightest from the threat of an impending attack. I took it as a good sign.

A rowdy looking private was holding court with five of his buddies. 'It's official. The Germans have a new strategy,' he proclaimed loudly.

'Oh?' said another.

'They're to attack to the north and the south of us. They plan to isolate the Corps, and then make a separate peace with Canada!' They all laughed.

It was a good line. I found it a tad too close to the truth to find much hilarity in it. The current line at headquarters, predictably humourless, was that the Germans would soon launch a heavy attack to the south, near Arras, to cut us off. On the other hand, the soldiers were right, what better time to laugh than when you were in the shit? Three years of war had given me virtually unlimited opportunities to hone that philosophy to perfection.

I was still thinking of them, and their cocky self-confidence, when we tumbled out of the lorry at headquarters to get back to the daily routine. In my case, describing it as daily routine was like saying the Red Baron drove a plane. I'd lost half a day already, so the decent night's sleep I was looking forward to was in as much peril as we were.

The daily intelligence summaries definitely made for depressing reading. And that wasn't solely because I was doing the writing. The outburst of enemy activity portended nothing good. Normally, the tiresomely upbeat London newspapers could be relied upon for a dose of optimism. They were plainly struggling, though, to put a brave face on the German breakthrough in the north. As for Army command, it was in a state of near panic.

"With our backs to the wall, and believing in the justice of our cause, each one of us must fight on to the end", Haig's special order read. Somehow, even *my* imagination failed when it came to picturing the field-marshal wearing a tin helmet and wielding a bayonet.

Haig's worries were real enough, however.

Up on the wall at headquarters there was a huge coloured map depicting the entire British line on the Western Front. It showed more eloquently than words could, the reason for all the disquiet. The map wasn't even ours. We usually had enough on our plates figuring out what was in right front of our noses to worry about what was going on fifty miles away. Some HQ before us must have bequeathed it to their successors and, in time-honoured army tradition, it became a permanent fixture.

The British line was a hundred miles long, held by sixty-odd divisions. Deep bulges were drawn in it, one south from Arras all the way to the French lines, and another in the north, near the Salient, where the Germans were threatening to expand it. In the middle, the Corp's four divisions were stretched like thin gauze across a length equal to a fifth of the entire front.

'Amazing, isn't it?' said Tibbett, appearing out of nowhere.

I glanced enquiringly at him. 'Your skill as a marksman?'

'Oh, no,' he said, and grinned awkwardly. 'Why do you think they put me in a staff position? No, I meant that Fritz has attacked every inch of the BEF's line, except ours. And strategically it's one of the most important areas.'

'Hmm,' I replied. 'They have a healthy respect for us, by now. Speaking of which, it's a good thing they didn't observe target practice this morning.'

'Enough, Malcolm,' he said with a sigh. He refused to call me Mac. I'm sure it stuck as awkwardly in his throat as mindless pleasantries did in mine. 'Still, you can see what Currie is worried about. We're already in a salient of our own. The Germans wouldn't have to go more than a few miles at Arras and we'd be risking complete encirclement.'

There was no arguing with that. 'That's why I'm so relieved you're in the Last Resort Reserves, Paul,' I pronounced. He groaned good-naturedly. I couldn't help it, the man was the reason why they'd invented sarcasm. Then, ashamed of myself, I gave him a big pat on the back, although it might have been more to assuage my feelings than his.

By this time next week, there was a good chance we'd be fighting for our lives.

My face was virtually planted on my desk, a not uncommon sight for those who know me well. I was squinting intently through a small three-legged looking glass at an aerial photograph, when I heard someone loudly clearing his throat. That wasn't terribly unusual, and at first, I didn't bother looking up. Then, with a creeping sense of unease, I noticed a peculiarly stilted silence had descended on the hitherto buzzing office. When I did raise my head, I immediately realized why.

It was General Lipsett, standing unsmiling in the doorway. 'Major, if you have a moment? I'd like to speak with you,' he said, in a neutral tone that could have meant almost anything, except that the general never, ever, dropped by to shoot the breeze.

'Of course, sir,' I said, and grabbed my hat, rushing to catch-up with him as he strode away.

Oddly, the room behind me emptied and followed at a respectful distance. That should have been my first clue. The second came as we approached the officers' mess.

The officers' mess at HQ in Sains-en-Gohelle was becoming a favourite, not that there were a lot of other options in this ugly duckling coal mining village, ten miles west of Lens. Its white-washed walls were decorated to the taste of an exclusively male, military and generally stuffy clientele. There was a charming assortment of regimental standards, pictures of assorted military commanders in the pompous unsmiling poses that masqueraded as fashion in more senior echelons, and a large framed portrait of the King prominently displayed on the far wall at the end of a long rectangular table with matching chairs, which dominated the centre of the room. A handful of comfortable leather club chairs and a small mahogany wood table for drinks, newspapers and a large candle standard filled three corners of the room, and a doorway the fourth. I liked the warm glow from all the candles;

they almost made me forget where we were and what was awaiting. The poor lads in the trenches could only dream of places like this.

What was unusual was that it was four-thirty – not a time anyone ate dinner, and no one had the time to lazily pass away the afternoon in the mess – and yet I could hear a chorus of voices washing down the hallway as the general and I approached.

I'd totally forgotten. What with my sickly health, Lipsett on my case, and the prospect of the German Sixth and Seventeenth Armies stomping on us, I had other things on my mind. Given the occasion, I was reluctant to fob it off as the collateral damage of old age, how inevitable that is.

Set out in the middle of the table were two fruit cakes – some kind soul had donated his package from home – a bottle of Old Orkney Scotch, and a battered German Stahlhelm with "29" and two huge exclamation marks painted on it in white.

Lipsett stopped and looked at me. 'Malcolm, I've been meaning to tell you.' I glanced over at him uneasily. 'You're doing fine,' he said. 'Enjoy yourself for an hour. And Happy Birthday!'

The entire room broke into that familiar song that at my age you know so well.

CHAPTER 19

20th of May, 1918
Auchel/Lozinghem, France

The gloom had lifted. The line had held. We'd been spared.

And spring had arrived. That such a thing was possible in this war was too much to hope for, and I found the leafy green woods and grassy fields to have a bizarrely peaceful, almost dreamlike quality to them. It had been beautiful all week. Early this morning the sun was already shining with that bright joyful intensity that foreshadowed a scorcher of a day.

The village of Auchel, much like its little cousin Lozinghem further down the road, was not the place of dreams to where the wealthy of Paris fled at the weekend – fled *from* it, more likely. It lay in the shadow of a mountainous pyramid of slag, stone-sized tailings that came from the Fosse no. 3 mine shafts so prominent on its outskirts. The spire from a church that would have done a large and prosperous town proud, towered over the rows of humble red-brick coal miners' houses. But spring had come to Auchel as well.

The few trees and shrubs that dotted its simple dirt streets were painted in a palette of vibrant greens. Against the clear blue sky, the monotonous functionality of the town faded into the background so as to make it almost palatable, if not pretty. Driving through, its dour-looking inhabitants were much in evidence going about their daily chores. The sun had even coaxed a smile or two onto worn faces, as natural a sight as if the townsfolk had donned black top-hats and evening gowns. Tomorrow, the under-used muscles in their cheeks would be aching.

It was the sort of day on which you could very nearly envisage peace breaking out. Needless to say, that was a pipe dream. If anything, it was pretty much the opposite. I was here to observe two of the division's brigades training for open warfare. And while fending off the Germans was reason to celebrate, we'd only landed back in the same bloody stalemate. At this rate, the war was never going to end.

I had no idea how long Auchel had existed. But I was certain the village had rarely been as popular a destination as it was today. The tickets for the midday scheme were all but sold out. Obviously, the brigade commanders themselves were on hand, while General Lipsett and Colonel Hore-Ruthven were attending as the most critical audience, in addition to their roles as hosts.

Not only was the Corps Commander making an appearance, he had brought along his new chief of staff, Brigadier-General Webber. Webber replaced General Radcliffe a few weeks ago. Radcliffe must have made quite an impression with our Vimy tour, for shortly thereafter he was promoted to Major-General and made Director of Military Operations – an awfully important sounding title, at the awfully self-important War Office in London.

Currie was also accompanied by the CO of the British 61st Division and the senior staff training officer of the First Army. With all the riff-raff that escorted a high-powered delegation such as this it made for an impressive, not to mention stuffy, congregation in the large tent that had been erected for the occasion in the flowing grassland between Auchel and Lozinghem.

Too unimportant to be hobnobbing with the brass hats in the tent, and glad for the fresh air, I was outside. In the absence of anything productive to do, I was trying to exude a poised casualness, my hands clasped behind my back as I surveyed the scene. I didn't have a cane and as I mulled it over, it seemed obvious why so many officers did, even inactivity looked dynamic. It did raise the question of how much was getting done considering the sheer number of canes in active army service.

Fortunately, I saw a familiar face appear. It was Major McAvity. He had thrust his own hands into his trouser pockets, and then apparently thought better of it, for he quickly pulled them out with a pained look, reminiscent of a visit to the dentist. I resolved not to make any jokes along those lines, and dashed over.

He grinned enthusiastically when he saw me coming, and I waved in return.

'Major Malcom MacPhail, congratulations on your promotion!' he beamed. 'It's been a while!'

'Thank-you, Major McAvity. Good to see you. I'm still awaiting your knighthood, but you don't mind if I call you Sir Malcolm, all the same?' I said, jokingly, aware that to a casual bystander I sounded completely off my trolley. Anybody who knew me wouldn't have been surprised in the slightest. 'How are things at Corps headquarters?'

'I always thought that if I made it that far, I'd understand this whole war straight away. From that perspective, it's been a bit of a let-down. Otherwise, it's fine,' he said. He took off his cap and was vigorously tousling his hair. It hardly looked worth the effort given how little of it there was. It was approaching 11 o'clock, and I too felt the moist rivulets of sweat forming under my cap, as the sun beat down unremittingly.

'You know, I'm still a little perplexed,' I began. Seeing his features twist into an expression identical to that of a two-year-old fresh from painting your nose with mashed potatoes, I paused to collect the obligatory ribbing.

'The Great Malcolm MacPhail, perplexed. That's about as rare as an eclipse of the sun,' he said, his eyes twinkling.

I sighed. 'What I was going to say... prior to the eclipse of the sun coming into it... was that I can't make out why we were pulled from the line. And placed in GHQ reserve?' In fact, I'd been puzzling over it since early May, when it happened.

Three of the Corps' divisions, including ours, were abruptly ordered away from the front and relieved by two Imperial corps. I was happy about the move, but canny enough to query the motive. After all, the Germans were still pounding away with their typical fervour, so somebody must be hatching a plan.

'And only two weeks previous we were preparing our last stand, you mean?' said McAvity.

'Exactly.'

Despite the many signs to the contrary, the Germans refrained from attacking us the entire month of April, aside from the usual painful grind of gas, shelling, raids and sniping. It was a welcome surprise, and a considerable relief, not least to me. I'd never completely reconciled myself with the idea of holding the line with Tibbett's Lee-Enfield swaying blithely off my flank.

German restraint was not much in evidence anywhere else. Fritz pressed hard to break-through in the north and again, for the second time, at Villers-Bretonneux near Amiens. Frightened by the large advances, the politicians agreed to make Général Foch the Allied commander-in-chief, though as our first "Generalissimo", you'd be hard pressed to recognize him as such. The diplomats had worked tirelessly to negotiate an appropriate rank that pleased all concerned. It began to dawn on me how diplomacy had so utterly failed in 1914. But with Foch in charge, he eventually sent French divisions north to relieve the beleaguered Second Army. They were in time to lose Mount Kemmel, but the line steadied, and the German offensive was stymied – for the time being.

Finally, McAvity made a stab at answering my question. 'Perhaps after four months we were due for relief?' he suggested. I could tell from his voice he didn't really believe it.

'And you must have been in high school when you finally caught on about Santa Claus,' I said. I grinned to soften my words. 'Don't you think it might have something to do with all these manoeuvres, like today's scheme? Offensive warfare tactics, of all things. I can't shake the notion that somebody is thinking ahead, and wants to make a big splash. And that splash is going to involve us,' I added. I was testing out my latest theory, hoping he'd dash it to pieces with some logical explanation. Instead, he slowly nodded his head, ruminating over the idea with altogether far too much seriousness.

Before he could answer, an officer emerged from the tent and beckoned him over. It must have been urgent, for he departed in a hurry.

I had trouble believing that we were planning to go on the offensive, when it wasn't clear we'd successfully concluded the defence.

One lesson I'd learned in my years at the front, though; never dismiss anything as unthinkable, it has a way of boomeranging back.

At Zero Hour, 11.30 a.m., the guns boomed out. For an exercise it sounded terribly realistic. The 7th Brigade was playing the German defender along a line not far from our observation post. The 9th Brigade was to attack from the other direction. That appeared to place us squarely in the middle of the battle zone, but few around me seemed concerned. It's what makes exercises such a draw for the denizens of headquarters; the only danger involves spilling your tea, and when it's as lukewarm as mine was, that's hardly a danger.

The tent emptied in time for the festivities and I was attempting to find a decent vantage point behind the row of officers arrayed in front. Off to my left was a Brigadier-General. I guessed it must be Webber, seeing as how he was in deep conversation with McAvity, who wasn't the sort to accost generals he didn't know. With them was a third officer, whom I didn't recognise. Never one to pass on a chance to gather some real intelligence, I sauntered up behind, so I could eavesdrop.

The other officer turned out to be the training officer from the First Army, a colonel. He was referring to some training manual, and my thoughts automatically began to wander, until I heard the title. At once my ears pricked up. It was then McAvity spotted me. He motioned me forward, and introduced me to the brigadier – it was indeed Webber – as well as the British colonel.

Once the pleasantries were out of the way, my curiosity got the better of me. 'I couldn't help but overhear your conversation about the training manual for offensive operations. By chance I met the author, a Captain Montgomery, a couple of months ago. He sent me a copy, in fact,' I began to say.

Webber appeared amused, and interrupted, 'The author? Is that what he told you?'

I nodded cautiously. I had a vague feeling my innocuous comment might somehow have landed me in a wasp nest.

Luckily, Webber's face remained calm, a picture of affability. 'It's true he was involved. As was I, and several others. The captain suffers, at times, from a touch of myopia when it comes to the importance of his own role in this war,' he said with a chuckle. The colonel must have known him too for he was wearing a big smirk, the kind that drips scorn like a waterfall drips water.

'Yes, I noticed that,' I said.

Webber inquired, 'Forgive me, Major, you had something else on your mind, if I'm not mistaken?'

I hesitated. 'Well, sir, it strikes me that we're doing a considerable amount of training for open warfare, and offensive operations. And there are a lot of useful things being taught. Only it's a trifle difficult to reconcile with our current predicament of hanging on by our fingernails,' I said.

'Ha!' he exclaimed. 'An officer who's not afraid to call a spade a spade! I'm afraid I don't know much more than you do. Don't underestimate the damage this entire offensive is doing to the enemy, however. He's losing many of his best men. We're not the only ones having a hard time, and the worst would appear to be over. You might view all this training, as contingency planning, for when we finally fend off the Boche for good.'

Put like that it made all the sense in the world. The panic of early and mid-April, from Haig on down, was indeed dissipating fast. The Germans must be having a worse time of it than I'd assumed.

Alerted by the rifle fire, I watched a group of soldiers sprint forward, only to fall prone on their stomachs after a hundred yards, their rifles pointed forward, and firing as soon as they hit the ground. In their wake a second group stormed over them in the direction of the "German" line. A flash of colour caught my eye. There were red and blue flags waving energetically. They were supposed to simulate machine-gun posts opening fire.

The attackers were now crouching low to the ground on one knee, their rifles held like medieval pikes, butts braced on the earth protecting against a charge from the cavalry. Only pikes didn't fire grenades, and these did. After firing their salvo, the soldiers rose to their feet and rushed the line. Their comrades further back ran to join them. I noticed one soldier lying crumpled behind, clutching his arm. It didn't take me long to figure out it wasn't part of the act. His grenade might have been a blank, but his arm had gotten in the way, and he was screaming in pain. That kind of realism I could do without. It was bad enough in the real attacks not to want to repeat it during manoeuvres.

Within half an hour the show was winding down. The air was still hazy from all the smoke bombs and the soft breeze was doing little to dissipate the smoke, or the heat. From our viewpoint the 9th Brigade seemed well on its way to its objectives. All those captured German documents on their tactics, painstakingly translated, plus our own critical notes on the recent fighting, were being put to good use. The army's hidebound ways were cracking. It was none too soon.

'An impressive exercise,' said McAvity. Most of the other officers were making ready to leave or to join in the post-mortem.

'Who's that?' I asked, staring at the unfamiliar officer ducking into the tent. A sullen-looking subordinate was slinking after him, as only trained lackeys or the most docile house pets do. My black Labrador never did seem able to master that kind of obedience.

'That's Major-General Mackenzie, the Commanding Officer of the 61st.' McAvity lowered his voice. 'They say there hasn't been a battle where the 61st was involved that wasn't lost. MacKenzie hasn't got what you'd call the most stellar reputation in the army.'

'In other words, he's right at home in the BEF High Command,' I concluded, with a brusque no-prisoners-taken précis of the situation. 'What's he doing here?'

'His division was mauled at the Somme on the first couple of days of Fritz's big offensive. They were moved north to recuperate. Then they got mauled again when the attack shifted there. Talk about bad luck. There's not much left, by all accounts.'

'Ah, with no division left, he's got time on his hands,' I said unmercifully.

McAvity showed some teeth at that. 'I'd guess that's why he's here,' he said. 'Sent to figure out how to make a better go of it the third time round. Believe it or not, he was Chief of the General Staff before the war, until he got in a fight with old Sam Hughes.'

'He was *our* Chief of the General Staff?' I asked, incredulous. 'Well, quarrelling with Hughes... he's got one good thing going for him.'

Sam Hughes was a legendary sort of character, especially in his own mind. He also happened to be the former Minister of the Militia. I tended to emphasize the *former* aspect of that whenever his name came up. I hadn't much use for him since early 1915. Among other things, he'd saddled us with a rifle that didn't shoot, which when you're fighting a war is a fairly considerable handicap. The problem was, since being dumped in late 1916, he didn't know how to slink gracefully into a hole, and stay there.

'Boy, you sure have something against that man,' exclaimed McAvity. He meant Hughes.

I snorted dismissively. 'I wouldn't if he didn't keep meddling where he's not wanted. He reminds me of another halfwit I spotted lurking around here earlier.'

'Oh, who's that?' McAvity was watching me in amusement. 'I'd forgotten how exhilarating it was to watch you rant,' he said.

'Colonel Whatley-Wigham from GHQ. Do you know him?'

'Sure. He drops by Corps headquarters every few weeks. I understand he's an adjutant or something for the field-marshal. Very prim and proper and all that. Not really your type.'

'You can say that again. He's the sort that thinks it's about him when they talk about the sun never setting on the British Empire.'

McAvity grinned. 'Don't underestimate him, Mac. He's not stupid, and he's definitely not a man you want to make an enemy of.'

'Underestimate him!? Whatley-Wigham is ballast. Now if we were in the Navy that might be useful…' I began to say in a loud tone. That is until I noticed McAvity.

His flushed face had lost its colour and he was staring awkwardly at my feet. I opened my mouth to ask, when I saw him cringe in response, and in one of those disconcerting moments you replay in your head afterwards, I understood. Without turning I said, 'Come. Let's have a look over there,' indicating a group of grenadiers behind him. We moved off into the field.

'Jesus, Mac,' whistled McAvity. 'He was ten feet behind you. He just popped up out of thin air. I hope for your sake he wasn't listening.'

'The man is shadowing me,' I said, as my breathing slowed. Later, I would reflect on this incident with more than passing regret.

My performance of stoic indifference must have convinced McAvity, for shortly thereafter he asked, 'What are you doing tonight, Mac? Perhaps we could have dinner together. Auchel looks like a dump, but there must be somewhere to eat.'

183

'Don't count on it,' I said, 'but sure. Hey, there's also a show on tonight at the YMCA theatre in Auchel. I was thinking of going. I don't suppose you'd like to go, perhaps before dinner? The Dumbells are performing.'

'That sounds right up your alley, Mac,' he chortled.

I'd walked straight into that one, too. The self-inflicted wounds are always the most painful.

CHAPTER 20

1st of July, 1918
Tincques, France

My eyes were watering, my lungs ached, and I was trying not to think about my pounding legs that felt like they might give out at any moment. I was running for all I was worth. If only I could put on an extra spurt, I might have a hope. In a daze of adrenaline, and with a determination I didn't think I had, I willed myself forward, straining my muscles in search of that last little ounce of momentum that could make the difference. There were parts of me hurting I didn't even know existed.

Vaguely, off in the distance, I could hear shouting. I stared in front of me, but my sight was a blur of shapes and movement. I kept running.

I crashed across the finish line, barely avoiding the kilted officer who was acting as timer, and somehow managed to keep my footing.

The crowd was on its feet cheering.

'Well done, MacPhail, you sportsman!' I heard someone shout amidst the applause.

'Second to last, we knew you could do it!' bellowed another voice from close by. It sounded familiar. It was immediately followed by a loud chorus of laughter. The Brits called it "taking the piss", which seemed appropriate.

I ignored them. I was panting, bent over with my head down, my wobbly knees threatening to give out at any moment. As the blood rushed to my brain I felt dizzy. With my left arm I reached out, unsteadily, and a sturdy olive green one grabbed mine. Soon, someone else had my other arm in a firm embrace and I felt a pat on the back. 'Easy on, fellow, you'll make it,' said a voice. At moments like this I really hated sports.

It was the 1ˢᵗ of July 1918 and it was Dominion Day. It was also the Corps Championships. While the tradition had begun modestly enough, today was a day of superlatives rather than modesty, my run notwithstanding. I don't think I'd ever seen anything to match it, perhaps some huge sporting event, but then minus the spectators, and with thousands upon thousands of carefree soldiers in their place. This was an army event, needless to say. It's one thing to read about it in the newspapers; seeing so many in the flesh, I was astonished at how big the army really was.

A dirt terrain adjoining the village of Tincques had been transformed into athletic grounds of near Olympic proportions. There was an oval quarter-mile running track I was now painfully familiar with, complete with a grand-stand, thanks to the engineers, and a full-sized baseball diamond in its centre. Along one side of the grounds a regulation-sized football field had been carved out, and the whole terrain was spotted with tents and little huts serving eggs and chips, and drinks, or simply offering a place to pray – earlier in the day I'd sniffed at the need for a chapel at a sports event. In retrospect I was more humble; I should have skipped the pre-run warm-up and gone straight to prayer.

Ironically, the only reason that I'd run at all was that we'd gone into the line to relieve the 2ⁿᵈ Division. I didn't begrudge them their relief. They'd spent three long months facing off against Fritz in a high-stakes game of chicken. They stuck it to him with relentless raiding and harassment and had battered the division opposite them into a state of near docility. Believe me, when it comes to Germans, that's saying something. It had come at a cost, as was to be expected. The boys of the 2ⁿᵈ Division had earned their rest, and we were to provide it.

An unfortunate side effect of this decision was that it placed our division's two best runners in the trenches near Arras, at a critical moment. The same clods from headquarters, who today were beside themselves in glee at my performance, had therefore begged me to run, something about not letting down the division. Eventually, I was worn down by their pleading appeals, the same campaign of attrition that had worn down the Germans. Next time around I was going to stick to time-keeping, or baseball, as I observed all the other officers had.

I couldn't help noticing that the children of Tincques were out in droves today. It was a beautiful day with a brilliant blue sky, and for any kid it was an exciting place to be. They were only slightly outnumbered by the dignitaries who'd made the journey here from all over France. A day of sun, sports and leisure had universal appeal it seemed. Prime Minister Sir Robert Borden and several cabinet ministers had come all the way from Canada, and the Duke of Connaught from England. But there was also Field-Marshal Haig, and the American general Pershing – the latter as starchily fearsome as his photos – as well as General Birdwood of ANZAC fame, and what seemed like half the British and French generals in the field. With their generals enjoying a day off, there were a lot of divisions rejoicing at a new holiday they'd never heard of.

At 4 o'clock the activities paused for afternoon tea. I stared enviously at the long twisting lines of other ranks queueing up on the dusty field to buy a beer. God, what I wouldn't have given for a nice cold beer. I'd barely had time to change and I was feeling semi-fit at best. A cool drink would have gone a long way to speeding up my convalescence. But I knew it wouldn't have done to join them. As an officer, I was consigned to mingling with my peers and sipping hot water. It would have been an altogether different matter if the Duke of Connaught had expressed a spur-of-the-moment desire for a cold brew, but he was talking to the Prime Minister under the watchful eye of General Currie. Drinking beer was as improbable in that crowd as removing their hats under the blazing sun.

Funnily enough, in the trenches, grouching about the officers' lifestyles was a popular pastime. In particular, those of us marooned at a headquarters were the butt of a lot of humour. I was out of the trenches, and working at a headquarters, and I was still at it. Some habits die slowly. I couldn't help thinking, however, these young carefree privates simply had no idea the sacrifices some of us made on a day like today. I gazed down unappetizingly at my lukewarm cup of weak tea.

'Is there a fly in it?'

I looked up, blinking. It wasn't from the bright sunshine. Brigadier Webber was standing in front of me. His face was glowing red as if he had a bad case of sunburn. He probably did. I'd seen corpses with healthier skin tone than many of the Englishmen I knew, and sun was an apparent novelty for the majority of them.

'Sir!' I exclaimed. It took me a second to regain my composure. 'No. No fly. I was merely contemplating the joys of being an enlisted man,' I said, my eyes dolefully following a crew of cheerful privates, all carrying a glass of golden froth.

Webber couldn't help but grin, as if he wouldn't mind one himself. He was no fool I could tell. He'd instantly discerned precisely which element of being a private I was so envious of. 'So, Major, are you enjoying yourself? MacPhail, wasn't it?' he asked. Both he and I knew he already knew the answer. It was the sort of sneaky rhetorical question lawyers favoured, to which silence was usually the best response. 'What did you make of all the exercises?' he queried, by way of a follow-up.

'I thought the exercises went well, sir. A lot of it is very innovative. I'm of the mind that the more we practice, the better. That's what always worked for us in the past. Especially when there's something new planned, such as *offensive* warfare,' I said wryly, emptying my last mouthful of cold tea unceremoniously onto the ground.

'You sound sceptical about going on the offensive, Major MacPhail. You know that after the Boche's latest offensive, the French are still holding firm in front of Compiègne?'

'Yes, I know, sir,' I said. 'The only thing is, at the beginning of June they were holding a line 15 miles further ahead than where they are now. Who's to say where it'll be in August?'

'True enough. Still, as I told you the last time we met, all those miles the enemy has penetrated are not coming effortlessly. Fifteen miles may seem far, but not when you consider his losses. And his line becomes more stretched, and more indefensible, the further he gets. He's a very long way from Paris yet, Major, make no mistake of that. Don't worry, our time will come.'

'That's precisely why I *am* worried, sir.'

He wiped at his brow with a handkerchief he'd conjured from his breast pocket. I wasn't sure whether he was merely hot, or just frustrated at my lack of enthusiasm. Then he smiled, which confused me even more. 'Your name came up not long ago. General Currie told me you were a real character. Not afraid to swim against the current were the words he used. He also said you were smarter than you look. I told him that didn't promise much.'

Not expecting it, I sputtered, as the laugh came bubbling up. I felt myself turning redder than the general.

'I was serious when I asked your opinion of the exercises. We're blessed with an exceptionally long period to regroup, get up to strength, and to train. And we had best use it to maximum effect.'

'It's not that there's something amiss with the training, sir. If anything, it's been remarkably thorough. From an intelligence point of view, learning to use the enemy's own tactics against him is also wise. Lessons have been learned, and we're making lots of useful changes. The problem, as I see it, sir, is that the enemy always knows we're coming. We only have to move into the line somewhere, and once he's discovered it, he's immediately expecting an attack. We can practise tactics all year long, but without surprise, it's like fighting with one arm and a leg tied behind our backs.'

'Yes, you're right, of course,' he said. 'That's the downside of the Corps' reputation. The Germans are on edge whenever they get wind that we've arrived. There's no easy way around it.'

'That's one thing I *have* been thinking about, sir. In hockey, when you want to move forward and there's a defender in your face, you feint. You don't crash into him. You stare him in the eye, throw your head sharply to the left, and when he moves to follow, you go right.' It made me think of Frank McGee. What a player he'd been. As a teenager I remembered reading with enthusiasm how he'd scored a mind-boggling 14 goals in a single game in the playoffs against Dawson City. He was killed two years ago at Courcelette, during the first battle of the Somme.

Webber was English and immune to the charms of hockey, but he'd been around the Corps forever. I saw that he understood. 'A deception? Yes, that's good. That's very good,' he remarked, slowly articulating each word. It was as if I could see the gears in his head chewing something over. The more he chewed it over the more curious I became. Finally, he asked, 'And presumably you had some ideas in mind, Major? Regarding feints, that is?'

'I do have a few thoughts on the topic,' I admitted. 'They all more or less come down to pretending we're somewhere else, instead of where we actually are.' It sounded so terribly mundane put like that.

It was then a bi-plane flew low over the grounds, followed by a second. Fortunately, I knew they were ours for they were Sopwith Camels – Lieutenant Smith had insinuated that any self-respecting intelligence officer had to recognize the basic plane types, and I fell for it hook, line, and sinker. Naturally he'd volunteered as mentor. Thinking about it afterwards, I was convinced he simply wanted to lecture *me* for a change. Regardless, if there'd been any doubt about the planes' allegiance, they started doing rolls.

'That's Billy Bishop and Raymond Collishaw, our aces in the sky,' said Webber, as we watched them buzz over and bank to make another run. 'Thank you for a most interesting conversation, Major. I'll keep what you said in mind. I found it quite intriguing. Perhaps when the time is right, we might discuss this further. Do enjoy the rest of your afternoon.'

'Thank you, sir,' I said, and watched as he walked over in the direction of a couple of the brigade commanders. One of them had what looked like lemonade in his hand. Beer was out of bounds, but I wouldn't say no to a lemonade.

I was on my second glass when I saw McAvity. He was a de-cent-sized man, shorter than I was, probably five-foot-ten or so. Unvaryingly, he had a friendly air to him, and his infrequent scowls were no more menacing than those of a puppy dog wrestling with a piece of rope. Partly it was his round, almost chubby face. That and his inquiring wide eyes parked under his broad forehead. Today he looked ecstatic, albeit slightly flushed. I never really took him to be an athlete. However, either he'd walked here from Corps HQ or he'd been up to some sports.

'Sir Malcolm!' I cried. 'You look pleased with yourself.'

'Hey, Mac,' he said, grinning. 'Second place in the doubles, and the singles too.'

'I didn't know you were a tennis player?' I said. 'Not bad for a man your age! Congratulations!'

'Oh, I used to play a lot at home. I'm a bit rusty. And, by the way, I'm only a month older than you, wise-ass!'

'Don't rub it in,' I said.

'Aren't you fellows supposed to be doing something useful, like manning the trenches?' he asked.

'Us being in the trenches is precisely why I'm here,' I said. 'Our star runners are mucking about with Fritz at the moment, those that aren't down with the Spanish flu, that is.'

He pursed his lips as if to say bad luck. 'You ran the half-mile, didn't you? I saw your name on a list of participants. How did you do?'

I shrugged casually. 'Let me put it this way, if the last runner hadn't gotten lost in the final bend, it would have been worse.'

'Not bad for a man *your* age. Anyways, don't fret about it, all the important people were watching tug-of-war,' he said sympathetically.

'Incidentally, I don't suppose you read one of the papers, a few weeks ago?' I said quickly, aiming to change the topic from my advancing age and scant athletic achievements.

He looked puzzled. 'I usually read them, why?'

'Then you'll have read about the solar eclipse in North America. I recall you described it as rare.'

'Ah! Don't tell me you've been brooding over my innocent little remark for an entire month!?' he said. I hadn't been really, but it seemed too much of a coincidence to let it pass unmentioned.

'So, what's it to be, football or baseball?' I asked, referring to the two finals still left to play. 'I had a peculiar conversation with Ox Webber I wanted to ask you about.'

As it turned out, we watched a bit of both. The games were considerably more exciting than what McAvity told me; he was as much in the dark as I was. I began to think calling what we did, "intelligence work", to be a misnomer.

Finally, we came to my favourite sport of the day, the *après-sport*, a delightful concept I'd learned from Benoît. When it came to describing the good things in life, French speakers had a nimble dexterity with words that made us English speakers ploddingly inarticulate in comparison. There was some consolation in the fact that actions speak louder than words, and we Anglos were no slouches in having a good time.

Whatever the High Command had in mind for us was a concern for later. Tonight, a gentle cooling wind was blowing over the grounds, the Volatiles were playing their latest revue and the beer taps were open for officers. It promised to be an enjoyable evening. When you're fighting a war you take your leisure time very seriously.

PART THREE

CHAPTER 21

21st of July, 1918
Château Blanc, Flixecourt, France

For the first time, in a very long time, a sense of hopeful anticipation was in the air. I felt it too. Yet I was bothered. A thought nagged at me, and I couldn't seem to get it out of my head, no matter how positive the news from the front was. When would we be thrown into the cauldron again?

Captain Richardson, my witty drinking companion from the Connaught in London, was still talking. 'The Germans are as good as finished at the Marne. They won't be up to much for a long while,' he said assuredly. I wanted to share his carefree optimism, but I was a pupil of the see-it-before-I-believed-it school. War has a tendency to do that to you.

Richardson and I were sitting beside each other in the brilliant afternoon sunshine. We'd parked ourselves on the left-most of the two white wooden benches. They stood pontifically underneath the château's main entrance, which was atop the landing of the stately staircase at our backs. Separated by a small sidewalk, the apex of the long semi-circular gravel driveway curved lazily before our feet. From the bench we had a fine view overlooking the château's front lawn, a modest one by the standards of most châteaux. Beyond it was Flixecourt's main thoroughfare. In London, the snobs might have called such a modest dirt street an alleyway, but this was Flixecourt and, truthfully, there were few streets in London that saw the exalted traffic this road did.

I was slouched with my legs extended and my arms clasped behind my head in a pose that suggested I might be taking an afternoon nap – an idea that had more than a cursory attraction to me. Richardson also looked as if he might doze off at any moment. No one in the château could see us. The large ivy-fronted staircase, with stairs to left and right, shielded both benches from view – something I suspected Richardson knew full well when he suggested we sit here.

'You're right, it's incredibly good news,' I said, finally. Richardson appeared to think the Germans would shelter meekly in their trenches from this point on. However, I'd learned from bitter experience not to write them off prematurely. 'One thing to keep in perspective, Niall, is that General Foch used half the French army at the Marne to counter-attack. I would have been a little disappointed if they hadn't made any progress.'

'It wasn't exactly *half* the army, Malcolm. But there were 30 or 35 divisions – mainly French, as well as some from the Americans. Plus they had hundreds of those new Renault light tanks,' he said.

I whistled softly. '30 or 35 divisions! And hundreds of tanks! It makes you wonder where they all were a couple of months ago when everybody was pulling their hair out. Enjoying late lunches?'

He shrugged. 'I see what you mean. However, the important thing is it worked like a charm. The Germans are pulling back. I dare say they're a spent force offensively, certainly for the time being.' Surely Richardson was right about that?

For the second time since 1914 the Germans made another go of crossing the Marne River and threatening Paris. It began less than a week ago. They were thwarted just as they had been four years earlier. This latest desperate plunge had all the signs that Fritz was running out of steam, men, or both. It was high time as far as I was concerned.

'It was a brilliantly well-timed counter-attack, I'll grant you that. And it sure would be a relief if Fritz took a holiday,' I admitted. 'I was beginning to wonder how long the Germans could keep their offensives going. It gives a whole new meaning to the word stubbornness.' I took a deep breath, enjoying the fresh air and the sunshine.

'Hmm,' agreed Richardson. 'Of course, if they do stop attacking, it does raise the question of what comes next.'

'Exactly!' I said. 'Fritz has been staved off, but they're already saying the war will go on well into next year. I can't shake this feeling we're going to be thrown into the breach soon. We're over-strength, we've been training non-stop the past few months and almost entirely in offensive warfare. As much as I appreciate a quiet spell, I don't imagine our generals see it that way…'

Before I could ramble any further, Richardson interrupted, 'There's your answer, then, don't you think?' he said matter-of-factly. I couldn't tell if he was amused at stopping me thus, as dead in my tracks as Ludendorff's offensives; his cap was tilted too low over his face to make out much of anything.

'That's precisely what I hoped you wouldn't say, Niall. You could have at least *tried* to sugar-coat it. Or have you heard talk of plans involving us?'

Then another Vauxhall staff car turned off the road into the drive-way and made its way gingerly towards us. It was the fourth in the past ten minutes. This one, like the one before it, was flying the red and white pennants that visibly identified its occupant as a British corps commander.

Instinctively we straightened up and I placed my cap on my head again. 'I thought this was supposed to be a quiet spot,' I muttered a little irritably, more to myself than to Richardson, as we rose to our feet. Two officers stepped from the car. Without wasting so much as a glance at us, they quickly mounted the stone stairs, where I heard them being loudly welcomed. The car crackled past on the gravel and parked behind the others at the end of the drive.

'I'm not sure what you expected, dropping in unannounced at army headquarters?' said Richardson. He'd obviously heard me. 'We actually do some work here, whatever rumours to the contrary you may have heard. That was Lieutenant-General Butler of III Corps, by the way.'

I hadn't planned on coming at all. In fact, I drove down to Flixecourt in the early hours of the morning to visit a training school for tank-infantry tactics the Australians had set up nearby. After their huge success at Hamel in early July, a school was a natural next step. It was a 35-mile journey or so and the road was remarkably good. The weather was even better and I'd made excellent time.

Lipsett had suggested I visit to see if it would be worthwhile for the division's officers to learn about working with tanks. He was infused with a new energy, too. At the time I hadn't seen much point. The tanks were invariably either stuck or broken, as Richardson and I had earlier ascertained, and cooperation was therefore a whimsical notion at best. Still, any suggestion of the general was as good as an order in my books. Not that I minded. For the most part I rather liked being Lipsett's jack-of-all-trades. And the idea of a relaxing day at some sun-drenched Aussie training centre in the tranquil French countryside behind Amiens appealed to me. It sure beat hanging out in a lice-infested trench near Arras, all the while waiting for a Boche trench mortar to dump a pineapple on my head. Besides, there was always Smith to fill in for me.

The morning went very well. The Aussies had a demonstration on. I watched with mounting amazement how the clanking steel beasts slowly plowed their way forward across trenches, obliterating the wire, machine-gun nests and other obstacles that fill an infantryman's nightmares. In turn, the infantry followed carefully in their shadows. They used them as moving shields to close in on their opponents, darting out to attack gun positions from the flank. I was going to have to revise my thinking on the tactical merits of these contraptions.

After a short and disappointingly sober lunch – frankly I'd envisaged more from the Australians – I was ready to hop into the Ford for the trip back, when one of my guides joked that I should keep my speed down. At least until I was well away from town, in case I should run down a Fourth Army bigwig. Who but an Aussie would think of that?

I had no idea whether Richardson was still with the Fourth Army, or even alive – though the chances of the latter were high if he'd survived London traffic. HQs are not particularly renowned for their danger. So, I decided to make a spontaneous detour into town, to Fourth Army headquarters.

Flixecourt itself was a pleasant enough little village. Its location was undeniably attractive, set on the gentle incline of a hill with pastoral meadows and small stands of trees leading up to it from the valley floor. Beyond, further up on the crown of the hill, like an uncropped head of hair, lay a leafy green forest of splendid oak, beech and chestnut trees.

The Château Blanc was an elegant four-story stone mansion. It was virtually square-shaped and entirely as white as its name suggested, making the black and red flag of an army commander flapping on a rooftop flagpole all the more conspicuous. As I hadn't stumbled in here by accident I knew it belonged to General Rawlinson.

Captain Richardson himself hadn't been difficult to find. The pudgy-faced lieutenant in a double starched uniform who helped me did firmly insist I move my car down to the street, before agreeing to summon him. If I'd known then that half the High Command was visiting, I wouldn't have been so put out. That's the curse of hindsight.

With the freshest batch of generals safely inside, Richardson and I sprawled ourselves out once more, and I casually tossed my cap onto the bench.

'What do you make of Rawlinson? You've been with him a while,' I inquired, stifling a yawn. It had been an early morning.

'Rawly the Fox? Oh, he's alright. He's personable and certainly clever enough. Energetic too. One thing I'll say, he's definitely not afraid to do his own thing. Though that doesn't always work out as it should. Or endear him to Haig. Apparently, they squabbled,' he said. I gathered he was referring to one of the cock-ups at the Somme, in 1916, where Rawlinson had been one of the principal commanders. In Rawlinson's defence, you don't lose a half-million men from a single blunder.

Richardson was plainly enjoying playing host, or possibly simply getting away from his desk. Either way, I was glad I'd made the effort to come see him. You can never be entirely certain, after a night lubricated by Scotch, whether you want to see your new best friends again. Happily, in the case of Richardson my first impressions were entirely correct.

'I like him already,' I said, referring to the Fox and his independent streak.

For some reason Rawlinson was called Rawly the Fox. To me it conjured up images of a sly, lithe, sure-footed man. I'd never actually seen him, except in a grainy photograph in the papers. Perhaps he once looked sly, but it couldn't have been the poor quality of the photo that made him appear as gangly as a new-born fawn wearing extra-large, black trench boots. Gangly or not, after Gough's dismissal, Rawlinson had inherited what was left of the Fifth Army in the wake of the German onslaught. Initially that wasn't much. More quickly than anyone expected, the reborn and redubbed Fourth Army was already spreading its wings.

'What's all this?' I asked perturbed, as yet another pennant-adorned staff car crunched its way up the gravel driveway to the grand balustrade stairway where the car ground to a halt. We rapidly assumed a posture more becoming our rank.

'Your guess is as good as mine. I'd say the general was entertaining if I didn't know better,' Richardson replied. 'It does explain all the whispered preparations this morning.'

'You've got a procession of generals turning up on your doorstep and you're on the staff of this army. Surely you must have heard something?'

'No, it's got very secretive around here the last couple of days.'

'Oh no,' I puffed melodramatically, as the car approached, and the fluttering flags took on a form and a colour I could identify.

He turned to me with a start. 'What's wrong?'

'The Australians... I can't seem to escape them,' I said, sighing deeply.

Richardson replied seriously. 'Oh, they're not too bad. A little full of themselves, perhaps. And somewhat rough around the edges...'

'Don't I know it,' I groaned. His defence of the self-proclaimed "diggers" was well-meaning, so I continued, 'In my experience, the diggers need a periodic shovelful of dirt on their heads to stifle their natural boisterousness.' Richardson grinned. It also helped if you didn't behave like you'd sauntered out of a tea party with the King – not that I was keen on those types either. I kept that thought to myself.

I noticed the pointy elven ears first. They were hard to miss. Then I saw the crisply tailored form belonging to General Monash as he emerged from the car. Together with a second officer I didn't recognize, the general stepped smartly up the steps. When I considered it, there was nothing extraordinary about the Australians being here. They were part of Rawlinson's newly reinvigorated army.

Another figure slipped from the front seat beside the driver. He looked vaguely familiar. I watched as he looked furtively up towards the entrance. After seeing his superiors disappear inside, he turned in our direction. Even at a distance he had a lost-in-the-desert-without-water look written on his face.

'Ha!' I sputtered, loudly enough that he heard me from twenty-five feet away. It was Banting.

'Mac! What in God's name are you doing here?' he blared, as the recognition clicked in. He promptly barged down upon us.

'I was enjoying some sun, quiet, and fresh air with Captain Richardson here, until the Aussie Corps blew in,' I said, trying to appear peeved at the interruption. My grin gave me away. 'It's good to see you, Dan!'

He pumped my hand for what must have been thirty-seconds. Finally, after retrieving the pale and crumpled version of the one I'd extended, I introduced him to Niall. Banting's epaulettes revealed that he was now a major. Richardson, a long-time staff officer, oozed army etiquette from every pore and was poised to primly salute until Banting and I intervened. That's one thing the dominions categorically have in common, little patience for pomp or pompousness. I had the impression Richardson was beginning to appreciate that.

While Banting was as mystified as Richardson about the nature of the conference taking place today at Château Blanc, it didn't take long to catch up on his news. Monash had been promoted and made commander of the newly formed Australian Corps. He'd taken Banting with him to corps headquarters. I guess a promotion to major was part of the package.

Cheerfully I said, 'Congratulations!' Naturally, I couldn't leave it at that. 'But you know, Dan, given your driving skills I rather assumed you'd be in a unit worthy of them – say, the tanks?' The very thought of Banting, with an Aussie slouch hat on his head chugging along at four miles per hour in thirty tons of steel struck me as unbelievably comical at the time. On the Western Front, it's sometimes a question of taking your humour where you can find it.

Banting grunted. I'd forgotten how monosyllabic he could be.

Right as I was on the verge of telling about my morning visit to the Aussie camp, and asking him about their victory at Hamel, we heard a car approaching – fast.

By this stage, the three of us were comfortably installed on the bench and I wearily raised my head at this, the umpteenth interruption.

We watched as the car careered wildly into the driveway. It was twelve minutes past the hour, so it wasn't a stretch to think that one of Rawlinson's guests was running late.

'Friends of yours, Dan?' I asked innocently. 'The restrained driving style is positively unmistakable.' Rawlinson's neat gravel drive was being spewed about in a cloud of dust so thick you'd be excused for thinking von der Marwitz's Second Army had unexpectedly dropped in. Though, on reflection, the Germans were nothing if not well-ordered.

Richardson looked quizzically over at Banting. Banting managed a sour frown, as if he too had lunched on a variant of the same dry biscuits and water I had. More likely he was furiously devising witty comebacks on behalf of his countrymen.

Then I gulped as I made out the two flags on the front of the car's hood fluttering pertly in the slipstream. I shook my head in disbelief, but there was nothing wrong with my eyes.

It took the other two a long moment before they also caught on, and Banting began to chuckle – the last laugh was to be his. Never had the red dominion flag of Canada been so amusing.

The car shuddered to a halt before the staircase where, at the appointed spot, a couple of orderlies stood dutifully waiting. A yellow-brown trail of dust that had rippled out from the rear tires as the car drove up was drifting in from behind, like a gas cloud in the calm warm air. With the Vauxhall's soft-top roof down, I immediately spotted Generals Currie and Webber sitting in the rear seat. What were they doing here!?

'They must have been in a hurry,' I said quietly. The current silence felt awkwardly painful, if only because I knew my two companions were revelling in my embarrassed discomfort. I could just make out the two smug faces beside me.

The orderlies were quick to open the car doors, and Currie and Webber wasted no time in clambering out.

Webber glanced cursorily in my direction as he walked around the front of the car to the sidewalk. Then I saw his head snap around again, as his mind seemingly registered the image his eyes were recording. He stared at me unabashedly. I couldn't really make out whether he was pleased or displeased, surprised or indifferent. Not knowing what to do, I saluted. Currie, who'd exited the car on the right, was already bounding up the stairs. Webber turned away, ignored my salute, and followed.

'Oof,' I said.

Banting thumped me on the back and started to laugh. Richardson, by now, saw an ironic humour in it as well, and was grinning broadly. This time I wasn't rescued by the arrival of some general.

My own thoughts were elsewhere. Specifically, why on earth would Currie and Webber visit General Rawlinson's Fourth Army? We were assigned to General Horne, and he and the First Army were responsible for the Arras front. There were only 40 miles separating Arras and Flixecourt, but it might as well have been 400. Flirting with another general's army was about as socially acceptable as doing it with another man's woman. While Currie wasn't one to mince words, he hadn't gotten where he was by needlessly riling his superiors.

One thing was certain, Rawlinson had invited a crushing concentration of firepower to this meeting. With us, the Aussies, and the Imperial III Corps, there was an awful lot of infantry and an awful lot of artillery. And what to think of the cavalry corps, the tanks, and the officer none of us knew from the Royal Air Force? You didn't need squadrons of horses or aeroplanes, let alone a fleet of tanks merely to hold the line. What had the Aussie officer at the training school said this morning? 'In future, no attack will be complete without the use of tanks and aeroplanes.' The generals hadn't gathered here in secret to discuss the weather, no matter how nice it was.

An attack was coming, and from what I'd seen today, we were to be in the thick of it. Knowing Lipsett, he'd have me squarely in the vanguard.

CHAPTER 22

22nd of July, 1918
Le Château, Camblain l'Abbé, France

I was dumbfounded. 'Orange Hill,' I exclaimed loudly, for the second time. 'Are you positive about that?'

'Trust me. That's what they're discussing. They've been in there for almost two hours. An attack on Orange Hill. When I entered, General Watson was in a fierce spat with Currie about it. Something about the number of tanks he was to be assigned. You know how worked up those two can get. I was glad to leave my message and be gone,' said Major McAvity. 'Why? Is there something I should know?'

'No. Nothing. Just thinking,' I replied.

Another day, another bench, another château. At the rate things were going I could look into starting a new business after the war: The MacPhail Guide to the châteaux of France. Either that or the similarly named guide to French trenches. I figured the former had more chance of commercial success. That assumed the war ended soon, before the châteaux all ended up looking as torn and disfigured as the ruined centre of Arras where I couldn't see a tourist appearing anywhere in the next several decades. On the other hand, if the war didn't end, there might be a future for the trench guide after all.

This particular château was in Camblain L'Abbé, a hamlet tucked away in the corner of France behind Arras where we'd been on and off for years. It was in immaculate condition. Not surprising, perhaps, seeing how many illustrious guests had passed through: Pétain, Joffre, and Haig were amongst the most famous of its inhabitants. There was also a sizeable contingent of lesser names such as England's Minister of Munitions, Winston Churchill. Our very own General Currie also called its walls home. Currie was what you might describe as a long-term resident, though most decidedly not the kind usually tagged with that moniker – they typically are to be found in dingy downtown hotel rooms and high security penitentiaries.

The general's extensive headquarters – it took 70-odd lorries to transport it all – was planted here a month or two ago, and it wasn't for the first time. Not that it was a bad place to call home. I'd been here often enough to know, and Currie could be excused for thinking he was on to a good thing.

The château itself wasn't really much more than a large, white plaster, two-story house. It was disarmingly modest by the standards of your average shipping tycoon or allied general, but it had a homey charm to it for all its present military haughtiness. A large stand of tall trees to the right of the courtyard, their high tops swaying audibly in the breeze, lent an oasis of shade on a hot summer day, and a dash of colour. The trees were a welcome distraction from the blatant ugliness of the half-dozen or so Armstrong and Nissen huts that were erected in the garden – with the army's utter disdain for aesthetics in full display.

Thoughtfully, there were two white-painted wooden benches on the area in front of the building. They faced a modest courtyard of grey cobblestones with a carefully tended circular flower bed in the centre, full of reds, purples, and whites, around which there was exactly enough room for a large Vauxhall staff car to approach, turn, deposit its passengers by the front door, and return in the direction from whence it came. As benches go it was uncannily similar to where I'd been sitting yesterday. And it was a lot less crowded than inside. The company wasn't as fearsome either.

I turned again to McAvity. 'As far as I recall Orange Hill is a few miles east of Arras, on the left bank of the Scarpe River, right?'

'Yes.'

'And Arras falls squarely under the First Army's area of operations? Under General Horne?'

'Yes, of course. You know that.' McAvity was staring at me, befuddled.

'One more thing,' I said. 'Could the Fourth Army theoretically be involved with an attack on Orange Hill? Maybe you heard some news at headquarters, late yesterday, or early this morning. A joint operation, perhaps? Or some form of cooperation?'

His eyes widened and he didn't immediately say anything. Instead he shook his head. Finally, when he answered, he said, 'No. A joint operation with the Fourth Army? Not a chance. It's a recipe for disaster if you make two armies responsible for a single objective. The only way the Fourth Army would be active near Arras was if the two armies were to swap positions and that never happens. And even if it did, can you imagine the confusion? What would be the point? But you know all this, Mac. What in heaven's name are you getting at?'

I was puzzled. In some ways I would have been less surprised had McAvity told me the Germans were on the verge of surrendering. The news that we were to attack Orange Hill was a total shock. Yesterday, on the trip back from Flixecourt, I had everything so neatly plotted out. Today I was as confused as ever. Right when I thought I was getting the knack of being an intelligence officer, something inevitably occurred to persuade me otherwise.

'Oh, nothing,' I fibbed. 'I'm not trying to get at anything. The objective surprises me, that's all.' I had an uneasy hunch I should hold my cards close to my chest on this whole business – at least until I understood what was truly unfolding.

All this week I'd planned to come and see McAvity. We had a few semi-important matters to discuss. It was only this morning, as I was preparing to actually leave, that Smith informed me the Corps' commanders were converging here for a conference around noon-time; he couldn't be more precise.

Briefly I thought of cancelling – gate-crashing two conferences in two days was a bit much, even for me. But cancelling and rescheduling inevitably requires three times the effort it takes in the first place. I knew McAvity wouldn't mind, as long as he didn't have to perform at the conference himself. And that was worth taking the chance. As important, I had no intention of letting him off the hook on his promise of lunch. Another week of procrastination would surely have put paid to that rare offer. I was also very curious to hear about Currie and Webber's visit to the Fourth Army, which surely would be discussed.

After what McAvity told me, my curiosity was off the scale.

'Orange Hill,' I mumbled, thoughtfully, as if repetition alone would clear away the cobwebs. It wasn't a trick that had ever worked before, but on the off chance…

'Hmm, hmm,' affirmed McAvity, nodding while he scratched some itch on the back of his head. 'Orange Hill it is.'

Voices spilled out into the courtyard as the double French doors swung open. The meeting had adjourned.

McAvity and I sat as inconspicuously as we could, not five leaps from the door, as the assembled generals and their GSO1s poured out onto the sidewalk to await their cars. I wasn't sure how the drivers were going to sort it out; no general wants to wait behind another, and the competition to pick their man up first was going to be fierce. It was all so different going over the top in the trenches, no one wanted to be first then.

And then I saw him – Brigadier-General Webber. He was talking amiably to Major-General Burstall, the commander of the 2nd Division, when I noticed he'd spotted me as well. I could tell that from his open mouth. It was stuck in mid-sentence as surely as Tibbett had been stuck in the Ypres mud, and perfectly positioned to capture any random fly that happened along. Burstall was saying something to him. It appeared to be going in one ear and out the other. All he seemed capable of was staring at me. I'd even shaved this morning. Nervously, I rubbed my chin, double-checking, just to make sure.

I don't think I've ever made such an impression on a superior officer. I found it strangely disconcerting, especially for what seemed a mildly amusing coincidence. The only explanation I could think of was that I'd stumbled onto something I wasn't supposed to – now I had to figure what that was.

General Lipsett and Colonel Hore-Ruthven came through the doorway at that very moment. Upon seeing McAvity and I, they brushed past Webber, who had his back to them, and stepped over towards us. Their timing couldn't have been better. There was nothing more effective in warding off a Brigadier-General than a Major-General.

They had a friendly exchange with McAvity whom they presumably hadn't seen for some time and inquired how he was faring. After a few minutes the conversation ran its course and Lipsett turned to me, 'You could have driven here with us, MacPhail.'

'I would have appreciated that, sir. Only I didn't know you were coming to Corps HQ, until this morning, right before I left myself.' Feeling a need to explain my presence, I added, 'Major McAvity and I had a few things to discuss.'

'Where best to eat in Camblain L'Abbé. Yes, I can picture that,' he said. The general's sense of humour was never more finely pitched than when I was in his sights. I couldn't imagine he was truly aware of our lunch plans; otherwise his wittiness would have been a few shades more caustic.

I grimaced by way of response. That made the smiles only grow wider.

'I hope you two majors find some time to discuss preparations for the forthcoming attack. We'll need all the intelligence you can gather. Finely-tuned antennae that you have, I presume you already know where?' he said, in his characteristic half-facetious manner.

'Yes, I understood it was Orange Hill. Today's plan that is,' I replied. 'I'm still of two minds whether the objective will last the week.' This sounded a tad more enigmatic than I intended, not to mention irritatingly cocky. But before I realized it, it was too late.

Lipsett looked at me with interest, a small frown forming. 'I don't know what you're referring to, Major, but I've spent the last two hours with the Corps Commander, and his four divisional commanders, discussing in considerable detail precisely that objective. I have a feeling you and I ought to have a conversation soon.' He might not have meant much by it, but it sounded ominous, and I racked my mind for a suitable response.

Right on cue, the general's car rolled up and a tall, wiry private I recognised, by the name of Donaldson, sprang out to open his door. Last-minute rescues don't come any better executed than that.

We said good-bye and saluted. As the car edged away, I glanced over my shoulder and could see an adjutant excitedly vying for Webber's attention.

It was half-past one and an excellent moment for lunch. I was so thirsty I could have sworn I'd done calisthenics all morning, instead of simply exercising my behind. Granted, I was a little on edge.

One of the highlights of Camblain L'Abbé, for those less inclined to admire the local architecture or mingle with staff officers, was a visit to the *Strong Point*. The *Strong Point* was a large *estaminet*, so named for reasons it didn't take a genius to guess at, namely its drinks menu and noticeably formidable location. It was hard to believe that a tiny village could have spawned the marketing genius responsible for such an alluring name, and that was an unmistakable hint that the current clientele had played a role.

From a previous visit I recalled drinking a *vin blanc*, lovingly known as vin blonk, or just plonk to the other ranks. It had been surprisingly tasty, if my memory was anything to go on. Mercifully, it wasn't doused in a vat of sugar. War or not, sugar seemed to be in full supply. Many other *estaminets* did precisely that, supposedly to appeal to the taste buds of the typical Tommy. The typical Tommy wasn't crazy, however. I knew it was a not so subtle subterfuge to camouflage the sour bitterness of their dubious wares. But there was nothing dubious about this café's wares. In addition to their drinks, they served a short but appealing menu consisting of simple, French country food, in a cozy ambiance that just about made you forget why we were all here. That probably explained its popularity... that, and the extra-strong beer.

As we strolled down the dusty, yellow dirt lane towards the Strong Point, I could see there was something on McAvity's mind. He had that concentrated look that I'd learned was a precursor to some penetrating questions and he didn't disappoint. My plan was to lull him into a comfortable state of lethargy with a few of his own drinks while I conjured up a convincing story. Like most plans, this one went astray almost immediately.

'What's going on, Mac? Webber looked like he saw a ghost when he spotted you,' he said. 'And that bizarre response you gave Lipsett. Were you *trying* to piss him off!?'

209

I sighed, as if I didn't know where to begin, which more or less accurately described the situation. Normally, I would have told him straight away about what I'd seen at Flixecourt. For some reason I didn't. Instead I said, 'It's complicated.'

'I bet,' he responded.

'Look, I'm not convinced Orange Hill is the objective.'

'That's abundantly clear,' he said. 'But why not?'

'It doesn't fit. Strategically, it's hardly crucial. Meanwhile the Corps is fit, way over strength in terms of numbers, and we've trained all summer in open warfare. And we're to take Orange Hill? No. High Command hasn't been saving us for that,' I said. The real reasons for my scepticism I left unsaid.

'Don't underestimate it… it won't be a walk-over.'

'No, of course not. But if you were commander-in-chief and desperately short on resources, with Foch demanding an offensive, would you pick Orange Hill to attack with your largest, strongest and hardest-hitting corps? Not to mention, with the Germans expecting it before you even gave the order? No, that can't possibly be it,' I said resolutely.

Determinedly, McAvity went on, 'What about Webber, then? What is it with you and him? I didn't know you even knew him. Or, in any event, not well enough to annoy him. He looked like he saw a ghost.'

'He might have been irritated you invited me to lunch, and not him?'

McAvity groaned.

I was relieved when we finally arrived at the L-shaped, two-story farmhouse with a dark thatched straw roof that was the Strong Point. Despite being in the middle of town it was set on an imposing earthen embankment. It required a stiff climb of a dozen steps or more to reach an outdoor terrace surrounded by white picket fencing, where – in the absence of a hurricane – the evening's festivities would burst out into the night air. It was an easy enough feat to climb the embankment in the warm radiance of the afternoon sun. I had a suspicion the descent was rather more challenging in darkness, after an evening spent imbibing. I stormed the steps two at a time, looking forward to leaving McAvity's interrogation far behind, and made quickly for the door leading into the cool, dimly lit interior. By this time, I was not only thirsty, but ravenously hungry. I hoped McAvity had brought a well-padded wallet.

A thought came to me. What if today's conference was Currie and Webber spinning their own web of deception?

CHAPTER 23

27th of July, 1918
Château d'Hermaville, Hermaville, France

'Nine-thousand?'

'Yes, sir. We've had nine-thousand casualties since mid-March. Since the Germans launched their offensives,' said Lieutenant Smith.

'It's a lot of casualties for four months,' I said, 'considering we neither attacked, nor repulsed a major attack.'

'Yes, it is, sir.'

The rain was coming down outside with a vengeance and I was in a dark, gloomy, contemplative mood. The cautious optimism I was feeling of late had ebbed away for the moment. It wouldn't be long now before we were back in combat, and the casualties soaring.

9,000 was a number that barely registered in a war that was devouring life with such abandon. The Germans attacked where the pickings were easiest, and that apparently included the entire British front, except for Lens and Vimy where we were. Not that the daily shelling, gassing, aeroplane bombings and raids passed us by. 9,000 dead and wounded testified to that.

I knew more than a few personally, and the names of numerous others. Outside of a sporting event it was impossible to picture that many faces. It was the population of a decent-sized town. All killed or wounded. All with families. All who had done their bit, but not in some decisive battle, or glorious victory – not that glory mattered anymore, it lost its meaning long ago. The unrelenting, senseless grind of war had claimed them. It was a sobering epitaph and one well suited for the nearly four years of conflict the world had endured.

Replacements streamed in all summer and the spirits of the men were high. Compared to others we'd had it easy. There was palpable pride that our section of the line was the only one on the entire hundred-mile British front that hadn't budged an inch.

Yet the whispered innuendo gnawed at me – that the army had faced down the Hun without us. The condescending words were especially galling for some. The 2nd Division, the machine-gun brigade, and the cavalry – they'd all been thrown in elsewhere to help stave off the advances. They made a difference, and suffered heavily for it, not that much recognition, let alone gratitude, was forthcoming.

'The rumours have it that we're heading to Ypres.' Smith was addressing me. His voice had a relaxed pleasantness to it; no matter the subject, his tone was unfailingly reasonable. 'There's an expectation the Germans will attack there again.'

'Ypres,' I mused. 'There might be something to it. I rather doubt the Germans will be the ones doing the attacking, though. I don't think they're in much shape to attack anything.' It was only a rumour, but God knows, I'd spread enough rumours myself to know when there was actually some meat on the bone. This one was quite possibly the fattest T-bone I'd ever come across. Ypres was never far from our generals' minds and a new offensive there ticked off a lot of boxes. The only thing it didn't explain was the peculiar conference near Amiens with General Rawlinson. Nor the meeting about the Orange Hill attack near Arras, come to think of it.

'I can't say I'm looking forward to returning,' said Smith. It hardly needed saying. Nobody was. Ypres is a destination you should only have to see once in a lifetime, particularly if you made it out okay the first time. And I'd already survived three visits.

'Where did you hear this?' I asked.

'Oh, a fellow I know at Corps HQ. He's usually in the know about a lot of things,' he replied. 'Oddly, Higgins told me the exact same thing, not two hours later.' Higgins was a staff officer, one of ours. He'd transferred into the division only this summer from the 5th Division, who were training in England. He was by far the smartest dresser at HQ, but had precious little experience. His contacts were reputedly top-notch, I'd been told.

'And Orange Hill? Any news on that?'

He shook his head. 'Not that I've heard. The planning for the attack goes on.'

'And the Fourth Army? Any word about them? No imminent warning orders that we're to move south?'

He stared at me, puzzled. 'No, sir, of course not. Is there something I should know, sir?'

I ignored his question. 'Well, there's one reassuring thing about all this,' I said.

'What's that?'

'If we're this confused, think how poor Fritz must feel.'

By noon, the rain showers passed, the skies brightened considerably, and my mood with them. There was no point in brooding. Like most soldiers I'd long since come to that conclusion; in my case in the trenches, not long after arriving here. It was the only way to stay sane when everything around you was conspiring to cause the opposite. We had a job to do, and the sooner it was done, the better. Only, every so often I strayed. That was one of the invisible, unspoken hazards of being where I was now. Most days I escaped the worst of the blood-shed, but I couldn't escape knowing exactly how horrific it was.

After lunch I ducked out of the office on my way to Tibbett and DuBois, who'd surreptitiously spirited away the latest batch of aerial photographs, when I saw a familiar figure. Actually, I almost bowled him off his feet. It was Ox Webber.

'I'm sorry, General,' I said. 'I wasn't looking.' He smiled graciously. As an afterthought I mumbled, 'I'm surprised to see you here.' A visit from Currie's right-hand man was not a commonplace occurrence. Briefly, I debated mentioning that it was several days since I'd seen him last, but thought better of it.

'It's not entirely coincidental,' he said. 'I had some business to discuss with General Lipsett. And I've been meaning to speak with you. Do you have a moment?' It was all very polite. Naturally, there was as much chance of me pleading demands on my time, as a minister pleading ignorance of the bible. Anyhow, it's not every day a general tracks you down for a chat – unless there's something pressing, and usually unpleasant, on his mind. Webber didn't appear to have it in for me and I was intrigued to hear what he had to say.

'Naturally, sir. If you'd like, we could talk in my office. There's only Lieutenant Smith in there at the moment.'

'Perhaps we could take a stroll outside? A little fresh air would do me good.' I understood his meaning immediately. Whatever he had on his mind, was meant for my ears only.

'That's a good idea, sir. I could use a little fresh air myself, and it appears the showers have passed.' What I didn't say was that it would spare me considerable embarrassment if I'd misjudged him and he was, indeed, planning to ream me out.

The splendid château at Hermaville was ideal for a stroll in the garden, set as it is in the midst of a park of almost regal proportions. The front lawn was a vast expanse of bright green ringed by a darker-tinted wall of majestically tall trees, many of them chestnut.

I breathed in deeply as we stepped outside. The air was still heavy from the morning rain and the lawn sparkled as the sun's rays peeked through the clouds to reflect off the moisture-covered blades of grass. There was that sweet, fresh grass smell I'd always loved. It reminded me of when I was boy with the chore of mowing our lawn every few weeks – an obligation I'd whined about at the time, but came to think of more fondly with age. If I ever made it home, there were a lot of things I was going to think about more fondly.

'It's nice here,' remarked Webber, as we walked away from the doorway in the direction of the trees off to our left.

'It is,' I said agreeably. 'I find that I appreciate serenity a lot more than I used to.'

'Yes. Don't we all,' said Webber, and for a fleeting moment I could see his thoughts were far away. Then he pulled himself out of it. 'You'll no doubt recall our conversation in Tincques, at the sports day?'

'I certainly do, sir. I'm surprised you remember.'

'Oh, I do indeed. It was most instructive. Currie warned me, you're an unforgettable sort,' Webber said. Then he chuckled softly. 'Not that I'd be able to overlook you even if I wanted to. Your face has been popping up in very unusual places recently and at the strangest possible moments. That's another thing I wanted to discuss,' he added, stopping in mid-stride to look at me. I wasn't entirely sure what he meant with his first comment – reminiscing about what a nice day we'd had in Tincques seemed improbable – but I clearly had some explaining to do regarding the second item on his agenda.

I tried not to look sheepish as I turned my head to hold his gaze. 'At Flixecourt, I was as surprised to see you and the General as you were to see me. I went there to tour the Aussie training centre. You know, the tank-infantry course they've set up, sir. Only afterwards did I decide to drop in to visit an old acquaintance at the Fourth Army. I met him on my last leave. It was a bit of a spur of the moment thing,' I said.

'No, no,' said Webber, clearly amused. 'You misunderstand me. I'm not asking you to explain your eccentric travel itinerary. Come.' With that he beckoned me to follow, as he turned into a little path between the trees barely wide enough for the both of us. 'No. What I mean to say is that surely it struck you as remarkable that General Currie and I should be attending a conference at the Fourth Army with General Rawlinson? And what to think, only a day later, when we're discussing an attack in the Arras sector – First Army territory – with the divisional commanders?'

I nodded. 'I still haven't figured it out, sir. Not for want of trying, I might add.'

'Nor should you,' he said. 'No. That's not quite true. You can do all the mental gymnastics you want to, Major, so long as your conclusions remain firmly up here,' he added, tapping his head lightly with his forefinger. 'I'm afraid I'm not able to explain to you at the moment. I do have to ask you to keep what you've seen, and heard, to yourself. It's very important.'

'Of course, sir. I'll do that. Fortunately, I haven't discussed it with anyone,' I said, thankful for whatever sixth sense had led me to hold my tongue, thereby in all probability saving my skin.

'That's good to hear. I'm glad I had the chance to discuss this with you,' he said. 'What else have you heard?'

'That we're to be sent to Ypres.' It came out in a burst.

He nodded. This bit of news was clearly not news to him at all.

'We've been warned that XVII Corps will relieve us shortly and we should prepare to move to the Second Army,' he said. I guess he figured this would provide me with an explanation. Only it left me more confused than ever.

The Second Army meant Ypres, and Ypres was logical enough. Only if Ypres was our next destination, why go to the trouble of warning me off discussing my stopover in Flixecourt? That was surely irrelevant. Or not? And what was the rationale behind all the planning for an assault on Orange Hill, if our next stop was, in fact, Ypres? There were enough twists and turns in this plot to confuse even the most avid reader of detective novels. By my reckoning, we were linked to three different armies, and since the disbandment of the Fifth Army, the BEF only had four. At this rate we'd be taking over the entire front ourselves.

The path we were following exited the treeline. We emerged at a spot directly opposite the front of the château. From there we could look back to admire the distinguished grey stone edifice looking its best in the midday sun. I was glad to be back in the open; the trees were dripping rainwater and my tunic was annoyingly wet, as a result. Webber must have thought the same, for he now avoided the trees. We sauntered off across the lawn. He looked over at me. He could see the puzzlement. He was smart enough to know that my mind was working feverishly to turn his handful of apples into a pie.

And then it came to me. 'It's a feint! A deception! We're deking left,' I exclaimed. 'If it's not to be Ypres, where will the real attack be, sir?'

'I couldn't possibly comment and nor should you,' said Webber sternly. His face revealed nothing; he'd assumed a stonily impassive look. His eyes, however, showed something else. He was an accomplished chief of staff, but not much of an actor. It was a feint alright. 'Two days from now, two infantry battalions, the wireless signals units and two casualty clearing stations will move north as part of the Corp's advance party. One of the battalions will be from your division. I've asked General Lipsett for you to accompany them to facilitate our move north. He's agreed to that.'

I had to think about this development. Things were moving very quickly. 'And what precisely am I to do in Ypres?' I asked.

'The Corps HQ will be in Cassel I should think. Obviously, some basic preparations need to be made, and I expect you will need to coordinate locally to alert all involved of our arrival. The battalions will go into the line without delay near Mount Kemmel,' he explained.

Mount Kemmel – really only a hill to the southeast of Ypres – was the lynchpin to the Salient, and commanded the city and its immediate surroundings. Its loss in the spring offensives had been a heavy blow. The Germans knew full well that a counter-attack to regain it was inevitable.

Webber continued, 'Some aggressive patrols to test the German lines would be useful. Given the uncertain situation it wouldn't be unhelpful if they discovered our presence – a shot across the bow, so to speak.' I noticed any mention of acquiring useable intelligence was conspicuously absent from General Webber's briefing.

'So, if I understand correctly, sir, I'm to do everything possible to trumpet our imminent arrival with as much fanfare as I can muster?' I said.

'I knew you were the perfect man,' he replied. I wasn't sure what that implied for my career as an intelligence officer; this assignment seemed to revolve solely around pumping out misinformation. Before I had any more time to reflect on it, Webber went on. 'Remember, the divisional wireless units need to be up and running. If signals security slipped in the haste of it all – well, that would be perfectly understandable.'

'I see,' I said, ruminating on his words. As far as I could recall, I'd never heard a single solitary instance in my entire army career in which a slippage in signals security was acceptable, let alone "understandable". There was a lot Webber was leaving unsaid, and for an army that excelled in issuing orders down to the last-minute detail, that said a great deal.

'One final thing. The responsibility is yours, but you'll require some assistance from others. Try to keep your explanations as short and plausible as possible. Also, it's best if you discuss this with no one other than me, at least for a day or two until General Lipsett is fully informed.'

Great. I was off to the Salient and even General Lipsett was oblivious to the real purpose. One aspect of this whole hazy business was abundantly clear – if it didn't work out, no one would have far to look for a scapegoat. On the other hand, I'd never seen anything like this. Maybe we would surprise Fritz.

CHAPTER 24

29th of July, 1918
Arneke, France

The train was moving at considerable speed. Our scheme was in motion.

The French countryside was obscured in darkness, but the tell-tale clacking of the wheels as they rolled, shrieking and clanging over the steel rails, and the steady shuddering of the carriages at each new length of track, were as sure a sign of our progress as any sight of a farmhouse passing by. After departing the town of Hazebrouck we were on the last leg of our journey. I was looking forward to arriving, in the blissful and, as events would make woefully apparent, somewhat naïve supposition that a warm bed was awaiting.

We were told it was a strategic train. While I've heard of many different sorts of trains, this particular species was a novelty. It didn't seem especially strategic. To my inexpert eyes, it looked exactly like any other train I'd ever seen, although it was fast. Regardless, the announcement we'd boarded such a beast proved to be good for half an hour's worth of jokes and general merriment, which might have been the strategy all along.

I entrained, together with the rest of the 800-strong battalion, the 4th Canadian Mounted Rifles (4th CMR), at four o'clock sharp this afternoon, at the small village of Acq. Acq was an important transit point, midway between our HQ at Hermaville a few miles to the west, and the city of Arras not much further to the east. General Lipsett and Colonel Hore-Ruthven had come to the station to wave us off in person. It was an unusually magnanimous gesture, even if it wasn't a long drive. Not for the first time since my stroll with Ox Webber, their presence made me wonder what I'd been plunged into. Of course, from one perspective, with the destination being the Ypres Salient, the answer was blindingly obvious. I hoped the weather had turned.

Lipsett had taken my arm, on the platform, and steered me aside.

'General Webber told me about your little deception,' he said quietly, acutely aware the platform was teeming with men. While elderly ladies may be the ones with the reputation for gossip, I'd hazard to say they run a distant second to your average soldier, and Lipsett must have felt the same way. However, I couldn't help noticing how he openly described it as a deception; two days earlier Webber had warily skirted around even the merest hint of that idea. There was only one possible explanation; Lipsett had been fully briefed on the forthcoming operation. I wanted to ask him what was going on, but whatever it was, it was so cloaked in hush-hush secrecy that I knew I'd be wasting my breath. And, by now, I was forming my own theories.

One other word Lipsett said was still echoing in my head – it had become *my* deception. I wondered how that had come about. It didn't take a genius to realize it was a description that could very well stick, particularly if things went wrong.

Lipsett had his head down. I could have sworn he was mumbling if I didn't know how completely contrary that was to the general's character. He wasn't entirely at ease with this cloak and dagger stuff.

'I've asked the battalion commander, Colonel Patterson, to offer you all possible assistance,' he murmured. 'I explained to him the importance of your work in preparing for the arrival of the Division and the Corps. Also with carrying out your intelligence duties. He promised me he'll do everything he can should you require men, material, or anything else. And, MacPhail – do try not to step on any general's toes,' he concluded, before wishing me good luck and a safe journey. If you'd missed his opening sentence, no one would have guessed the meaning lurking behind these seemingly innocuous words – I'm sure it was intentional. Normally he hated ambiguity.

I was sitting in an officer's compartment. As always, there was a strict division between officers and other ranks; everywhere that is except for on the battlefield, where survival rather than comfort is the first thing on everybody's mind. And nobody in their right mind wants to be an officer in the field, knowing a pip on your shoulder doubles your chances of landing on a stretcher, or buried in a dirt grave.

Beside me, on the hard wooden school bench, sat a captain and a lieutenant. Two knee-lengths across from us were three others, also captains. The officers were all from the 4th CMR. They'd gotten the dubious honour of shipping off to the Salient as a thread in the elaborate web being spun.

On occasions such as this I was glad I was an officer; it spared me the sardines-in-a-tin like conditions further back in the train, not that I had any delusions I was travelling on the Orient Express.

'It shouldn't be more than half-an-hour, I'd guess,' I said hopefully, to no one in particular. It might have been a fast train – though there was no advantage to speed when we spent half our time kicking our heels at stations, and being shunted back and forth – it certainly wasn't a comfortable one. I was longing to escape.

'Beats a trench,' said the captain opposite me, who was comfortably curled up against the wooden bulkhead adjoining the gangway. Likely he'd noticed my discomfort. It wouldn't have taken much. A mere glance at my face was a dead give-away, as was my constant fidgeting. The others in the compartment were either asleep or lost in their thoughts – soldiers being infamous for their ability to sleep pretty much anywhere, and anytime. Myself, I preferred a bed. I was fast becoming everything I'd looked down on two years earlier.

The captain's name was Thomas Dixon. He was Tom to his friends and I felt like I'd known him half my life. Really it had only been seven and a half hours. He shone a quirky, engaging grin at me and straightened up. I felt a conversation coming on. Somehow, he reminded me of a stand-up comedian. It was because of the pair of bushy black, shoe-shine bristles that passed as eyebrows. One was now bent into a bemused archway, while the other remained dead straight. Under his nose there was a wisp of a dark moustache that hardly looked the bother. With his cap on and a stern expression, all this might have made him look intimidating, were it not for his sparkling eyes and his demeanour; they both radiated affability.

Dixon had a remarkable story. He was from Toronto. He'd joined as a mere private around the time I had, in late 1914, not long after my wife's death. While I hadn't so much joined a cause as fled my misery, Dixon had enlisted out of principle. Miraculously, he'd survived the regiment's epic stand at Sanctuary Wood and Mount Sorrel in 1916. I remembered all too well that scene of horror as we fought to retake the hill, a week later.

That battle claimed the division's first commander, General Malcolm Mercer, and ninety percent of the mounted rifles, and Dixon won a Military Medal and a commission in the process, much as I had. He added a Military Cross at Vimy. I gathered he'd fought in all the big battles, with the exception of Passchendaele, when he was attached to a training camp. That might have explained his cheerful demeanour heading off to Ypres. I honestly couldn't think of another explanation. He was now a captain, and the commander of B Company.

Dixon began speaking. 'We spent most of the winter and spring with mud up to our knees in a trench near Lens, with Fritz shooting his heavies and field guns at us twice a day. I would have died for somewhere warm, dry, and safe like this,' he said. 'Even if the company leaves a little to be desired.' He gazed amusedly at the two officers beside him. One was sprawled over the other in sleep, with his head resting on his mate's shoulder, like two kittens in a litter.

Naturally he was right. *Put me in a château for a day and I'm spoiled for life.*

'Yeah, I tend to forget the trenches all too quickly,' I said. 'Habit, I reckon. I'll grant you this beats a trench, but it's still a bloody hard bench to sit on all these hours.'

Dixon nodded, as if commiserating, although he'd looked comfortable enough two minutes previously. 'So, what do you make of our move north?' he enquired. Surprisingly, it hadn't come up earlier. With the six of us we'd talked about everything except the war, including our plans for when it was over, and the first hours had passed quickly.

I hated to lie; besides, most of what I thought I knew was pure speculation, so I tried to keep as close to the conventional script as I could. 'The word I hear is the whole Corps is moving to Flanders.

That's one of my tasks, to prepare the way. What happens then, who knows,' I said.

'Ours not to reason why, but to do and die,' he said, and grinned. Exactly why this was humorous would have escaped most in civilian life, but I knew, and I returned his smile. I'm not sure Dixon realized he was paraphrasing Tennyson's *Charge of the Light Brigade*, nor how that bloody episode in the Crimea ended, more than a half century ago. I couldn't help thinking that was for the best.

There was a harsh squeal from the train's wheels and the compartment shook violently as we came to a sharp curve in the track. One of the duffel bags stowed in the netting overhead tumbled out, and fell with a thump onto Dixon's neighbour, his second-in-command, Captain Poyser. Poyser groaned and then rolled a quarter-turn, knocking the bag to the floor, and clamped himself more fiercely onto his equally comatose sleeping companion beside him.

We both smirked at the sight.

'No mistaking him for anything other than an infantry man,' I said, meaning Poyser.

'How do you figure?'

'Well, if he was a staff officer, he wouldn't have been sleeping in the first place, and seen it coming. An engineer would never have stowed his tote so precariously it would fall, and an artilleryman might not have heard it, but he would have felt it. Simple process of elimination,' I replied. 'Don't worry, infantrymen have their qualities as well.'

'Such as being deaf, dumb, and blind you mean?'

'It takes all sorts, Dixon,' I said. He laughed, for he knew I was from the infantry as well.

We chatted about this and that for a while, and then, with earnest seriousness, he asked, 'How did your wife die?'

'Tuberculosis,' I replied, to which he grimaced. He didn't ask any more and I didn't volunteer.

'I've never had a wife,' he said, after a length.

'It's nice having a wife,' I said. 'I'm sure you'll find a sweetheart to marry when this is all over.'

He couldn't have been more than four or five years younger than me, but he reflected on this as if the thought had never occurred to him.

Finally, he said, 'Yes, I hope so. I'd like that.' Whereupon, he paused again for a long while, before asking, 'Did you have any children?'

'No. No we didn't,' I replied. 'We were planning to someday,' I began, and then paused to clear my throat. Either the words or the courage left me for I went quiet. I could see he understood.

'Children would be nice, I think,' he said quietly.

I nodded. He didn't say anything else on the topic, and after a spell we began to talk baseball – the divisional league to be precise. It was odd. It all seemed another lifetime ago, and it had been a long time since I'd spoken to anyone about such things, let alone a complete stranger.

I liked Thomas Dixon. He reminded me a lot of myself and I suppose that's a way of saying that the old saw, opposites attract, doesn't cut much ice. That expression probably referred to women, though.

Before long the train slowed to a crawl, and I glimpsed the sign with Arneke on it as our carriage crept past, and a platform appeared out of the darkness. I grabbed my bag and my helmet, anxious to be on my feet again and in the fresh air.

The train emptied with alacrity – I wasn't the only one glad to arrive. In the middle of the platform stood Lieutenant-Colonel Patterson, and I made my way over to where he was engaged in conversation with two British officers. One was apparently the Rail Transport Officer (RTO) and I presumed the other was the Town Major. Patterson didn't appear overly pleased with what he was hearing.

'I have a map here for you, sir,' I heard the RTO explaining and saw him meekly pass over a large two-coloured map to the colonel, almost dropping it in the process.

'So, beyond telling me that we're now part of X Corps and kindly giving me a map, that's it?' said the colonel. 'We're on our own?' I saw my hopes for a warm bed, any bed, evaporating before my eyes.

The RTO shifted uncomfortably on his feet, while the major studied the ground with an avid keenness. 'I imagine so, sir, I don't know what else to say,' he stuttered.

I took a closer look at them. The RTO was a pale, spectacled, unhealthy-looking lad. He was holding himself in an unnaturally stiff pose, as if at any relaxation on his part the whole house of cards would collapse, which it might well have done. His companion, the major, wasn't much better.

They were sterling examples of what the British army classified as "B category" men. I understood the primary requirement of the B category was the ability to breathe. The army may have had to relax the criteria somewhat for this particular pair.

The colonel quickly cut his losses and was now conferring with his officers. It didn't take long before a decision was made, and the ranks were assembled into marching order, and we set off in search of our billets. Billets proved to be a slightly optimistic description of our sleeping arrangements as I soon came to appreciate. After a ten-minute march we arrived at our apparent destination: a field.

We'd barely begun to unpack when a scruffily dressed man – I took him to be the farmer whose field we were to inhabit – hastened towards us. He was all smiles and I could hear him calling: '*Bienvenue! Bienvenue!*' a hospitality I found remarkable at one in the morning, with hundreds of uninvited soldiers milling around his land. Nor was he content to solely welcome us. He scuttled about lending a helping hand as the men bedded in.

There were pleased looks all around when it became clear the officers were to be offered lodging in the farmer's barn. I had the distinct impression this was an improvement on their normal accommodation. In the middle of the night, after a long day, I certainly wasn't going to complain, not that I was under any illusions how seriously the army treated complaints about the housing. With a thick blanket from the farmer, and a cushy haystack, I was as cozy as a pig in a mud-bath. I must have fallen asleep before removing, or even untying my boots, for that was precisely how I found them the next morning.

And that was when the real work started.

CHAPTER 25

30th of July, 1918
Cassel, France

Today was going to be busy. General Webber had impressed on me the need for haste. My plan was to begin at Second Army HQ.

I woke with the rest of the battalion, which is to say far too early – the army and I tended not to be entirely of one mind on that subject. By noon, we'd packed up camp and begun the march to Cassel, an easy enough walk straight down the road for 7 km, according to the farmer.

There was no car to collect me, and that was a mildly disturbing omen, given all that certain generals were expecting. Apparently, I was on my own. That left me with no other choice than to accompany the 4th CMR as they marched towards Belgium.

And so it was that I entered the town of Cassel at around one-thirty in the afternoon, bathed in sweat, in a long column of soldiers marching two abreast. The march itself had hardly been arduous. Without their heavy packs – they would follow by lorry – the men were in fine form. That was a good thing, too, seeing as how the battalion had only covered a third of the distance they needed to, to reach Steenvoorde and, eventually, Abeele, across the border into Belgium. It was scorching hot. Despite the heat, or perhaps because of it, the air was heavy with a wet clamminess that positively weighs on every sinew, and leaves your skin sticky to the touch, and your clothes damp. I was too damned old to be playing infantryman.

At Cassel I said my farewells to Dixon and the others from the 4th CMR, with a promise to catch-up with them soon, and made my way to General Plumer's headquarters. But not before grabbing a quick bite and a drink at an *estaminet*. It's never wise to show up at a general's headquarters looking like you've walked out of a rainstorm, and irritable from the hunger and thirst. Feeling refreshed and a little chipper – I'd splurged on a *demi* of *vin rouge* – I reached the Castel Yvonne.

It was perched midway up the slopes of Mont Cassel – I've seen snow banks higher than some of the so-called mountains in this region.

Castel Yvonne was a weirdly eclectic, five-story square house, topped by a tall thin spire on one corner of the roof. It required only a dark and stormy night, and a few bats, and Count Dracula – a grisly character from a book I'd read – would have felt right at home. I had the impression General Plumer felt right at home, as well, but he was probably enamoured of the view in the direction of the Salient.

Unfortunately, I wasn't able to see the view, as I didn't make it further than the first-floor office of a florid-faced Captain Givens. The only view I saw there was of him, mopping his brow at intervals, and a large map taped on the wall behind him.

'Ah, ha,' he pronounced dubiously, on hearing my request.

'As you no doubt are aware, Captain,' I told him, trying to butter him up, 'the Corps requires a building in Cassel for its headquarters. As I heard the *Schoebecque* is presently unoccupied, it seems an ideal location.'

He thought about it for a moment. 'The *Schoebecque*. Yes, I see. You do realize, Major, that Field-Marshal Foch lived there for some time, and Field-Marshal Haig still resides there regularly?'

'Oh, really?' I replied.

Naturally, I'd hardly have gone to the bother of asking by name if I hadn't known. It's not the sort of name you stumble upon by chance. I was beginning to think Givens owed his puffy red face to something other than the heat.

Curiously, the topic of Haig's second residence came up in the train. Stranger still, one of the captains from the mounted rifles knew a great deal about it, including its name. That had put me onto the idea. The *Schoebecque* was one of the better-known buildings in town, aside from the city hall and Plumer's residence. It was therefore a terrific place for a high-profile headquarters which, when I thought about it, seemed to be precisely Captain Givens' concern, even if he worded it more diplomatically.

'I'm not convinced it would be entirely suitable for a corps head-quarters,' he began. 'There's not a great deal of space for offices. And the house is rather elegant.'

I brushed his objections away, with a nonchalant dash of my arm. 'Oh, that won't be a problem at all. General Currie runs a small, tight ship. A disciplined one, too. After all, Captain, it wouldn't be the Aussies moving in,' I said.

He wasn't entirely convinced. 'You must understand, sir, General Plumer would have to give his approval. And I'd have to consult with the local French officials,' he said, sighing. This was sounding better and better.

'Yes, Captain, I can certainly appreciate how frightfully difficult it is to arrange something like this. And at such very short notice. It's fortunate I was referred to you. I wouldn't know where to start, quite honestly. But I do know General Currie would be extremely pleased,' I said, and then paused. Pensively, I looked up, as if the thought had just struck me, and added, 'Apparently, General Currie and General Plumer got to know each other very well during the battle for Passchendaele. You likely know that already from General Plumer, I expect. Anyhow, the generals will have a lot to discuss when they see each other.' I hoped I hadn't overdone it.

'Well, sir, under the circumstances – it is unoccupied as you say – I believe I should be able to get it arranged,' said Givens.

'That's fantastic,' I said, beaming.

As I was leaving, nearly two hours later, I thanked Captain Givens profusely. We'd also created a detailed dispositions map, together with a colleague of his, outlining in bold red pen where each of the Corps' four divisions was to be deployed in the area of Kemmel Hill, with the Corps HQ at Cassel. I made a show of insisting copies be distributed as soon as possible, as widely as possible. It wasn't yet five o'clock and the whole Second Army would soon know we were coming. The way

I saw it, that was a necessary and important precursor to the whole German army knowing it.

Givens thoughtfully arranged a car to take me to Zuytpeene, a pleasantly short ten-minute drive from Cassel, thereby sparing me the unpleasantly long one-hour walk. My feet were feeling tender enough from the march earlier this morning. Post-march, and after two days of forced confinement in my boots, it would be wise to liberate them tonight in the open air.

Here in Cassel, they normally had few troubles from gas. They did get the occasional aerial bomb. The fighting and the mud were a very long way off, speaking figuratively, if not literally – Plumer probably saw it all out his window. And that was very obvious from the Second Army staff cars. They were as spotless as their drivers, a combination I'd seldom come across. It must be said this was the Imperial Army, not some wild tribe from the colonies. A well-mannered young private greeted me with exaggerated deference as he held open the big Vauxhall's door, allowing me to deposit myself on its spacious leather back seat. Painfully subservient or not, I'm sure I would have done exactly the same, knowing the alternative was employment in the trenches.

'X Corps headquarters in Zowt-pain, sir?' he asked. It was a lucky thing I didn't speak Flemish, his pronunciation might have left me mortally wounded.

'Yes, that's right. I do have one question, first. The *Schoebecque*. Is it far?' I said something like 'shoe beck', hoping he'd understand.

'You mean where Field-Marshal Haig stays?' Languages were not his thing, but he evidently knew his way around.

'Yes, indeed.'

'Oh, it's only a two-minute detour. Would you like to see it, sir?'

'Would I ever,' I said.

It was everything I expected. Frankly, I would have been disappointed if it hadn't been. It was a shame Currie wouldn't be moving in.

'Let me out here,' I said, 'I'm going to have a quick look around. I'll be back in a couple of minutes.'

Crowned by a bluish-grey attic, it was a large two-story brick house in an elongated square horseshoe form, built for a modest family of ten and their thirty closest relations, making it the perfect choice for a field-marshal in need of a bed in a strange town. The front of the house was walled off, creating an enclosed courtyard ideal for receiving important guests. Coincidently, the King had already dropped by, according to my driver.

I walked through the gate that hung invitingly open and headed for the door. 'Major MacPhail. What a remarkably curious place for you to turn up,' I heard from across the courtyard. The clipped nasal drawl was worryingly familiar and I turned. Colonel Whatley-Wigham from GHQ stood with his hands on his hips, frowning.

'Uh, yes, sir,' I replied. 'I'm making preparations ahead of our move here.' I might have said it was also odd seeing him, were he not a colonel, and of the 19th century mindset that subordinates speak only when addressed.

'And why is it, then, that I've heard no such thing? Tell me that, Major.'

'I wouldn't know, sir.'

He clasped his hands behind his back, as he strolled casually towards me, his nonchalance a cruel counterpoint to my own rigid discomfort. 'Could it be that you're simply slacking off?'

'Oh no, sir. Those of us in the *front lines* seldom have that opportunity.'

Whatley-Wigham looked as if I'd kicked him in the shins, which given half a chance, I would have loved to. 'I do say. Mark my words, Major, this won't be the last you hear of this,' he eventually sputtered, whereupon I hastily excused myself citing pressing matters, saluted, and made for the gate in a quick trot. The colonel's threat was vague, although the expression on his face was anything but, and I didn't want to stick around to find out the details. Sightseeing would have to wait.

We didn't dally and shortly thereafter we pulled into Zuytpeene, home to X Corps. Any delusions of grandeur I might have had were mercilessly swept aside when I noticed one of the sentries wave a hand in dismissal to his mate as we approached. He knew what the real brass looked like and, gleaming staff car or not, I didn't fit the description.

I hadn't come to X Corps on a whim, but nor did I know who its commander was, or much anything else about them. I was intending to visit the wireless units. They were sent here to add to the confusion. And I was planning on turning it up a notch.

At the canvas tent, where I was told they were set up, I ran into a private with a blue patch on his sleeve. There was no mistaking where he was from.

'Welcome, eh,' he said. 'I mean, sir.'

The blue patch was 2nd Division, and he'd recognised me as a fellow countryman, likely from the cap badge. He may have recognised the maple leaf, he was obviously shaky on the whole concept of ranks.

'Thanks, Private. I'm glad I found you. I'm Major MacPhail. Brigadier Webber from Corps headquarters sent me to check in on you.'

'There's not much to check on, sir, but we're in here,' he said, motioning at the tent from where he'd just exited. If there'd been any reason to doubt his word, the large aerial sticking through a small hole in the roof sealed the case.

'There's just the three of us at the moment. That's Flaherty over there,' he added. He pointed at a skinny youth seated at a makeshift table behind a large, black metal, hinged box. I assumed that was the wireless set. 'The corporal's off for some tea. Oh, and my name's Dunbar, sir.'

'Where's the rest?' I asked puzzled. I'm not sure what I'd been expecting, but three men and a box wasn't it.

He shook his head. 'As I told you, sir, we're the entire contingent at present. Another set is coming up later tonight from the 1st Division.'

I meant to reply until I heard, 'FUCKING HELL! Bloody no good teapot!' It came in an indignant roar from immediately outside the tent. The two privates were exchanging huge grins. The flap opened and I saw a battered tin teapot appear, followed closely by a fair-headed corporal in dark-stained trousers.

He looked ready to take a piece out of his two fellow signallers, when he spotted me.

'*Earl Grey* would be lovely, Corporal,' I said. I said it quickly, before he recovered his composure, which funnily enough now showed even fewer signs of recovering forthwith.

'Ah yes, sir,' he mumbled. 'I had some trouble getting the flap open.'

'So we gathered,' I said. 'As I told Dunbar and Flaherty here, I'm Major MacPhail. I've been sent here by Corps HQ.'

That seemed to stir him. 'Isn't that something,' he said. 'The CO and the lieutenant were here only yesterday, to look things over. And today you've arrived, sir.'

'And you're wondering why all the sudden interest in your work?'

He nodded. 'Exactly, sir. No offence. We're not typically on the *show and tell* tour when generals come visiting, that's all.'

'Well, leaving aside the fact I'm not a general, there's a very good explanation. Sit down and pour us some of that tea, and I'll explain. Assuming there's any left?'

I stuck to the basics, but the problem with this bunch was that they had more than a passing acquaintance with how army communications worked. And they weren't stupid. They were already mystified at their orders to send a stream of signals to receivers they weren't convinced even existed. Whatever happened to the timeless military tradition of mindlessly following orders, I wondered.

Webber was right; it was better I dish up some semi-plausible explanation than have them cook one up themselves, or worse, mull it over with half of X Corps.

'Consider this secret,' I said. 'It is not to be discussed with anyone else. Is that completely clear?' They nodded their assent. 'There is a serious concern at High Command that the Germans will renew their offensive here. I came with two battalions, but it could be some time before the Corps arrives in strength. Obviously, should the Germans attack before our divisions are in place there's a significant risk the lines won't hold. The intention is to bluff them that we're stronger than we are, so that doesn't happen. That's where you and a couple of wireless sets come in.'

They seemed to accept that. It wasn't altogether too far removed from the truth. Myself I was beginning to lose track. One moment we were coming to attack Mount Kemmel, the next we were on the defensive. If I kept at this sort of work for long, I'd soon have trouble telling left from right.

The signallers, however, were firmly onboard. Before long they were coming up with all sorts of suggestions of their own, many worthwhile, but a few were patently absurd. I had to rein in their boyish enthusiasm. 'You may be about to become the sloppiest signals unit on the Western Front,' I said, 'but don't get carried away, the Germans aren't fools.'

'Send this,' I said to Flaherty handing him the message I'd written down: TO 3RD DIVISION HEADQUARTERS. MOVE PROCEEDING WELL. 4TH CMR AND 27TH BTTN EN ROUTE. ANTICIPATE IMMINENT ARRIVAL ELEMENTS 1ST AND 4TH. SIGNED STAFF 3RD DIVISION.

'Would you like it encrypted, sir?' asked Dunbar.

'Encrypted? Oh no,' I replied. 'That won't be necessary. We'll let this one slip out. One other thing, while I think of it; use the old call signs occasionally. You know, CAO for Canadian Corps, and so forth.'

'But the Germans have cracked those, sir?'

'You don't say?' I responded. 'Until we're fully in position to repel any attack, it might be best if Fritz at least *thinks* we're ready. Don't you agree?' I said, with a wink. He nodded conspiratorially.

I had to repeat the whole spiel at eleven-thirty, after the promised contingent from the 1st Division reported in, and my encore performance went smoother still. It helped that Dunbar, Flaherty, and Corporal Hanson were there to participate, particularly when my knowledge of signalling and wireless sets came up short, which it did more than once. Finally, I left them, with a handful of messages I'd written as a souvenir, to throw in amongst all the others over the next couple of days. The local church bells sounded one lonely, clanging ring, and I headed off to the quarters that a thoughtful English staff officer had conjured out of nowhere for me.

I felt immodestly pleased with myself – I'd sowed enough confusion for one day. I'd almost managed to convince myself of our imminent presence at Kemmel Hill. I could only hope the Germans would be as confused by it all as our own troops seemed to be. And if they weren't, I had a few other ideas, just to make sure. Convincing the Germans we were in Flanders was one thing. How was Currie going to move the entire Corps into position without them noticing? The attack would need to follow quickly. No wonder Webber was in a hurry. Particularly if the attack was to come where I suspected it would.

CHAPTER 26

2nd of August, 1918
La Clytte sector, Kemmel Hill, Belgium

I glanced at my watch. The ruse I'd concocted would soon begin. The faces opposite me talked on, blissfully unaware I had motives ulterior to theirs. I felt a twinge of guilt, but there was no choice. Webber had made that abundantly clear. Absolutely *no one* was to know.

Strictly speaking, we weren't in the Ypres Salient, although the approaches to Kemmel Hill looked, and felt, well-nigh identical to everything I remembered of it. It was raining, and had done so for most of the previous night. The front line was a miserable wet, muddy blubber. You don't forget the mud, or the smell. I certainly couldn't.

Unlike the elaborate trench systems further south in France, the front line here was little more than a patchwork of holes, humble outposts, and make-shift dug-outs of timbers and dirt. They weren't quite Passchendaele's moonscape of shell-holes, and they kept you out of sight – even if their defensive value was decidedly questionable. What there was, had been hastily dug in the frantic rear-guard action after the Germans successfully took Kemmel Hill from the French in April. It was the German's second attempt in less than two weeks, and the Boche's perseverance – pigheadedness, really – paid off in the end. I groaned at the thought.

'Sir?' Captain Poyser, was staring at me.

Lost in my meditation, I looked up, startled. 'Oh,' I said. 'You know, Poyser, I hadn't realized what a blow it was to lose Kemmel Hill until I actually saw it. It's one thing to read the reports, or the newspapers, but quite another to see it at first hand.'

'Tell me about it, sir. It's terribly hazardous here.'

'Which is why the first words I heard after arriving were, "Keep your head down, sir".' Poyser nodded. He'd only been here a day or two, but he knew all too well.

The reason was obvious. A thin coarse stubble of destroyed trees and assorted structures was all that remained to enliven the stark flatness of the Flemish earth. Bulging out of it was the shorn, dark pimple of Mount Kemmel.

I'd seen it from miles off as I approached in the open-top staff car – the rain, obligingly, held off on the first day of my return to Flanders. From the hill you could view Ypres and Poperinghe to the northwest and, with a good pair of field-glasses, look far into the Salient. In the other direction was France. To observe what the 4th CMR was up to in its line, less than a mile from the crest of the hill, you could skip the field-glasses, altogether. When I thought about it, you could probably skip an eye or two, as well.

Unfortunately, as far as I could tell, the current crew of Huns manning the hill were anatomically complete. There was positively no belittling their eyes, nor their artillery skills. Even poking a hand out of a hole resulted in a torrent of shells raining down in your vicinity. I began to understand why the line was in such horrific condition. Working at it in daylight was akin to suicide, and the night shift had all the visceral thrill of being dropped into a lion's cage at dinner time. It was a shame the city work crews back home couldn't experience it – I'd often joked their biggest worry revolved around how to bridge the period between morning coffee and lunch.

Seeing Kemmel, it wasn't hard to envisage why Field-Marshals Foch and Haig wanted it back – badly. Happily, whatever rumours to the contrary I was spreading, it wouldn't be our job to do so. At least not straight away.

La Clytte was a hamlet to the south of Ypres, a few miles under it, at the mouth of the Salient. Not that there was much of the Salient left, not after the second of the Germans' spring offensives at the River

Lys. When Ypres was threatened with encirclement, General Plumer had sounded the retreat. The great bulge in the line around Ypres to the north had shrunk as fast as a balloon with a pin applied to it. Three years of war, countless attacks and counter-attacks, more dead friends than I cared to think about, and the front was little different than it was in May 1915, right after the second battle of Ypres. I was still alive, and that left me with the dubious privilege of being able to contemplate what the point of it all was, not that any answer was forthcoming, least of all a satisfactory one.

Nobody wasted a second on the relief; certainly not the departing 15th Hampshires who cleared out in record time, thanking their lucky stars for this unexpected blessing. The 4th CMR was already in the line. It was only a few hundred yards in front of La Clytte in the direction of the hill. A little further south, the boys of the 27th from Winnipeg were manning the trenches near a village called Locre.

Near Arneke another diversion was also underway. The 1st and the 4th Casualty Clearing Stations were setting up. I regretted not visiting. With their sea of red-cross-emblazoned canvas a CCS was hard for any German airman to miss, errant or otherwise. Presumably that was why they were given the laborious task of packing up, moving north, and pitching their tents and gear in French Flanders.

Somebody was being very clever. You didn't require a casualty clearing station, let alone two of them, if you weren't expecting casualties. And the Germans knew as well as we did that the surest reason to expect a lot of casualties, was to plan an attack. One plus one is an attack on Kemmel, you could say. My guess – more a dead certainty at this stage – was that Currie and Webber were fervently hoping Fritz would conclude exactly that. For if we were attacking Kemmel, we couldn't possibly be attacking somewhere else, wherever that might be – although I had my suspicions. Webber had made it clear that my task here was to add fuel to this wee fire, if not start it outright.

That wasn't why I regretted not visiting a CCS. In good conscience, there was little I could contribute. No, my lament was altogether more mundane: nurses. My experience with nurses was brief, mercifully brief viewed from one angle, woefully brief from another. I hadn't much reason to see any nursing sisters and when I had, I was in pain and half-comatose, and she was as approachable as the north face of Mount Robson, and not nearly as attractive.

Women are a topic soldiers are always on about. Seeing as how nurses are some of the few women you run across anywhere near a battlefield, they're never far from anybody's mind. I'd heard some lurid tales. The wounded who returned sang their praises virtually to a man, such that you almost forgot it was a hospital they stayed at, and not the Etaples Country Club and Resort. I wasn't so taken in by these vivid portrayals of clear-eyed goddesses that I forgot there was a lot of creative embellishment at work. Still, I would have liked the chance to visit on my own accord, to see for myself. Perhaps over tea, in a dry tent, I could have gotten to know one or two.

DuBois was going to mock me mercilessly when he learned how I botched my once in a lifetime opportunity. He would make it sound like the title of some heartbreaking French romantic novel I'd never read, but should have.

Rather than being at Arneke with the nurses, I was at B Company headquarters with some soldiers, trying not to get too wet, and feeling uneasy. There was a lot that could go wrong tonight.

The most impressive thing about B Company headquarters was its name. Otherwise, it was a flimsy lean-to, held together by a handful of scavenged wood beams and a sheet of corrugated steel. Rain was driving down on the roof, and it had sprung a leak or twenty. Despite the layer of dirt and assorted flotsam on top, which had since dissolved into a mud-like stew, the rain made a fearsome clatter.

'It's a bit like being under the shower,' I remarked. 'More water than most showers, but the same general idea.'

There were chuckles from the others – three officers, and a sergeant. Astonishingly, they'd all squeezed into the HQ with its table, handful of chairs and a few cots. It wasn't large.

'Will it be dark enough, sir?' asked the lieutenant. Lieutenant Knowles had been on raids before; however, this was to be his first in command, and he was noticeably edgy. So was I, and I was just along to "observe". Edgy was understating it. The pit of my stomach was filled with a heavy numbness of the kind when your nerves completely seize up, and before the adrenaline takes command. Raids were hardly a novelty to me, but I don't think I'd ever be like the scouts, for whom it seemed second nature. In the darkness, you never knew where your foot would land next, or what that little hole or rise in the earth might reveal. Every sound was amplified a thousand times and, regardless of how dark it was, I always felt like I was walking with a spotlight trained on me with a Boche gunner leering wickedly down his sights. I was resolved to keeping a stiff upper lip.

'Oh, I don't think with this weather you need worry too much about the light,' I responded. 'By ten o'clock, it'll be plenty dark, and there's no danger of moonlight tonight.'

Captain Dixon was staring at him, probably inwardly questioning his choice of leaders. Outwardly, he said, 'I know you'll do fine, Knowles.' It was precisely what needed to be said, and that said more about Dixon than Knowles.

This was the culmination of another of my "brilliant" ideas. Somehow, they always seemed more brilliant in the afterglow of their births, than on the eve of the events themselves. It was to be a raid on the German lines a few hundred yards ahead of us, ostensibly to get identifications. No one from either side would think twice about that. We were forever sending out soldiers to grab prisoners, or anything else that might give a clue to which unit was positioned opposite us. Myself, I must have initiated twenty in the tense months of March and April alone. The Germans were also at it, all too frequently. Only, unbeknownst to the rest of the patrol, I had a wholly different scheme cooked up.

'The least they could have done was to make some identifications before they bolted,' lamented Captain Poyser, referring to the 15th Hampshires. He was looking tired, damp and not especially comfortable, even though the rest of his evening was destined to be spent safe, if not dry, at HQ. I could have set the record straight, by piping up that identifications were the last thing I was concerned with. Instead I bit my tongue.

At 10.03 p.m. – I was watching the seconds tick by – I motioned to Knowles, and said, 'Shall we?'

It was time. We stood up, shook hands with Dixon and Poyser, and together with the sergeant, exited the dug-out. By sheer chance I avoided one of the half-full buckets on the dirt floor that Dixon and Poyser had artfully placed here and there, two rows deep – a desperate attempt to prevent the rain from transforming it into a bog. For obvious reasons, they kept the dug-out as dark as a tomb.

Outside, the rain had thankfully abated, but the wind had picked up, ensuring it stayed every bit as miserable. As I'd predicted it was indeed dark, not that I reckoned there'd be many Germans glued to their posts staring into No-Man's-Land in this gale. Of the hill there was no sign. Then I saw the flash of a German gun far off in the distance and it lit up the rain-streaked horizon in a yellowy-red glare. For a fleeting instant, the hill stood menacingly silhouetted before us, until darkness returned.

We reached the others, who were huddling in a small line of trench, barely big enough to hold them all. There were eight. Including the lieutenant, the sergeant and me, that made for a party of eleven, or *dix et demi* as DuBois would have wittily put it.

Lieutenant Knowles was bent over, whispering instructions to the two sergeants – it could have been shouting, the howl of the wind was all I heard. The second sergeant had been waiting with the troops. Soon, I was following them out of the trench, crouched over low, and walking foot by measured foot into No-Man's-Land, towards one of the abandoned Nissen huts I knew was our first objective.

What was today No-Man's-Land had not so very long ago been the rear lines of Mount Kemmel: *our* rear lines. Old Nissen huts and habitations littered the landscape, like broken bottles strewn carelessly over the grass after an unruly summer party.

When we reached the Nissen hut, we squatted outside for a minute, waiting, while one of the sergeants and two men entered the ragged black hole that had once been a doorway. Hearing nothing, we followed them inside. The air was damp and heavy, and smelled like shit, which there must have been in abundance judging by the swarm of flies. I saw one of the finned, blue-grey French helmets lying in the corner with a gaping hole in it. Its owner was presumably one of the bodies we'd passed along the way. The French had had a tough go of it at Kemmel. There was no sign of anything German.

'Not much here, sir,' whispered Lieutenant Knowles.

'No,' I said. 'Let's move on.'

As we turned to leave, I straightened my right arm, and held it parallel against my body so that my balled fist rubbed tight on my thigh. In it was a brass-coloured metal badge. I let it slip to the ground. It landed with a faint thump.

The badge was molded into the form of an ornately antlered bull moose's head, fearlessly staring down from his mount on the letters: 4 CMRR Overseas. I'd surreptitiously snatched it when I was visiting battalion stores earlier this afternoon. Ever since, I'd had the conscience of a remorseful criminal. However, you didn't need to be a Prussian aristocrat, an *Oberst* in the intelligence service, or a combination of both, to decipher what it was. As clues go, this one came with its own instruction book – assuming they found it. With the smell in here, I would have stayed well away myself.

In well-spaced single file, we slowly edged through the mud, trailing the two scouts who'd gone out in front, moving in the direction of the German lines. There was a decent map of the line in this sector and we had a very good idea where the enemy should be. With this visibility, following the map to get there was going to be no easy thing; I could barely make out two men ahead of me. Wetness aside, the weather was in our favour. If we couldn't see, at least Fritz couldn't either.

Our pace slowed to a crawl, and the men were bent over almost horizontally, their Lee-Enfields grasped tightly at the ready – in two hands – and I quickly saw why. The entrance to a dug-out jutted from the mire less than a hundred yards away.

There was a muffled crack. It was a rifle shot, and not one of ours. Then we heard a cry of '*Englischer!*' I had to fight the urge not to shout, "Wrong army", were I not fighting to remove my Webley from its holster.

Suddenly, there was action everywhere. The soldiers in front rushed the dug-out. It was the reflexive instinct of men acting on their experience and training, and buoyed by the same rush of adrenaline coursing through me. I broke into a run.

Half the squad had already entered the dug-out. The others were on one knee, their rifles aimed outwards. Together they covered an arc in the direction of the hill, now virtually in front of our noses. I pushed through and clambered down the half dozen or so steps of the rough wooden ladder.

'There were only a couple of them,' said the sergeant from company HQ. He stood relaxed. Casually, he was leaning on his weapon as if it was a walking stick, and he'd returned from a stroll. 'We saw them high-tailing it out of here.' The Germans had wisely scrammed at the first sign of trouble.

'Alright,' I said. 'Let's search it quickly and go. Before this bunch returns with half the German army in tow.'

'Have a look here, sir.' It was Lieutenant Knowles. He was holding a bag. I peered into it. Seeing only some unrecognisable item of clothing and what looked like a can of food, I nodded.

'Take it with you,' I said. 'We can search it later. What else is there?'

Other than a couple of potato mashers – stick grenades to the uninitiated – a rifle, and two *stahlhelms* with no markings, there was nothing of interest. Not much in the way of food either I noticed. The Navy blockade of Germany was having its effects.

'Take the grenades and the rifle,' Knowles said to the sergeant. 'No sense leaving those here.'

'Lieutenant!' A soldier was leaning down, calling through the entrance hole. 'There's a lot of activity out here, sir.'

'Okay,' said Knowles, 'let's get a move on then.'

Awkwardly tucked away, under the inner liner of my trench coat near my armpit, was a canvas tote bag, containing a tattered gas mask. There was a serial number on it, stamped prominently in black letters. It was from a battalion soldier who went missing in July. The quarter-master had told me when I'd asked him for one to "replace" mine, and he'd offered up this. I rolled the mask up as best I could, but its bulge left me looking like an ageing prize fighter with his arms posed on his hips and immortalized in marble. I felt gawkily self-conscious. Fortunately, it was dark.

I undid a few buttons on my coat and, for the show, flapped my arms to shake off the water. I felt the bag slide down to my waist where I caught it with my hand, halting its descent. When I saw the sergeant and lieutenant turn and line up behind each other to climb out, I let go. It tumbled to my feet. In some ways it was a pure gamble. I was hoping the Germans were as tenaciously efficient as everybody assumed, including me. If they weren't, the message was as good as lost on your typical twenty-year old private from Oberhausen; he was uninterested in anything that wasn't edible. On the other hand, the Prussian intelligence *Oberst* from Potsdam – he ought to recognize it for what it was. More importantly, he'd recognize from whom it was, and ring the alarm bells. I always found that to be a fascinating aspect of the human mind; the more you work on something, the more you believe your own conclusions – I'd just have to keep my fingers crossed Germans weren't so very different.

Quickly, I moved over behind the sergeant, brushing up against the back of him as if to hurry him along, preventing him from turning for one final look behind. As the last man, I clambered out of the dug-out.

The troop was moving at a brisk walking pace, which is fast when every footstep sinks for a few seconds after it hits the ground, and requires a good yank to get it out again. All the while we were trying to avoid stumbling into a hole; or over wire, or a body, or any one of the many other obstacles that clutter Flanders fields these days. We were spread out, and keeping low, not tempting fate by offering an easy target to some eagle-eyed German machine gunner.

'Any flares?' I asked one of the soldiers, as I caught up to him. I was puffing from the exertion and the excitement.

'No, sir, not seen any,' he replied. I was worried they'd call down an SOS barrage. On second thought, it was too close to the front slope of the hill and their own positions. *Luckily*. They might, however, shell No-Man's-Land and our lines. That would be messy.

I needn't have worried. The German artillery men weren't sufficiently bothered to rouse themselves, and brave the violent gusts of rain, which were blowing down like sneezes from some foul-tempered giant above. They were leaving it to the poor slobs from the infantry to investigate. Certain things in an army were universal, no matter where it was from.

'I'm sorry, sir, we didn't get those identifications you wanted,' said Knowles, after we reached our lines. He was taking stock of our paltry loot. He looked downcast.

I was pleased as punch. I'd done what I wanted to and no one was hurt. I tried not to let it show. 'Don't worry, Lieutenant. You and the men did great. Sometimes you need a little luck on these raids. We're all back in one piece, and that's a success where I come from. There's always the next time.'

CHAPTER 27

3rd of August, 1918
Dug-out in La Clytte sector, Kemmel Hill, Belgium

A swarthy, beady-eyed German in a *Pickelhaube* and moustache was standing in front of me, his bayonet pointed straight at my heart.

I was pouring sweat. Then, in a flash, it came to me – where I'd seen him last.

He was a carbon copy of the fiendish Hun depicted on the late 1914 propaganda posters. They'd popped up everywhere, not long after the Imperial German Army was unleashed on "little old" Belgium in August that year. At the time, I'd laughingly dismissed the childishly exaggerated images and bombastic text. You had to be a pretty simple soul to fall for that. Or so I thought. One way or another, those posters must have left a deeper impression than I thought possible. If I'd ever read any psychology – this new-fangled science of the mind – I might have known why. On the other hand, its leading light, Dr. Freud, would have a tough time explaining why I was awake at this hour.

My Borgel put it at a little after four. I looked at it twice to make absolutely sure.

I can't remember the last time I woke so early, voluntarily at least. A Moaning Minnie roaring overhead was ordinarily no more than a signal to shift sides. I glanced over at my companions, Dixon and Poyser. They were still lost to the world.

Last night I returned to their little dug-out, intending to briefly relay how the raid went, and then carry on to the drier surroundings of the derelict battalion farmhouse at La Clytte. Only one thing led to another, which led to finishing an unfinished bottle of Scotch, an animated discussion and, eventually, a late bedtime. They offered the hospitality of a cot and I gratefully accepted.

I closed my eyes. Usually I found it to be a fail-safe method to fall asleep – but not this morning. I tossed and turned in the small crude bed. It must have made quite a commotion for Poyser grunted irritably, which took some doing, as I'd already discovered. There were too many thoughts tumbling around in my head.

Webber gave me an important task, but I felt hopelessly out of touch. I was on my own, and it was up to me to get it done. I didn't know what the division or the Corps were doing, let alone where they were. The only information on the war was from *The Times* and the *Daily Mail*, and they were a week old. It was as if I was marooned at the North Pole. Only it was raining, so I knew categorically it had to be Ypres.

I was also curious whether we had any new intelligence. Were my exertions in Flanders being noticed by the Germans? And if they were, was Fritz convinced the Corps was poised to attack Kemmel? Perhaps he was scratching his head in confusion. Or had he simply waved it off as the hoax that it really was? I didn't know. When in doubt, keep going, I figured. So that was the plan for today. I had a few good ideas still.

However, the next thing I knew I heard Dixon and Poyser noisily rummaging around, and I saw that it was five-thirty.

I stifled a groan, or meant to.

Apparently, Dixon heard it, for he said, 'Rise and shine, Major. A brand new day is dawning.' I hated morning people – even if he meant it sarcastically – and I wasn't sure he did.

'You two look the picture of health and happiness,' I grumbled.

Dixon put an arm around Poyser, smiled, and said, 'Aren't we now?' I laughed.

From the absence of water dripping through the holes in the roof I surmised that the rain had ceased. It looked very dark, but five-thirty in the morning or not, Dixon and Poyser didn't seem inclined to raid their stock of candles to reinforce the lone flickering example sticking out of a bottle on the table – they'd acclimatized to their new lives as cave dwellers.

There were probably countless worthy reasons why I should get out of bed, only they weren't coming to me at the moment. I gave my face a vigorous rub with the palms of my hands. That sometimes does the trick, but it fell short this morning. I was still totally bagged, so I put my head back on the pillow and listened dreamily to the two captains gossiping.

'Whatever happened with that rumour about the abandoned guns? You know, the ones supposedly abandoned at Nameless Farm?' Poyser was asking.

Dixon half laughed and half snorted. 'I sent MacLachlan and Coxford out yesterday to investigate. You were at Battalion HQ at the time. Turns out it was absolutely true. Amazing when you think about it. There's a constant shortage of guns and we find four 18-pounders, two of them brand spanking new, lined up and abandoned in some hedge.'

'That's a fine place for four guns,' Poyser said.

'That's what I thought too. I informed Colonel Patterson and headquarters, and they swore they passed it on to the division, straight away. I even offered our assistance to man-handle them back.'

Despite myself I was getting interested in this tale. 'You'll have to help me. Which division is the battalion now serving under?' I interjected from the peanut gallery, annex cot. 'I've been on the move every day, and I'm having trouble keeping track of which foot is left, let alone anything else.'

'The 41st,' said Dixon, 'with Swanky Sid... sorry... Major-General Sir Sidney Lawford at the helm.'

'And what happened then?'

'Oh, nothing.' Dixon had the most expressive eyebrows I've ever seen, only now they remained as immobile as the bear-skin hatted guardsmen at Buckingham Palace to which they bore a definite resemblance.

'What do you mean, nothing?'

'Division didn't seem particularly interested. The guns are still there.'

Poyser, who was a lot more awake than I was, looked incredulous. 'You mean to say they lost four field guns, and they can't even be bothered to let us collect them, after we found them again?'

'No,' said Dixon. 'Apparently not.'

'Don't be too harsh, Sid was likely sleeping in,' I said. I looked at my watch, terribly envious of Swanky Sid's hours. It was a quarter to six. The sun wouldn't be up for another half hour, or so.

I tried to freshen up a little. With all the buckets around there was no shortage of water. In Ypres, provided you had a bucket, there never was. 'God, I'd die for some coffee,' I said, after a spell.

'Yeah, I wouldn't mind a cup myself,' said Dixon. 'I'll see if I can round some up.'

'Let me go. I'm not exactly gainfully employed here,' I said.

And that was how it came to be that I was 300 yards away, trudging back to La Clytte and the battalion field kitchen, when the shell hit.

I heard it coming.

One moment it was a faint wailing whistle I barely noticed, the next it was positively screaming in my ear. I was enough of a veteran to know from the sound that it would likely land a safe distance behind me. So I didn't bother to sprawl prone, or even turn. That gave you away as a fresh recruit faster than the absence of dirt under your nails, or starched creases in your pants. Maybe I was simply too weary and fatalistic to make the effort – that's something else that marks the old veterans.

The blast from the high explosive detonated with a powerful deep CRUMP.

I was expecting it. I even braced myself. All the same, the concussion's force surprised me. It reverberated against my upright body as if somebody had placed an unfelt hand on the small of my back and then, abruptly, and forcibly, shoved.

What I didn't reckon on, deep in my sleepy reverie, was what was behind me. I walked on. The awful realization hit, a fraction of a second later – sparked by a sudden vision of young Philips on the Spur. I pivoted, every sense in my body pulsating. B Company HQ!

My stomach plummeted, as from a cliff, while the blood rushed from my head in a sickening whoosh that left me feeling faint. I hadn't walked far, but the dug-out was hard to see. No, I thought – my eyes straining in the pre-dawn gloom – there *was* something. I looked closer. Only there wasn't. The dug-out was gone – obliterated. The ramshackle roof had disappeared, and one of the wooden beams that supported it was sticking up almost vertically.

The dark colossus of Mount Kemmel was dimly visible, and the first shy rays of light were peeking over the top. Another shell detonated nearby in a thunderous eruption, a column of oily smoke and a shower of mud spewing outwards. Vaguely, I was conscious of the roar of other shells tearing like express trains through the air. I began running, pell-mell, as if my life depended on it, back to the dug-out.

The dug-out had become a crater. 'Dixon! Poyser!' I screamed, and then again. Around me, I could hear the explosions, and felt the land shudder as the bombardment ripped into the line. Distractedly, I felt the earth raining down on my helmet from a blast many yards away and smelled the coarse pungent odour of the explosives. It was from one of the howitzers, the 5.9s, I found myself thinking, mechanically analysing the shot. I felt no fear.

By some terrible fluke the shell had hit the dug-out practically dead-on. And then I heard a moan. It came from a spot to the side of the crater. I looked closer and I saw a man lying prone. As I approached, I made out Captain Poyser, covered in dirt and debris, and the contents of his make-shift shelter in the mud.

'Thank God!' I cried. 'You're alright.'

He moaned louder this time. He may have been alive; he wasn't alright.

'STRETCHER!' I shouted, 'STRETCHER!' And I ran to him. Frantically, I tore at the thick plank mired in the wreckage that pinned him to the ground. It was rough and sharp, and I could feel it cutting in my hands as I swung it off him.

I grasped the hand he extended between mine, and squeezed it. 'You'll be fine,' I intoned, 'you'll be fine.' I said this looking into his eyes, not knowing if it was truth or fiction I was selling. He had a placid serenity to him I found worrisome, yet his eyes were bright and vibrant and alive, and I was encouraged by this.

'Sir, we heard you shouting.' It was a pair of soldiers from the company, from one of the holes in the line out towards the hill. They looked down at Poyser and, as if for the first time, saw the crater where their company headquarters had been. Either they were sleeping, or keeping their own heads down, when the explosion went off. The tall one shook his head in disbelief. The other said, 'Shit,' in a soft awestruck voice. It was a well-chosen word. It described the situation better than a thousand pictures could have.

'And Captain Dixon? Did you find him, sir?' asked the first.

'No. Not yet. I will though. You take care of Captain Poyser. Get him back to La Clytte. And hurry now. But as carefully as you can. And send some help.'

'Yes, sir, we'll get him back. Don't worry, sir,' one of the soldiers said. They stood astride him and, with my help, we gently lifted his body so they could each clamp an arm under his and around his back. He was in pain, but his limbs were attached, and I had the impression he'd be okay. I squeezed his hand again, nodded to them, and watched briefly as they hurried in the direction of the rear lines.

But where was Dixon? I stumbled down into the crater and up the other side. And then I saw him: Tom Dixon, the fearless commander of B Company of the 4th Canadian Mounted Rifles, decorated at the battles of Mount Sorrel and Vimy Ridge, and a veteran of untold others – a survivor of three and a half years of the most horrible war in the history of man. He lay crumpled under one of the wooden beams.

For some reason my mind returned to the train and our late-night talk; of the wife he wanted to find, and nervously questioned whether he ever would, and the children he desired and so very much deserved. It streaked through my head in an instant, shorter than the flash from a shell flaring and then extinguishing, and it melted my defences, the mental armour all soldiers build for themselves.

Of his body below the shoulders I could see virtually nothing, save for a solitary arm twisting unnaturally upwards and a hand reaching out to the sky from under the rubble, as if seeking deliverance. The back of his head rested cruelly on the earth but his face was unscathed. His open eyes, always so full of life, stared emptily. Perversely, he had a look of peace to him. Even in death his full black eyebrows still teased playfully. I knew already it was a scene I would bear forever.

I collapsed to the ground and sat there. I hadn't ordered the 4th CMR to Ypres. I hadn't sent them to Kemmel, or put the two captains and their company into the line in the shadow of the hill. I hadn't fired the shell. Yet General Lipsett had called it my deception, and I had played my small part. Now, through some fortune I neither understood, nor asked for, I was alive. And Tom Dixon was dead. Justice may not have survived the horrors of the Western Front, but guilt had. As had the guilty – that was the only possible explanation for why we were still at it.

Many minutes passed. The bombardment ceased. The sky was a hazy grey and the light was brightening fast when I felt an insistent tapping on my shoulder. I don't know how long he'd been standing there, addressing me in vain, before he gathered his courage. It was a battalion runner. His helmet was strapped tightly under his chin, the rim low over his eyes, and he had an expression of dead seriousness sandwiched in between the two. 'Major MacPhail?' he asked, when he got my attention.

Grimly I nodded.

The runner handed me a folded piece of paper from the leather message bag hung diagonally across his chest.

I read it quickly. Caught off guard, and not understanding it at first – there couldn't have been more than two or three lines – I read it again.

The runner stood waiting, watching me expectantly, and sensing I guess that his patience would be rewarded. The devastation could scarcely have escaped his attention.

I squeezed my brow with my hand in contemplation as I'm wont to do, and held it there for a long while. When I lowered it, I could see it was smeared in blood. The runner was staring at me. I must have looked a proper sight. Finally, I cleared my throat and said, 'Could you send an acknowledgement, please?'

After he left I glanced down at the sheet again: YOU ARE TO PROCEED IMMEDIATELY TO DIVISIONAL HEADQUARTERS, the first line began – harshly precise and unequivocal – the language of picking yourself up and getting on with it. Tom Dixon's funeral would be tomorrow. It didn't feel right that I wouldn't be attending, to pay him my last respects. Right or not, the war was calling, and it was doing so in ugly, blaringly shrill notes. It wasn't the *Last Post* but, in many ways, it seemed to me it ought to be. I would have to say my good-byes here and now.

CHAPTER 28

4th of August, 1918
Château Dury, Dury, France

It took some considerable doing simply to find divisional headquarters.

I stumbled to La Clytte and gave a terse and sombre report to the battalion commander and his staff, before solemnly taking my leave to walk to the 41st Division. Once there, I must have made a sorry impression, for a kind-hearted staff officer offered me a car and a driver when I explained my orders. Even after I told him I wasn't sure where my division was presently located, he waved off my objections with a breezy nonchalance, chortling something about the driver wasting away the day, otherwise.

'Where to, sir?' the driver asked in a thick Scottish lilt. He wasn't taking it personally, the fact I was depriving him of his day of blissful indolence. Neither of us could then have imagined he would tour a broad swath of France before eventually returning, let alone the adventure he was unwittingly enrolling in. But then, anything was better than here; Hell itself would be an improvement on the Salient.

'Arras,' I said. 'Hermaville, to be precise, although it's only a few miles from there. I can direct you when we get closer to the city.' It was a gamble, but I had no better idea where to start than the last place I knew our headquarters to be. And if the division had moved, the new inhabitants would surely know where to.

The driver was friendly and, on any other day, I would have enjoyed chatting with him. There's a lot you can learn from a soldier, and especially a soldier assigned as a driver at a divisional HQ. His name was Donnan McNally and he was as Scottish as they come. How could he not be with a name like that? Before the war his parents had moved to some place in middle England; Surrey, I believe he said. Eventually, discouraged by my tepid responses, it dawned on him that my mind was elsewhere, and he gave up his good-hearted attempts at conversation.

That left me to sit and brood in the back seat of yet another battered Ford Model T staff car. I'm not exactly the brooding type; I shy more to the glass half-full side of the spectrum, I think, but this morning I yearned to brood. Also, I wondered why I was being summarily recalled.

When we eventually arrived at the Château d'Hermaville, it looked every bit as impressive as I remembered. I saw immediately from the flags that hung listlessly from their poles that a new group had moved in. Nevertheless, it gave McNally and I a chance for a hurried bite, while I asked the rotund and impeccably polite sergeant who offered assistance if, by chance, he knew where my division was.

'Hornoy-le-Bourg, sir. That's what their orders said.'

'Where?' I exclaimed, not daring to repeat the mangled mix of French and English consonants he'd just sputtered.

'Horny, we call it, sir.' That I understood.

I smiled weakly. 'Sounds wonderful, Sergeant, but I have no idea where or what that is.' Normally, I would have said something like: 'Aren't we all, Sergeant,' but I wasn't in the mood for petty jokes.

He pulled out a map and after studying it briefly, stabbed his finger down, and the figurative lightbulb went off in my head. 'There it is, sir.'

Amiens! It was behind Amiens.

I knew it. Fourth Army terrain. Not far from where the battle of the Somme was fought two years ago. More recently the Germans beat a massive concave into our lines there in their quest to seize the city in the spring. The attack was to be near Amiens. That mysterious conference I stumbled upon at Flixecourt wasn't a coincidence, after all – not that I ever seriously thought it was. And the meeting on the Orange Hill attack; it was an elaborate charade. Currie and Webber had played everyone masterfully. With all this secrecy, something very big was going on.

It took us the better part of three hours to reach Hornoy only to discover, upon arrival, that the division had picked up and moved again. This time to Dury. Dury was to the east of Hornoy they told us, nestled up against the southernmost extremities of the city of Amiens. We were calmly assured it wasn't far, only twenty or twenty-five miles, an easy drive of less than an hour. As it turned out, it was much longer. It didn't help that we ran out of petrol not far from the city.

The small roads were a tangle of lefts, rights, stops and starts, and even with a rudimentary sketch of the area, we got lost more than once. Several times we halted, and asked for directions from one of the traffic control men, who began appearing with startling regularity as we approached Amiens, now an empty and desolate place. They stood wearily, miserably shuffling their feet, without shelter from the frequent showers. They were only too happy to exchange a few words to relieve the boredom. The role they were destined to fulfil, soon became increasingly clear.

The roads themselves weren't excessively crowded, but the country-side was positively swarming with life, chock full of men and horses and motor vehicles of every possible description. We passed a small pond where horses by their hundreds stood good-naturedly waiting for a drink. There wasn't a stand of trees, or a small crop of buildings that had escaped the olive green and accompanying accoutrements of war. They all appeared to be ours, from the Corps.

'I've never seen anything like it, sir,' said McNally, with some astonishment after we passed another grove bursting with soldiers. 'There's an entire army packed away down here.'

'Yes,' I said. 'It's stunning. I'm at a loss for words.' I would have explained just how incredible that was, only he was a private, and I still didn't feel much like talking.

'What do you suppose it's all for, sir?'

I straightened up and, with mock seriousness, looked forward so he could see me plainly in the rear-view mirror. 'I could tell you, but then you'd have to swear an oath,' I said. He smiled uncertainly.

I was only half kidding. This was definitely no joke, of that I was certain. I was equally certain that a gregarious Scottish private from an Imperial division in the Salient didn't mesh well with the extraordinary secrecy shrouding this operation. Sort of like a match doesn't mix well with a vat of petrol.

Darkness was falling by the time we arrived in the deserted little settlement of Dury. We bumped along the cobblestone streets, eyeing desolate and abandoned houses to either side, their grey walls forming long canyons along the road, interrupted only by shuttered windows and double-chained gates. The war had done Dury little good.

The château of red and white brick – although it would be this morning before I could properly admire its pretty lines – was a welcoming beacon, despite the blackout curtains. My heart leapt as we pulled around the semi-circular drive and I spotted the familiar blue-grey patch of my division on a soldier loitering outside the front door, smoking a cigarette. We'd finally arrived. I was relieved.

I arranged a bunk for Private McNally, who must have been as knackered as I was, and found one of my own. I plunged into it, a lust for sleep possessing me that was exceptional even by my sorrowful standards.

This morning, I awoke with a start. I'd slept like a log and I was groggy when I came to, my bearings way out of kilter. A shout – probably from a soldier calling his mate – had shocked me awake, and for a dazed, confused moment I was in the dug-out. When I discovered I wasn't, I was astonished to discover my brow was moist.

After I rose, I ambled over to the main building in search of the officers' mess and some food to quell the ominous rumblings coming from my stomach. I was starving. I'd barely eaten in the past day. Almost immediately I ran into a familiar face. 'Sir, welcome back!' said Smith, grinning exuberantly and making me feel like a long-lost uncle. It was hard not to feel touched.

I gave him an affectionate clap on the shoulder and smiled back at him. 'Thanks, Lieutenant,' I said. 'You can't begin to imagine how glad I am to be back. How were things here?'

'Busy. We've had little rest since you left, sir. We moved a day later and have been on the go ever since. We only settled in here yesterday. There's a big operation coming – I'm sure of that. Though they've told us nothing. Only that we're here to support the French at Reims, or maybe the Fourth Army, or French First Army, near Amiens.' Fortunately, he paused to draw breath. 'If you could have seen it, sir, the entire Corps was on the move. Something very big is going on and I don't think it's got anything to do with Reims.'

After what I'd seen yesterday, I had no trouble believing that. In fact, anything else would have sounded ludicrous. I shrugged and said, 'And do you know if we're moving again?'

'Not that I've heard.'

'And any preparations for an attack?'

'That's the strange thing, sir, there's been no reconnaissance, no urgent requests for identifications, no detailed maps, nothing. And nobody seems to know anything.'

'You're obviously new to the army, Smith,' I said. I knew full well he wasn't. 'It's a nice place this,' I added, after a bit, looking around the ornate hallway.

'It certainly is,' he replied. I could tell from the way the corners of his lips twisted, and his eyes sparkled, that he had something else to say. I didn't have to wait for long. 'You'll enjoy the irony of this, sir. Until recently this very château was the headquarters of the Fifth Army under General Gough. At least until he got the sack.'

'Was that before or after he'd mulched through his army?' I asked, meaning it rhetorically. I couldn't help it; the man brought out the worst in me.

A hundred years from now some historian, chasing glory of his own from the gloriously safe confines of his study, might attempt to burnish all the reputations this war had tarnished. Gough was only one name he'd come across. For me it was a name that personified the sheer inanity even a hundred years would have a hard time erasing. 'Say what you want of him, he has good taste in property,' I said, determined to end on a positive note.

Smith kept silent, avoiding any controversy. He was wholly reliable that way. 'By the way, the colonel wanted to see you as soon you appeared,' he said.

'Well, I guess I'm off to the coal mines, then. I'll see you in a little while, assuming they don't ship me off to God knows where in the meantime. There wasn't a problem was there?'

'Oh no, sir. I don't think it's anything like that. You were needed here, that's all.'

'That's a relief,' I said.

Lieutenant-Colonel Hore-Ruthven looked strained and tired when I found him. But he greeted me with genuine friendliness. Unusually for him, he didn't comment on my appearance which, in the absence of a change of clothes from my chest – I still had to track it down – bore the reminders of my stay in Flanders. My uniform was streaked with mud and blood and who knows what else. I wasn't a pretty sight, and that was not something the colonel typically overlooked.

I briefed him on what I'd done in Ypres. His frequent nods and the absence of any piercing questions revolving around my capabilities, or lack thereof, suggested he was satisfied. My intuition was not far off. When I was done he said, 'Well done, Major. I believe you earned your five dollars a day last week.' From anyone other than him it was hardly a resounding endorsement. Fortunately, I knew him.

There were any one of five different biting retorts I could have made. Instead, I said, 'One thing, sir, I borrowed a driver from the 41ˢᵗ Division. We arrived late, and he slept here last night, but he'll be wanting to return to his division today. As it is he's been gone an entire day. What should we do about him? We can't send him on his way?'

'Oh, no. That won't do,' said Hore-Ruthven, shaking his head. 'That won't do at all.'

'I more or less promised his division. They were very good about lending me a car and driver in the first place. It was rather a long walk,' I said. I knew what had to be done. We weren't going to risk everything so one private wouldn't feel homesick, but this was a decision the colonel had to make. I knew what he was going to say.

'The guilt, you'll have to live with, Major. As to his division, they'll need to put him down as missing, I'm afraid. He's not going anywhere.' The colonel had made up his mind and only God or a superior officer – the two often blended seamlessly into one in the army – was going to convince him otherwise. Actually, I didn't think McNally would be bothered one whit; after nine hours rattling along beside someone in a tin-bucket car you tended to have a fair idea what they thought. And it got him out of the Salient for a spell – a priceless advantage.

'I'll take care of it, sir.'

I'd barely settled into my new surroundings, in a beautiful second-floor office with a decent view – sadly obscured by Smith's head opposite me – when a private appeared with a summons from the general.

'Good to see you, Major,' said General Lipsett as I entered his elegant office. The room could have doubled as a small ballroom, not that there were many self-professed dancers at headquarters, aside from

DuBois. And apart from the total absence of the fairer sex, Dubois' fearsome appearance and size fourteens would have dissuaded most partners, anyhow. 'I understand from Colonel Hore-Ruthven that it went very well up in Flanders. You should be pleased.'

'Yes, sir,' I replied automatically. I said it without really thinking. When I did, it made me wince. To atone, I said, 'A good man from the mounted rifles got killed... needlessly, I'm afraid. His funeral was today.'

'Captain Dixon?' he asked. 'Yes, I know. Colonel Patterson included it in his report from this morning. It's a shame. He was a very fine soldier.' His features turned starkly serious. 'Major, in wartime, no death is needless. Or perhaps they all are. Either way we don't get to choose. We follow our orders and we know the risks. And I, for one, would prefer to have my death from a chance shell not written off as needless.' He looked at me sympathetically. While he couldn't have known much about what transpired near La Clytte, I had the impression he understood more than he let on. He definitely understood rather a lot about me. General Lipsett had been a soldier for many, many years.

He poured me a cup of tea from a plain china pot on his huge mahogany desk and offered a biscuit from his tin. It was the first time in two years he'd done such a thing. 'I'm happy you made it back in one piece, MacPhail,' he said.

'Thank you, sir. No happier than I am to be back. I never much liked the Salient,' I said, sipping on my tea and nibbling on my biscuit.

And then he frowned. 'There's something I need to tell you. Even in your absence you were able to create a right ruckus – that's the correct word, isn't it?' He'd heard me say it once. Curious, he'd asked about it; it wasn't the sort of word the King used.

What was he on about? I'd been in Flanders for close to a week. How could I have created a ruckus? I must have looked puzzled, and a little worried, for he shortly felt compelled to explain.

'A representative of the Belgian King submitted a complaint about you to GHQ,' he said.

'The Belgian King,' I said, the surprise in my voice obvious. 'Complaining about me? To GHQ?'

'Hmm,' said Lipsett, looking perturbed. 'Well, to be fair it wasn't strictly about you, more about a lack of manners in general. And a bull in a china shop. Naturally, I couldn't help but associate both with you.'

'Naturally, sir,' I grumbled.

'The Belgians were somewhat miffed the Corps is moving north to Flanders and planting our headquarters there without the "common courtesy" of informing them.'

I exhaled. The Belgians had gone for it. The Germans were altogether tougher prey in that respect, but it was encouraging news. 'I'm glad my efforts weren't in vain,' I said.

'No, you've just single-handedly managed to drive a deep wedge between the allies,' he responded. For a split second I believed him, and then I saw his face. 'Well done, MacPhail.'

'And what do you suppose happens next?' Lipsett asked.

'I expect we'll be launching a large attack near Amiens, soon.'

'Correct, Major. We will, indeed, together with an Imperial corps, the Australians and the French. Our role will be to spearhead the centre of the advance along with the Australian Corps. They've recently extended their line to the south taking over a section of the French line, and are holding a huge front.'

'Oh, that's smart,' I blurted out, my mind whirring. 'To make them look overextended and convince the Germans that an attack is the last thing to be expected. Only where do we come in, sir?'

Lipsett nodded. 'The Corps is assembling in secret a few miles to the west of Amiens, near the villages of Boves and Gentelles. The southernmost half of the Australian front lines is only a mile or two further east, and they will provide cover for our approach. There are also a couple of large woods in the vicinity we can shelter in, and considerable lodgings. We'll slip into the line and replace the Australians shortly before the attack commences. It's absolutely critical the Boche don't catch on, or the game will be up. Our success depends on surprise.'

'Yeah,' I said. 'With those two corps together in one spot, Hindenburg would have a heart attack if he knew. On the other hand, that's a strategy that might be worth a try!'

'I wouldn't have put it exactly that way,' said Lipsett, 'but you've got a point. The Germans are suspicious wherever we are, and if we show up next to the Australians, they'll know for certain something's on. As to your suggestion, I'm not convinced High Command is willing to sacrifice this operation on the bet Hindenburg has a weak heart.'

'And when does the attack commence, sir?'

'I'm afraid I can't tell you, MacPhail. What I can say is there's very little time to prepare. I'd like for you to reconnoitre the section of the line the division is assigned to. It appears we've drawn rather a tough nut. The colonel and I have already had a quick look. As you would expect, we have aerial photos, detailed maps and intelligence from the Australians, but nothing beats some more eyes on the ground. However, to avoid any unnecessary risks, and possibly reveal our hand, I'd like you to do it incognito.' He threw the last bit in, almost as an afterthought, concealed in a muffled rush of words. 'General Rawlinson is insistent on maintaining secrecy.'

'Incognito?' I asked, the bewilderment no doubt plastered all over my face.

'Yes,' he replied. 'That means in disguise,' he added helpfully.

'Yes, sir, I'm aware of what incognito means. And how exactly am I to be disguised?'

'As an Australian,' he said. At that moment I recall rolling my eyes.

'As an Australian!' I exclaimed. Playing cops and robbers as a kid, I never wanted to be the robber either.

Lipsett's face was curled into a look of smug delight; he was clearly relishing this little twist.

'Brit, no problem. I'm sure I can pass fairly well as a Kiwi, or even a Newfie. On a good day I might just manage a convincing impersonation of a Frenchman. For that matter, you could dress me up as a tree. But an Aussie?'

'There's no one in the division better suited to the task than you,' said Lipsett. I didn't much feel like asking why he thought that. In my experience, what's left unsaid is sometimes better left that way, particularly if you're being thrown into a pot with a bunch of rough and ready diggers from a penal colony.

'Well, I suppose if I practice my swearing,' I said. Even to my ears I sounded dubious.

'You'll do fine,' he said. I expect he meant it to be reassuring.

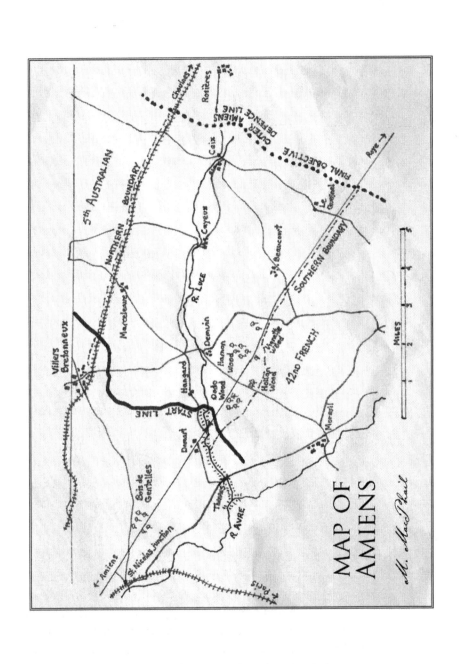

MAP OF
AMIENS

M. MacPhail

CHAPTER 29

5th of August, 1918
Domart-sur-la-Luce, France

I was a newly minted officer of the 51st Battalion of the 13th Brigade of the 4th Australian Division, complete with slouch hat. The uniform had been delivered very early this morning. I knew that because I was woken by the motorbike churning up the drive as it departed. Not only had I become an Aussie, I'd been demoted in the process. Talk about calamities coming in twos. I guess I should have been thankful they made me a lieutenant; being an Aussie private would have been too much for my fragile self-confidence to handle.

As far as I could make out, slouch hats were a sort of wimpy cowboy hat: take a big felt one, shave the brim down to a woman's size, curl the left side up a little effeminately, and straighten the right so it's flat. Before you know it, you're ready to lasso a koala bear or whatever it is they lasso Down Under.

There was a small oval mirror hanging on the wall above the sink in my room. I was using it to fit my hat. I might have saved myself the trouble. No matter which way I twisted or turned the bloody thing, the final result left me looking, and feeling like an idiot. Then there was the ludicrous cuckoo-like bird eating a worm carved on the silver cap badge. Fortunately, he'd been relegated to the upturned left side of the hat, so we didn't have to share the mirror.

I looked ridiculous.

It was no particular surprise that Benoît spotted me straight away, as I slipped through the hallways in search of breakfast – he'd always had a nose for the absurd. He began to laugh, and there was a palpable danger the whole German army would hear it ruining any element of surprise we might still have.

'What the fuck are you on about, mate?' I growled. 'I'm looking for bacon and beans, not ridicule.'

His hacking cough was so severe as to warrant a hospital bed. I patted him on the back, and he seemed to calm down. Slowly he sputtered back to life.

'I feel like one of the poor lads from down the road,' I said.

He'd largely recovered his composure. However, he looked puzzled. Finally, in a sudden enlargement of the irises, it dawned on him. 'Oh, you mean the lunatic asylum!?' he said, wiping the last of the tears from his eyes. 'Don't worry, Mac, there's no room there now. The medical corps beat you to it. They moved into the asylum three days ago.'

'Precisely,' I said. 'And did you ever pause to consider where all the inmates went?'

And so it was that I turned up later that morning as the Australian Corps' newest digger at the 51st Infantry Battalion HQ near Domart-sur-la-Luce, a small village 8 ½ miles east of Amiens down the road in the direction of Roye. Roye itself was miles behind German lines. Even the handful of Aussies present in the dug-out seemed amused at my costume. For the life of me, I couldn't see the difference between mine and theirs. If I'd kept my mouth shut I might have got away with it. It was a considerable blessing Dan Banting wasn't here to see me.

'I understand you'd like to visit the observation post and survey the line, sir,' said the stickler of a boy lieutenant who welcomed me. At first there'd been some natural confusion about my rank. When I briefly explained, the "sirs" and stilted language had flown in abundance. General Monash must have been laying down the law on his unruly rabble.

'Yes, exactly,' I replied. 'I want to see the lay of the land for myself. And get to know the topographical features for when we take over the line.' I was taking no chances – the less they knew the better. The only problem being, a Canadian turning up in an Australian uniform was as common a sight as a kangaroo in the Prairies. 'Lieutenant, seeing as how we're both the same rank, this is a wonderful opportunity to dispense with protocol, and cut out the *sirs.*' Exaggeratingly I eyed the double pips adorning my right shoulder. 'We wouldn't want any watchful Germans getting wise, would we?'

The lieutenant looked as solemn as a mortician. 'No, sir,' he answered. Compared to the profession's average client, the lieutenant wasn't quite as quick on the uptake.

'Where's your colonel and the major?' I asked.

'They had pressing matters to attend to, sir. Captain Holmes is in charge.' He indicated the bronze-faced captain who'd pulverised my hand with his grip when I first arrived. He was now bent over a table, scribbling furiously.

'Well, we can be on our way, then,' I said. The timetable was vague, but Lipsett had made no secret of the fact it was a short one. Dawdling around a battalion headquarters wasn't going to make anybody happy, least of all me.

'We have several rules, sir. In particular, we have strict instructions there should be no more than two officers at any time observing the line,' he said.

Thoughtfully, I rubbed my chin. 'Hmm,' I said. 'That could be a problem. Particularly seeing as how I brought along not only *me*, but *myself and I* for this reconnaissance. It appears as if one of us will have to stay behind. We'll do eeny-meeny-miney-mo to sort it out, if that's okay?' I paused to let him stew in the absurdity of it all. 'Good. Now that we've got that all arranged, perhaps you can point the way?'

The lieutenant was a curious shade of red. 'Oh, no, sir. I didn't mean it like that. I, uh, just...'

'Yes, Lieutenant?' He was writhing like a fish on a hook, and I wasn't going to let him slip off too easily.

A sergeant was watching with growing amusement, and he stepped forward. 'I'll take you, Lieutenant,' he said to me with a conspiratorial wink. 'I'm Sergeant Perkins.' He was only in his mid-thirties, but his weather-beaten face told a different story. His dark brown eyes had the world-weary look of someone who'd seen more than a little war, and the furrows on his cheeks and brow were deep enough to shelter half his battalion, should the need arise.

'Remember if you're captured, sir, you're from Western Australia,' he reminded me, as we left. 'That's where most of us are from.'

'Fuck me, mates. I'm a digger from Perth. Where's the beer?' I said, in my best imitation of an Australian accent. They all cracked up. Even the stern young lieutenant smiled. I think it was the accent.

'Don't mind him, sir,' said the sergeant, after we left. 'He's a good lad, but he's just arrived from officers' school. He hasn't yet figured out it's not all on page twenty-three of the manual.'

'Ah,' I said. 'That explains a great deal.'

'I don't know if you heard, sir? We had a lot of excitement here yesterday morning. The Boche launched a big raid against A Company. They're a half mile further down the road towards the front line. We beat them off in the end, but they captured one of our sergeants and five privates in the process.'

'Really!' I said, whistling softly. That was far bigger news than the sergeant realized. If those soldiers suspected anything about an attack, or even that the four divisions of the Corps were ranged up behind them, and then spilled the beans to their interrogators... it didn't bear thinking about. There were going to be a lot of people on tenterhooks at High Command today. And not only at High Command, I thought grimly; I'd hate for Tom Dixon's death to have been in vain.

'It's not the first time we've lost men in a raid, but there's been mild panic ever since. Can't say I recall such a commotion before. That explains why the colonel and the major are AWL today, in case you were wondering.' Seeing my questioning look, he explained, 'Absent Without Leave. They were summoned to divisional HQ early this morning,' he said. 'Although I guess that would make them absent *with* leave, when I think about it.'

'How are the Germans acting?'

'Nothing out of the ordinary. If anything, it's quieter than normal. Course, the weather is miserable.' He motioned to the grey overcast blanket that had lain across the skies for a couple of days, and which was spitting rain again. 'Not that a little rain ever stopped the Hun.'

How right he was. But the weather did limit the visibility, and given the beehive of activity that was Amiens and its surroundings, that was a stroke of luck. Strangely, there weren't many enemy aircraft overhead. Come to that, I hadn't seen a single one – without exception all the aeroplanes were ours. It was very different than Passchendaele.

The observation post was built into the slopes of a grassy, but otherwise barren hill with an excellent view eastwards down the Amiens-Roye road, and through the valley of the River Luce. The ruined village of Domart and the Australian trenches were in the foreground and, beyond them, those of the Germans. It wasn't much, the OP. No more than a few timbers sheltered the top and the sides, and there was a small length of trench. If you stood on an earthen step, it gave an unencumbered view towards the next hill, three or four miles distant in enemy territory. And that is what we did.

'Follow the road,' said the sergeant. 'Just beyond the bridge on the other side of the river. Can you see those trenches that bisect the road? That's our beachhead. That's A Company, where the Huns raided. And just in front of them is Elbe Trench, where the Germans fled to. Our boys could hear them talking after the raid.'

The Aussie bridgehead on the enemy's side of the River Luce was an oblong spit of land immediately to the southeast of Domart village. It was situated around the even smaller hamlet of Hourges – at least that was how the map, in a font of small neat capitals, assuredly described it. All I saw was a mid-sized pile of rubble and a couple of houses astride the Amiens-Roye road.

I'd brought a telescope with me – it was more powerful than my Lemaire field glasses, albeit far more awkward. I stared through it following the sergeant's directions. 'Yes, I see it,' I said. 'And the Elbe Trench, that's their front line?'

'Yeah, it's only a couple of hundred yards long on both sides of the road. They have others like it on our front, spread here and there. It's not a continuous line like up north. The fighting has been too recent for much construction to be done. And the Hun we've got don't seem like real builder bees, although they're deadly enough. They've filled the gaps in the line with machine-gun nests. They're awfully nasty works, and they're spread everywhere, including the towns.'

I had a decent picture of the general topography already. On the way here, I paused briefly at 13th Brigade headquarters close to the Bois de Gentelles – one of the large woods, and its abundant summer foliage, in which thousands of our troops were sheltering. The HQ was a roomy dug-out where a constant low murmur of conversation hung like a persistent cloud of smoke, swirling, but never dispersing. The staff had set up a large table in the corner, and guests were welcome to peruse the information on hand. Presumably this arrangement kept us, the visitors, out of their hair. And I could see why that might be a concern, even for the talkative Aussies. By midmorning, there were five of us jostling for a spot, each interested in essentially the same things. I greeted a couple of the officers I knew from other divisions, and one from my own. It was Hancock, he was arranging accommodations. Myself, I was more interested in the intelligence summaries, and the maps and photos of the sector.

Outside of Amiens the road to the east split into two, with one arm branching due east going through the hard-fought town of Villers-Bretonneux, while the other heading southeast, was the Amiens-Roye road. It was the path I'd taken this morning, the continuation of which I now saw in front of me. These two roads, more or less made up the Corp's northern and southern boundaries. Together, on a map, they formed a shape I found oddly evocative of a huge bullhorn, its mouthpiece at the gates of Amiens.

Our task would be to blow out of that horn, pushing the Germans back towards the old Somme battlefield to the east, and away from Amiens, and the crucial railroad south to Paris.

The boundaries the Fourth Army had arranged invoked another resemblance with a bullhorn. When using a bullhorn, if you get your mouth stuck in the opening it doesn't matter if you have the lung capacity of an elephant, you'll soon be blue in the face. Likewise with an army, and a plugged bottleneck, which this had the potential to all too easily become. Our divisions were packed together, waiting in a tiny area of a couple square miles from which they'd stream outwards after Zero Hour, hoping not to get bogged down, or shelled to pieces as they did so.

'Tacking to port,' I warned, as I swung the extended telescope left, tracing the path of the River Luce as it cut almost perpendicularly across my view. It wouldn't have done to knock this veteran Aussie warrior out of the fight before it even began.

'And here I thought I'd joined the army,' said Sergeant Perkins. I saw a quirky smile on his face when I glanced over. 'My dad had a boat. He was always going on and on with his naval terms. Drove us mad, he did. It's probably *why* I chose the army in the first place.'

'That and the fact the Australian Navy's rowboat was full, leaking, or both,' I said, eliciting a groan from Perkins.

What wasn't a laughing matter, was the section of the front we were assigned to. The 3rd Division had the most southernmost sliver of the piece of pie served up to the Corps. And it was brutal. The problems revolved around the Luce, and Dodo Wood.

'Am I mistaken, or are there only two bridges across the Luce near here, Sergeant?' I asked. That was one of the few things I'd learned in my short time as a practising lawyer: never confuse *thinking* you know the answer with actually *knowing* it. Which is why I'm a firm believer in double checking. It seldom amounts to much, but breath's cheap I figure, and there's no place on earth where that's more true than on the Western Front.

Perkins shook his head. 'Nope, that's them. Only two. The one down the road in front of you, and the other is in the Frog's sector.' I recalled it from the map. The 42nd French Division was only a dash to the south, on the right side of the road.

'Thinking about it afresh, it's a shame you didn't join the navy, Perkins. With a river like that, your skills as a sailor might prove useful.'

The river itself wasn't particularly large; the Luce was a lesser tributary of the River Avre, itself a tributary of the Somme River, making it less daunting than your average swimming pool. However, including its marshy banks, it was a good 200 yards wide in places. Crossing it without a bridge was a near impossibility, especially for the 50-odd tanks that were to accompany us. And the Luce curved diagonally across our front, so there was simply no avoiding it. Before any troops in the bottom half of our sector could even get to the starting line, they'd have to cross one of those two bridges. It would mean some tricky manoeuvering; deadly manoeuvering, too, if the Germans on the hill were on form.

'And I presume that's Dodo Wood?' I said, indicating the large wooded hill beyond the river and to the right of the road. Curiously, there was a difference of opinion about that forested rise. The Brits called it Rifle Wood, and I'd seen a captured German map where it

MALCOLM MACPHAIL'S GREAT WAR

was entitled the *Schwarz Wald*, the Black Wood. The latter seemed the most appropriate name given the frightening proliferation of weaponry atop it. From the hill the enemy could directly observe the vital Paris-to-Amiens railway.

'Dodo Wood it is, sir. The boys in the line have to keep their heads down, the enemy can see most of our front from there,' said the sergeant.

'Just to make sure I'm not missing anything. Your boys in the beachhead are completely cut off by the river to their rear – it seems to bend around behind them – except for one bridge they can cross. 200 yards in front of them are the enemy trenches. And beyond them is Dodo Wood, which is not only bristling with machine guns and artillery, but has a clear line of sight to both their trenches, and the bridge.'

'Yes, that's pretty much it, sir,' agreed the sergeant.

Of all the tactical nightmares I'd ever seen this topped them all. How were we going to get the entire division across a single bridge, in range, and sight, of a hill full of Germans? I wasn't looking forward to briefing Lipsett. 'I see why you're anxious to be relieved,' I said, finally. That wasn't exactly the story, but it was bad enough I was here posing as an Australian, I didn't want to leave him with too much to chew over.

'No chance Dodo Wood refers to the current inhabitants?' I said, studying the hill through my telescope.

'No, not a chance, sir.'

'Well that's just great,' I muttered crankily, more to myself than to Perkins, although naturally he heard it.

'What's that, sir?'

'I was hoping it was merely a question of me not being good with a map,' I said. 'I'm not, but the view from here hasn't done much to cheer me up. Tell me, aside from the Boche in Dodo Wood, how are the rest of them in this sector?'

'Good to average,' he said.

'And here I was hoping you'd say wretched.'

'No, sir,' he said, frowning, 'wretched they're not. Aside from the raid yesterday, they haven't been too much trouble, all things considered. Mostly they keep to themselves, and throw a few shells across now and again. We're thinly stretched but they don't want to mess with us. Before we came, the French left them largely alone. Our battalion has the best part of a Hun division lined up against it. They're Prussians, the 225th Division.'

'Lucky thing we in the…' I glanced at my shoulder patch to make sure I got it right, '…51st Battalion, are the roughest, toughest lot in the entire BEF,' I said. Lipsett was correct, after all. That Australian swagger wasn't too difficult with a bit of practice. Perkins, to his credit, took my teasing gracefully in his stride. After we returned to battalion headquarters, I had more time to practice my swagger, by which point I felt like I'd lived in Western Australia half my life.

The Aussies had a loud, brash, self-assurance about them that rubbed many the wrong way, especially the well-groomed types from the Imperial Army. Modest they weren't, but at least there was some substance to the bluster. They were a good bunch to have on your side. Australia being a sister dominion, it seemed only appropriate the elder sister put the young upstart in her place every so often. I tried my best, but frankly it was a thankless, and altogether endless task.

By mid-afternoon there was still no sign of the colonel or the major at the battalion dug-out. Sergeant Perkins, I'd discovered, was an absolute fountain of information, and I pumped him for everything he had, hoping for some glimmer of light. He even took me down along the banks of the Luce to see it up close. Fortunately, he didn't ask many questions himself.

I was not looking forward to my briefing with Lipsett. There was an excellent chance I was going to get an earful: "I promoted you and put you on the intelligence staff to come up with solutions, not to take leisurely afternoon strolls by the river…" As I thought about all that I'd seen, dinner arrived. It came in great piping hot metal tins brought from the rear in a small lorry. I didn't need much coaxing to accept their offer to eat. There was rarely a day since I'd joined the army that I wasn't hungry, and after playing Aussie for hours on end, I was ravenous. I wolfed down the curry and rice like I hadn't eaten in days. And then it came to me: *Could that be a solution?*

'Don't worry, ladies, the Aussies are here,' I loudly proclaimed, with a grin, to a couple of familiar faces as I strutted into divisional headquarters in my new attire, later that evening. Months earlier I'd heard a slouch-hatted soldier bellow precisely that as his unit marched through a French village. Before the stunned look on their faces wore off, I strode rapidly past them. It was the exact same strategy of hitting them hard, and moving on before they could react, that we'd been practicing all summer long. Open warfare was what General Webber had called it.

Not that I had any use for that where I was presently headed: to General Lipsett to relay my findings. With him it was more a question of meticulous preparation, tough slogging and keeping your head down, all of which bore the hallmarks of being back in the trenches. But I did have the outlines of a plan.

CHAPTER 30

6th of August, 1918
La Roseraie, Sains-en-Amiénois, France

The sun was rising fast, but I was already up and ready for action, mulling over the events of yesterday. Last evening, I presented my extensive report. And for the second time in a month, I put my head on the block with another idea.

After hearing the results of my reconnaissance, Lipsett brushed uneasily at his moustache with one hand, and drummed out a nervous beat on the table with the fingers of the other. He looked unusually pensive, even for him.

Finally, he said, 'That river. That infernal river.' The fierce intensity took me aback for General Lipsett was by nature calm, cool, and collected, to the extent I'd call it spooky, except when riled; then, it was an imprudent man who didn't batten down the hatches or flee, assuming he had his wits about him. I could see the River Luce was preying on the general's mind. At least he wasn't berating me.

'Half the division and the tanks will have to get across that bridge at Domart, the 4th Division is coming in our wake, and the 3rd Cavalry Division and Brutinel's armoured cars later as well,' he said after a moment, his calm returning. I'd forgotten about Brutinel's Brigade.

The two motorized machine-gun brigades with armoured cars, 60-odd motorcycles from the cyclist battalion and two lorry-mounted

271

trench mortars, had been brought together in Brigadier-General Brutinel's Independent Force. With their mobility, and the awesome firepower from their Vickers machine guns and the mortars, they would be a potent addition to the attack – assuming they could get across the Luce, and into action.

Colonel Hore-Ruthven, who was also listening, added, 'And let's not forget all the traffic in the other direction, like ambulances, prisoners and so forth. The engineers are busy building footbridges for the infantry, although it's very tricky with the Germans so close, even if they are working by night. The bridge risks being a major bottleneck.'

'There is one possibility, General,' I said, cautiously.

Lipsett and Hore-Ruthven looked at me expectantly.

'You could put a brigade on the far side of the Luce *before* the attack, sir.'

'You want me to move a four-thousand-man brigade, in the middle of the night, across that bridge, and into an enclave of a thousand by a thousand yards currently manned by a couple of hundred strung-out Australians?'

'Actually, I don't believe it's quite a thousand by a thousand, sir. Including the marshes, it's more likely 500 or 600 yards wide and a thousand long. And I don't think the Aussies have more than a hundred men there, sir.'

Hore-Ruthven and Lipsett stared at each other in disbelief. It wasn't the best rejoinder I've ever come up with.

'You do realize, Major, if the Germans catch on it'll be a slaughter?' said the colonel.

'Look at it this way, sir. As soon as the attack commences the Germans are going to bring down a bombardment on that bridge to level a city. There's a good chance we won't be able to cross in any numbers at all. At least this way we'd have enough troops across the river to push forward, and hopefully take the hill and Dodo Wood, and some of their guns.'

'It's audacious, Major, I'll grant you that,' said Lipsett.

'Or stupid,' added Hore-Ruthven.

'It all depends on your point of view, sir. This entire attack depends on the element of surprise. If we don't surprise them there's a good chance of a slaughter, anyhow. However, if we do surprise them, but don't get past the starting line in our sector, the centre of the attack will be in jeopardy. And if the Corps doesn't advance because we don't, the overall attack will fail.'

'You make a convincing case, MacPhail. Let us think about it.'

I cleared my throat. 'I don't mean to add to your concerns, General, but there's one other thing I heard today that you should know – if you don't already. The Australians in the enclave were raided yesterday morning. Apparently, the Germans took five soldiers and a sergeant prisoner.'

I saw the two men look meaningfully at each other, sharing some confidence I wasn't privy to. Then Lipsett spoke. 'General Rawlinson has ordered our relief of the Australians to be postponed. He's worried about a repeat if we're in the line. If the Boche were to capture any of ours it would be a blatant red flag, and as you rightly point out, it's paramount we achieve surprise. The relief will have to take place the night of the attack… and now you suggest I do it with 4000 men…'

'Really,' I said, whistling softly. 'Relieve the Aussies on the night of the attack? That's cutting it awfully close, sir. Am I allowed to know when the attack will take place?'

His hands stopped fidgeting. 'The morning of the 8th.'

That stopped me in my tracks as effectively as a regiment of the Prussian Guards. It was less than three days away.

We'd had little chance to properly reconnoitre, the plan wasn't even finalised, and the troops would need to spend most of the preceding night slipping unobtrusively into their jumping-off positions. Everything about this endeavour was unprecedented.

There were a lot of moving parts that needed to be greased if this was going to succeed. And that meant an uncomfortably narrow margin for slip-ups. Thanks to my big mouth, the margin may have got smaller still. It was going to be a busy couple of days.

This morning Lipsett was up at the crack of dawn to go to the red-brick ruins of Domart and the marshland of the Luce to view the situation again, together with the colonel. I'm sure my plan was uppermost on their minds. If I'd known they were going, I would have happily offered one of them my Diggers' disguise, not that General Lipsett or Colonel Hore-Ruthven looked like the types for a slouch hat. The lieutenant's pips wouldn't have been a big hit either.

Once dressed – in my own tatty but trusted major's tenue – it didn't take me long to find Lieutenant Smith. There wasn't a lot of time to waste.

'I forgot to tell you earlier. We have a car and driver at our permanent disposal,' I said.

'Oh?'

'Yes, a trusty little Ford and a pleasant chap from Scotland by the name of McNally from the 41ˢᵗ Division, both of them borrowed from the Brits.'

'He's a Brit? What's he doing here? The 41ˢᵗ are nowhere near here, are they?'

'A Brit, did I say that? Well, yes and no. As a Scot he'd probably say no, but for our purposes he is. As to why he's here? You might say he's on a form of indefinite leave with us. Keen to avoid the Salient for a few days, you understand. His superiors, I fear, may see it a little differently. As long as we can avoid any talk of kidnapping we should be in the clear, Smith, just remember that,' I said, mischievously.

Smith's expression resembled something akin to an open-mouthed fish looking for bait – the kind you sadly never run across when fishing. It was the kind of reaction which made him such a delightfully tempting target. 'However, as I told you, he and the car are all ours for the moment. So, don't hesitate if you need some transport,' I added.

Smith looked perplexed. 'I didn't know anything about it until you told me, sir. I'm afraid to ask more,' he mumbled.

'And right you'd be,' I chirped. I wouldn't have been so carefree if I didn't know that Swanky Sid – assuming he was out of bed – would have to take up any complaints with Lipsett and Hore-Ruthven. And I had a good idea how that match would end. 'Let's be off to Sains-en-Amiénois then, Lieutenant. You see how convenient it is to have a car? Unless, of course, you'd prefer to walk?'

The whole divisional travelling circus – minus a few of us who spent the night at Dury – had packed up again last night and moved a few miles east to this small collection of houses where our next residence, la Roseraie, stuck out like a sore thumb.

It wasn't the two-story brick house, which was fairly large but otherwise unremarkable, nor even the tall square castle tower anchored on the left side of the façade; they were common enough in France. Mainly, it was the curious, round, pointed minaret with glass windows near its peak, which soared from the roof another two stories into the air. It could have been a lighthouse were the sea not 50 miles distant. In front of the building was a modest lawn and a fair-sized pond, not large enough to require a lighthouse, although I was hardly an expert on the subject. On a sunny day with nothing to do – neither of which appeared remotely likely – I could have pictured myself lazing on the grass by the water, a blade of grass between my teeth, and a cool drink in my hand.

We were bumped out of the much larger and more ornate Château Dury by General Currie. He was to arrive there with his staff tonight, or possibly tomorrow morning. He was coming from Molliens-Vidame, affectionately known as "Molly-be-Damned" to the troops. Molly-be-Damned was a dozen miles east of Amiens and Dury was unquestionably a lot closer to where the action would be. Considering the château's chequered recent history, the move told me that Currie was not a superstitious man.

Smith had already christened our new office in his own inimitable way, by dumping the sizeable pile of reports, photos and messages that had arrived overnight unceremoniously onto the large table we shared. He must have been a lot more tired than I realized, for normally he would have sorted everything meticulously into neat piles – Smith was neat, there was no denying that.

I was halfway through a Fourth Army intelligence summary when I heard someone come in. It was the divisional paymaster. There were worst ways to be interrupted. By now I was used to most of them, so this counted as a pleasant surprise.

'Ah, there you are, Major. You're a tough man to track down, I'm glad I finally found you. Here's your pay book, if you're interested, sir,' said the paymaster, and he dropped it with an audible thump – the legacy of three and a half long years at war – onto the table in front of me.

Distractedly, I picked it up and started thumbing through the pages, curious what my fortune amounted to after another month of pay and few opportunities to spend it. Glued to the inside was an official notice consisting of a short text: "KEEP YOUR MOUTH SHUT!" it began.

Well, that was pretty unambiguous. Knowing the average guy in the Corps, the jokes were already rife. I couldn't wait to use the line myself; here at headquarters there was certainly no shortage of worthwhile targets. Levity aside, the message was deadly serious. If I hadn't just returned from a week churning out misinformation in the Salient, I would have been amazed at the lengths we were going to, to keep this operation secret.

By lunchtime, Smith and I had worked through the night's haul of information. We were busy plotting the changes to the enemy dispositions on the large map we kept updated for the staff, when Smith looked up. Something was on his mind.

'Sir, why do you suppose Field-Marshal Haig picked us for this?'

'I don't think he did, not exactly. The way I heard it, was that General Rawlinson asked General Monash who he wanted beside him: Brits, French, Americans... and it seems Monash wanted us. The Aussies likely thought our food was better.' There was a glimmer of a smile from Smith. 'However, I'd guess the field-marshal is thankful he didn't have his way when he wanted to break up the Corps last March.'

Not long ago I overheard snippets of a conversation between Lipsett and Currie. From those few words, it was apparent that Haig had been livid at the time, bemoaning the political interference, and questioning our allegiance to the Empire. War has a way of making short shrift of bad ideas, though. Even if sometimes it requires a devilishly long time, and a bloody nose or two, before it happens. Fortuitously for all concerned that particular idea died a quick death.

'It also can't hurt that we kept our twelve battalions per division, while all the rest went to nine,' said Smith, referring to another of the bad ideas the spring of 1918 had sprung. Unfortunately, that one *had* seen the light of day – in the rest of the BEF.

'That's true. And our divisions are the strongest on the Western Front, as a result. Well, aside from the Sammies. And they're gung-ho, but awfully green,' I said. Smith bobbed his head in what must have been agreement. Smiling, I continued, 'Foch and Haig haven't let me

276

in on their thinking yet, but I'm sure they know the numbers very well. In fact, we're over-strength thanks to the dismemberment of the 5th Division. With the additional machine guns, artillery, and engineers that gives us, plus all the Corps troops, I wouldn't be surprised if we're three times the size of any other corps in the army. Just think what that means for the next football championship, Smith!'

But Smith was not to be waylaid by jokes. 'And what if the Germans are expecting us, sir? We'll battle ourselves to a pulp.'

'Then we'll have no choice but to show our true mettle,' I said. It was a flippant response to a good question, one I'd been worrying about non-stop ever since I returned from up north. The attack was either going to be a big success, or a colossal failure. And the second didn't bear thinking about.

'The Germans attacked III Corps this morning to the left of the Aussies,' he persisted. 'It could be they're trying to pre-empt an attack.'

'It's possible, but I don't think so. More likely they're trying to straighten out some of the bumps in their own line. You've seen all the intelligence. What do you think? There are no signs of reinforcements, or new defensive works, or artillery movements. Their aeroplanes are nowhere to be seen. There's absolutely nothing that suggests they're suspicious.'

He nodded. I could see he wanted to believe what I said, though my words were probably as much for my benefit as his. His curiosity momentarily quenched, Smith put his head down to concentrate on his papers and, after a while, I did the same.

The work wasn't exactly gripping, it was primarily a lot of checking and rechecking small details. Identifying units and matching them to a map. Pinpointing machine-gun nests, trenches, and artillery positions after some downbeat hungry prisoner of the xyz infantry regiment uttered a careless word, or a Royal Air Force pilot snapped a cluster of dark spots in a wood. It helped to remember these were the sort of abstractions that were anything but for the man in the field; his life might depend on them. Every so often a staff officer would pop his head around the doorway to ask a question or reconfirm some small detail on the map. Smith and I weren't the only ones checking and rechecking.

The dining room of *La Roseraie* was a modest affair, barely large enough to fit the combined population of Sains-en-Amiénois and its sister village of St. Fuscien, when they gathered to eat, drink, and dance the night away after a local couple sealed their vows. Not that there was a lot of celebrating going on these days. The country was under siege, all the men were in uniform and there was precious little food and drink. There were scant, if any, reasons to dance. Under army purview the faded cream dining room served as a conference room, when it wasn't in service as the officers' mess. It was lucky somebody had absconded with the chandelier, it being precisely the sort of thing I could imagine tree-height Benoît felling with a head-butt, in a careless moment.

I had a hard time recalling the last staff conference. It must have been weeks ago. With all the moving, and the staff scattered from here to there, Hore-Ruthven evidently decided they weren't worth the bother. It was an insight I'd come to much earlier, though my reasons may have been a little more self-serving than his.

Lieutenant-Colonel Hore-Ruthven stood before us readying his notes. Naturally his uniform was pressed, creased, and immaculate. There was nothing to indicate he'd spent his morning mucking about the Luce. Mine hadn't looked like that since the tailor on Maddox Street had folded it carefully and wrapped it in brown paper.

Everyone was present, including the general, and that constituted a miracle not far short of the parting of the biblical seas. Everyone that is, except for Lieutenant Hines. Fresh-faced Hines was on leave in London, blissfully unaware of what the rest of us were up to. Unwittingly, he'd gained himself a free pass out of fear that his recall might tip off some temptress of a German spy or, more mundanely, the inordinately efficient London rumour mill.

Lipsett had been looking at me and when he saw me return his gaze, he motioned me over to one side, out of earshot of the others. His face was drawn and from the way he was anxiously rubbing the balls of his hands together I knew something was wrong. I couldn't begin to guess how wrong.

'MacPhail, I'm afraid I have some very unpleasant news,' he began. 'I had a visit this morning from Colonel Whatley-Wigham. He informs me he intends to lay formal charges against you.'

'I beg your pardon, sir?' I said, my heart pumping, and my own words echoing in my ears.

'He accuses you of behaving in a scandalous manner unbecoming the character of an officer and a gentleman, and using insubordinate language to a superior officer. According to him you have a history of such behaviour. He mentioned a number of occasions, most recently in Cassel, where he says you comported yourself in an insubordinate fashion. He also referred to an instance of public drunkenness in London last year, which he witnessed.' Lipsett looked at me questioningly.

'I was in a bar, sir. I had several drinks, as did my companions. That's what you do in a bar. But it was certainly not public drunkenness, sir.'

'You can state that in your defence. Although I should tell you it will be largely his word against yours. And, as you know, the colonel is on the general staff. Regardless, once he formally lays his charges, I'm afraid I'll have little choice. I will have to convene a court martial without delay.'

'A court martial, sir?'

Lipsett nodded, not unsympathetically. 'Yes. These are serious charges, Major. The military code gives me no leeway.' He handed me a handkerchief and I gratefully dabbed my brow with it.

'I see,' I managed to say, the feeling of nausea overcoming me.

'I have, however, been able to convince the colonel to delay laying his charges until after the attack. I impressed upon him the importance of our assignment and the need for secrecy. And I told him I needed every man I had, and especially my intelligence officer. He was most gentlemanly in agreeing.'

'What then, sir?'

'I wish I knew. I can't say I haven't warned you, MacPhail. The only advice I can give you is to do your duty as best you can – as you've always done. This attack must succeed. If it does, I believe your chances will be improved. I'm sorry to come with this news and, of all times, on the eve of battle.'

'I see, sir.' Honestly, I saw nothing, other than three years of toil and danger ending in scandal, disgrace and quite likely worse. Being an officer, I probably wouldn't face the death penalty, but a stay in irons was a distinct possibility.

The meeting began minutes later. Lost in a world of my own, I sat with the others, unable to concentrate or even hear what Hore-Ruthven was explaining. It was only when I saw the others tense as the colonel raised his voice that I broke out of my trance.

'Gentlemen. The Fourth Army issued formal orders today for the attack we've been preparing. Zero Hour is set for 4.20 a.m. on August 8th.' A murmur swept the room.

'From left to right, III Corps will attack on the far left between the rivers of the Ancre and the Somme. Beside them, to their right, the Australians will take the section between the Somme and the Amiens-Chaulnes rail line. From there to just beyond the Amiens-Roye road is our sector. We have been assigned the largest front with a width of more than 8,500 yards. To our right, the French First Army will be in action with seven divisions, initially. Their 42nd Division will adjoin our right boundary. Finally, the Cavalry Corps, including the Canadian Cavalry Brigade, is in reserve to exploit any breakthroughs, and more than 600 tanks – an unprecedented number – will be supporting.'

This was no mere raid. The preparations were too extensive for that. Half the air force was flying overhead. Still, I was astonished at the sheer scope of it, so soon after the German offensives and the French counterattack at the Marne. This was to be a smack the Boche wouldn't soon forget, assuming they hadn't puzzled it out and were lining up behind their Maxims. Despite all the precautions, and my breezy dismissal of Smith's concerns, that was what I usually worried about in the minutes after my head hit the pillow and before my brain pulled the plug.

'The Corps Commander has given this operation the code name Llandovery Castle. I'm sure I don't need to explain the significance of that.' The murmur grew louder.

There wasn't a man amongst us who didn't know of the Llandovery Castle, a Canadian hospital ship making its way back to England from Halifax at the end of June when it was torpedoed off the coast of Ireland, and the survivors machine-gunned. Only two dozen lived to tell the tale. They'd told us exactly a month ago today. It was horrific news, and emotions were running high. Fritz had become the Hun.

'On the Corps' front, from left to right, we will attack with three divisions: the 2nd, 1st and the 3rd. The 4th Division will leap-frog through us after the second objective. Our third and final objective, probably sometime on the 9th, is the Outer Amiens Defence Line.' Somebody whistled softly. Most looked stunned.

Jesus, I thought, that must be seven or eight miles. At the battle of the Somme it took almost five months to get that far. We'd spent the last two years bashing away furiously to get nowhere – an advance of a mile or two was considered a major victory. All of a sudden, the generals wanted to push eight miles in two days. It seemed preposterous. At the end of March, even the pride of the German army had taken more than a week to steamroll through that old British line protecting Amiens, to where we were now, before the defences stiffened.

But how were we going to get past that bridge at Domart-sur-la-Luce, and then Dodo Hill, without attracting the wrath of von der Marwitz's entire Second Army?

'The 3rd Division will attack on a two-brigade front,' said Hore-Ruthven, maintaining a merciless tempo. He wasn't the type to go slow just because half the room was nervously eyeing each other. 'On our right, the 9th Brigade will cross the Domart Bridge under cover of darkness immediately prior to the attack. They will relieve the Australians and await Zero Hour in the beachhead on the east of the river.'

They'd gone for it!

Benoît was whispering, 'Your idea?'

I nodded.

'Thought so. Nervous?'

I nodded again and looked down. Benoît didn't know the half of it. To my astonishment I saw that my right leg was twitching uncontrollably. I rested my hand on it. There was a lot riding on my plan, not least the lives of four thousand men. And since twenty minutes, ago, seemingly my entire future.

The meeting was coming to an end. There were no questions, which for this group was unheard of. I expect most were as anxious to get on with it as I was, even if none had the incentive I did.

'The orders are going out tonight,' concluded the colonel. It was Tuesday afternoon. The attack would begin early Thursday morning. It was only a day and a half away.

CHAPTER 31

7th of August, 1918
Boves–St. Nicolas junction, France

'We may be here for a wee moment, sir,' said Private McNally, his youthful enthusiasm undaunted by the scene in front of us.

Smith and I were in the back of our borrowed car, and even with the onset of dusk, and having to peer over the front seat and through the streaked and insect-splattered windshield, I had my doubts about his choice of adjective – "bloody long" seemed more appropriate.

We'd made good time as we'd sped down the gentle incline of the curving road from Sains-en-Amiénois into Boves, and across the ancient stone bridge and the trickle that was the River Avre. We came to a screeching halt at the junction on the other side of town.

One of the massive wheels of a heavy cannon had sunk into the soft earth navigating a left corner in the direction of the *Bois de Gentelles,* and was tilted angrily to one side. The gun being towed was one of the 8-inch giants – the kind which had a barrel you could easily fit your head inside. Alternatively, facing in the other direction, it could shoot a 200-pound shell seven miles and, with any luck, land it smack on top of a troublesome Hun battery. A large rectangular-tracked vehicle capped by a tent-like structure, otherwise known as a Holt tractor, was pulling it. The tractor stood still, safely around the corner, its motor lazily chugging away. Behind the tractor a wooden two-wheeled cart, a limber, was attached and behind that, the gun. All in all, it made for a fiendishly long and unwieldy contraption requiring some polished driving skills. Precisely the sort of skills that made it fortunate the Aussie guns were already in place. That spared us what could have been a really severe traffic infarct.

The junction was blocked and traffic was piling up. I could see men madly scrambling in the ditch in a blur of ropes and timbers and shovels. My gut decision not to join the artillery had been inspired brilliance. A team of horses stood by, and I saw another Holt tractor being hooked up ahead of the first one. There was little to do but wait it out.

I got to thinking about Benoît and Tibbett.

I ran into them this morning, at around eight, shortly after I rose. I turned the corner out of the administration office and there they were. They looked terrible. Benoît was gaunt, his normal carefree face creased by lines of worry and tiredness. If anything, Tibbett looked worse. In fact, almost worse than when I pulled him from the mud in Ypres.

'What happened to you two?' I inquired. 'Was the bacon all gone at breakfast this morning?'

Benoît sighed as if steeling himself to answer, but the effort seemed to overcome him. Eventually Tibbett responded. 'We've been up all night... again,' he said. 'And we've still got a mountain of things to do.'

Admittedly it was a little naïve, but I said, 'I thought all the plans were in place?'

'Sure the plans are. That's the first ten percent. Implementing them, that's the real work.'

'But there's not even to be a preliminary bombardment?' What I meant to say was, surely there couldn't be that much work without a bombardment, but fortunately I minced my words.

Benoît sighed again and this time he answered, his French accent unmistakably stronger as his grey cells wobbled on their last legs. 'No. But there's a barrage to be planned for Zero Hour and it's the biggest ever. Captain Tibbett and I need to target all the Boche guns, the important cross-roads and many other targets. It's a hell of a job, Mac.' I still had a lot to learn about the life of a counter-battery officer.

As if anticipating a snide rejoinder from me – though, honestly, I felt too sorry for them to add to their woes – Tibbett quickly added, 'And without a pre-attack bombardment, we can't afford to make any mistakes. We won't be able to destroy their artillery and defences ahead of time. To keep the element of surprise we're shooting at their guns only sporadically. We've plotted every battery we could find, and after Zero Hour we need to destroy as many as we can, and quickly too.' He was dead right about that. If the German artillery was on form and began shelling our packed little enclave and the bridge, the whole venture risked falling down around our ears.

Weightily he went on. 'On our front alone we have 650 guns, as well as another 150 or so from the Royal Artillery. And every one of them needs their own target map. 650 individual maps, not counting the British guns! Malcolm, the guns haven't even been live registered.' I must have been wearing my time-worn expression from science class for Tibbett wearily added an explanation. 'You know, practice shooting. To see if the shells land where we want them to. The gunners will be shooting solely based on the maps, so those guns and the maps need to be exceptionally accurate.' I began to see their predicament. 'It almost makes me wish I was doing your work,' said Tibbett tiredly. He had taken off his spectacles and was polishing them with his tie. They were in sore need of a shine, I could see.

'And here I was, thinking I should have been in the artillery, Paul. The work pace seems so much more relaxed.'

Tibbett's cheek muscles eased into a thin smile. 'You stick-handled around that one real pretty,' said Benoît, his eyes sparkling and with a big grin – his first of the morning and likely the week.

I smiled back. I'd never met a French-Canadian yet, who didn't pepper his speech with hockeyisms.

'I can't wait to explain stick-handling to Field-Marshal Haig the next time we speak,' I said.

It was Tibbett's turn to look mystified. I don't know what those two talked about if DuBois still hadn't explained a few basic hockey terms; unless they just stared into each other's eyes all day. Perhaps that was why Tibbett didn't bother cleaning his glasses.

In all likelihood it was the sudden thought of home that caused DuBois's face to take on a resigned, almost philosophical look, one I'd only seen very late at night, and always after far too much liquor.

'This damned war goes on and on,' he said. 'It makes you wonder why we're here.'

'For King and Empire, Benoît. For King and Empire.'

DuBois snorted like a bull in heat. Under the circumstances, that was altogether the most appropriate response. I was never a big fan of the recruitment posters myself.

'You take care of yourself, Mac. It'll all work out. You'll see,' he said as I was leaving – I'd told them about my predicament last night – and the three of us solemnly shook hands. Benoît knew we wouldn't see each other until it was over, and by then, you never knew. And besides, even if I survived, there was a good chance I'd soon be in irons.

The relative calm of the hopelessly jammed crossroads was shattered by the roar of a motor; two of them to be precise, belching oily smoke. The Holt tractors were roaring in unison, a dozen men were pushing the gun, a couple of others lent their weight to timbers pried under the wheel, while the horses pranced skittishly from one foot to the other. With a jolt the whole train began to move. A flexed timber sprang up sending a man flying into the field. But the gun was back on the road. There was a loud cheer. It was only that we were five miles from the frontline that I didn't worry the enemy had heard the whole unholy commotion.

'We're moving again, sir,' said McNally, unnecessarily, although he could have been excused for thinking we were dozing, so quiet was the back seat. I glanced at my wrist. It was nine-thirty.

While moving was the correct word, it didn't come close to describing the tortoise pace we were crawling along at in the wake of the moving throngs. I felt like putting my foot out the door and helping to push, not that it would have helped.

Dusk was turning to night and the tree-lined roads were packed solid. Every road, lane and dirt path in the direction of the jumping-off lines was pulsating with the slow advance of an army on the move. It was one vast medieval army on the march to war, streaming out of every nook and cranny in the landscape, converging on the few paths eastward, soldiers with their arms in hand and siege engines trundling along behind.

Only this was no army of bows and arrows, pikes and catapults. It was an army of the modern age, with all the awesome firepower that man had perfected in the many years of this, the greatest war the world had ever seen. There were columns of rifle-bearing soldiers marching two or three abreast stretching to the horizon, tractors towing great guns, lines of ambulances, and long ammunition trains of horses and lorries bearing the countless weight in shells the guns would soon hunger for. And then there were the steel colossuses, the tanks, as they lumbered forward with a deep penetrating rumble, punctuated by periodic rattles, and creaks, and the incessant but invisible cloud of petrol fumes that enveloped them.

In little more than a week, the entire Corps, more than 100,000 men – an entire city – plus 20,000 horses, hundreds of guns, motor vehicles and the miscellanea that accompany such a vast host had surreptitiously moved southwards, passing from one army to another, and prepared for battle. It was an astonishing feat. And in less than seven hours that battle would erupt.

'Listen, McNally. Let us out here. It's going to take all night to get to Domart at this rate. We can walk faster,' I said. 'You carry on. We'll see you when you arrive.'

'Are you sure, sir?' asked McNally.

'Yes. Lieutenant Smith needs the exercise, anyhow,' I said. Smith gave a muffled laugh. He was with me long enough to be conditioned to my little jabs.

The sky had turned a dark bluish-black, and it was clear and warm, and a cooling breeze danced upon our faces as we walked purposefully along the grassy shoulder, skirting the many trees that lined the road. It was a lovely summer evening. The stars shone brightly. I'd almost forgotten how beautiful they were. From above came the whining drone of aeroplanes. Without seeing them, I knew they were ours.

The road itself was an endless procession of men, beasts and ma-chines, all headed in one direction: southeast. We hugged the empty roadside and had soon left McNally and the car far behind. Not long after, I heard the curious notes of what sounded like singing from ahead. I looked over at Smith. I could see he'd heard it too. Singing!

As we approached the marching column the sound was unmistake-able, and when we came alongside, I saw they were marching slowly but smartly, their backs erect, rifles slung over their shoulders, chests proudly forward and, to a man, singing boisterously.

'It's a long way to Tipperary… it's a long waaay to gooo…' I shivered, as my neck hair stood erect and goose bumps raced up my arms at the sound of that deep, haunting refrain. The lads were singing as they marched to battle. Singing of all things! They hadn't done that in two long desperate years of futile bloodshed, and now they were singing. I don't know if it was an omen, but it sure felt like it was.

We pushed onwards. Behind us came a dull thud as a heavy gun fired its solitary shell and, long afterwards, a flash illuminated the horizon as it reached its destination. The singing, and even the talking, had abruptly ceased. There was a crunch of countless feet on the dirt road and the deep rumble of some tanks further on ahead, but otherwise it was still – the sort of stillness that sharpens every sense, and amplifies all the doubts and uncertainties that burdened each of us. We were only a few miles from the German lines.

The pungent odour of petrol was overpowering as we came to within a street's length of the steel, rhomboid-shaped, tracked monster. It was the last in a squadron of a tanks that was hogging the road for as far as I could make out in the dim silver illumination of the stars. They could do 5 miles per hour, but rumbling along in second gear to keep the noise down, their pace was such that Smith and I easily overtook them. Not that that was much of an accomplishment, I reminded myself, thinking again of my eighty-year-old grandmother.

We kept well to the side as we walked past. The six-pound gun and the Hotchkiss machine gun, protruding menacingly out from one side, gave good reason even if being squashed under one of the tracks, each the circumference of a small barn, held no particular fear. Regardless, I almost jumped out of my skin when I heard a whistle, and a soft shout, beside me. 'Hello! Major MacPhail!'

'I thought it was you.' A skinny bespectacled officer on the tank had his hands cupped to his mouth. It was Captain Turner – Ewan, from the Connaught bar. I recognized him instantly. He lowered his hands and smiled broadly. After all the teasing I subjected him to last December in London, it was a sheer wonder I hadn't found myself under one of those tracks.

He scampered deftly down from the machine, and I went over to him, a hand extended, braving the exhaust. 'What are you doing here?' I asked, trying to keep my voice down, but with enough volume to be heard over the growl of the motor. It wasn't what I'd describe as one of my more perceptive inquiries. But Turner seemed very pleased to see me, judging by the way he exercised my hand up and down.

'Here, get in,' he instructed us. Smith was shifting awkwardly along behind, transfixed by the behemoths. Turner motioned us towards a smallish hatchway in the side of the iron wall that he'd yanked open. It required an awkward moving jump with head bowed, a manoeuvre even my grandmother might have thought twice about before attempting. Unlike me, she had the advantage of being built like a tanker, short, thin and a whole lot tougher. I managed it with my body intact, if not my dignity.

After we settled into the steel cavern that Turner called home, he pulled the door tight, and secured it. The latch fell ominously into place with a loud "clunk". 'At least we can talk in here,' said Ewan, half shouting to be heard above the motor and the clanking of the treads that reverberated around us.

'Yes, it's a veritable oasis of calm,' I shouted back.

I turned to Smith, 'This is Captain Turner. He's with the tanks.'

'You don't say, sir.'

Ignoring him, I said, 'Ewan, this is Lieutenant Smith. Allegedly he's in intelligence.' Smith sighed.

'He must quite like you, Lieutenant,' said Turner. For someone I barely knew, it was an insightful comment.

Smith, visibly enthralled to be in a tank, addressed himself to Turner, 'There are eight of you, is that the normal crew, sir?'

Turner was only too glad to have the opportunity to show it off, and he launched into an elaborate explanation. It gave me a good chance to look around. I'd never been in a tank before.

We sat three abreast on a small bench along the left bulwark. I sat next to the well-oiled breech of one of the 6-pounders. In the front I saw a driver pulling at gear sticks and peering through a narrow slit, following the firefly of a man with a cigarette, seeking to keep the contraption on the road – with admirable success I had to say. Ticking along at slow speed the engine opposite us was radiating a furnace's worth of heat, oily fumes and enough noise to make permanent deafness more than a passing concern.

'...it's a Mark V,' Turner was saying. 'The most modern tank in the field. The Germans have nothing like it. You'll see – it's a marvel at clearing out machine-gun nests. Usually the Boche turn tail when we get anywhere close.'

Smith was captivated by it all. I, on the other hand, was preoccupied; calculating how quickly we could make an exit, without appearing impolite. There was a sudden jolt and I knocked my head painfully on some protruding piece of metal. There was no shortage of protruding metal in a tank. The bloody thing was a death-trap.

We shouted at each other for fifteen minutes, about what we'd seen and done since our brief encounter in London. Turner chuckled at my story of Richardson living the good life at his château in Flixecourt – I embellished it a tad. Then I saw the driver wave to Turner to get his attention. When Turner returned from consulting with him, he made a cutting motion with his hand at his throat. Ultimately, it turned out to be a more innocuous signal than I first feared. 'We've reached our first halt. We're stopping shortly,' said Turner, after he sat down again.

I shook my head. 'It looks like we'll have to hoist those weary feet back into action, Smith,' I said. Smith looked genuinely disappointed.

Turner saw right through the veneer of regret on my face to the elaborate landscape of relief painted beneath it. To Smith, with a wink, 'I'm trusting you'll help your ageing Major adjust to warfare in the twentieth century.' Smith grinned from ear to ear.

It's funny how those little coincidences can change your life more than you can ever imagine. This whole adventure in Amiens had begun for me with my impromptu visit to Niall Richardson. And what more fitting way to storm off to battle tomorrow – it was less than six hours away – than to meet up with Ewan Turner and his beloved landships?

To our surprise, and my amusement, Turner had told us that "tank" was a term dreamt up as a subterfuge to confuse the enemy as to what the boffins were really up to. *Tank* was supposed to conjure up visions of water tanks. Just what German intelligence was to make of a building spree in water tanks was a question better left unasked; Turner had enough on his mind. By mid-1918, *tank* was a firmament in the dictionary, at least the kind soldiers consulted. And whatever my qualms about riding in one, I was glad they were riding into action with us.

Turner was a good man. And immeasurably tougher than I'd made him out to be, when he casually cavorted through the door of the Connaught Bar, half a lifetime ago.

'Good luck, Ewan,' I said. 'We'll drink to your feats next time we meet!' I didn't envy him one bit, no matter how imposing the steed he rode in on.

Smith and I reached the deserted ruins of Domart-sur-la-Luce around eleven, and map in hand we pushed on to where we were told the advanced divisional headquarters was located.

In the direction of the German lines, a plane was flying low, slow, and noisily down the front line.

'What a racket,' I said.

'It's a bombing plane, sir. One of ours. A Handley-Page, I believe.' Smith was an encyclopedia of trivia, sometimes useful, sometimes not, but indispensable all the same.

'It's awfully loud,' I said. 'It almost drowns out those bloody tanks.'

'I suspect that's entirely the intention, sir,' he said. To which wisdom I didn't respond. In my defence it was past eleven and I was tired, hungry, and tense.

I checked my watch. Again. The attack would commence in a little more than five hours.

CHAPTER 32

2.35 a.m., 8th of August, 1918
Falcon Trench near Hourges, France

'Good morning, sir,' whispered a lieutenant, as I slid into the crowded trench.

'Good morning,' I murmured. 'You're all here?'

'We relieved the Aussies half an hour ago,' he replied.

I looked at my Borgel. It was 2.35 a.m. I began counting forward.

But he was already ahead of me. 'One hour and forty-five minutes to go, sir.' He was keeping a close eye on the time, as well.

The lieutenant was a tall, well-built man with a deep reassuring voice. He exuded the sort of natural authority you instinctively knew would have his platoon following him anywhere. It had nothing whatsoever to do with his rank. That was invariably the case with the best officers. He must have been young, even if his features were obscured by the night and the standard, olive-green steel Brodie helmet he wore tilted low over his brow.

'Not long now,' I said. 'I'm glad you made it. We're cutting it very close.'

He nodded knowingly. The battalion, and its two sister battalions to the left, were the very last units to relieve the Australians for fear of tipping our hand. Four battalions, the entire 9th Brigade, with well more than four thousand men had silently slunk into this tiny knob of ground. The front-line troops arrived only a mere two hours before Zero Hour. It was as if the population of London had decamped to Portsmouth in an afternoon.

'And did it go well? The relief?' I asked him. It was the only question that really mattered. We'd soon know whether all the deceptions, the precautions, and the preparations had succeeded. So long as we didn't give it away at the last moment.

'Without a hitch, sir. There were a couple of flares, but things quickly died down. I don't think the Boche noticed anything.'

'Nothing? Surely they must have heard something?'

'Perhaps, but aside from a burst of machine-gun fire, and the flares, they didn't react at all. And now it's quiet. It was their normal twitchiness, that's all, sir.'

'Let's pray that's the case. For all our sakes.'

My plan avoided a bottleneck at the bridge. The only thing was, if the lieutenant was wrong, and the Boche *had* heard something, the Hun would be training their guns on this very spot. It would be like sheep to the slaughter, so tightly packed were the troops in the handful of trenches and holes that made up the front line. I didn't much like any of our chances then.

'Early morning,' said the lieutenant, making idle conversation.

It hardly needed saying. I'd managed to close my eyes for a couple of fitful hours under a canvas sheet strung between two trees. It was just long enough to make me feel completely worn-out – the sort of rest that leaves you more tired than you were to begin with. It didn't help, that while my wake-up instructions were crystal clear, the sergeant exercised precious little subtlety in applying them – major or not. But then the army was never renowned for its subtlety, and the sergeant probably enjoyed it.

'I hope you and the men got some rest,' I said. 'We have a long day ahead.'

'Bit difficult to sleep, sir.'

'Yes, I know. I'm MacPhail. What's your name, Lieutenant?' I asked, curious, perhaps for posterity's sake.

'Holland, sir, B Company, 5 Platoon.'

'Good to meet you, Holland. You're from the Camerons, aren't you?' It wasn't entirely intuition on my part; he and the others were wearing kilts. If ever there was an appropriate occasion to wear a kilt, and offhand I wouldn't have necessarily said there was, August in France was probably it.

'Yes, sir.'

The Camerons were young Philip's battalion, the same 43rd Cameron Highlanders whose perseverance in the cold wet misery of the Salient helped swing the tide at Passchendaele. If this bunch had half the spark that group did, Lipsett and Hore-Ruthven had nothing to worry about.

'I had the privilege of seeing your battalion in action on Bellevue Spur, on the first day of the attack on Passchendaele Ridge, back last October,' I said, extending a hand. 'I'll never forget it. It truly was an incredible show. I hope you rise to the occasion again.'

He shook my hand. 'Yes, sir. Thank you. We'll do our best.'

The waiting was the worst. It always was. I remembered all too well my first time in the trenches, my stomach in a knot, waiting for the whistle that would send us in a mad frenzied scramble off across No-Man's-Land. The whistle was gone nowadays. More often than not we settled for a couple of hundred guns going off in unison. That way no one could pretend they hadn't heard it.

The men around me hadn't slept much, either, though they didn't show it. Several were conversing in whispers, others were nervously fingering their equipment or distractedly playing cards. It was far removed from the ebullient games of deep concentration, and even deeper laughter, that I was accustomed to.

One soldier, a big bull of a man, was laboriously scratching away on a sheet of a paper, on his knee, with a small pencil stub buried in his bowling-ball fist. A last letter home. They were all anxious, but eager, too. They were as ready as they would ever be – only the waiting seemed endless.

But it only seemed that way.

Soon the NCOs came along, and the men began forming up. *An hour and twenty minutes to go.*

Then a group of 30 Frenchmen emerged out of the darkness, bearing a *Chauchat* light machine gun. Their insignia indicated they were from the adjoining 42nd Infantry Division.

I looked over at Holland, puzzled. He was waving to their captain.

'They're here for me,' he explained. 'The Inter-Allied Platoon.'

'The what?'

'That's the name they came up with for my platoon and the French. We're to move along our boundary with the French army, and secure it, off to the right of the road and Dodo Wood, and past the Andrea Ravine.'

'It's a good idea,' I said to him, as he left to greet the French captain. After the endless cock-ups over the years when confusion over who was responsible for what ended in painful debacle, somebody – at last – had come up with a grand idea: jointly tackle any objectives close to the dotted boundary line, the arbitrary division dreamt up by GHQ to separate us in the first place. It just went to show, good ideas needn't be complicated.

One hour. I could feel the tension.

For all the activity, it was deadly quiet. The air was warm and I welcomed the occasional wisp of wind that blew softly on my cheeks. A bombing plane still continued to buzz low over the lines. Every so often, a sporadic Boche shell burst far behind us. Uncharacteristically, it went unavenged; our own artillery was silent. A mist was beginning to form, a white steam that seeped up from the ground all around us, as is if the Earth's crust was struggling to contain it.

The first assault companies were lined up and ready.

The plane was making a terrible hullabaloo now. It wasn't enough to conceal the unmistakeable clanking rumble that was approaching from behind.

There were eight minutes to Zero. The tanks were moving forward.

I held my breath, awaiting the inevitable fierce rush of activity from the Germans as they awoke to the onslaught now approaching. But strangely, there was nothing. The minutes ticked by in painfully slow rotations of my Borgel's small hand. Its luminescent paint had long since faded and I had to squint. I'd have to buy a new one next time I was in London.

Suddenly, a deep THUMP from a naval gun sounded. It was 4.20 a.m.

As the retort subsided the heavens exploded. The greatest barrage of the war began.

The heavy guns boomed, the massive howitzers joined in and the

60-pounders began firing in frenzied succession, shell after shell. A sharp piercing hurricane of noise from the whizz bangs blew mercilessly in my ears. Field guns by their hundreds were firing high velocity shells up over our heads and into the enemy trenches and gun positions that lay waiting. The sky shrieked and whined. All the trains of France were roaring overhead, the express route southeastwards, their whistles blowing.

I stared in awe, looking back.

Contrary to what you'd expect, experience taught me to look to the rear when an attack begins. I had the luxury of not being in the first waves and could therefore afford to gawk shamelessly, fascinated at the sight. From left to right, as far as the eye could see, the entire horizon glowed a fiery yellow so bright I could have read a book huddled at the bottom of this trench. The ground shook and the steady roll of the concussions pounded in my chest.

When I turned to look forward, I gasped. A boiling foam of red and orange lava enveloped the German lines, spitting upwards at each new blast that came in a rain of explosions. A raging and greedy forest fire had spontaneously erupted along a front twenty miles long. I could see the soldiers watching, awestruck. It did them good. They were heading that way soon enough.

From the German side, solitary S.O.S. flares of double red, and then green, wobbled desperately out of the fiery cauldron into the sky above, calling for help. If our counter-battery guns had done their work, it wouldn't be coming.

B Company was now rushing forward, eager to keep up with the creeping barrage. Speed was of the essence. They were to rush the hill in a frontal assault. Other companies would slip around to attack it from the side and behind. The sooner we moved out of this cramped space, and ahead, the better.

I saw Holland and his platoon, and the blue-grey forms of the French infantrymen, swallowed up by the mist, heading in the direction of the woods and the ravine.

The mist had begun forming around four. With the smoke shells that were falling it was thickening to a dense fog. Despite the light of the barrage, the battlefield at hand was obscured in an impenetrable cloud. A road width or two ahead, I could make out almost nothing, no matter how I strained my eyes.

The last men of the company moved on into the veil of smoke. The next company was preparing to follow. The tanks were lumbering past on the road as well. Their throttled engines were revved up, and through the gloom came the terrifying clanking of the massive treads as they propelled themselves forward. I could only imagine what the young German soldiers woken from their sleep were experiencing.

The German response came within five minutes. By their standards it was tardy – inexcusably tardy. But their artillery was encountering problems of their own, of the variety that arrived in a metal casing. Tibbett and DuBois would be pleased. I was relieved.

Too late I heard the brief whine. The blast blew me square across the trench and up against the rear wall. Anxious to see what was taking place through the fog, I'd stupidly climbed up the side, to squat like a spectator at some sports event. I should have known better. It was the same unthinking recklessness that got new recruits killed. I was getting soft.

'Damn,' I exhaled, as I slumped ungracefully down into a chastened pile beside the private who was calmly huddled on the trench's earthen floor. My back ached and my heart was thumping. But I was in one piece.

'They're off their form,' said the private matter-of-factly.

I stared at him as if he was nuts, the thought passing fleetingly through my mind that my reappearance in living flesh was perhaps a disappointment to him. After a moment, I collected myself, and said, 'You're right. The bombardment, it's erratic.' The shells were still falling, not too far away, off in the direction of the river and the bridge. They lacked their usual Teutonic intensity.

'All the same, sir, the boys from C and D companies, and the 52nd, will be taking a beating,' said the private. He was referring to the units still in the assembly area as well as the Brigade's reserve battalion. The 52nd Battalion was closest to the riverbank, precisely where most of the shells were landing. He was a perceptive kid. Or maybe he just knew someone back there.

Shakily, I picked myself up to peek cautiously in their direction, pulling my helmet tight down over my forehead. Sure enough the road and the bridge were the targets. Judging by the muffled explosions, many shells were falling harmlessly into the wet marshland. Without warning, there was a bright flash, and a large bang.

By sheer chance the Hun had hit what must have been one of the last tanks to cross the bridge. As I often said, it was better to be lucky than good, although my witticism hadn't contemplated the luck being with the enemy.

'It's a damn good thing they *are* off their form, Johnson, or we'd have a real mess on our hands. As it is they just hit one of the tanks,' I said, slouching down next to the private again. Private Johnson had been my parting gift from Hore-Ruthven early this morning. He was a runner and, should the need arise, he'd be my lifeline with headquarters.

In the improbable event I sleepwalked through the past couple of days, the colonel had helpfully reiterated how critical it was we seize Dodo Wood. I recognized one of his phrases. Admittedly, it was hard to forget, about Dodo Wood being the key to our whole right flank. It was something I'd said to him three days earlier. Nerves, I guess. I nodded. Somehow, in my stupor, I found the reassuring words even colonels require occasionally and I told him I'd appraise the situation, and report back, as quickly as possible. He seemed satisfied.

I coughed. The air was so thick with smoke I could taste it on my lips. Early on, another errant enemy shell had hit a stack of smoke bombs piled in the trench off to our left. The mushroom cloud that erupted, together with the smoke shells from our own barrage, was turning the heavy air into an acrid soup and my throat itched. Any notion of a breeze was no more than that. 'How are you feeling?' I rasped to the private. Thankfully, the German bombardment, such as it was, was trailing off.

'Fine, sir,' Johnson said. He looked like a runner should: thin, lithe, and healthy, and he was coping with the lack of oxygen a lot better than I was. Where he'd been when the half-mile was chewing me up and spitting me out at Tincques, at the sports championship, was a topic I had a damn good mind to revisit when this was all over. *If* I made it out.

I gathered myself together. 'Good. Let's go take a gander at Dodo Wood, then,' I said. I was glad to be finally moving.

By now it was almost five o'clock. All four companies of the Camerons were long gone. The intermittent small arms fire we'd heard near the enemy's Elbe and Heidelberg trenches, in front of the hill, had ceased. The first German defence line had snapped.

The walking was easy enough and the fighting sounded far ahead. What increased the difficulty level was the fog. As the officer I was naturally expected to navigate, providing a wonderful opportunity to embarrass myself, or far worse should we go terribly afoul. At first, the going wasn't overly strenuous. Only, after ten minutes of blundering ahead through the toxic mix of mist and smoke, seeing maybe ten yards ahead, I began to fear we might be walking in circles. It was an ominous sign for the assault troops. Poor Turner in his tank would be lucky if he hadn't landed in the Luce already.

I could only hope there were a couple of souls with that innate feeling for direction that I always thought I possessed, but which, to my dismay, was currently leaving me in the lurch. There was one saving grace: the Germans couldn't see us coming, and that was a not to be belittled advantage.

'The trench appears to be empty, sir,' said Johnson, almost immediately after we stumbled into it. And indeed it was if you overlooked the corpses strewn here and there. Almost all were clad in field grey. Behind the trench, I knew, would be the infamous wooded hill packed with machine guns and artillery.

The hill had dominated our discussions for days, and preoccupied everybody from General Rawlinson on down. I listened carefully for shooting, alert for any hint to confirm the direction we should take. Suddenly, audible above the thunder of the barrage, I heard the crackle of rifle fire straight ahead. We pushed on, and began the climb up what seemed like a steep incline.

The firing sounded closer, and I recognized the rat-tat-tat of the German Maxims. Dodo Wood was absolutely packed with them. There was no doubt about that. But no matter how closely Smith and I had studied the aerial photographs, figuring out where they were amongst the thick stands of trees hadn't been easy. For certain, we'd missed half of them. I wiped at my brow.

As we reached the treeline, I signalled Johnson to halt, and I pulled the Webley from my holster. 'Keep your wits about you, Johnson, we don't want to stumble into a company of the Boche with you picking your nose with a bayonet.'

He unshouldered his rifle. If I'd had half my wits about me a couple hours earlier I would have brought one as well. The Webley was a fine revolver when you couldn't miss, only by that stage, neither could they.

The mist cleared slightly as we entered the wood. Climbing further the visibility improved markedly. The smoke was starting to dissipate, and while it wasn't yet light, it would be shortly. I didn't much like the idea of Johnson and I, facing off against a concealed light machine gun and its three-man crew, with us caught in the bright sunlight.

I heard movement ahead. Frantically, I waved at Johnson to get his attention. Apparently, he'd heard it too, for he was moving to crouch behind a tree and I quickly did the same. My heart was pounding like the pistons of a fifty-car freight train climbing a mountain slope when I saw a file of a dozen Germans emerge only steps away. In my hand, the polished wooden butt of the Webley was squeezed in a clammy ball of sweat, my forefinger poised far too tightly against the cold metal trigger guard. It was only then I noticed they were unarmed.

As soon as I saw the distinctive upside-down bowl of a helmet, the familiar olive-green tunic, and the bayonet-clad rifle held horizontally, the tension sissed out of me in an exhilarating rush, like a balloon pricked by a darning needle. I rose from behind the tree. The soldier, who was herding the prisoners before him as if they were a flock of docile sheep, was nonplussed. He greeted me with a cursory nod and a friendly, 'Hello, sir! I almost didn't see you there. I'm off to take this bunch back to the prisoners' cage.' Almost before I could reply they eased away into the brush, and the lingering smoke, heading downhill.

Johnson and I pushed on through the wood. We sheltered when a burst of machine-gun fire sounded not far ahead, and moved on again when the silence had endured long enough that to remain still any longer would make us both seem like cautious fools. Not that I cared, but Johnson was full of fire.

'Sir!' hissed Johnson. He pointed his finger off to our right. I saw them instantly through the mangled trees and tangle of heavy under-growth. They were Germans alright. Thank God they hadn't seen us. It was a machine-gun nest.

I motioned with my head for Johnson to follow. Softly, foot by cautious foot, we circled around in an arc until we were able to approach from the rear. We crept forward. There appeared to be five or six of them. At least those I could see. And I didn't want to miss any.

They were manning two machine guns in a small pit. That must have been their commander's intention, but as we approached they seemed more concerned with keeping their heads down than engaging in heroics. The guns weren't even manned, and were jutting absurdly upwards. These were my kind of Prussians.

'Good morning,' I said cheerfully, in English, as I stepped out. I tried to look fierce, with the revolver in my right hand, and the French F-1 grenade I'd found in the Camerons' trench, in the other. With Prussians, you never knew how they'd react. And these were from the 225th Division – a solid unit, by all accounts. From the corner of my eye I could see Johnson coldly peering at them down the barrel of his Lee-Enfield. I'd heard he was a crack shot. Whatever my initial reservations, our tactics proved to be singularly effective.

'*Kamerad! Kamerad!*' they shouted. Arms raised high, their helmets lost or discarded, they were not exactly the stuff the legend of the Imperial German Army was born of. They looked scared, hungry and suspiciously pleased to be taken prisoner. Given the alternative I can't say I disagreed with their logic.

There were seven of them – one had been dangerously hidden from view in an adjoining hole – and I hadn't a clue what we should do with either them or the two MGs. Leaving them and the guns behind wasn't an option. But neither of us could afford the time to escort them back to a prisoners' cage – at least not if I intended to stay in General Lipsett and Colonel Hore-Ruthven's good books. They hadn't sent me to play soldier.

We stood there, Johnson keeping them under shot, while the sun rose and I deliberated on a course of action – the rotation of the earth moving embarrassingly fast compared to my thinking. Then, miraculously, a solution presented itself in the form of a small group of kilted soldiers. The Camerons! They were led by a sergeant, and were picking their way carefully along, rifles extended – presumably a mopping-up party.

'Excellent timing, Sergeant,' I said as they approached. 'I'm Major MacPhail from divisional headquarters. We have a few prisoners here

I'd like you to take charge of.' Seeing his expression, I added, 'Don't worry, they seem like a meek bunch, even if they are Prussians.'

He might have had other plans, but whether it was my rank, the mention of headquarters, the thought of bringing in six prisoners, or he'd simply caught his breath, he now became very accommodating. 'Certainly, sir,' he said. 'They can join the column.'

'The column? A column of prisoners you mean? The attack must be going well, then?'

He grinned. 'Yes, yes you could say that, sir. You certainly could. We hit them hard in the flank and they're surrendering in droves. We must have more than two hundred prisoners already, and scores of machine guns like these. In fact, we've almost secured the wood.'

'Really!' I said, not daring to believe him, although the sergeant's lined face and serious dark eyes didn't give him the look of a comic. Most sergeants I've encountered, weren't famous for their sense of humour.

'And who's in charge?'

'I don't know, sir, but I've just come from Captain Verner, from D Company,' he said. To indicate he pointed further up the hill, not far from where the Amiens-Roye road passed parallel along the wood's northern border.

I was eager to be off, but not so eager to realize a casual wave of the hand wasn't much to go on. I made him repeat the directions in more detail.

We ran into several small groups of soldiers along the way and large parties of prisoners before I finally managed to track down Captain Verner near the top of the hill. By that time, it was around seven. Due to the fog, many units must have been mixed up, and when I accosted him he seemed to be supervising an improvised roll-call of sorts. The men looked in high spirits.

'The sergeant was right, Major,' he said, after the introductions were made and he'd briefed me on his unit's progress. 'The wood and the hill are in our hands. We've had some real trouble from a battery at Vignette Wood that's firing at us, on the other side of the hill. They knocked some of our tanks out of action. But we've managed it all the same,' he said smiling. 'Except for the odd machine gun, Dodo Wood is now ours.'

I could barely contain my excitement. 'You realize what this means, Captain,' I said. 'The division's whole right flank. Hell, the Corps' whole right flank depends on what happens here. If we didn't crack Dodo Wood the Germans could have held up the entire advance. The road would have been useless, and God knows what trouble the Hun would have got up to with the commanding position they have here. It's the trickiest part of the entire front. And you've taken it!'

He shifted uneasily on his feet, uncomfortable how to respond to my praise. Nor did he realize he'd likely salvaged my career, not to mention my life. The whole plan I'd impetuously convinced Lipsett of, would have backfired if we hadn't made it past Dodo Wood. The bottleneck at the bridge would have been replaced by a bottleneck at the wood.

'You know, everyone is waiting with bated breath for what happens on this hill, Captain?'

He shrugged. 'No, I didn't, sir. I've been a little preoccupied with this and that.'

Suddenly I felt like the archetypical red-tabbed staff officer flexing my muscles, safely ensconced behind a towering mound of paper. 'Of course, Captain. I didn't mean anything by it. You and the battalion have done great, that's all,' I assured him. Prompted by his comment about the tanks, I thought of Turner. 'How has it gone with the tanks? Have they been helpful?'

He smiled. 'You could say it was a weak first period, but much improved since the first intermission. We had one here, not long ago, firing with great perseverance – only we were the target. Mistook us for the Boche no doubt, eh. Lieutenant Hanson marched right up to it, pounded on the door hard enough to break the bloody thing down, and put things right. You should have seen him! Ever since it's gone well. The tanks are off now towards Hamon and Vignette Woods. That's where we're heading, also.'

'And has anybody passed the word back you've taken Dodo Wood?' I asked, the thought suddenly occurring to me.

He frowned. 'No, not that I know of. All the smoke's made it tough to figure out left from right, let alone communicate. And we've had our hands full, as I told you, Major.'

'I don't doubt it. But your Brigade commander, Brigadier-General

Ormond, must be waiting anxiously. I know for a fact General Lipsett is, and I suspect General Currie and General Rawlinson are as well. And, if that's not enough brass for you there are two field marshals, Haig and Foch, who are more than a little intrigued about the progress here.'

Verner looked pale. He'd been bombarded in the assembly area, fought his way through the fog and up the hill, attacked one of the strongest defensive positions the Germans had, and captured a barracks full of soldiers along the way. But the mention of a few generals was making him queasy.

'Don't worry, you've done exceptionally well, Verner. I'll take care of it,' I said. Afterwards, I heard he captured the troublesome battery of 5.9s at Vignette Wood.

From my tunic pocket, I wrestled a small battered notepad and a pencil, and kneeling down, furiously scribbled two short notes. I handed them to Private Johnson.

'Time to earn your pay, Johnson,' I told him with a wink. 'The first is for Brigade HQ. When you've delivered that, take the second to Division HQ. As quick as you can. And whatever you do, don't get lost or shot, or I may very well have to shoot you myself.' He gave me a cheerful grin, and a knuckled salute, and he was off.

Lipsett and Hore-Ruthven would be relieved – assuming they could decipher my handwriting – the road was clear for the next wave.

CHAPTER 33

12.04 a.m., 8th of August, 1918
Quarry near Domart-sur-la-Luce, France

Sometime around noon I arrived back at HQ, the hitherto unknown Château of the Abandoned Stone Quarry, an unpretentious collection of dug-outs and tents in a limestone quarry near Domart. I was tired, but relieved, and eager to hear how the attack elsewhere was going.

The sun was shining at its midday fiercest, the sky was a dazzling clear blue and the trees were swaying in the wind. It was a gorgeous summer day in the French countryside. But nothing shone as brightly as the familiar, once haggard faces that soon began popping up around every corner. I had a premonition I knew why.

'Ah, Major MacPhail,' Lieutenant-Colonel Hore-Ruthven said jovially, emerging out of the blue from a dug-out. 'I'm very glad to see you. Good afternoon!' I swore the man had a crystal ball when it came to my whereabouts.

When he'd cornered me early this morning, he'd tersely asked if I would monitor the attack on Dodo Wood in the field, and report back. He was far too much of a gentleman to refer to my plan, or to suggest it was only appropriate I see it through with the troops – to share the pain if it all went wrong. If I'd been in *his* shoes, I suspect I might have.

Now I glanced uncertainly at my wrist, convinced it was still morning. It was the sort of wasted effort I usually try to avoid for naturally Hore-Ruthven knew the time down to the minute.

The tense, distracted man of one o'clock this morning was positively giddy. I put it down to lack of sleep and the abundance of afternoon sun, and good news, particularly the latter. 'It's going rather well, isn't it?' he asked, offering a rare smile for my benefit.

It was the sort of open-ended question where the desired answer is blindingly obvious, and that I'd learned as lawyer to avoid like the plague. Under the circumstances, the question seemed eminently reasonable, reminding me why nobody much liked lawyers.

I shook my head. 'I can't believe it, sir. We've made astounding progress. We got past Dodo Wood by early morning, as I believe you know.'

The colonel nodded. 'Yes, your message came in the nick of time, Major. We were on pins and needles. Shortly thereafter the 116th took Hamon Wood. It was a very tough fight.'

'I figured as much,' I said. 'I happened to run into a column of prisoners. They were all emblazoned in chalk.'

Hore-Ruthven frowned.

'They had "captured by the 116th Battalion" written on their backs,' I explained, and he smiled. The boys were proud of their accomplishments and having some fun.

'I don't suppose you know what happened with the Inter-Allied Platoon, sir?' I asked, the jargon sticking awkwardly in my throat. 'I saw them leaving this morning. It was a dramatic sight, kilts and Gallic blue rushing off to do battle together.'

'The Germans surely agree with you on that, MacPhail. It appears that our joint platoon was a grandiose success. They secured the boundary with the French and even captured two small copses of their own.'

I whistled appreciatively.

'However, tell me, do you know how the second wave is faring?' I heard in his tone that it was the question that been burning in his mind since he first spotted me.

Fiddling with the leather strap around my chin to pry the helmet from my sweaty scalp, I could see the colonel's patience was wearing thin. With a rough yank I pulled it loose. 'I followed the second wave after it leap-frogged through the first, sir. In fact, I'm returning from the front line now – perhaps you've heard?'

'No. I haven't heard anything. Go on, Major.' He stared at me, waiting. In another of the morning's small miracles, I'd seemingly beaten all the runners, pigeons, and aerial observers.

My hat was finally off, and I tucked it away under my arm. 'The second wave is on its objectives, sir. They reached the red line an hour and a half ago.'

'They've reached the red line, have they?' The red line demarcated the second of the three objectives General Currie had set for today. 'Oh, that's simply *splendid* news, MacPhail,' he enthused with a mouth full of acorns, like only an Englishman can. In his pent-up excitement Hore-Ruthven was reverting to his old military college days.

I wiped my brow with a rolled-up handkerchief I fished from my trouser pocket – despite my initial misgivings, my parents' gift was *still* proving more useful than I anticipated – and asked: 'How's the rest of the division faring, sir?'

He looked at me for an instant, confused. 'Oh yes, of course, you wouldn't know. On our left, the 8th Brigade also reached its objective. Their casualties were remarkably light. They didn't face all the obstacles that we had on the right, but they've done extremely well. From what you tell me, the division has done its duty for the day. It's up to the cavalry and the 4th Division now to carry the final objective in our sector. Did you see them, by chance?'

'The roads were full, Colonel. The engineers did an amazing job on the roads and the bridges, but I had a tough time getting back with all the horses, men, and guns moving forward. You know, sir, I figured the cavalry's role was played out in this war, but seeing them two abreast, columns long, they make an impressive sight. Not as fearsome as the tanks, mind you,' I added.

Sensing his impatience, I said, 'I expect the 4th Division will be at its starting line, sir.' His query had surely referred to them, not my views on the future of the cavalry.

'Excellent,' he responded. 'Thank you, Major. I'll inform the general. He'll be relieved to hear.'

'Very good, sir.'

'Oh, and MacPhail.'

'Yes, sir?'

'Congratulations. I had my reservations, but your audacious plan proved its worth. I should mention, the general is very pleased with you.'

'Thank you, sir.'

With that he turned on his heel, and disappeared as rapidly as he'd come, leaving me with a mouthful of my own unanswered questions – such as how the rest of the attack was faring. But the colonel was keen to be the bearer of happy tidings. I understood. Perhaps the general would see fit to put in a good word for me now at the proceedings.

Lieutenant Smith positively glowed when he spotted me sticking my grimy head into our modest tent, in a row of others, staked out in a corner of the quarry. The day was very warm and inside the canvas tent it was stiflingly hot – Smith's red-streaked brow and flushed cheeks weren't solely because of his excitement at seeing me.

Smith was full of news. With my trusty aide there was categorically no need to ask questions; the answers came in a flood. So, I flopped into a chair and listened. After a stress-filled morning traipsing up, down, and around trenches, orchards, grain fields and hills, it felt good to sit.

After a couple of minutes, I sensed a slowing in the torrent, and I interrupted. 'You mean to say the entire Corps has already reached their second objective?'

'Yes, sir,' he replied. 'The 1st and 2nd Divisions reached it by mid-morning. There's only one battalion which is a little short. Unfortunately, there's only a few details from the Australians. But the initial reports are encouraging. I don't know how it's gone with the French...'

'From what I heard the French are making good progress,' I said. 'And no counter-attacks, yet?'

'No, sir.'

'It's a shame you can't see it all, Smith. On the way back from the front I passed the cavalry moving up. Truly stunning. Our brigade was in the lead, pennants flying. And the prisoners! Well, you can't picture how long the lines are. You remember Passchendaele? This must be ten times that many.

'Oh, and I saw a dogfight,' I said, excitedly. 'You'd be fascinated by the aeroplanes, Smith. The air is positively filled with them.'

'There's almost 2000 of them,' he said wistfully. I had the feeling he missed seeing the aeroplanes most of all.

I took a swig of warmish water from my canteen. 'By the way, you may not have realized this, but it's the second time in a half year we've captured Dodo Wood. Depressing, don't you think?'

'No, I didn't know that, sir. Is that true?'

I nodded. 'Our cavalry brigade retook it at the end of March, along with Moreuil Wood, during the German spring offensives. It's to the south of us in the French sector. I'm sure you must have seen it on the map. It was an epic battle.'

'That was when the Germans were pressing on Amiens in the spring?'

'Exactly. In the first of their spring offensives. And they got pretty damn close. However, a few days after we recaptured Dodo and Moreuil Wood, the Aussies held them at Villers-Bretonneux, and Ludendorff called off the offensive on Amiens and attacked up north. At the time I thought he was crazy. But the going got too tough, I expect.'

'So, if it was already ours, why did we need to capture it again, sir?'

I shrugged. 'A fine question, Smith. You're not in intelligence work for your looks alone.' I was repeating what somebody once said to me. Now he rolled his eyes much as I had then. 'But to answer your question, I don't know,' I responded. 'Whatever happened, it evidently ended up back in German hands.'

'I have the feeling *that* won't happen, again,' Smith said.

I shook my head. 'No, I expect you're right.' After this morning it was positively unthinkable. The annoying part of it was, the unthinkable had recurred at frustratingly short intervals in this war.

Smith brushed away a fly that was madly circling a few crumbs on the table. It had all the tenaciousness of one of the Red Baron's Flying Circus. I watched him track it as it looped, swirled, and went in for the attack. SMACK. In one sudden blow, he crushed it with a thick report. The report looked suspiciously like one of mine. You disregarded the lieutenant at your peril.

It wasn't something I said, but Smith's face was beaming. 'I was forgetting something,' he said slowly.

'Alright. Enough. Spit it out, Lieutenant,' I said wearily. Whatever it was, it was coming my way anyhow. Better to get it over with.

'Have a look at this, sir,' he said brightly, handing me a single typewritten sheet.

It didn't take long before I understood his sunny expression. Without giving me a chance to finish reading, he blurted out, 'It's a summary of a prisoner interrogation. One of their officers. Have a look, it's near to the middle. I've underlined it. The officer being questioned states they were completely surprised by the attack. And then he goes on to say, "the Canadians were believed to be at the Kemmel Front". Congratulations, sir. Your deceptions worked.'

'Hah!' I cried. So, all our tricks *had* been worthwhile.

I must have looked relieved, for he added, 'We all agreed, what a wise choice it was that General Lipsett picked you to send to Ypres. You being the *ideal* man, and all... sir.'

Irony hung heavy in the air, like mustard gas. I looked sharply over at him. He'd heard me whining about my conversation with first Webber and then Lipsett. Smith's face had assumed a deadpan stillness, except for his eyes, which gave him away. They sparkled like the stars would later tonight. He was discovering a wicked sense of humour, my assistant, and whether I'd had something to do with it or not, I was paying the price. It served me right. I smiled tautly, trying desperately not to laugh.

It couldn't have been much past seven o'clock, when the flap was roughly thrown aside and a bull moose stormed our modest tent. Predictably it turned out to be DuBois.

'Hello Benoît,' I said quietly. 'Nice of you to drop in. Check the antlers at the door, would you? Can I get you some tea?'

Panting, he ignored me completely. 'The line's been reached! The Aussies are there, and we are as well. We've done it!' And then, in a soft aside, as he caught his breath, 'Hi, Mac.'

'Slow down a touch for us old-timers, Benoît. My hearing is not what it used to be. *Lentement,*' I murmured.

He didn't hear a word or if he did, he didn't listen, for he slowed not at all; his words tripped and stumbled and swept over each other in his haste and his eagerness.

'The attack is a complete success! The French went five miles. And the Aussies seven. Seven miles, all the way to the Amiens Defence Line! Can you believe it, Mac? We're at the old British line.' He swallowed. 'And we've gone even farther than the Aussies, more than eight miles today. The "Old Red Patch",' he enthused. 'The boys from the 1st Division made it almost to Rosières. We've routed the Boche!'

After this morning, I hadn't questioned our success – only this was too much to hope for.

Benoît began to cough and hack uncontrollably. He was short of breath, and he leaned forward with both arms on his knees, his mouth open, gulping for air. I felt a sharp pang in my gut as the fear shot through me he was having a heart attack.

I jumped to my feet, but he lifted a hand, to call a halt to my advances.

'Asthma,' he wheezed.

I steered him to the wooden chair I was sitting on, and he collapsed gratefully onto it. He pulled out his canteen and took a small sip. He was sweating. Soon, his breathing moderated and the wheezing disappeared. His colour was coming back.

'So that's why you're no longer in the infantry,' I said softly.

He closed his eyes and nodded. I could see he was embarrassed.

'I'm very glad you're not, Benoît,' I said, and patted him on the shoulder. 'Don't worry, mum's the word.'

With no apparent sense for the moment, Smith then asked, 'And III Corps? How did they do?'

They were on the Aussies' left and conspicuously absent from Benoît's summary. As it transpired, he didn't leave them out because of trouble in the translation.

'Two.' When we both looked puzzled, DuBois felt compelled to explain. 'Two miles. They got two miles.'

Smith and I sighed. 'They had the misfortune they were attacked yesterday, and were still trying to sort it out when the attack began,' I offered. To which, Smith and DuBois politely nodded. Politeness was the last thing I expected from III Corp's neighbours, the Aussies, whose left flank they held; their commentary was undoubtedly slightly more scathing.

'I can't believe it,' I said. 'Eight miles. It's a bloody wonder.'

There was a long silence as we digested the marvel of it all. It was unheard of. Advances in this war were measured in yards, not miles. All the great battles, all the thousands upon thousands of young men sacrificed. In four years of war there'd never been such an advance, nor such a victory. Never had the German lines buckled as they had today.

'You know we wouldn't have carried it off without surprise,' said Smith. 'You were absolutely right about that, sir. The surprise was crucial.'

'And we sure surprised them,' said DuBois. 'They didn't see us coming at all.'

'After all the worrying and second-guessing you did, sir,' said Smith, 'it turns out all our deceptions worked.' Considering all the time we spent together I should have expected it; my inner doubts were not the closely guarded secret I always assumed.

'Thankfully,' I agreed. 'For the first time since this war began we really, truly, surprised them. It's a shame it took us four years to figure it out.' Then a thought came to me and I grimaced.

'Why the glum face, Mac?'

'I was thinking, that's all.'

'Dixon? The court martial?'

I nodded.

Benoît stood and put an arm around my shoulder. 'Perhaps Dixon had to be. But it means something this time, Mac. There's hope. Dixon would know that. We made a difference. *You* made a difference.'

I shrugged.

'You did real good, Mac,' he said quietly. 'I'm sure they'll take that into account.'

'We all did good, Benoît. Even those that didn't make it. Especially them. But I'm afraid my prospects are bleak. That colonel is not going to rest until he has me behind bars or in front of a firing squad.'

The flap to the tent rustled again and then opened. General Lipsett stood in the opening, looking at me.

'Sir?' I said, a nausea bubbling up.

'I wanted to tell you myself, MacPhail. I spoke briefly with

Field-Marshal Haig a few moments ago. He wanted to congratulate us on our success. He was most complimentary.'

'That's very fine to hear, sir.'

'Also, I took the opportunity to discuss your case with him.' I felt the knot in my stomach tightening. 'He agreed that in view of your contribution to today's success, it would be most unfortunate to lose an "officer of your calibre", as he put it. He intends to ask Colonel Whatley-Wigham to withdraw his charge.'

Stunned, I just stared at him.

A quirky smile lit his face. 'Cat got your tongue, MacPhail?'

'No, sir. I mean yes, sir. Thank you, sir.'

'I thought you should know. Have a good evening, gentlemen.' The flap fluttered shut.

I looked over at the others, Benoît thoughtfully stroking his beard beside me and Smith watching closely, his earnest face glowing from the excitement. *They didn't come any better than these two.*

I stepped out of the dark confines of the tent, and climbed a narrow path that twisted from left to right, as it coiled up and out of the rough-hewn grey limestone walls that boxed us in. Emerging from the quarry, I found myself in a field facing eastwards under a vast sky of pinkish orange. The sun was setting in a blaze of colour no painter could ever hope to match. In front of me were the splendid miles of France's fields and orchards and villages we'd conquered this day. They could return to how they were meant to be. It was breathtakingly beautiful.

In the distance, I heard the occasional dull thud of a field gun and a brief staccato of rifle fire. Despite that, a curious serenity hung over the battlefield, as if not to distract from the sheer beauty of it. I sat down cross-legged in the grass with a straight back, Indian style, and gazed off into the distance, eastwards. The sun was at my back.

We were victorious and it was magnificent. I'd survived another ten months of war. It would continue, just as it had every day in the three and a half years since I arrived on these shores, but after the hardships, the lost friends and the frustrating futility of it all, I'd glimpsed something else: an end. What would my future bring when the war did end? It was a thought I'd ignored for a very long time and I found it strangely daunting.

Perhaps tomorrow we could force the total breakthrough that narrowly eluded us today. Lipsett would be expecting mountains from me, especially now. But it did mean something. Benoît was right. There *was* hope. At last – at long last – there was a sliver of hope. And for today that was enough.

'SIR!!'

The shout stirred me from my thoughts. Lieutenant Smith was standing, near the quarry, waving furiously.

I pulled myself up and headed back. There was work to be done. My war was not over yet.

AUTHOR'S NOTE and ACKNOWLEDGEMENTS

Writing this book was a labour of love – a strange choice of words, perhaps, for a novel about one of history's most horrific conflicts, however, researching the men of the war and their feats and sacrifices, I found it impossible not to feel anything but admiration. Malcolm's tale, from Passchendaele to Amiens, highlights the remarkable and largely unknown saga of the Canadian Corps. It shows, I think, how much more there is to the history of the Great War than the senseless slaughter in the mud we associate with it today. I hope I have done justice to the men who were there.

Many readers, recognizing names such as Field-Marshal Haig, will understandably wonder how many other characters in the book really existed. Besides Colonel Whatley-Wigham, who is purely a figment of my imagination, the other higher-ranking officers (lieutenant-colonel and up) did exist and are part of the historical record. Malcolm MacPhail and most other characters are my own creations. There are a few noteworthy exceptions. Sergeant Travis of the New Zealand Division did reconnoitre the wire at Bellevue Spur. Later he was to win the Victoria Cross. Major Pearkes, Lieutenants Ellis and Shankland, and Sergeant Mullin all fought on the Spur. Pearkes and Mullin won the Victoria Cross for their actions. Interestingly, Captain Bernard Montgomery of IX Corps (and future field-marshal) did observe the attack at Passchendaele. Although I was unable to ascertain the exact date my fictionalization of his "visit" became Chapter 11. Writing home shortly thereafter, Montgomery extolled the Canadians' fighting qualities, but was little charmed by their self-confidence, a theme I returned to. Lieutenant Jucksch really did carry out the remarkable raid on Comfort Trench which has gone down in the annals of the 58th battalion. Malcolm's friend, Malcolm McAvity, served with the 3rd Division and later the Corps HQ, and his tennis exploits are a matter of record. The story of Captains Poyser and Dixon of the 4th CMR, the latter whose tragic death near Mount Kemmel so troubled Malcolm, is part of that regiment's history. Finally, Lieutenant Holland and Captain Verner were in action on August 8th, their part being told in the battalion war diaries.

As is almost always true with historical fiction, the dialogue is invented. How could it be otherwise when writing of events of a hundred years ago, or more? However, there are a few instances where the words spoken are taken straight from the history pages: Lieutenant-General Currie did strongly object to the attack on Passchendaele as written in Chapter 6. Presciently he also forecast the number of casualties and I find it truly remarkable, in light of his objections, that he kept his job. Also, Field-Marshal Haig did visit the Canadian Corps to "ask" for its cooperation and his words in Chapter 8 are really his.

The events of August 8th 1918 were later famously described by General Erich Ludendorff as the "black day" of the German army in World War One.

When researching, I benefited greatly from the vast amount of information available: official and regimental histories, many outstanding history books, maps, memoirs, letters, academic dissertations, radio interviews and others. The treasure trove of war diaries and photographs accessible on-line and for free at Library and Archives Canada and the Australian War Memorial were invaluable. Sadly, the UK National Archives have locked away much of that country's heritage behind digital pay walls where the coin of the realm reigns.

I am indebted to my sharp-eyed first readers, Dr. Gary Grothman and Diann Duthie, who cheerfully read multiple versions of my early drafts and between them were responsible for many improvements, large and small. I especially want to thank my editor Edward Fenton whose extraordinary insight, creativity and ability to put his finger on the sore spots, whilst somewhat painful at the time, was truly invaluable. My deep thanks also go to my second editor Dexter Petley. His review of the text was both astonishingly perceptive and encouraging.

If you enjoyed reading *Malcolm MacPhail's Great War* I would be grateful if you wrote a review on the website where you bought it.

Malcolm MacPhail will return in 2018 with *My Hundred Days of War*. Please sign up for my email list at www.darrellduthie.com to receive all the details and publication date when they are finalised.

Darrell Duthie, Amersfoort, September 2017

Made in the USA
San Bernardino, CA
03 November 2019